The Sum

Michelle Medhat

MINDBLOWING
BOOKS LTD

THANK YOU FROM MICHELLE MEDHAT

I would like to thank you for reading this book.

If you've picked this up, and you haven't read the earlier books, please check out The Trusted (book one), The Dominant (book two) and The Resonance (book three) and The Refracted (book four). Direct links to these books can be found at the end of this book.

Also, at the end of this book you can find details on how to get my exclusive, free eBook **Operation Snowdrop.** You can only get this book through sign up to my newsletter *'Fearless Spies, Amazing Realms and Ice-Cold Villains'.* It's not available anywhere else. Operation Snowdrop is the mission that is cited throughout *The Trusted Thriller Series.* Together with this free eBook you'll get early bird discounts, the latest news on this series, and what I'm up to. You'll also get access to incredible free thrillers bundles to keep you entertained.

But for now....

Dive in, hold on tight and enjoy!

Chapter 1

18 June 2017

The blond, permanently tanned man known as Richard Ashton, British Prime Minister, lounged back on the ivory, leather sofa, the type only found in first-class lounges and VIP club suites, and he sighed contentedly. He pulled the casually slung seatbelt a little tighter across his toned stomach as he noticed a slight dip in movement. He took in his surroundings. Much had happened in the past couple of months. And all for the good. *His good.*

Quantum Force, the incredible, abundant, clean energy source had dramatically changed his fortunes, enabling little luxuries like the sleek, private jet he was on, and all the trimmings private ownership brought.

"Prime Minister, we'll be arriving shortly. Would you like anything before we begin our descent?"

Ashton smirked as he eyed up the raven-haired beauty at the drinks trolley. He licked his full lips salaciously. *Well, a quick blowjob wouldn't go amiss.*

The man seated opposite him looked up as the flight attendant spoke.

"G and T thanks, darling."

The man was Jensen Stalbridge, promoter of Freedom Earth and the PM's business partner and confidante. Unlike the PM, whose features were softer, bordering on effeminate, Stalbridge's features were sharper, angular, with a hooked nose that led up to searching, always interrogating eyes. He looked like an eagle on a constant hunt for prey.

"How about you, Richard? What're you having?"

"Just another glass of bubbly."

"You're getting a taste for the finer things."

"And why not? We're all entitled."

"And some are more entitled than others." Stalbridge laughed, knocking back his drink.

"I have no idea what you mean," said Ashton in a coy voice, and then the two men laughed raucously.

Startled by the sudden loudness, the attendant flicked her head back. She caught Ashton's eye. *Finer things, why not?* He motioned her over.

She leaned in towards the prime minster. "Yes, sir?"

"Listen, sweetheart, there is something you could do for me."

Stalbridge's eyebrows rose. "Rich, I'll go and…well, just check on those papers," he muttered hurriedly, and got up. Heading for the back where the office paraphernalia was, he didn't turn around. The attendant noticed him leave.

"Sir, we'll be descending shortly. Could you take your seat?"

"Sweetheart, the only one descending around here is you." Ashton grabbed the attendant's head and pushed it forcefully down toward his crotch. "Now off you go," he said, unzipping his hand tailored trousers.

The flight attendant, too terrified to refuse, acquiesced without a further word.

Ashton's long arms stretched out across both cushions of the leather sofa and his head tilted back. He let out a deep groan. He could feel it. Beyond the climax, something else.

At that moment, it was blatant. Revealed to him. The surge that every human craves but tries to hide. They shun even the mention. But deep down, Ashton knew humans wanted to control others. Dominate them. Hold the balance of life and death in their hands.

That was ultimate power. An unquestionable primal need unfettered by twenty-first century morality.

And he had it.

Chapter 2

11 Days Earlier

Reggie Wellwood looked out from the northern end of the Terrace in Westminster Palace. The expanse of the Thames spread out before him, glistening in the morning sunlight. He'd stared out from this place before when he had just been made a Member of Parliament. His life in politics had then been an unturned page. An expectation still waiting to be fulfilled.

He remembered watching the gentle waves and imagined streams of horses galloping just underneath the surface. Their eyes, the sparkles of light that caught his attention. He would be like them. Running ahead, sweeping up the top positions, being the star politician. His ascendency would shine bright over the palace.

But all that had been a lifetime ago.

His close-set eyes scanned wearily the horizon for movement. No airborne Surv-Motes out today. At least not around Westminster. Other parts of London would be under observation by the strange surveillance drones the prime minster had instigated almost immediately following the systematic decimation of his family.

Life in Westminster had become very different following that moment. He hadn't seen that much of the prime minister since then. Understandable, considered Reggie, trembling inwardly as he imagined how he'd deal with such a devastating act of terror. How does a man deal with his family's annihilation? Even in a hypothetical context, such a consideration delivered an unthinkable level of pain. Reggie knew, in truth, if he'd been in Ashton's shoes, he'd have been crushed to the ground.

Reggie recalled the days following the prime minister's return. The hushed whispers. The incredible respect, not pity, that Ashton received from not only his party faithful but all the opposition as well. He was virtually venerated. A man who could do no wrong. A man who had suffered for peace and for his country. Everyone somehow felt that they had to honor whatever the PM wanted, for rejection of his wishes could be tantamount to treason.

Initiation of the Surv-Mote devices hadn't been something Reggie had wanted. As defense secretary, he thought, despite the PM's circumstances and the dreadful massacre, that it was a form of provocation and would only create more problems. But Ashton was not prepared to engage in any such discussion. Reggie shivered, remembering their conversation after the PM had returned from his short leave.

"Prime Minister, I'm not sure that this is necessary. We already have one camera too many as it is. Intrusion into the public lives of people has gone too far. These drone things…well, their lives won't be their own."

"Wellwood, do I have to remind you that terrorists are everywhere, and they can still get to anyone?"

Reggie looked down, embarrassed by having to face the PM about his family's demise.

"Yes, Prime Minister, sir, I know they can. But not all the people in the UK are criminals. Most are good people."

"Unfortunately, Wellwood, you are naïve. Most people are not good, and they take no responsibility in their lives at all. When they eventually decide to live their lives with responsibility away from evil temptation and become law-abiding citizens, then their lives can return to be their own. Until such time, their lives are mine."

Ashton smiled at Reggie. It wasn't a joyous smile. Reggie could feel bile rising in his stomach. He nodded, accepting the inevitable.

Ashton slammed him hard on the back in a faux-comradery gesture. Reggie gasped as his spine vibrated under the PM's impact.

"Good man. Will help with our civil defense agenda. Work with the home secretary and the energy secretary to make this a reality, old chap. I want it expedited without delay. First, the delivery of the Surv-Motes."

"Surv-Motes?" enquired Reggie, confused and still a little dizzy from the 'don't cross me again' endearment.

"Surv-Motes, yes. It's the new people-friendly term for the surveillance automated drone. It's much more genial to the impressionable masses. I've even commissioned a public information advert on TV and across the web. A cute, cartoonish Surv-Mote zooming around, talking to kids, and keeping people safe. We may even run production on the cuddly Surv-Mote toys and games. Make a killing at Christmas time!"

Ashton laughed at the joke. Reggie tried to laugh too. But the laugh mutated into a cough as his lungs tightened in his body, agitated by the PM's earlier hit, and he puffed and wheezed.

"You're in a bit of a state, aren't you, old chap? You do need to take better care of yourself."

Ashton proffered a chair to his coughing defense secretary and continued.

"So, as I was saying, Reggie, delivery of the Surv-Motes will be arriving Friday."

"That's very soon, Prime Minister," muttered Reggie through his heaving.

"Can't wait around. Need to get things moving." Ashton rubbed his hands together. The action completed his interaction with his defense secretary. It also signaled his closure to any argument, if anyone would dare to bring one forth.

Reggie stood up from his seat and left the PM's office in a numb silence. He likened the feeling to a visit to the dentist, when he'd just been injected with cocaine and had things done to him he had no control over. His mind floated on a peripheral consciousness, aware of things happening but not actually partaking in their activity.

Reggie slid out the PM's office and into Private Secretary Milburn Cumberford's domain. A thoroughly nasty little fellow, thought Reggie. All Oxford Blues, the classics, and stiff upper lip. Reggie doubted he'd ever felt a true emotion in his life. He had a round, pudgy face, boyish in a way, which could display quite an affable, even vulnerable, appearance had it not been for those dead eyes of ice-blue and the permanent condescending sneer he carried and delivered to everyone except for Cabinet Secretary Sir Martyn Redfern and, of course, Prime Minister Ashton. Two peas in a pod were Redfern and Cumberford, realized Reggie, as the Cabinet secretary pushed past him in a hurry to jump at Ashton's next request, as always.

Redfern was the type of person who could probably remain immaculate in a 60-mph gale, thought Reggie begrudgingly. Tall, as one sees a basketball player, with an almost concave body despite gorging on the best fare in the Common's dining hall. His startling, green eyes reflected disregard and condescension to all except the prime minister, a man for whom he fawned and brownnosed unashamedly.

Redfern was a stickler for detail on everything. Nothing happened without him knowing and no one got to the PM without going through him first.

"Morning, Sir Martyn," ventured Reggie, wanting to appear the better man.

"Oh yes, good morning, Minister. Hope all is well in the world of defense?"

A slit of red venom curled across his face. The Redfern smile. It showed utter contempt for having to deal at all with Reggie. He could see, although he held his ministerial position, who really held the power. He was nothing but a minnow against the barracuda might of the Cabinet secretary.

"Never better," mumbled Reggie.

"Getting those Surv-Motes sorted for us then? Good chap." Redfern flicked a conspiratorial look at Cumberford, who sneered, as expected, in return.

Reggie turned away from his colleagues, his face flushed with embarrassment. He was nothing more than an errand boy to them. He didn't have their public-school sensibilities. He hadn't been brought up to bully, victimize, and belittle those around him. Respect for himself and others had been the code he'd lived by.

He heard the malicious sniggers behind him. Like being back at school, he thought, and closed the door.

Reggie returned from his reverie and sighed. The intelligence elite had their eyes and ears everywhere. No one could keep a secret anymore. Oh, how the world had changed in a few months.

His gaze bounded over the flowing river, and he had a sensation he'd come to recognize and, with reluctance, accept: being under observation. He moved his head toward the feeling, and a Surv-Mote popped up almost of out of nowhere in front of him and hovered just above the railings on the balcony. It had no sound, but human instinct always informed on its presence.

The Surv-Mote was a strange machine. It was like a tennis ball only a fraction larger and adorned with small apertures like the compound eye of a fly. The small eyes were nanocamera or nancams, and they picked up movement across a three-hundred-and-sixty-degree field of vision. If the Surv-Mote detected movement, its nano-eyes would suddenly flicker and flash independently. The Surv-Mote in front of Reggie was flickering and flashing but was not issuing any command. Had the Surv-Mote's surveillance of the scene indicated signals of movement above the threshold criteria of acceptable behavior, its real-time data-feeds flowing back to Freedom Earth HQ would have been analyzed by an artificial intelligence system, and according to the AI's established rules and current learning, a prediction on the likelihood of criminal activity would have been made. The Surv-Mote would then emit an eerie, high-pitched whine and announce, "Your actions are identified as unacceptable. Police have been called. Remain where you are."

It was now understood that since all data was streamed and stored at Freedom Earth HQ, insufficient evidence was a defense plea that had no standing in Ashton's brave new world.

The Surv-Mote's presence had disturbed his thoughts and Reggie no longer wanted to be outside. He wandered over and opened the door to return inside the Terrace. In his mid-fifties, of slight frame and average build, even the exertion of pushing down on the handle made him puff a little. Moving to the city after Ashton had given him the UK defence secretary position had brought back his asthma.

The pollution of the city hung uncomfortably inside him, constantly at the back of his throat. Before any talk, he'd cough, trying to clear the mucus, but that sour taste would still stick. If he got too irate or too passionate about a subject, the coughing would kick in rendering his delivery inadequate and embarrassing.

His doctor had given him various medicines but none of the remedies had been lasting enough. Only getting out of London would help, and that wasn't going to happen now.

All the ambition, the drive for stardom, had been burnt out of him decades ago by the ruthlessness of the political game. He wanted a quiet life. He was quite satisfied with being culture minister, attending nice, dignified events and getting paid for the pleasure. He really didn't want such a high-profile position. But with Godley's untimely demise, he was suddenly in the spotlight.

His appointment still bemused him. He had no experience in defense. No experience in anything really. As a minister, having too much knowledge was sometimes a disadvantage. You couldn't uphold the impartial position the role demanded. Far better to know a little but rely on your advisors for the drilled-down details. That's how Reggie had operated, and although that ascendency to political stardom had evaded him, he'd been a survivor. Many of his other feistier colleagues couldn't claim the same.

It was, however, all very strange, his appointment. Reggie knew there were at least three other ministers who could do the job ten times better than he could. But it seemed Ashton wanted him. And lately, what Ashton wanted, he invariably got.

Chapter 3

Fluffy, ice-blue sofas.

They're everywhere throughout Kudamun. Our quarters are no exception. We have our share of those requisite sofas, and I especially enjoy their fluffiness. It feels like I'm sitting on a cloud, although I've never done that. Not sure if I could. But anyway, that's the feeling the material projects. The Kudamaz love them. They push a sense of calm in your body and when you sink into them, everything feels so right.

So perfect.

I'm on the sofa, stretched out with Sam Noor, my husband. Kudamun is our home. Well, partly home. Our other home is Earth. You see, I'm Ellie Noor, Protector of Earth, and until recently I was just a hard-working businesswoman with a husband I thought was a boring diplomat who actually turned out to be a badass, saving-the-world type spy.

Over the last few months, things have changed.

Life has changed.

I've changed.

I'm not human anymore. I've taken the form of a Kudamaz-human hybrid attuned to every resonance vibration on Earth. Plant, animal, or mineral, including man-made things, I can connect to at the molecular level and communicate with those base elements. I'm also quite a fighter, and I've cornered the market in rainbow light annihilation.

Sam is also Kudamaz but he's different to me. Instead of having light energy networks inside him, Sam's human makeup, his blood, bones, organs, and brain, through the reconstitution process, have been separately turned into Kudamaz energy rather than obliterated and recreated. Imagine a body is digitized and all that information is used to produce a super-pixelated image. Well, that's my hubby. Sam's being is like a rasterized image, with every part of his human internal make-up recreated as billions of light cells instead of human cells. He still has the human scaffolding, but he's held together through Kudamaz energy.

We both use our shimmer ability to transport between Earth and Kudamun, an inner dimensional world out of time, space, and the known universe. The positioning of Kudamun was perhaps best summed up by the Dalai Lama, who Sam and I met back in May this year. He said, "You are from the world in between." That's exactly where Sam and I are from. The places in between. We are always there, but hidden by the Reality Gap. That constantly fluctuating quantum field where the degree of tilt of shooting quantum particles keeps Kudamun from being seen by anyone in the physical world, or the reality plane as the Kudamaz call it.

I close my eyes and stretch my body down languidly toward Sam. He tickles my feet as they nestle into his lap and I pull away suddenly, my eyes open and alert.

"Still makes you jump!" says Sam, smiling with naughty delight.

"Yeah, a little. More a retreading of old memories. Difficult to shake."

Sam grips hold of me, staring hard. "Shake? Why would you want to?"

At that moment I don't know why I made such a crass comment. The words came out of my mouth as if I wasn't in command in that split second. I scowl, annoyed with myself.

"Of course I don't want to."

"Then why say it?" snaps Sam.

The relaxation vibe has vanished.

"I don't know. I... I...haven't been quite myself. Everything that's happened. Al Nadir's obliteration, Ashton, the massacre, Freedom Earth. All that religious and new energy stuff. It's been a whirlwind even for us. I guess my head isn't quite clear yet. My databanks aren't blasting on all eight cylinders!"

Sam nods. "I know what you mean, darling. It's been a wild ride."

"I know I got a lot when I become Kudamaz, but I had to give up so much."

Sam puts his arm out and drags me closer to him. I rest my head on his chest and try to hide the emotions building. The Kudamaz are not meant to submit to feeling emotion. The way in which we function is through our knowledge banks, reliving memories that are used to create energy to materialize the emotion into reality and, with it, our tears of joy or sadness.

I can feel the tears pricking at my eyes. I blink, and they sparkle away.

"I know you did, darling. But there wasn't any choice."

I listen to Sam's voice. Pragmatic. Commanding. Infuriatingly sensual.

I curl my legs underneath me and sit up, resting my chin on Sam's shoulder.

"I know. It's just sometimes I think, why me? Why did it happen at all? I know it had to. Destinies are written. I'm aware of what I'm saying and, of course, I'm grateful to Aby-od for saving me, but…" I stop and look into Sam's deep pools of dark brown.

"But?" repeats Sam, edging me on as he pats my thigh.

"I wonder what would have happened if I hadn't insisted on you coming back that Friday from Oslo. If I'd just accepted that you were away on business. I'd probably still have had the nightmare, woken, had that awful experience with Aby-od and Aswa-da's wicked intervention, screamed and burnt my hand, but you wouldn't have heard anything. There would have been no revelation. Even if MI6 had seen, they probably wouldn't have put so much emphasis on it had I not known about your MI6 status. That moment changed it all. And it was down to my petulant, schoolgirl tantrum that I wanted you back sooner. I really do think I caused it all."

Suddenly, I can't hold back. Tears drop and sparkle as fast as I produce them.

"I almost lost everything, Sam. My life. You. All because I wanted the last say on everything. I had to win. I just didn't want you away from me anymore."

Sam rubs my arm. "You didn't lose me, sweetness. We got through it. We survived. Being Kudamaz is the most incredible experience I could ever have dreamed of. I love every moment."

"Don't you think about the things you've had to let go?"

"What, all those human things, like being hungry, tired, having aches and pains, using airports, getting stuck in traffic, handling politics?"

"We still do that now," I counter, and grin,

But Sam isn't smiling. "Not being afraid of dying."

Sam says it. It's a truth I know he values. Probably more than me.

"Fear makes you human," I say.

"But we're not human anymore, Ellie. We have gained more than we have lost. You must be able to see that."

"I do. But even though you're not admitting it, I have lost too. My business, for one."

"Ellie, sweetheart, you can't put losing your business on the same level as not being human."

"I'm not." I sound peevish, and I tone down the testiness in my address. "But it was still something I cared about a lot. Remember, darling, it became my obsession, so much so, I didn't even realize you were a spy!"

Sam strokes my leg. "Alright, point taken."

I glance at Sam, turning my head sideways. I see he's considering what I've said.

Ever the analytical mind, he retaliates, "Come on, sweetness, you're being myopic in your recall. You know you didn't lose it. You sold it. Ashton found you a great buyer."

I thought about Richard Ashton, British Prime Minister and current pain in my backside. It was true, he found a very deep-pocketed tech company who happened to be branching into virtual warehousing. The blockchain capability I'd developed with my tech team was an attractive, differentiating feature. The acquisition made sense for them – cheaper to buy than to develop the new business organically – and for me. Being the Protector of Earth, I couldn't kid myself I could continue as CEO of Cloud Nine. I'd made sure all my staff were kept on and all were given pay rises. Securing Palmer Pharm and their deal in several orders of magnitude larger than the twenty million I'd secured from their rival a month before made Cloud Nine a sought-after asset in the tech world.

Sam and I never had money worries. With the funds from the sell-off only boosting our very healthy bank balances, I decided to keep a small amount in trust, with the majority of the funds going to key charities I cared about. I left enough in our main bank account to pay for utilities. Even though we were Kudamaz and, for all intents and purposes, superbeings, we still had to pay the bills for electricity, gas, and water on Earth.

Some realities stay constant!

"Yeah, I know he did. But besides you, Cloud Nine was my only love. I gave part of myself away when I sold it."

"I know you did, darling, but we're beyond all that now."

I look at Sam. Beyond it, I think. Right. So that's why you always slip back into your MI6 agent mode whenever you possibly can.

But I say nothing. Just smile and grab his hand.

"I know."

"So you're okay?"

"Yes and no."

"That ambiguity again, darling. You're fond of that."

I know what Sam's referring to. When I first explained about me becoming Kudamaz, and I spoke of Mark I and Mark II versions of Ellie, he asked, 'Are you Ellie? Yes or no?' I replied, 'Yes and no.'

"It's not intentional. It never was. But life isn't always black and white, Sam."

"For someone whose life is about balancing dark and light, that's a hell of an ironic thing to say."

This time I do laugh. It is ironic, but it's also true. Lately, I've been unable to discern dark and light. Nuances of grey are all I can pick up on. Actions that I think are honed with evil intentions have turned out to be delivering good. Ashton is a prime case in point.

"What do you think about Ashton?"

"What? As in, do I think he's good or bad?"

"Yes." I keep my response short, like I'm scared my mouth will run away again and say something weird or out of keeping with who I am.

"He's a good guy. No question. And one unlucky son of a bitch too. That stuff with his family, it would send a man crazy."

I stare at Sam and purse my mouth, unsure of his conclusion.

"You don't think he's good?"

"I don't know, darling. He seems good. But there's a ruthless streak in him. I feel it."

"Ellie, he's a politician, of course he's going to be ruthless." I hear Sam's voice playing down my fear, dismissing it as paranoia. My need to be wanted as the Protector. Couched within his voice is mocking.

I stiffen as I listen. "Don't think I'm a fool. I'm not paranoid. Nor delusional. But Ashton is still an unknown quantity."

"Unknown! Ellie, we know him completely. The High Council cleared him to work with us on religious unification, Freedom Earth, and Quantum Force. He's open and honest. Ellie, he shows his hand to us all the time."

I stare at Sam and cannot believe, with his constantly questioning background defined by his time in MI6, why he can just accept Ashton.

"Shows his hand!" I say with scorn, raising an eyebrow at Sam. "Well, let's hope he doesn't have any cards tucked up his sleeve."

Chapter 4

4 Days Earlier

Ashton lifted the glass to his lips and watched as Redfern, his Cabinet secretary, mirrored the gesture. A considerable amount was riding on the Thurso meeting. He hadn't confided in Redfern as to what was going to happen, only that 'Eyes Only' security clearance for the participants was a requirement, and they had to sign agreements that 'if any leakages occurred from the meeting, those found responsible would be deemed traitors and executed under Freedom Earth law'.

He recalled Redfern had approved of his 'no nonsense' approach to meeting security.

"All is in place, Prime Minister. The correspondence needed for the meeting has been drawn up and the participants you identified have been informed of their requirement to attend."

Redfern's solemn voice gave Ashton reassurance that his ducks were all in a row.

"Excellent, Redfern. I knew I could rely on you." His Cabinet secretary issued a swift nod. He paused as if in sudden contemplation and looked sideways at the PM. From the interrogative glare in Redfern's eye, Ashton knew what to expect.

"Prime Minister, may I enquire as to what this meeting is about?"

"Al Nadir clean-up and Quantum Force rollout," said Ashton without taking a breath. His words shot off his tongue, and Redfern noticed. He smirked and crossed his arms, staring at Ashton.

"So why, may I ask, is there a need for a top level 'Eyes Only' security clearance on members of the Cabinet and Security Services who already have such SC on their personnel files? And why do we need to go to the end of the country to have a meeting when the contents of which could be addressed in a Cabinet or COBRA meeting in London?"

Ashton detected a slight tinge of vexation toward the end of Redfern's question.

"Don't fancy flying then?" quipped Ashton, attempting to deflect.

"That's not quite so. I fly when there is reason to. But that it is the thing, Prime Minister, from this meeting agenda, Al Nadir and QF rollout, we could easily hold it in Whitehall. Why the need to hold it in…" Ashton could see Redfern holding down his displeasure. "Thurso?"

Ashton could tell that it wasn't the location that was the problem for Redfern. It was the fact that he'd only been told half of the story. Or more accurately, none of the story. In Redfern's immaculately inimitable way, he was pushing Ashton's hand. The PM sneered. It was an obvious play by his Cabinet secretary, and it underlined his great need to be in the confidence of the PM and take his place in his inner circle of trust.

"You remember when, back in April this year, you asked how I was achieving the religious leaders' buy-in so quickly, and I said I'd tell you, but not just now."

Redfern's eyebrows rose, and Ashton knew he was replaying the scene. "I do recall that, yes, Prime Minister."

"Well, in four days from now, you'll learn quite a lot more about how that buy-in was secured."

"Really, Prime Minister? That will be most fascinating."

Redfern moved his buttocks around on the leather-backed chair he was seated on in front of Ashton's desk, and the leather made a squelching noise. Redfern blushed.

Ashton snorted, asking crudely, "Everything alright downstairs, ole boy?"

Standing up, Redfern looked peeved and stated indignantly, "Absolutely, Prime Minister." But his expression cast doubt on his positive status. Ashton discerned something was bothering him.

Ashton slid to the side and withdrew the bottle of JD. He poured without asking whether Redfern fancied another tipple. He liked Redfern. He was a great drinking companion and Ashton could enjoy himself with him. It wasn't normal practice for a PM and his Cabinet secretary to be buddies, but Redfern had a similar upbringing to himself: private boarding school, parents abroad, Eton then Cambridge, gone into law, and eventually decided on the civil service. Okay, some differences. No MI6 and no journalism. But, in many ways, realized Ashton, the two of them were very similar. And at least if they both got up to no good together, neither could play the righteousness card. So, of course, daggers would thus remain firmly away from backs.

"Here, sit down, take this, and for God's sake loosen up. You've been as stiff as a board lately."

Redfern sat back down, took the proffered drink, and swigged it immediately back.

"Is everything okay?" asked Ashton, scanning Redfern's face.

"Not really, Prime Minister. Wellwood has ignored my request for a meeting to talk through the upgrades to the Surv-Motes. Permanent Secretary for Defense, and he's been giving me the run around. And that just isn't on."

Ashton pulled in his mouth tight and frowned. "No, that isn't on. What the fuck is Wellwood playing at? I thought the upgrade was all in hand."

Ashton dove into his private filing cabinet at the side of his desk. He pulled out the Surv-Mote upgrade file and flicked through it. Sam had undertaken the diagrammatic for what the upgrade would look like. The upgrade was now a necessity. Other countries had adopted Surv-Mote technology. There was already talk of many wanting an upgrade, and he was damned if he was going to sit by and watch as other countries took leadership of the technology.

"Get that little shit over here. I want to see him this afternoon. Say five in the Commons bar. Usual protocol. I'll shove that upgrade down the little fucker's throat if I have to, but he'll make the upgrade happen!"

Redfern smiled. "Sounds like a perfect idea."

Ashton returned his usual smirk. "Martyn, what do you say, after we've put the frighteners on Wellwood, we head out to one of our haunts? Give our livers a good seeing to and find a couple of fillies to have some fun with."

"That, Rich, sounds like another perfect idea!"

Chapter 5

Reggie sat down at a table in the Commons bar and waited. It was unexpectedly quiet for a late Thursday afternoon. Normally jam packed. Redfern must have sent a note to his minions. The Redfern Protocol. When the PM wanted the bar for a private discussion, everyone cleared out. Not that they wanted to; it was just expected behavior. Another change the PM had made. One of so many. Reggie had lost count. And it was all down to 'that massacre' that nobody in Westminster was allowed to mention.

Reggie realized life in Westminster was just a series of 'don't mention that's. Long before the terrible attacks, the 'don't mentions' had been the PM's country-hopping on his Freedom Earth and Quantum Force junkets, involving things like new energy powers and religious stuff that Wellwood didn't know much about, and couldn't mention even if he did. And before that again, it had been the weirdness of those days at the end of March. Little was really known. Wellwood had seen a change in Ashton. He seemed to become someone totally new, driven and impassioned by whatever he'd seen.

But what he'd seen, Reggie could only speculate. There had been murmurs. Something to do with superbeings or aliens, and about a terrible fate that had been averted. Armageddon had been avoided, others claimed. Reggie didn't know the facts. Not yet anyway. He hoped his defense appointment would now open previously closed doors.

One thing, however, he did know. On March 27 at 10:47 p.m., his very understanding of the world around him changed dramatically. Reggie saw something that would have the date and time forever seared into his mind. The Chinese whispers that made up the account of what had happened on that day couldn't dispel what he'd witnessed with his own eyes.

He'd just finished a sumptuous Italian dinner at Al Duca on Duke of York

Street. He'd been entertaining friends from France with whom he'd studied with at Oxford. It had been a lovely evening but one that would have been relegated to the confines of his memory as just another 'good evening out'. But emerging onto the street, he realized very quickly that relegation was not to happen. The moment he stepped outside, he heard the shouts, the screams, and, as he made to turn right and head toward his parked car in St James Square, he knew the night was not as it should be. People milled around in the road, drinks in one hand and pointing with the other to the sky above their heads. Reggie followed the path of their fingers. What he saw chilled and amazed him.

The star-lit sky he expected to see was not there. In its place was an arc of sparkling red that grew ever stronger as he watched it. The color that started a pale red turned in seconds to rich crimson. It glittered like a million tiny sparklers had been lit. And it moved, or rather undulated, like a red sparkling sea had materialized above him.

He shuddered. Was this just London? As he looked, he knew it wasn't. This was global. Of that, he was sure. People called from a pub further up the road, "It's on the news." Crowds piled into the pub as the landlord pushed up the volume to max on his TV.

"No one quite understands this strange aerial phenomenon, but reports are coming in from across the world, so this is not localized to the UK."

Reggie heard the newscaster, but inside, he already knew it.

He watched the TV a while longer. Experts from the worlds of astronomy, physics, and the environment came on delivering a range of explanations. New-age philosophers, astrologers, and all manner of people across the ecumenical spectrum then came on delivering a diatribe of doom.

After he'd been pushed and prodded in the back, he decided that he'd received enough bruising for one night and slipped back, letting others take front viewing of the TV. He filtered his way through the people who had gathered in the streets. Following the screams, they had left their buildings and come out to see what was happening. Several hundred people now blocked his way to the square. He pushed through and eventually got to his Audi A6.

Climbing inside, he suddenly realized that more and more people had exited from their homes to look at the strange phenomenon. With that many warm bodies out, the streets would be difficult to navigate.

"It's Armageddon," someone screamed.

Reggie placed his gear stick in reverse, determined to get the hell out of there. All the time, as he drove through the throng of growing hysteria, he prayed.

Dear God, let them be wrong.

A buzzing in his pocket brought Reggie's attention back to the present. He answered it with brusque "Yes" and listened to the caller.

"I understand. I'll try," stated Reggie, his tone non-committal. After a lifetime in politics, he knew such a reflection was the only way to respond. Any affirmations of any kind could end up being a noose around one's neck. Reggie was clear that wasn't going to be his exit path. He closed the connection and returned the phone to his inside jacket pocket and waited.

Redfern hadn't shown up, and he was getting tired. His mind began to drift again. This time news headlines burst in: 'UK leading on new energy technology', 'PM backs new energy source', 'UK secures energy security for life'.

Amazing headlines, but what really lay behind this weird energy source everyone seemed to be talking about while actually saying nothing? Some confirmed it to be a form of cold fusion or a low energy nuclear reaction, but unlike anything ever seen before. The capability for reproducing the energy was touted as exceptional and inexhaustible.

Similar to the events in March, the new energy source was virtually a closed book.

The PM had given his assurances of its valid, robust, and rigorous research program. Claims of associated testing that had been undertaken for decades. Actual evidence that he'd been privy to appeared sparse.

Reggie felt it was all a smokescreen, and like the particulates that hung in the air, the lies that lingered around him were difficult to swallow.

He listened as voices got louder and footsteps sharper, more pronounced. He stared at the door expectantly. It opened.

The prime minister, Richard Ashton, walked in followed by his Cabinet secretary, Martyn Redfern.

"So good to see you, Reggie," exclaimed Ashton, smiling. "What's your poison?"

Reggie startled, not knowing that this meeting would include the PM, shuffled in his seat, tried to stand up, and knocked his drink over his trousers. He noticed Redfern's eyes shoot to the ceiling in dismay.

"Oh, Reggie, how long have you been drinking? You look a bit squiffy already!"

Reggie noticed Ashton glance at Redfern, who guffawed at their ridicule of him.

He flushed red, moved the glass to an upright position, and mumbled, "I've just arrived and that was only mineral water!"

"Yes, and the rest. Still, I'm sure you could do with a refill. Give him a double whiskey, Redfern, and be quick about it. Haven't got all day!"

Reggie watched Redfern, and jealously pricked at him mercilessly.

I bet you know what happened in March.

Chapter 6

Temenos slipped into the Observation Room. He swiped his hand across the crystal wall next to the massive Observation Screen, and the crystal structure melted away to reveal a lattice array of crystals and sparking arcs of light. The crystal light circuity was everywhere; up and down into the wall, and deep in front of him, going into heart of the wall. Temenos couldn't see its end in any direction. The top seemed to align with the Reality Gap. The bottom carried on going until the crystals and lights faded into darkness. In front of him, flickering lights refracted by the glistening, multicolored crystals continued far to the vanishing point. He looked at the small, tear-shaped, pale-blue crystal with a tiny, raised ruby at its base in his hand. It vibrated, as if discerning its purpose was close.

Temenos followed his dark lord's instructions and placed the crystal between two pale-lilac crystals that were arcing, glittering lights. The arcing paused whilst Temenos inserted the crystal. The sentient nature within it initiated fully. The lights between the two lilac crystals commenced their arcing back and forth. Only, this time, the crystal Temenos had inserted caught the arced connection. Temenos watched as the ruby sucked in the light from the lilac crystal on the left-hand side and then emitted the sparkling light back out to connect with the lilac crystal on the right-hand side. Within an Earth moment of looking at the activity, the new crystal started to change color. Its pale-blue mutated into a pale-lilac, and the ruby assimilated itself into the now-lilac crystal.

Temenos smirked with satisfaction. His inserted crystal had hooked successfully into the matrix of lights within the Observation Screen circuitry. The function of Temenos' crystal could be likened to that of a Harmon gun. When it emitted the light again to the other lilac crystal, it had embedded within the quantum light particles a specific harmonic frequency. But this frequency harmonic was emitted to disrupt, not destroy.

Previously, he'd used the device manually to prevent the Observation Screen from recording and playing back feeds from particular events. Namely, the meeting of Prime Minister Richard Ashton with US President Al Hutchinson on March 30, 2017 to discuss papers the president had found in President Treeborne's personal safe, which described a new source of energy linked to the harvesting of quantum spin.

The intention had been to install the disrupter device into the crystal light circuity of the Observation Screen. At the time, he'd been disturbed by Ellie and Sam running a playback on a query referencing Prime Minister Richard Ashton, US President Al Hutchinson, and quantum energy prior to April 1 of that Earth year.

He had to initiate the device from a sub-shimmer position at the back of the Observation Room. Unfortunately, he'd been a few Earth seconds too late in synchronizing the trigger and Ellie had caught a glimpse of something she never should have seen. Ashton and Hutchinson talking together about quantum energy.

For the Observation Screen to record all events across the universe, the resonance of the time stream of the targeted planet had to align exactly with the resonance wave of the Observation Screen. The resonance of the time stream was captured at the quantum level, and symbiotically linked with the resonance wave of the Observation Screen. Without this symbiosis, errors would be broadcast in live-view and playback. If a difference in resonance frequency at the quantum level of the targeted planet was detected by the Observation Screen, it would deliver the stream with interference. If that same observed moment was watched in playback mode, the difference in the resonance frequency at the quantum level of the targeted planet with the Observation Screen's resonance would, thus, render the observed moment as void. This void status would signal to the universe at the quantum level that the event never happened, and the universe, in association with the Observation Screen, would delete the event from Kudamun's Observation Room databanks to avoid a time-space anomaly.

Aswa-da, the previous Leader of the House of Etima and Temenos' predecessor, had devised the disrupter device with the express intention to manipulate what the Observation Screen showed. Usage of the device leveraged Kudamun's antediluvian laws under the Order of Kudamun, which denied any Elder the right to lay claim to the act of malfunction or sabotage on the functionality of key technologies in Kudamun, unless full evidence was substantiated and provided at the time of the claim.

If this evidence was not provided, the plaintiff making the claim would face summary execution for incitement to treasonous activity and unwarranted assertions of High Council malfeasance. As the Observation Screen was one of Kudamun's key technologies covered by the Order of Kudamun, no one would dare to make a claim of malfunction or sabotage for fear of their life being extinguished by a Harmon wave. The Balance Shift Indicator also fell under the Order of Kudamun and, thus, was also protected by Kudamun's lethal antediluvian laws.

The disrupter device that embedded itself into the family of glittering crystals and lights had now started to run the program Temenos' predecessor had devised. Temenos didn't know the exact programming, only that it would curb the view of what Kudamun and, more importantly, Aby-od would see in live-stream viewing or playback mode.

This restricted view gave Temenos the assurance that Aby-od would only see what was necessary for him to see.

The rest of the time, he, like Kudamun's High Council and all humans, would remain blind.

Chapter 7

Three double Scotches were deposited on the table and the team launched into their meeting.

"What do you think about the Surv-Motes then? Great, aren't they?"

It wasn't a question; it was an affirmation that Ashton's idea was tops. His hubris had manifested as almost a separate entity and he really required nothing but the massaging of his massive and growing ego. What he didn't need was anyone to go against him.

"They are certainly changing behaviors, Prime Minister," answered Wellwood.

Ashton discerned a degree of careful consideration. He smirked. *Know where your bread's buttered, old chap!*

"Absolutely, and we're out to make sure they stay changed. Aren't we, Redfern?"

His Cabinet secretary nodded, smiling in his supercilious way.

"Permanently, Prime Minister."

"Got to keep things in order. Mustn't let any bad apples into my basket." Ashton sneered, and tapped a file that Redfern had placed on the table. "The way the Surv-Motes currently operate is not sufficient. This should have been added at its inception. The designers were remiss in their estimation as to how the device would be used. But no matter. That failing, with their design upgrade, is being addressed. I want the new Surv-Motes distributed across the UK immediately. Get it done, old chap. Sign it off. I just want to know when the upgrade is operational."

Ashton stood up behind his defense minister, gripped tightly on Reggie's neck, and pressed hard into the gap above his collar bone. Reggie winced.

"We do understand each other?"

Reggie nodded and muttered a small, "Of course, Prime Minister."

"Jolly good. Now I'm tired of this shit hole. What says we head for where the action is?" He raised an eyebrow and gave a side smirk at Redfern.

"Best idea you've had all day."

Ashton looked faux-annoyed. Their gameplay energized him greatly. "Really, Sir Martyn?"

"Oh, Prime Minister, apart from the tremendous one we have left our good friend Wellwood to implement, of course!" Redfern turned to Reggie. "Not joining us?" he enquired, knowing full well that Reggie never partook in their drinking jaunts.

"No, Sir Martyn. I still have a few red boxes to attend to."

"Oh, good show, old fellow. Keeping our end up."

Ashton sniggered like a schoolboy. Reggie stared with distain at the PM and his Cabinet secretary. Ashton clocked the stare. Infuriated, he stood up straight. His eyes, piercing and cold, drilled in Wellwood. The defence minister swallowed and attempted to stop his hand from shaking.

"You're a good man, Wellwood. Someone we can rely on," said the PM.

Ashton gripped Reggie's hand and held onto it, squeezing it tighter and tighter until Reggie could feel the tips of his fingers numbing. Reggie's eyes widened in a mixture of fear and indignation.

"We can rely on you, can't we?" asked Ashton, as his other hand closed over Reggie's like a spider's mouth over a fly.

Reggie flicked his head from Ashton to Redfern. Neither cared about the pain that was being inflicted upon him. Indifference showed on their faces.

Reggie breathed deeply and found his voice. "Yes, Prime Minister. You can rely on me."

Ashton nodded, sneered, and removed his hands from Reggie's throbbing digits.

"Get this sorted, Wellwood," snapped Ashton, and he touched the file on the table.

Reggie turned the file over, stared at the picture, and ice poured into his veins.

"Prime Minister, erm, are you…y-you-"

Reggie stopped with an abrupt stutter as Ashton roared, "Are you questioning my judgement?"

Redfern shook his head, looking on with pity. Such a stupid act to engage in. One should never cross Prime Minister Ashton.

"No, sir. No. I'm just…well, is this really necessary?"

Reggie's raspy, whiny voice had no backbone, and it sounded like he was pleading to the PM. Ashton enjoyed Reggie's inadequacy. He was surely the best choice of defense minister. Such a pathetic specimen of a man. Ashton thought he could take a shit and then wipe his ass on Reggie's face, and he'd just lie there and take it. Ashton smirked on that thought and Redfern wondered what the joke was. Perhaps he'd share it a little later after a good few shots of the fine stuff.

"Just do it. Okay?" Redfern said with a brutal tone, and looked at the PM, who indicated it was time to move on to their usual 'less than delicate' haunts.

Reggie attempted to ask the PM more questions. But Redfern shut him down. The two then left him alone in a state of absolute shock.

Chapter 8

Their talk concerned Sam. He tried to let Ellie's words filter from his mind, but they nagged him like a housewife to a wayward husband.

'More a retreading of old memories. Difficult to shake'.

'I really think I caused it all'.

'I almost lost everything'.

On and on, drilling into him, pushing him to consider something he really didn't want to.

That Ellie was unstable.

She even admitted that she hadn't been herself. Too much had happened and, although Ellie was an incredible force, the amount of change they'd both faced would hurl the most super of superheroes into a bit of a tailspin.

He could understand her feeling that way. What worried him was her sudden assessment that she'd caused it all. Somehow, she was to blame. Her acknowledgement of loss was also a new feature in her psyche. If anything, Ellie and he had gained by being Kudamaz. He never thought that she'd harbored any thoughts other than delight at having all her powers. But in her eyes, he had seen sadness.

Ellie had skillfully deflected his examination of her with her targeted regret at the 'loss of her business', just the way she'd done all those months before in March, in asserting a spider was the reason she'd screamed. Sam knew, in both cases, she was concealing something.

The desolation that flickered within her, that brought forth those sparkling tears, had originated from a place deeper than the hurt caused by losing a commercial enterprise.

Had the reconstitution process damaged her? Should he speak to Aby-od about her inconsistent attitude? Was this just a form of adjustment Ellie was still making? Could she maintain the power of The Protector within her? Could her psyche be breaking down?

Questions floated around like tumbleweed inside him.

Sam was directionless. At the mercy of the unknown.

As Sam considered the word, he remembered that it had been Ellie's description of Ashton: 'an unknown quantity'. Her constant wariness and unfounded insinuations of his evil doings grated at him. He'd retaliated and said, perhaps with some unfeeling, that 'her obsession with Ashton as the villain came from her need to be wanted as the Protector'.

If peace on Earth and a new level of enlightenment beckoned for the world, would Ellie find herself superfluous to their needs? Would she even be a Protector at all?

Thinking back over the past months up until Ashton's family massacre, Sam couldn't understand why she doubted Ashton and held so much vitriol against the man. She didn't know him the way he did. Ashton had been the same ruthless, unforgiving bastard as he'd been when it came to enemies of the state. But Sam recognized that, even though Ashton had carried out his atrocities for the greater good, he now wanted to find routes back to redemption.

Freedom Earth was one such way. Religious unification, another route to redeeming his soul for the sins of his past.

He could recognize this. Why couldn't Ellie? Surely, she possessed far greater powers of assessment than he did.

Or had she simply chosen not to accept them, as they didn't fit into the shape of Ashton she'd already formulated?

More questions.

Would there ever be answers that satisfied him?

Sam stared out through the enormous windows in the penthouse at people below walking along Chelsea Wharf. He enjoyed his time in Kudamun, but he had to always return to Silent Waters. There was something grounded about being able to see the sky and not just that weird, undulating Reality Gap above everything all the time. Having the sun on his face. Feeling a breeze. Even rain or wind. None of these happened in Kudamun. It was beautiful, peaceful, bright – well, certainly his House of Giznu side was – but something always felt clinical. Sterile. Like he was staying in an exclusive, exquisite five-star residence that didn't belong to him, and he was terrified of doing something wrong, breaking an object or tearing a fabric, and he just couldn't relax.

He felt Ellie's presence behind him.

"Hello, darling."

"Hi, sweetness. What's happening?" Ellie slid her muscular arms around his toned stomach and pulled him back into her. Her hands dropped downwards, and a light spark shot though Sam's body. She skillfully began to unbuckle his belt, at the same time kissing behind his ear.

He whipped around to face Ellie, grinning.

"Well I can see what's happening here," said Sam, slipping his arms around his wife's luscious body, just covered by a pretty, pink satin bra and matching panties. His mouth descended to encase his wife's soft lips. Ellie purred, dragging him down to the floor.

Absorbed in the kiss, Sam could release all his fears about Ellie and just give gratitude to being saved.

To being able to make love to the woman at the center of his universe.

Chapter 9

For a moment, Reggie stood staring down at the hideous diagrammatic in the file. His eyes locked on it and couldn't look away. Not even when he became aware of people around him. With the PM and Redfern now gone, his fellow colleagues had taken the opportunity to return to their Thursday afternoon drinking session. The bar filled up quickly. Reggie closed the file and brought it near to his body. The air in the bar seared. Reggie struggled to breathe. Faces and bodies closed in. Sudden claustrophobia stormed through him. He lurched out of the chair, stumbling into his colleagues. They gave him a little push away, with the retort, "Need to hold your drink better, matey!"

Reggie spied Janice Perkins, energy minister and his only true friend in Westminster (if one could have a true friend in Westminster).

"Janice, Sapori, ten minutes. This is critical."

Reggie stared at Janice, who nodded without another word. The inference was clear. Something was happening. And it was happening fast.

Reggie sat in the 'no frills' Italian café around the back of Whitehall. Fresh pasta dishes on the counter, wine by the glass; a long seat stretching the whole length of the café punctuated by small, wooden tables and rickety chairs. It was the favorite haunt of construction workers and taxi drivers. It was not the place frequented by Redfern and the Athenaeum mob.

Reggie held his cappuccino and his hand shook. He remembered Ashton's grip. He'd barely gotten away with all his fingers intact. Now he was going against the PM. A line no one dared to cross. After what he saw was being planned, he couldn't sit back and remain impartial. Civilian deaths were being flaunted.

It had only been minutes before Ashton had advised him as defence minister of the 'upgrade process' to the surveillance drones, or Surv-Motes as they were known. The upgrade consisted of weaponizing the Surv-Motes with lasers that would be powered by the weird quantum energy.

The door opened. Reggie raised his eyes up to see who entered. A short, small-boned lady walked into the café. She had an elfin face, and her brunette bob resting on her shoulders made her look more like she should be in a pantomime as Peter Pan than the British energy minister. Janice shuffled in and gave a furtive glance over her shoulder as if she had a feeling she was being followed. She looked around the café and spied Reggie. Janice made for his table, but a waitress cut her off, smiling.

"You want something to drink?"

Startled, Janice responded, "Erm, yes. A coffee. Macchiato."

Reggie watched her sit at the table next to him.

"Well, Reggie? What is this about? Why all the cloak and dagger?"

"He wants to do this." Reggie shoved the file underneath the table onto her lap.

Janice slid the file up so she could read it but kept it hidden beneath the table. She scanned it, quickly arriving at the diagrammatic of the upgrade on the Surv-Mote.

"Oh my God. He can't do this. Reggie, this is barbaric. Where would he use it?"

Reggie's voice wavered as he controlled his speech. Emotions tumbled over him. This wasn't what being a minister was about. He was a mere instrument of Ashton. There to do his bidding. But he'd be damned if he was going to sanction the murder of civilians.

"It says at any gathering. Crowd control. They'd get plenty of warning. Apparently."

Reggie's face was stricken. He had no one to tell. He couldn't back out of the upgrade. Ashton would find out. But how could he go through with this? He made a decision.

"We can't let him do this. We need to speak to-"

His sentence was caught in time, as the doors to the café burst open and heavily armed men stormed in firing MK2s. The waitress screamed and ducked down behind the food counter. Glass and food sprayed everywhere as the gunmen peppered the café with bullets.

Reggie instinctively grabbed Janice and the two tumbled to the floor between the seating and the table legs. Reggie's breath labored to rise out of his body. He could feel the onset of an asthma attack. He wheezed and tried to breath, but panic swept through him. His body turned into one giant sweat ball, and he knew he'd puke. He looked at Janice. Her eyes widened and her face seemed to shrink. Reggie thought how she resembled one of those strange aye aye creatures with bulbous eyes. He suddenly had the urge to laugh amidst his wheezing.

Suddenly the world around him was moving. Tables were flying everywhere. His hiding place was revealed. Janice screamed. One of the gunmen had picked her up with one hand, stuck a hood over her head and like a rucksack, and slung her over his back. She kicked out violently against him until the gunman punched at the hood, and her body slumped, death like.

Reggie's pulse raced fast, as he watched Janice's plight, until another gunman pulled him from the floor. He didn't have time to breathe before a hood was shoved over his head and he was forcibly dragged out of the café. Reggie could barely walk. Strong arms gripped him, pulling him through the rubble, and he felt the air on him for a moment. Then he was pushed from behind into a car. Reggie could feel the leather seats and the sense of space inside the vehicle. It must be an SUV, he thought, as he listened to the sounds around him. No one spoke. He could hear sirens.

Suddenly, a painful sensation hit his arm, and the sounds he'd tried so hard to hear drifted away.

Chapter 10

Xiao slipped his arms into the sleeves of his shirt and pulled the silken weave over his shoulders.

"Are you ready yet, darling?"

He could hear the fretful voice of his mother calling from downstairs. God! Why couldn't she leave him be? The second the thought passed his mind, a sharp, static jolt hit his nerves. No, he mustn't think that way. She loved him. She cared about him. He should be grateful for her attention.

"Almost!" called down Xiao, opening the door to his room. "Give me a minute."

"Okay, darling, but don't take too long. Fredericks is waiting in the car, and you don't want to be late for school."

"Okay, Mother," said Xiao with a conciliatory attitude, and returned to his dressing. He pulled on his silk-wool blended trousers his mother liked him to wear for school. She'd chosen them specially from his father's 'YouthDynamic' range.

She doesn't need to worry so much about me, thought Xiao, peering into the mirror and straightening his school tie. Maybe she's frightened I'll get ill again.

He didn't know much about the illness that had left him in hospital. Every time he tried to speak of it to his parents, they closed down, giving little insight except for claiming it was 'a nasty virus, but it's gone now'.

Thinking back, he couldn't remember much about when he'd been ill. Memories were sparse, and those he did have were filled with discordant images and confusing sensations. He'd just woken from sleeping, but his parents around his hospital bed had ecstatic expressions on their faces like they'd experienced something incredible.

Inside Xiao, he recalled a feeling of being terrified. He didn't want to open his eyes for a while. He was afraid to face a horror so dreadful his sight would be burned out just glancing upon it.

He'd also sensed peace, fulfilling and total, and it infused his body. It must have been a dream, but he could recall a lightness, akin to floating. Yet he was aware that he was still tethered to something. The floating, he didn't perceive it as being adrift, more like a gentle suspension above the surface of water in a calm sea. It was comforting, and he could discern a vibration of kindness and love.

From his parents doting behavior, he was well-aware he'd suffered a terrible illness but miraculously recovered. Coming out of the slumber, his body was feather light, as if he had no blood, muscle, or bone. A deep, comforting warmth had flooded into his being, and he'd been so pleased to see his parents there. All the animosity and rebellious attitudes he'd harbored seemed to have vanished.

It was strange why he'd been in hospital at all. Xiao didn't think he'd even been ill. He'd experienced no symptoms. Not like the ones he'd had when he'd contracted the flu last Christmas. He'd really suffered then. His throat had been swollen and raw, his phlegm-filled lungs had been heavy, making breathing painful, his nose had been stuffed with catarrh and green, nasty-looking mucus making his sinuses blocked, and his head had pounded continually with an ache that made him visualize his head exploding. Even his arms and legs were sore, and tiredness washed in waves through him as if he'd run a marathon.

But even with all that agony, he'd not ended up in hospital.

What had happened to him that warranted hospitalization?

A flicker of movement caught his attention, dragging him away from his contemplation, and his door burst open.

"Xiao, why aren't you down yet? You're going to be late for school."

His mother stood in the doorway and glared at him. Xiao frowned. The concern she constantly carried about him was getting into the realm of being suffocating.

"Mum, I did say I'd be down. Just give me time. You haunt me. Just let me be. Go down, please. Stop harassing me!"

His mother stared, worry lines etched across her sculptured face. "Sorry, Xiao. I just need to be with you. It's…it's…" His mother stopped talking and looked away, upset.

Xiao's arms flew up, annoyed, and he pushed his face in front of his mother's. "Why can't you leave me alone?" he shouted. "You've been like this since I came back from hospital. It's driving me crazy. I can't think like this."

His mother turned back to him. Xiao noticed her eyes were glassy, as if she was about to cry.

"Mum, what's wrong?"

Immediately, compassion for his mother overwrote his initial exasperated anger at her persistent coddling nature.

"Xiao, you've been very ill. We almost lost you."

Xiao glared at his mother, understanding the reason behind her constant fussing.

"Lost me? You mean I almost died?"

Xiao's voice dropped to a whisper. Could this strange floating feeling he remembered have been an out-of-body experience. A beyond-death encounter? Wow, this was almost too cool, thought Xiao, imagining how he was going to update his Facebook posts with this amazing information.

"Yes, you were virtually dead, Xiao. You were in a coma for many weeks. Your father and I didn't want to tell you as we thought it would frighten you, but as you've questioned my worrying nature, you had to know the truth."

His mother put her hand out to touch Xiao's shoulder. He could see love light up her eyes and inside of him, he sensed an inner vibration resonate in alignment with the love and care radiating from his mother. He didn't actually know how he knew this was happening, only that it was, and it made him feel content and happy.

He placed his hand on top of his mother's on his shoulder and grasped it.

"I won't leave you again, Mum. I'm sorry."

Xiao didn't quite realize what he was saying. His mouth seemed to be running off on its own. But the words brought a wide smile from his mother.

"Oh, my darling," said his mother, getting choked with emotion. "It wasn't your fault. It was something that just happened."

"How did it happen?" asked Xiao, fixing his mother with a steady look that told her, 'He had a right to know all'.

"The truth, my darling, is no one really knows. You collapsed on the plane coming back from Sharm El Sheikh, and you fell into a deep coma hours after we arrived in London. The doctors feared brain damage as the coma robbed you of your cognitive abilities in seconds."

"Cognitive?" said Xiao, confused, and he stared at his mother for an explanation. His mother sighed and shook her head.

"Stupid Lei," she berated herself. "You're too young to know that term.

What I meant was your brain functions. Your ability to speak, move, see, and hear. They vanished. You had a massive seizure and then fell into the coma. The doctors held no hope, but I never lost mine. Every day, I was with you. I stayed by your side. Spoke to you. As if you were there with me."

Xiao was spellbound by his mother's words. He never realized he'd been *that* ill. Why hadn't they told him earlier?

"And I said nothing all the time you were there?"

Xiao could see a distant look flicker in his mother's eyes. It was clear she was remembering something.

"Mum, did I stay silent? Did I try to make any contact with you at all?"

His mother's hand tightened around his and she looked straight into his eyes. Xiao couldn't understand his mother's expression. She seemed hurt, angry, and devoted, all at once. It was a weird look to see on one's mother. Like she hated him for a split second, and then was accepting of him, and then loved him unconditionally.

Chaos reigned inside of Xiao as he tried in vain to decipher what emotion his mother was really showing.

"Mum, are you okay?" said Xiao, feeling confused, and even a little afraid of the signals in his mother's eyes.

"You didn't say anything, but I felt you telling me one thing. That you wanted to survive."

Chapter 11

Reggie woke. His mind groggy and his sight obliterated by the hood still on his head. He ached. Coldness hit his bare skin. Someone had deprived him of his clothes, albeit his underpants. His hands had been affixed behind him with plastic ties. His short arms had been pulled around the back of the chair he sat on, and his legs had been pulled apart, with his knees positioned over the top of the chair's front legs and his ankles tied to the back legs of the chair. His tendons throbbed as his limbs strained against the wood that pressed into his flesh. Wellwood considered his state of undress and wondered what had happened to Janice. Had she received similar treatment? Or worse?

He heard a whimper close by.

"Janice. Is that you?" murmured Reggie hoping it was his political colleague. He kept his voice low.

"Yes, Reggie. I'm here. They…they've removed my clothes." Suddenly she sobbed. Reggie listened. He wanted to comfort her. However, moving was impossible. He pushed his shoulders back to gain better leverage, but the tightness of the ties prevented any maneuver and as he twisted and struggled, the ties cut into his wrists and ankles with unforgiving relentlessness.

"Janice, do you still have…"

"Yes, they left me with…I'm, I'm okay." Mumbled Janice. Reggie realized she didn't sound okay at all. She was terrified. So was he. Where were they? What was going on?

"Reggie, I'm going to try something," whispered Janice.

Reggie couldn't think what the petite brunette was going to try. "Be careful," he called back.

Janice didn't respond, but he could hear her breathing hard, as if she was pushing against something immovable. A creak sounded, and Janice breathed out and then in sharply again, and a guttural sound erupted from deep within her. Reggie thought he could discern a faint rocking and Janice made a growl, to encourage along whatever she was doing.

"What's happening Janice?"

No response, only another thrusting snarl, and now the rocking sound was clear. Oh God, she was going to tip the chair.

"Janice, no – don't!"

The chair tipped past its point of balance and crashed down. Hitting the floor boards, Janice was choked by startling pain behind her. She'd seen it done in films many times. The chair always broke so easily then. Why hadn't she managed it too? Janice lay on her back like an upturned turtle. Pain wracked through her. She felt exposed and stupid for trying such a dangerous stunt. Tears welled up in her eyes and she cried loudly.

"Janice, Janice, what happened? What did you do?"

Janice breathed in and a raging fire of pain engulfed her lower arm.

A rush of footsteps took her attention momentarily from a pain that was pushing her to unconsciousness. Hands came upon her, pulling her upright. They touched her arms and Janice screamed. Pain took hold and her head swam. She wanted to throw up. She breathed deep and ragged.

"Stupid bitch!"

The man's voice, with its hard, gruff tone made her cower. She wished they'd remove the hood. She needed to see what was going on. The darkness and the pain brought nausea, and she was certain before long she'd vomit.

"Please help me. My hands…" whispered Janice, almost frightened to say a word.

"I can see," retorted the man.

Another man's voice, sharper and well spoken. "Daft bint. It's fractured wrist. Looks like one of the carpal bones, maybe the scaphoid."

Janice listened, and he sounded clinically precise, like a doctor. She appealed to him.

"Please take the hood off. I'm going to be sick." Janice, through pain had become bolder.

"Not happening darling. Shut up otherwise I'll leave your wrist to mend by itself."

Janice swallowed down the nausea and remained silent. She didn't want to aggravate the men or cause them to take any harsher action than they had already done.

She noticed Reggie hadn't said anything to the men. She guessed he was pretending to still be out with the drug they'd given. Perhaps, he was figuring out what play to make with the men. She hoped he was, she couldn't take much more of this treatment. The agony of her wrist threatened unconsciousness.

"I'm going to release your hands. You try anything, and I'll cut your hands off. Understand."

His words brought her mind quick into focus. She felt the flat side of something she knew to be a knife draw down her forearm. Instinctively, Janice jumped at the touch of the metal against her skin, and nodded her submission; her body involuntarily shivering as he pressed his hands upon her.

She felt as the man snapped off the ties and brought her arms around to the front. The pain throbbed with agonizing regularity. A result of her reckless movie-inspired maneuver.

Despite his roughness, the man genuinely wanted to mend her breakage. He took in the fallen chair and knew Janice had been trying something rash. Her checked her wrist on her right hand and it was as he'd expected, the scaphoid bone beneath her thumb jutted at an unnatural angle. He shook his head, echoing some degree of compassion within him, and he took a syringe and injected the injured area with an analgesic to counter the pain. Janice winced on insertion and then settled as the drug kicked in. He dove into his bag and brought out a container. Inside was a nano engineered bio-material built from stem cells and virus sized programmable machines. The material was pre-programmed to attend to bone breaks and fractures. He knew it was actively used in Special Forces to heal bone breakages quick enough to have the soldiers back in theatre within minutes.

The material appeared at first like a metallic lattice bandage. He took Janice's wrist and wrapped the bandage around it. Rapidly, as he watched, the material changed its state from solid to liquid and absorbed into Janice's body. The wrist bone that stuck out started to straighten and pull back into alignment with the bones in the rest of Janice's hand. The man raised an eyebrow, amazed by the capability of the nano-bioengineering geniuses who had created the NanoBandage. He observed as Janice shook slightly, but she didn't speak. The breakage was fully mended. He had to ensure the NanoBandage extracted safely from Janice's body. The man placed a device, like a very small mobile phone, over her wrist, and the metallic liquid exuded out of her skin, and reformed around her as a bandage again. Solid in structure, resembling a metallic, fragile lattice fabric, the man gently unwrapped the NanoBandage and replaced it back into his bag.

"You're sorted, now let's get down to business."

Chapter 12

Temenos recognized the slight coldness and fuzziness in the chamber. These indications spoke of displacement within the quantum field. Above him, the Reality Gap fluctuated with greater ripples of vibration. Reasons as to why were numerous. The most likely one being a group of fellow Kudamaz Elders travelling through the Reality Gap to somewhere in the universe.

He wondered whether he'd affected the Gap when he'd carried out the Resonance Implosion. Temenos stared up at the Reality Gap. The startling blue and orange colors had appeared to fade. Not by much. Hardly noticeable. But this fractional difference in hue made him uneasy.

Anything affecting the Reality Gap would ultimately affect Kudamun. For the Gap was the balancing medium between their inner dimension of reality and the universal plane.

He thought back to what he'd done with the Observation Room, the Resonance Implosion. Did Kudamun sense his actions? Did the sentient crystals feel betrayed? Could that be the cause of the Gap's anomalous behavior?

Temenos swallowed. The thought that he'd ruptured the Reality Gap was unthinkable. Beyond his comprehension. The Gap had hung there, suspended, since Kudamun had been created. Before his forefather's forefather's forefather. When pure energy from the Ancient Ones had crafted and molded Kudamun. From that point on, maintaining balance in the universe had become their sole responsibility.

And a game, considered Temenos, with a customary House of Etima smirk.

He then realized that the greater plan was where his focus should be. Not worrying about the Reality Gap. That would always stay constant.

"Pleased you've come to your senses."

Temenos turned. The voice emanated from the shadows.

"It's the Reality Gap. Its colors appear to wane. I was worried that our activities...that maybe we had somehow been the cause."

"Concern yourself with what needs to be done. Not the furnishings." The voice, still in the dark, refused to enlighten Temenos with a body.

"Yes, Great Ensi."

The voice rasped, "Never refer to me that way. I am beyond that pomp and paraphernalia so befitting of all the others. Call me Your Helper."

Temenos, aghast, stood back. Such an action of disrespect. He could not countenance its initiation. He shook his head with vehemence.

"I cannot. You are too great for such a menial title."

"The coat I wear is of a different cloth. You will call me Your Helper. That is my title and I am dedicated to that remit."

Temenos lowered his eyes to the floor in respect. The voice showed humility and selflessness of great magnitude, unaffected by the current position and holding strong with an unerring resolve to see their plan to its conclusion. So overwhelmed was Temenos, he had the urge to fall to the floor and genuflect in honor of the obsidian oracle.

The figure smiled. Brief like stardust after fireworks, the smile disappeared. And, once again, dark enfolded the sacred sentinel.

Chapter 13

Reggie heard a man walk around him and his chair. He felt a hand on his head and the hood was whipped off. The removal happened so fast, Reggie didn't have time to prepare himself. His eyes were wide and questioning, but he would have preferred to have pretended to be drugged out. It would have given him the opportunity to assess the individuals around him.

The three men, now unmasked, were clothed in well-tailored, dark suits. Their faces were tough and cold. Their eyes glinted with intelligence, dispassion, and condescension. Reggie noticed they carried gun holsters just visible beneath the line of their jackets.

One of the men was taller and slightly younger than the other two. He had an air of authority despite his lack of maturity, and Reggie noticed that the men deferred to the younger man to make decisions.

Reggie watched a short, stocky man with an angry presence stand behind Janice. He grabbed the material and yanked the hood off her head with a rough gesture. Free of the claustrophobic hood, Janice flicked her head up toward the man who had released her from the purgatorial cloth prison.

"What is this about?" Janice shouted, raw with indignation at the removal of her clothes, and although terrified of her captors, furious at the still undetermined, and more importantly, unrevealed, reason for their incarceration.

The third man came into the light. He had broad, muscular shoulders, an almost square head exhibiting a crew cut, and a thick-set jaw. Of medium height, he looked as if he could have been a boxer in his earlier years.

He turned Reggie and Janice to face him, and then stood with his arms crossed and legs apart in front of the petrified Cabinet ministers, glaring at them without expressing a word.

The taller, younger man took up post behind Reggie, and the short, stocky man slipped in behind Janice.

Reggie looked at his friend. Her face was drained of color, but she sat still, defiant and silent. Despite the ordeal she'd gone through, she jutted out her chin and glowered with resolute insolence at her tormentors.

Something about the men's deportment implied to Reggie that they were not terrorists, but were, in fact, government agents. He was certain it wasn't a coincidence that they showed up at the exact moment he was showing Janice the weaponized upgrade to the Surv-Motes. Redfern or even Ashton himself was behind their imprisonment.

"Do you know why you are here?" Boxer-man asked, and looked from Reggie to Janice, and back to Reggie again.

Janice glanced down, indicating to her semi-naked body, and snorted with derision. "Well, it's not for your five-star hospitality, is it?"

Boxer-man raised an eyebrow at Janice's open rebuke.

"Protocol requires your present state," explained Boxer-man.

His matter-of-fact demeanor grated on Reggie. But it was Janice who stole his words.

"Protocol! What bloody protocol requires that you hood us, abduct us at gun point, disrobe us, and keep us tied in an excruciating stress position?"

Reggie admired Janice's courage but was watchful of the agent's response. Boxer-man carried a shallow smile, unsubstantiated by joy and held only to elicit discomfort. His eyes narrowed to slits at Janice's outburst.

"The protocol that is in place when we deal with individuals who engage in subversive and traitorous actions."

Their faces told their feelings. Reggie stunned. Janice furious.

"Do you know who we are?" Janice screamed, unabashed by her untenable position.

"Yes. We do. And we know that you are less than willing to conduct your patriotic duties in accordance with your public office. We have evidence to demonstrate this. Continuance of such acts constitute treason and, therefore, intervention was the inevitable consequence."

Boxer-man stared, his abhorrence of the Cabinet ministers evident. Reggie could see his eyes darken and his mouth turn into a horizon line. He looked to his colleagues behind the ministers and nodded. Stainless steel and glass flashed in Reggie's peripheral vision. He gasped as his frazzled brain computed its shape.

"We understand that you, Minister Wellwood, have been quite recalcitrant in your acceptance to carry through the prime minister's instructions. Your questioning at every turn is a clear articulation of your unpatriotic stance and shows a flagrant disregard of your public duty. Minister Perkins, you too have contravened the accepted norms of your public office through your association and intended collusion with Minister Wellwood. Your clear obfuscation of responsibility had to be addressed in the same way. From the intelligence collected, you have both been found guilty of unpatriotic behavior and dereliction of duty."

Reggie hadn't uttered a word until that point, but listening to the charges brought forth against him in the kangaroo court, he bit down on his lip then answered back. He tried to summon a deep, powerful voice. All he summoned up, however, was a wheezing, chesty coughing voice and a small officious tone that floated in the air resembling an uptight school mistress on a reprimand spree.

"How dare you! How bloody dare you! Janice and I are the very epitome of patriotism. We have upheld our duties. Never have we engaged in any act that could be interpreted as subversive."

Boxer-man interjected with swift authority, talking over Wellwood's words. "And what were you about to do before we arrived?"

Wellwood followed Boxer-man's eyeline to a small table where the file with the Surv-Mote weaponized upgrade lay.

"The very fact this 'Eyes Only' document has left the confines of your office confirms your ability to engage in subversive activity."

Reggie stared at Janice and she fixed her eyes at a point on the floor. Her cheeks blushed rose with embarrassment. Janice couldn't look at Reggie. He shook his head. He was the cause of their incarceration.

At least he knew with assurance that he wasn't at the hands of a new terrorist regime. The knowledge filled him with ambivalence. With terrorists, there was always a barter, something to exchange. With government agents, there was nothing. They had absolute power, by proxy, to corrupt and destroy anyone with whom Ashton took umbrage. Anyone who had pressed too hard or crossed the PM's red line of authority. Reggie swallowed deeply as his thoughts manifested further, producing a chilling clarity that his fear couldn't accept and his body couldn't countenance. He swiped a side look at Janice and saw she was trembling. The reality of their predicament had struck her with savage intensity, and her face was now scared and solemn in recognition of their on-coming fate.

The tall, young man stepped forward from behind Reggie and spoke.

"Ministers Wellwood and Perkins, you have been found guilty of the act of subversion and unpatriotic behavior. Prime Minister Ashton, however, is a truly tolerant and magnanimous leader who understands the confusion and the temptation to stray from the path of righteousness. He has thus decided to allow clemency for your crimes on condition that you conform to the accepted norms of your office, and that you never initiate in an activity such as the one we were compelled to remove you from following through. Do we have an acceptance of these conditions?"

The tall, young man awaited the responses from the Cabinet ministers. He stood, patient and calm, but his eyes pierced Janice and Reggie.

"And what if we do not accept your conditions?" asked Janice. Her sight bore deep into tall, young man's eyes, matching his laser-force strength stare for stare.

"Then we would have to commence with our initial investigation. An investigation, I might add, that could easily find you to be Al Nadir sympathizers."

The tall, young man stood in front of the ministers, his arms folded.

"So do you want us to continue our investigations? We're perfectly happy to do so."

Janice and Reggie exchanged horrified glances. Al Nadir sympathizers equaled treason and the death penalty. From a slightly reckless act to full blown treason. Reggie couldn't believe what he was hearing. Ashton had become a tyrant.

The tall, young man walked up to Reggie and then turned to Janice, and shook his head.

"Your silence issues a dangerous indifference to your current fate. You do understand that if we were to find you Al Nadir sympathizers and, by default, guilty of treason, you would be stripped naked, taken to a cell where you would become the property of Freedom Earth to do with you as we so wish, and following our usage of you, you would be executed. For, as you are well aware, Al Nadir terrorists are not given the luxury of a jury. It is the law that they are shown no mercy. 'Take no prisoners, accept no excuses'. So, therefore, I ask for a third and final time, Minister Reginald Courtenay Wellwood and Minister Janice Dorothea Perkins, do you accept the conditions that I have outlined?"

Reggie looked at Janice. She was catatonic. Her face of insolence and bold resolve had fractured revealing another face of fright and fear. The tall, young man sneered at Janice, and his eyes roamed over her breasts and between her legs. He licked his lips.

Reggie recognized his intention.

"That's enough! I may have been rash in taking secret documents out of Whitehall but this persecution and intimidation is overstepping the mark. You know we're not Al Nadir."

The tall, young man shrugged, and casually said, "You could be. Investigations could prove anything."

"Anything you want them to. Yes, I understand how this works. And yes, of course we agree to the conditions you've imposed." Reggie snapped out his words.

"And your colleague, Minister Perkins, is she of the same mind?" asked the tall, young man, and he sidled over to Janice, crouched in front of her, and reached out, touching her chin.

Janice trembled. She stared at the tall, young man. His arrogant, demeaning attitude sparked her ire and, somehow, she built enough strength to launch out of her terrified state and respond, "Yes. I am of the same mind. I agree to your conditions." Janice kept her voice even and paced to counter the shaking taking over her body.

"Excellent decision, Ministers," exclaimed the tall, young man. "Now time for a little trip."

The stainless steel and glass thing that had flashed past Reggie earlier came back into focus. Boxer-man and short, stocky man both held syringes in their hands. They advanced upon the protesting ministers, who both screamed.

"We've agreed to your conditions," cried Reggie. "Oh please God. No!"

Tall, young man watched as Boxer-man and short, stocky man took their respective syringes and stuck them, with some ferocity, into the ministers' necks. The moment the chloral hydrate inside the needles hit the ministers' bloodstreams, they slumped in their chairs.

The tall, young man gave his instruction, "Take them away."

As his colleagues snipped the plastic ties with pliers, the tall, young man's phone rang.

"Yes, Prime Minister, it's all done, sir. They will not be a problem to you anymore."

Chapter 14

"Ellie, darling, we've got a meeting with Ashton. Are you ready?"

I turn as Sam steps into the Observation Room where I've been flicking through the past incarnations of myself. I smile. Sam is still so very self-assured. So totally dominating. Selema memories flood me and I recall him as Dumuzi all those Earth millennia ago. His powerful, controlling presence remains with me. But not in a bad way. I enjoyed the feeling of Dumuzi handling things. As Selema, I had been much younger in Earth years than him. Of course, to a human, I was ancient. But, as I've said before, time doesn't register in Kudamun. Only through our symbiotic connection to other planets' time systems do we age at all.

I'm Kudamaz, but I have my human memories still. My physiology has changed. But has my psychology? It is a question I often ask myself. Am I thinking as Kudamaz, human, or both? What does it mean to be Kudamaz? And what is it to be human anyway? To be human cannot just reside in biology. A psychopath like Al Douri was made of flesh and bone, but he had no humanity. Could he be regarded as human when, really, he was a monster? Aren't humans just full of moments hard-coded into memories? The sum of your worth is the sum of your experiences. And if these experiences are rendered just as memories, am I really less human now than when I was biologically human? The memories are there with me always. Unfortunately, so is every memory reflecting every event that's ever happened to me throughout the many millennia of my time on Earth. Some wonderful. Some sad. Thankfully, I have a way to filter them and only see in my mind what I want to or need to see. My most recent memories as Ellie are the most horrific, and they seem to float to the top of my mind's contents page with unnerving regularity. I keep them contained, but when I sleep, it proves a harder task.

Control is much less. Just like humans, we Kudamaz appear to 'let go' whilst asleep. Not that we really need to sleep. Some Kudamaz choose just to rest. But, in truth, we never get tired. At least not the tiredness humans experience. Sleep for Sam and I is more a way to take the edge off not being human anymore. An active running memory from human time that cons my Kudamaz frame into believing I need to submit to slumber.

Putting my trust in a lie.

Again.

At first glance, the Kudamaz are like humans. We are, however, completely different internally. We are pure energy housed in a human form. We have no blood, organs, bones, or even a brain. Nothing that constrains us or makes us infallible. We are constantly connected at the quantum level through our quantum self, and our soul force is the center of our being, through which all our energy comes from and flows back to. It is our powerhouse and determines our light and dark balance. Even we as Kudamaz have to have a balance of both energies. But, as my house is Giznu, the House of Light, I am heavily predisposed to the light energy side.

Any seemingly human thing I do, whether it's bleeding, crying, getting drunk, or sleeping, originates from being manifested into reality by triggering hard-coded memory energies within my databanks that make up something humans call 'the mind'. A real case of thought energy makes matter.

"What's happening, Ellie? Are you ready or what?"

From Sam's irritated tone, it is apparent that whatever I was thinking, I was obviously thinking too much. My husband and timeless lover has been ignored.

"Darling, I'm almost ready," I say, flashing my brilliant ultramarine eyes to placate him.

I had decided to wear a cool, blue trouser suit, figure-hugging, of course. As Sam says, with a figure like mine, the only thing you can do is hug it. I smile, realizing that reconstitution has given me the physique that no amount of painful hours with a personal trainer could ever deliver.

"Well, hurry up. We're going to be late if we don't leave now. We mustn't keep the PM waiting. It doesn't look professional," snaps Sam, refusing to succumb to my charms.

The feeling of déjà vu hits me, strong. Back in March that year, after Sam had revealed he really worked for MI6 and not the Foreign Office. My databanks replay the scene so clearly. Sam had stood in front of me demanding to know why I'd screamed. At the time, I'd been unable to remember myself why I'd screamed, due to the reality pull that Aby-od had enacted to increase his ability to communicate with me. Aswa-da had interfered with said ability, and intentionally sabotaged Aby-od's 'calling process to Ellie as the Protector's lifeforce holder'. I'd told a lie. I'd said it was a spider. I knew Sam hadn't believed me, but he'd let it go. Then he'd spoken about how he'd kept the secret as a way to shield me from danger. 'What you didn't know couldn't hurt you. You were safe. But that's changed. The balance shifted this morning'. I recall Sam's ratty attitude. I'd been obsessed with 'balance shifted' but not really knowing why. I'd tried to hold Sam back and talk to him about the words, and as a result, he'd been late for another meeting with the prime minister.

Just what was happening now.

Had things really changed *that* much?

Chapter 15

Reggie waited outside the Cabinet office. All his life he seemed to be waiting somewhere. After what had happened a few days before, he knew he should have just upped and left the whole damn sorry state that Westminster had become under the absolute rule of Prime Minister Ashton.

But he was a coward.

That was something the PM obviously knew, hence his appointment. He'd wanted to surge against Ashton. Somebody must have listened to his brief exchange in the Westminster bar. For within minutes of meeting Janice in the little Italian café, they'd been abducted and rendered to a place that could only be described as a 'very dark hole'.

With an unexpected shiver, the memories flooded through him and he suppressed the desire to heave. He knew that the PM had been behind their sudden incarceration.

Distribution of the upgraded Surv-Motes had been undertaken swiftly and without further question. He agreed with Janice never to mention the horrendous experience again.

And never, ever to cross the PM.

Redfern strode into the waiting room. He stared at Reggie with complete distaste and the look of finding something unpleasant on his shoe.

Reggie took it without retort. Redfern would have known about the event. He may even have orchestrated it. Reggie couldn't win. He just had to accept the reality and collect his salary like a good boy.

"Wellwood, please come with me." Redfern's clipped tongue offered no warmth.

"I, erm, thought the PM was, erm…meeting us here?" Reggie stumbled over his words.

"Why would you think that?" asked Redfern, the disdain dripping from his lips,

"Well, I thought, I was, erm, well…I was told…because, well, I assumed as I was asked to be here…"

"My dear boy, never assume anything. Assumptions are bad things. Lead you into all kinds of pickles. Really not done. Trust me. Stick to the facts," Redfern sneered. His eyes danced mischievously over Reggie, taunting him to respond.

'What if I don't know the bloody facts?' was what Reggie wanted to say. But, instead, he just nodded dumbly.

"So to work. Come with me." Redfern opened the door. He motioned for Reggie to go through into the room.

Crossing the threshold, Reggie asked with a timid verging on scared tone, "Where are we going?"

Redfern answered confidently, "You'll see."

Chapter 16

Thurso, Scotland

One of the things that I miss is not shimmering together. I've tapped into my inherent knowledge on shimmering and I discovered that your soul force reflects how you shimmer. It's the soul force that connects with the quantum energies that effectively split me apart, only to restore me at the destination. As Kudamaz, we exist at every moment, everywhere across the universe, and at every instance of every universe within infinite possibilities. This is why we only have to think of a place, and we are there in that place, since our quantum self is already there and it is our soul force that brings us into reality.

Difficult for humans to comprehend, but very straightforward for Kudamaz elders. I guess humans are confined to three-dimensional space and ruled by time ticking. The notion of being everywhere at a single moment in time is inconceivable. The human brain is not developed enough to understand it, which is rather unfortunate as it would certainly ease up the jam on the Bakerloo tube line in the morning.

I used to enjoy shimmering with Sam caught in a loving embrace. His soul force entwined with mine. He could feel the wonders of life across the universe in the instant we shimmered. It blew his mind the first time, but I kept him centered. He was tethered to me and I'd always protect him.

Now, when we shimmer, it's different. He doesn't hold onto me anymore. He's independent, and I always feel the tremendous dominating power emanating from him just before shimmer. It's very masculine. Very primal. He's the alpha male of the shimmer.

The irony is for all this showmanship and posturing, I am still more powerful than Sam, even with his incredible Kudamaz life force given by Dumuzi.

I keep that knowledge quiet. When he was human, Sam had a hard time coming to terms with my metamorphosis. At first, he'd thought his Ellie had been possessed by aliens, and then he descended into a dark mind-set, announcing 'he'd wished we'd both died as that would have been more natural'. On hearing this, I refrained from immediately saying that there was nothing natural about being 'shagged to death by a group of sex-crazed, sadistic megalomaniacs'. I just admitted that his Ellie was 'a bit different to the girl he'd married'. We never resolved it and, at that time, I had no interest in idle discussion, as I was 'on the clock' trying to prevent a universal disaster. I must admit, the pressure I was under had made me rather snappy. Strangely, my sharp tongue had somehow connected and rung true for Sam more than the gentle, compassionate one I'd been using. Then he had accepted me as 'his Ellie' again.

I drag a little behind Sam as I emerge out of shimmer into the mansion house in Thurso in Scotland. The location was Ashton's choice. I'd suggested keeping it in Westminster, but he'd been adamant to have it as far away from London as possible, but still in the UK. I'd commented as a joke, 'Well, how about Land's End?' Ashton had laughed, but became suddenly serious and stated, 'No, but John O'Groats may just work. There's a lovely manor house I used to stay at back in the day, and it would make a super venue for our *unveiling event*'.

That was what Ashton called the meeting we were about to have. His unveiling event. I'd been against it from the start, but Sam had talked me around.

We arrive in the manor house and enter the board room. The place designated for the important meeting. Sam and I sit down. Him at the table. I take a window seat and gaze out of the window at the magnificent shoreline with its lapping waves and abundance of birdlife.

"Ellie, get up. He's coming!" says Sam, jumping up abruptly on seeing Ashton enter the room.

I can't understand why Sam is still feeling the need to be subservient to the prime minister. It is almost like he has a vestige of MI6 Agent Sam Noor still inside him. Which, of course, silly me, he does.

Unlike my reconstitution that completely obliterated the human Ellie, Sam's human side literally melded with Dumuzi, enabling a true hybrid to manifest. This is why he behaves differently to me. Sam still has his behavioral cellular memory which I have lost. I look human in my outer form. But my physiology, every part of me, is one hundred percent Kudamaz. My memories as Ellie have been integrated into my mind like a flash memory. If I wanted,

I could remove them, and I would cease to be Ellie. Or would I?

Ellie is made up out of a thousand past lives, their hopes and dreams, tears and fears. Removing my most recent incarnation wouldn't take away what Ellie is. It would only erase a fragment in time. In a way, it might be good. I wouldn't remember all that torture, that pain, and that horrible betrayal. But then I wouldn't be able to recall the good times with Sam and the sheer joy of waking up knowing I was a woman who had found her greatest love.

Caught in a philosophical thought, I neglect to realize Ashton's outstretched hand before me, and my husband poking my side to respond.

"Hello, Ashton. Sorry. Deep in thought," I announce authoritatively, shaking his hand.

The moment my hand slips into Ashton's, I feel it. The vibrations shake through me. I force myself to read his Balance Shift. Perfect equilibrium. No change. Just like last time. And every other time since I've scanned him on that fateful day when the end of life itself beckoned.

"Not too deep, I hope," says Ashton, smiling. "Want you on terra firma for a while. Need help with sorting out those Al Nadir stragglers that don't seem to want to back down. And some other business that I know Sam will be interested in."

For some reason, I have an uncomfortable twinge in the pit of my stomach. His voice is like treacle. Sickly and suffocating. The room's dark and light energy lanes, which are trapped in the quantum fabric and can be seen only by me, erupt with stark visibility as I take a reading of the environment around the PM. I know the energy lanes are made a reality for me by the interactions with things around them. All I can see are dark energy flows everywhere. Virtually no white light energy can be seen. Such flows, I know, are impossible if Ashton really is in equilibrium.

It doesn't make sense.

"Really sorry, but I have to go," I say.

I stare at Sam who looks incredulously at me, his lips mouthing, 'What the fuck?'

His face is a mask of embarrassment. With his lips thinned, he speaks to me, his reprimanding voice on full blast, "Ellie, we're about to start the meeting. What is more important than working on a blueprint for world peace?"

I notice Ashton looking quizzically at Sam and then at me. He seems to be enjoying Sam's discomfort. Ashton's expression brings back another face: Salim Al Douri, just after Sam had broken and revealed Malta as the location of the Peace Summit. And after that fucking, fucking bitch had all but ripped me apart. The eyebrow raised in anticipation at the mention of the 'floorshow'. That smirk on his face. All were Ashton's features now.

Am I crazy? Am I imagining it? Something is wrong.

I know that much.

"As I said, I'm sorry, but I really do have to go."

I shimmer rapidly away from Ashton's mocking eyes and familiar sneer. Sam's face gradually fading into a mist of hurt and confusion.

Chapter 17

The quantum energies describe a universe in constant fluctuation. I focus my soul force. In one instant I was on Earth, by the sea in Scotland in a private estate in Wick. The next, I am in the Hall of Umray in Kudamun.

Aby-od is standing by a light circuit embedded into the translucent crystal wall. Aby-od is the Leader of Kudamun, Head of the House of Giznu, also known as the House of Light, and the reason I am here and not shredded into pieces by the care of sweet Sabena.

On first glance, Aby-od looks like an ancient king of Earth civilizations thousands of years ago. If the truth be known, Earth's first civilization, the Sumerians, molded themselves on the Kudamaz. They received explicit instructions from Aby-od's predecessor, Dimkur. He had been a little too explicit by allowing himself to be seen, and such a sighting had resulted in man copying his image as a god. Humans reflected Dimkur in their own appearance, fashioning the Kudamaz corrugated beard and ringlets as part of their own image.

"Aby-od, I need to speak with you urgently." I have no idea how I am going to voice my suspicions, but I know I need to talk to someone about Ashton.

"Yes, Ellie? What's on your mind?" Aby-od's calm tone gently soothes me, as it always does.

"Ashton. He's not the man we think he is. I know I said I believed him and that he wasn't responsible for that Pain of Parsu stuff. And I know I've watched him bring the world together through Freedom Earth. But I have my doubts again."

I realize that what I have said, without clear evidence, is insane. Especially after what had happened to Ashton, all he'd gone through. With Aby-od's dark eyes widening, it is obvious he thinks the same. But he seems at least willing to hear me out.

"Why do you say this now?"

"His Balance Shift is in equilibrium. It hasn't changed. Not once. Not an iota. Even when his entire family was wiped out. Is that right? And he…" I look at Aby-od. Here is a man who deals in facts, substantiated facts, not inklings and hunches. I wonder on his reaction to what I will say next. "Reminds me of Salim Al Douri. I think he's evil, Aby-od. And he's fooling everyone."

Aby-od shakes his head. "Oh, my dear Ellie. Salim is dead. You killed him. You know that."

"Of course I know that."

I snort, still remembering his annihilation at my hand. That wonderful opportunity I'd been afforded to torture him before killing him with my rainbow light, representing all the goodness of the souls he'd so brutally taken.

"I don't mean he's come back," I continue. "I'm talking about Ashton's mannerisms. They mirror Salim's. I'm telling you, Aby-od, Ashton is not the peacemaker he makes out to be."

"I'm sorry, Ellie. I don't see that. Ashton is a man who has suffered so much for what he believes in. He lost his entire family and almost his life. Yet, despite all that, Ashton has gone on to deliver considerable peace and world security since the downfall of Al Nadir. He's orchestrated the restoration of a natural balance across the world. Through his Freedom Earth movement, he's done amazing things. I know. I've watched him. Ashton's a man who has even brought the faiths together. They'll be no more wars over religion. Mankind is close to achieving true harmony. You know this. You've been there with him."

I listen and, although it all sounds plausible, I'm not convinced. I know that the Observation Screen isn't infallible. I've had my experience of it before with its weird playback regarding Ashton's engagement with Quantum Force, and the real part President Hutchinson played in that. Only I cannot voice any suspicions. I recall having done that before and it was almost the end of me.

A key tenet within the Order of Kudamun is that the Observation Screen cannot lie. It records every moment across the universe. As I understand it, the Screen's internal mechanisms use the resonance of the time stream of the planet under observation, and the Screen then automatically aligns itself with the same resonance pattern to provide a live view and playback of any moment on any planet up to the current time on Continuum for the planet under observation. Jumping further ahead in a planet's Continuum is strictly forbidden under antediluvian law and any Kudamaz found doing so would be in breach of the Order of Kudamun and face summary execution. Given the incendiary, and virtually fatal outcome of even daring to question the accuracy of the Observation Screen, I hold my tongue regarding what Aby-od has and hasn't seen Ashton doing on the Screen.

"He's only been able to achieve such meteoric success because of our help. He's used Sam and me to take Freedom Earth to a different level. I helped him as I was unable to say no. I've been influenced by something beyond the Pain of Parsu that you said Ashton couldn't trigger. Something inside me couldn't refuse Ashton if it meant Earth achieving peace. I know it's to do with my Protector's internal make-up. Something hard-coded in me. An intrinsic need to protect. It's what I must live by. I'm not exactly sure, but I think it's the reason I could withstand torture whilst I was human. Ashton knew, or found out, or…Oh, I don't know. But with me, he always knows what buttons to press. I'd never have agreed to support him otherwise."

"Ellie, you have a sworn duty to protect Earth. His objective, peace on Earth, naturally forced you to accept his will. It means everything he was doing was good. You can't refuse goodness."

"Aby-od, you talk as if I didn't have any freewill."

"Where Earth is concerned, Ellie, you don't. Your objective is to protect Earth at all costs, wipe out evil, and maintain a white light balance. That is why you were created."

"If I don't have freewill where Earth is concerned, how can I know that these auto-will actions I'm taking are the right ones?"

"Because you'll only take those actions if they are right. Your auto-will, if you like to call it as such, can only be triggered by acts that are in favor of Earth's advancement. Essentially, they should be of a good origin and leading Earth to a good destination. Your auto-will cannot be triggered by any other circumstance."

"But how did Ashton know that?"

Aby-od looks at me wearily and I can see he is now irritated by my constant questioning.

"Ellie, we've been through this before. It's only you who has made such a judgement. All I can see from observed discussions is Ashton talking about peace, harmony, and man's evolution. I saw no manipulation and nothing malevolent in his demeanor to constitute your continual insinuation of his wrongdoings. If anything, he's a man who has had serious wrong done to him. He lost his entire family, Ellie. Doesn't that mean anything to you?"

Aby-od is showing signs of exasperation. I am caught in a vicious circle. If Ashton is doing something wicked, Kudamun would know, but Kudamun sees only a strong white light balance for Earth. So everything Ashton is doing must be right.

"Yes, I know, he's a big victim. He's lost so much. But you know what, Aby-od? All I have seen is what he's gained from those dreadful days in May. His status is elevated. The world loves him. But Freedom Earth, the religious unification, everything he's achieved is down to his association with Sam and me. Can't you see that?"

I am maddened by Aby-od's blindness.

"Yes, Ellie. I can see that. But however Ashton's done it, he's done it for good. I can't see anything wrong in what he's done."

"Maybe you're seeing only what you want to see." I'm not pleased. I feel my frustration building.

"What do you mean?" snaps Aby-od.

"Well, uniting Earth in a single cause for good, that's going to help the House of Giznu, isn't it?"

"Of course. But that's not why I believe everything is good with Ashton."

"Are you sure? Because right now I think you're going *fucking* blind. Something's not right. I don't know what it is, but I'm going to find out. I'll get the facts. I know how much evidence is so precious to you." I spit the words out with vitriol. I am burning with anger. Aby-od is blind. Really blind. And I am determined to show him the truth.

"Ellie, now, listen." I can hear Aby-od's voice is hurt, but I don't care. "Why are you always like this? Please don't be so-"

It's too late. Aby-od's words cut abruptly, sliced in two by the instant shimmer to my house in Winchester, England.

Back in Kudamun, in the shadows, a figure watched the interplay. He looked thoughtful and then smirked. It was time to pull those aces out of his sleeve.

Chapter 18

Ellie's sudden disappearance had left the meeting slightly tainted. Ashton took a moment to stare out of the window. The sky was a dazzling blue, with unbroken sunshine warming the golden beaches rolling around the crescent cove, washed by sparkling seas of azure. Plump, healthy sheep wandered the fields, grazing on verdant vegetation in front of the estate. If he took a picture there and then, it would surely win a 'nature's beauty captured' prize. The view, framed by the impressive windows of the manor house, was, by any measure, quite spectacular. For a few seconds, he wasn't British PM; he was just Richard Ashton, a man who could appreciate the wonderful joys of life, its diversity, its strength, its colors, and its abundance of light. He could feel what it meant to be truly alive.

The feeling touched his soul.

Unexpectedly, his head throbbed with a sudden, piercing pain, and his vision clouded. He shut his eyes to control the pulsing stabs behind his corneas. Instant blackness sucked him down, and he was caught in an avalanche of pure emotion that tumbled from him into a deep void.

And then a rising again of that surging power. So strong, so dominating. He could stand on the shoulders of gods; such was the strength welling up inside him.

Ashton opened his eyes. The view in front of him hadn't changed. But he turned away, tired of its pure wholesomeness. In the corner of his eye, he clocked a sheep, face down, feeding, with her offspring nestling close. That lamb will go down a bomb with a touch of rosemary. And he made a mental note to tell the housekeeper to arrange for slaughter later.

"Prime Minister, I do apologize for Ellie's departure. She's been a bit erratic lately." Sam could feel the tingle of humiliation erupting on his face.

Ashton shrugged magnanimously, indicating that it didn't really matter.

Sam bowed his head, grateful for the PM's understanding.

"So, shall we get started?" said Ashton, holding on gently to Sam's arm and leading him to a mahogany table with a stunning, gold-leaf crest embedded into its center.

Sam met the PM's pace and took his place at the table. Sitting down, he glanced around, wondering where Ashton's confidante was.

"Jensen's joining, isn't he?"

"Oh goodness, yes. He wouldn't miss a meeting like this. He's just sorting out a few things. As you know, we're expecting Martyn, Reggie, and the usual suspects. They're flying up from City. Should be arriving any time now." Ashton answered but didn't raise his head from reading the papers in front of him.

"That's, erm...good," answered Sam, feeling a little awkward sitting with the PM who was clearly ignoring him. Must be pissed off about Ellie leaving, despite shrugging it off.

Sam ventured to make conversation to ease the suppressed tension in the room.

"I'm pleased Freedom Earth is going well, sir."

"Sam, I think, given what you are, you can drop this 'sir' business. It's all pretty fucking meaningless."

The PM's ice-cold stare and sharp tongue delivered an even greater level of discomfort. From the tone of Ashton's words, he sounded very jealous and bitter. Sam's eyes locked with Ashton's and a shiver ran through him.

"Right, well, of course, sir, erm...Richard," said Sam.

"Friends call me Rich. You should do the same. You are, after all, a friend. Aren't you, Sam?"

The PM's intense stare made Sam question the statement.

Before either of the men at the table had time to regard their situation further, the door opened and Jensen Stalbridge, the PM's advisor strode into the room, followed by Nathan Cartwright, Head of MI6, Dudley Gibbs, MI5 Chief, Paul Weaver, Home Secretary, Janice Perkins, Energy Minister, Lance Remington, Foreign Secretary, Martyn Redfern, and, finally, Reggie Wellwood.

Stalbridge took his seat next to the PM, as usual. Redfern walked around the table and sat down next to Sam. Cartwright and Gibbs sat on the other side of Stalbridge. Weaver, Remington, and Perkins sat next to Redfern, leaving Wellwood dallying behind and unsure of where to sit.

"Reggie, take a pew for God's sake," said Redfern, smirking and Sam noticed he relished in broadcasting Reggie's inadequacy.

Flushing scarlet, Reggie sat down where he'd been standing. Sam watched as he flicked a stare back and forth at those seated around the table. It became apparent to Sam that Reggie had inadvertently ostracized himself from the rest of the meeting when he'd dropped into the nearest chair to save his embarrassment, only to realize he was far away. Reggie pushed back his chair and stood up. Sam swung a surreptitious glance at Redfern. It was what he'd expected. Redfern's eyes were glued to Reggie, casting derision at the defense secretary's actions. Reggie stared at the floor, pulled his new chair closer to the group and sat in silence with his eyes downwards.

"Right. Well, now we've all finished playing musical chairs," stated the PM, looking pointedly at Wellwood. "We can get down to business. Over to you, Martyn."

Redfern nodded swiftly, "Thank you, Prime Minister. Today we have two items on the agenda: Al Nadir mop up and full roll-out of Quantum Force's energy source within the UK. For the first item, I'd appreciate a brief update from Five and Six on where we are."

Redfern swept a look at Cartwright and Gibbs. Sam knew the Cabinet secretary would adhere to protocol in the case of security, which meant Five always delivered first. Gibbs, a dark hulk of a man, ex-army-general and an outstanding prop forward in rugby during his time at Oxford, went to speak.

Gibbs' sharp, brown eyes analyzed everyone at the table as he positioned himself to provide the intelligence update to the PM. His stare rested on Sam. He knew his background at Six. A magnificent spy who'd done everything for his country, but who had been shafted by Cartwright's predecessor. Something to do with his wife being taken by Six and interrogated without restraint. He also knew there was a cloak of secrecy surrounding the events of Sam's capture and eventual escape from Al Nadir on March 27. His wife Ellie had also been kidnapped by Al Nadir in the UK at the same time. Her escape was also shrouded in the same level of mystery as her husband's. Both Sam and his wife had been debriefed, but only in the presence of the PM. Even after the debrief, the account had been heavily redacted, and was only accessible to Cartwright. Gibbs concluded that the truth remained with the PM. The one person who knew the exact details.

What Gibbs did know was soon after Sam's return, he'd vanished again, and taken his wife with him on his mission. Cartwright had kept things quiet as to why she'd been recruited. Cartwright had only indicated her skillset had been 'impressive'. Both Cartwright and he had been told the couple were undertaking 'special duties as part of a global force alliance to bring down Al Nadir'. The authority for the mission had been signed off by the PM and the US president. Both had known not to question further.

When he'd questioned Cartwright, his equivalent in MI6, he'd told Gibbs that some kind of 'transformation' had happened to the Noor couple. He added that 'unexplained things were done in Pentagon'. All on March 27. The day everyone across the globe had been counting down to World War III. Gibbs had sought intel through his CIA back channels, but, once again, he hit a very sturdy and impenetrable brick wall.

Gibbs took in Sam. Transformation? He looked normal enough. Maybe it was just urban legend. Cartwright spinning a yarn. Gibbs stared at Sam thoughtfully. He did, however, provide the allusive answer to cracking the nano-bomb problem hours after whatever transformation happened on March 27. An answer that top scientists around the world in all their ally countries had been battling with since February of that year.

"The global inter-agency alliance with Freedom Earth Special Forces has made Operation Pancake a massive success." Gibbs took a beat and held down a grin. That name always made him want to laugh. It came from the idea of 'flattening Al Nadir like a pancake'. "The major cells in the UK have been removed completely. We are aware that there are still individual terrorists at large, but these are being hunted down as we speak. The biggest one was Cambridge, as we all know. But until OP got underway, the Acton plant, masquerading as a massive food processing plant, was one we weren't aware of. OP discovered cells in every major city in the UK. We've now incarcerated hostiles in Freedom Earth's specially built warehouses with Surv-Mote perimeters. All await execution under Freedom Earth."

Gibbs was aware of Ashton eyeing him with annoyance. "Terrorists at large?" Ashton asked. "So what does that resemble as a percentage of Al Nadir hostiles you've yet to take down?"

"I would say over ninety-five percent of Al Nadir operatives are in custody. There's only, at the most, five percent still out there. All the cells have been obliterated. They're running blind. They've nowhere to go. Their top line executives, Al Douri, Sanantoni, Russo, Lupez, and Stein-Muller, are gone. We've got their nanotech, the bombs and the masks. Their cloaked satcom networks have been located and disabled. From all the intel in cells' servers, we've got what we need to identify every operative that worked for Al Nadir in the UK. With Dr. Noor's solution that stops assimilation of nano-bombs once inside an operative's body, we don't have to worry about stragglers being loaded."

Gibbs scanned his notes and was making to speak again, but Redfern interrupted.

"How do you know it's over ninety-five percent you've taken down, if you haven't got a final figures from the servers? It's not quite on, to make sweeping generalizations when we're dealing with these terrorists. We all want to ensure every last one is captured. We can't afford to have, as you call them 'stragglers'. So we need specifics, not 'thumb in the air' intelligence of old." Redfern's lips curled back, showing perfect teeth. His haughtiness and razor wit had sliced the air like a scimitar.

Gibbs took instant umbrage. He straightened his back, stared fiercely at Redfern, and spat his response. "The intelligence so far taken and analyzed identifies almost all the terrorists we've capture, but not all. We have other data that spans across the UK and around the world still being analyzed through the global inter-agencies alliance. We'll cross-correlate and be able to finalize figures. All of Al Nadir will be out of the UK within months."

"I want it sooner." The PM's voice was deliberate and measured, and it chilled the room.

"I'm sorry, sir, that's not going to happen. The data is still being analyzed. It takes time. We're talking about tens of thousands of intelligence sources from across the world. By October, we'll be in better shape," Gibbs retaliated.

"Your protracted intelligence processes are of no concern to me. We have special help through Dr. Noor. Give him all the data files. I want this completed within three days, not three months."

Cartwright noticed the PM had turned to look at Sam. Suddenly everyone in the meeting repeated the motion.

"Only too happy to help. Shouldn't be a problem. I'll run the data through our systems and give you the answer in the morning." Sam's commanding voice shook the room. How could he do in a night what would take MI5 and MI6 months to achieve, thought Cartwright Who was this guy? These questions rolled undelivered from his lips.

The PM spoke, nodding quickly, "Thank you, Dr. Noor. I knew I could count on you. Can Six provide their intel from the global inter-agencies alliance direct to Dr. Noor?"

Cartwright took in Sam slowly. His posture. His delivery. It all said, 'utter power' with an underlying 'screw you all'. Sam always had been a bolshie bastard, breaking the rules and getting results, but the simmering power he now saw in the former agent's eyes was something different. It scared him. Who the hell was Sam Noor?

"Of course. I'll provide anything that Dr. Noor needs. But I'd like to know just how he's going to do this. I mean, he's not superhuman, is he?"

The expression on Ashton's face said it: Cartwright had inadvertently trespassed into guarded territory.

He watched as Ashton nodded to Redfern, and the Cabinet secretary rapidly took over.

"In your packs in front of you are papers. Security Clearance Level One, 'Eyes Only' authorization forms to be signed by you and authorized by the prime minister. Right now. Please remove this form and present it on top of your packs."

Cartwright, along with everyone around the massive table, opened his pack and took out the referenced form. As per Redfern's instructions, he placed the form on top of the rest of the folder pack.

"Please sign in the designated box and put today's date. And then give the forms to me."

Not a word was said. Pens were taken out of briefcases and Cartwright felt the room vibrate with the sound of scratching signatures. Redfern stood up and circled the table, rapidly collecting each form in turn. Cartwright signed and proffered his own form. He could see Redfern had purposely made the affair quite clinical in a bid to shift everyone's perception as to what was happening. Even Gibbs had been sucked into the Cabinet secretary's play. Cartwright knew they'd have neither time nor opportunity to read the conditions they were signing up to. But glancing at the PM, and then at the silently simmering Dr. Noor, Cartwright realized he really had no option. Backing out wasn't going to happen, and it was obvious by the 'Eyes Only' authorization form he'd just signed that he was on the cusp of being witness to something incredible. He didn't want to let his inherent cautious nature block an opportunity to experience the extraordinary.

Having collected the forms, he watched Redfern bend over the table to sign his own form and take all papers to the prime minister. Ashton grabbed them with a slight impatience. Cartwright held back a sneer. Redfern's detached theatrics didn't jive too well with Ashton's need to proceed.

Ashton already had his Visconti Forbidden City fountain pen in his hand, ready to sign. With a brief flurry, he scrawled his signature on one form after another. On the final signing, he placed the top back onto his pen and slipped the forms into his briefcase.

Still, nobody spoke.

But Cartwright knew the thought energy generated by the room, if harnessed, would have powered a town.

"Thank you for your cooperation," said the PM finally. "As per the signing. If it is found that you have revealed to someone outside of this group, what you're about to see and hear in this room, you will have committed treason, you will be branded a traitor of the state and Freedom Earth, and you *will* be executed immediately."

Not a sound passed anyone's lips. Cartwright flicked a glance at everyone up and down the table. No one dared to cross the PM on matters of treason. All knew that this was the law, and if broken, the price would be paid in their blood.

He watched Ashton smirk and turn to Sam. "Dr. Noor, would you please explain who you are?"

Cartwright breathed in. His suspicions as to what he was signing were about to be made reality.

The room, although silent, became even quieter. Those around the table held in their breathing. Anticipation electrified the air. Eyes turned to Sam, and each person held their stare, unblinking for fear they may miss what they had signed their life away to see.

Sam stood up. He smiled but no one smiled back. He'd planned this with Ashton. He knew what to expect. The only thing was, he'd arranged it all with the proviso that Ellie would be there too. On his own, he felt exposed, even before he'd said anything. He was unsure of their reaction. Ashton had been incredulous when he'd introduced Ellie in her Kudamaz form, but he'd been levelheaded. He hadn't screamed or passed out. But it had been only him in the room. Now Sam was faced with eight individuals he didn't really know at all.

Apprehensively, he started, "Okay. Well, the easiest way to know what I am is to show you."

Before the circle of glued eyes, Sam connected with his quantum energies at the end of the room, focused his soul force, and shimmered to the tip of the table.

"Fuck me!" screamed Janice Perkins, jumping back. Sam was surprised. He thought that Perkins would be the last person to react. Her file had said she was 'careful and controlled' but her reaction was hardly that. Within seconds of watching him, she flared up again, screaming, "This is trickery. Like that fellow David Blaine."

Sam grinned. He thought the famous illusionist might be referenced. Here we go again.

He connected, focused, and shimmered to the right-hand side of the PM, and then he decided that maybe they might think it's down to something in the room, projectors, mirrors and such. That it was all still an illusion. They needed to see him outside to truly understand what he was. He shimmered directly in front of the long Victorian window. Then he stood there for a second waving.

Sam could see everyone in the room had risen and were all now huddled around the pane, staring out, scared, fascinated, but in their faces, final belief that it wasn't an illusion they were seeing. This was for real. One last show. He shimmered to the very edge of the estate by the fence. It was a long way away. However, the onlookers at the manor house could still see him clearly. Sam waved again, bent down, and picked a few daisies. He then shimmered back into the room, directly into his seat, still holding the daisies.

"He's back," exclaimed Cartwright, stepping over to touch Sam hesitantly.

"Don't worry, Nathan. I'm harmless."

Sam waited for the stunned people in the room to return to their chairs. He offered the daisies to Perkins. The energy secretary, although dazed, took the offering. People sat down, their faces drained of color. Sam realized the very fabric of their belief system had been shattered in an instant.

Only Redfern appeared to be composed enough to direct a question at Sam. "And so what are you, Dr. Noor? An alien? A spirit? A government experiment?"

"None of those. I'm a Kudamaz-human hybrid, similar to Ellie, my wife."

Sam could see lips opening and eyes widening. They were getting ready to question him.

"Dr. Noor cannot say any more than this." Ashton stepped in before the interrogations started. "We have taken the decision to tell you as Dr. Noor will be working with all of you and, due to his abilities, things will be achieved much, much faster. Look at how quickly he solved the nano-bomb. No one will be able to stop our march of progress. Al Nadir are now history. We are the new tomorrow, my friends. Freedom Earth is the new way. The new way for all humanity."

Chapter 19

My house, my sanctuary. The place I always used to escape to when I wanted solace, to charge my batteries, or just to see my lovely wrens on the bird table.

I place my hand on the glass pane in the conservatory. Nothing is in the garden. No birds at all. The birds haven't had any food left for them for nearly three months. They've deserted me in favor of pastures new, sought out people and places that will look after them, nurture them, and not leave them stranded. Springtime is critical for birds and their newly hatched young. Suddenly, I think about baby birds, and I hope that my absence hasn't caused unnecessary suffering.

On thinking, I become aware of feelings, rapid heartbeats, deep awareness of surroundings, the need to protect. These sensations have a primal essence. They are not emotions delineated by humans. The heartbeats speed up and, through my eyes, I picture leaves, branches, and a rough twigged nest. I am SearchSighting my wrens.

Aby-od never told me I'd be able to SearchSight anything other than humans. My inherent databanks say the same. Is it because I have a strong personal connection? Or are my powers changing?

I draw my hand from the pane in contemplation, and, just on turning, a fluffy ball of brown comes close to the window. A black eye stares at me.

Opening the door to the conservatory, I step out and make for my little, green shed. Inside, I find the seed bags I need. I can't just watch without providing nourishment to nature's beautiful companions.

Unthinking, I grab a bag of wild bird seed, and take it to the bird table. It then strikes me that the same seed bag, some six kg of it, had made me heave a little when I carried it several months ago. But now it is like a crisp bag. The weight doesn't even register. I tip the seeds into the plastic container, and I barely have time to move my hand away before a family of hungry wrens fly down and feed quickly.

"Sorry about the wait, guys," I say.

Taking the seed bag back to the shed, I notice my striped green and white fold-up chair resting against the wooden joist. I grab it and unfold it onto the patio. I look at it for a few seconds, wondering what I am doing. Don't I have an important role to play? Do I even have the right to faff around in my garden trying to kid myself I am just a normal woman enjoying the everyday jewels that God has blessed on all of us?

I sit down.

Kudamun can wait. The universe can wait. I need this. My very own me-time. Apart from our initial love marathon, Sam and I had been focused on ridding the world of Al Nadir. I haven't been in my house since that terrible evening that started with Verity emotionally imploding and finished with my entry into Hell.

Chasing around the world with Sam and removing the commanders of Al Nadir operations has been my life up to this point. A life, I must say, I was quite happy with in the beginning.

Everything was delivered under a mission called Operation Pancake. I devised the name. And I thought it worked so well. I sold it quickly to Ashton and Hutchinson.

"I'll flatten those bastards like pancakes."

"And then maple syrup them to death!" Sam had added, laughing.

It was such an absurd name for basically the annihilation of fifty-six million people, but it seemed to confuse Al Nadir in the beginning, who'd been monitoring our comms, in bases where Allied Forces were given explicit instructions to pull back.

I worked with Special Forces, who incidentally never discovered my secret nor Sam's, locating Al Nadir bases and taking them down. I used my powers in association with my brute force, ensuring there wasn't any bodies to dispose of. Sam explained away the whole vanishing trick by saying he had a new biotech material that decomposed the body in seconds. They had seemed happy with this outlandish explanation. Much better than saying I'd vaporized them using harmonic rainbow light.

Al Nadir bases amounted to far more than where active wars were being fought. Through my SearchSight, I located each one. Sam and I wiped out those who fought and saved those who didn't. That amounted to nineteen million people who were too scared to fight Sam and me. It didn't mean, however, that they had been completely redeemed.

It took a few months, but even those who'd been saved initially were eventually executed under Ashton's new Freedom Earth laws of treason. Not an act I was comfortable with, but something world leaders, inspired by Ashton, and underpinned by Freedom Earth ideology, were impassioned to do.

Toppling the empire that Salim had grown with such dedication and precision had brought me immense satisfaction. I am only bitterly sorry that the fucker never witnessed me decimate his beloved terrorist corporation in the blink of eye. A fitting end, given Salim's fame was built on his ability to create Al Nadir in such a short time.

After two months, there are still the diehard fanatics of Al Douri wanting to be martyrs in his memory. That is fine by me. Anyone wanting to give their life in honor of a sadistic, sexually depraved psychopath has every right to feel my true wrath.

Sitting there, my thoughts flip back to those wrens again. I've been doing good things whilst I've been away. But those little birds might think I've done wrong by them. That I have somehow acted in a bad, maybe even evil, way by not feeding them. Especially when they'd grown to rely on my generosity. It was all down to perspective.

Do I have the wrong perspective on Ashton? Might I be like those wrens, thinking he was evil, but really, he is doing so much good? Only I don't know what he was doing.

Maybe it is all in my mind. I am seeing something that isn't there. My time in Al Nadir's clutches have warped my senses. Those memories now define how I view the world.

Freedom Earth has undoubtedly united humanity under one cause. I should be on Ashton's side too. I close my eyes and let the warm morning sun touch my skin. Although I no longer want or need the vitamin D the sun's rays help to generate, I can still feel the energy pouring into me through its solar vibrations.

Earth is a wonderful place. I love being on her more now than when I was human. I can feel nature and the gentle undulations brought on by birth, growth, and decay. My garden is an array of harmonic patterns only I can hear. The aligned, connected voice of Mother Earth. And she sings a beautiful song.

My SearchSight, the ability to see everyone and feel them, I have learnt quickly to control. Aby-od gave me a bracelet, a sleek, silver cuff with two crystal charms, one violet and the other mauve, that sits tightly on my wrist. Its purpose is to create a temporary block to my SearchSight through a particular vibration emitted by the crystals whilst I learn to control this power internally.

I don't really need the bracelet anymore. But it looks good and reminds me of days past when such things meant a lot to me.

It is quite strange. When I was human, I used to look at films depicting superheroes and I used to wonder: do they go to the loo, eat, sleep, shag, or even get lonely? I'm living in a world but I'm still beyond that world, with knowledge that spans the entire universe, with answers to questions that haven't even been posed yet.

And all the time I'm trying to mask the remoteness I'm increasingly feeling. Ironic, really, as I'm connected to all living things. But that remoteness is attached to being human. I'm not quite sure why, but I'm desperately hanging onto that last vestige I have of feeling human. Though, as time moves on, I feel that vestige is drifting farther away from me. Like a piece of shell in an egg that you're trying to catch before it gets fried, I never quite seem to be able to catch that piece of humanity.

I am remote. Ever more removed from the human race.

I realize now why Aby-od said I mustn't remain for long periods on Earth. Its exposure to that sense of inner loss. Reflective of the passing of a loved one. And the pain drills deep.

Forcefully, I push myself from the emptiness, that growing abyss inside, and embrace the tenderness of love.

The fast exuberance of those fluffy things flying around me flood me with multiple emotions. And the wrens and I are one, feeding and feeling in unity. I smile. Maybe this Kudamaz thing is all it's cracked up to be.

Chapter 20

It had been four days since Xiao had learned the truth behind his illness. Well, a form of truth. Neither one of his parents could definitively explain why he'd gone into a sudden coma. Even more strangely, no one could shed light on how he came out of it either. He'd been unresponsive for almost ten weeks. No sign of life at all. His vitals had been controlled by life-support systems. He'd been just an empty vessel.

And then, without any indication, he'd emerged from the darkness of the coma. To the joy and delight of his parents.

He'd regaled his life after death story to his closest school friends. Of how he felt like he'd been floating, and how comforting the sensation of weightlessness had been. His friends had gawped, open mouthed and incredulous to Xiao's claims.

Peter, eleven, bright, blue eyes, short, brown hair, a little on the tubby side, eased himself into a chair that resembled the red and gold hand from Iron Man. Xiao had met Peter's mum but had never seen his father. Peter had said he was 'doing something abroad' and that was it. Xiao hadn't liked to ask further. Each time he'd broached the subject, Peter had gotten edgy, and stuttered. "I'm…I'm n-n-not s-s-sure." Xiao thought his mum was lovely. They lived in Knightsbridge, in one of the mews houses around the back of Harrods, and Peter, who loved technology, had a bedroom stacked with some of the coolest tech he'd ever seen. Small cameras, finger-sized scanners, nanotech drones, flashing things broadcasting tiny holograms. Xiao had been amazed. In a bid to play more with the cool stuff, he'd quickly made Peter his best friend.

Simon, a thin, gawky twelve year old, dark brown, sharp eyes, black hair, and a drooping mouth sat on a swinging chair suspended from the ceiling.

Simon's parents were American. His father worked for the US government, and his mother did something with charities. They lived in the US Embassy. Xiao wasn't quite sure, but he thought Simon said something about his dad being the ambassador. Simon had a cool voice, and always played up at school. He answered the teachers back and flaunted their inability to reprimand him. He'd said to Xiao, "No one can touch me. I can say what I want. They just have to accept it. I'm special." Xiao had asked why he was special, and Simon had laughed saying, "Diplomatic immunity."

Xiao took to his bed, sat cross legged on top of the covers, and waited for his friends' responses.

"You really believe you were dead, Xiao?" asked Peter, his best friend.

"Who knows." Xiao shrugged, playing it nonchalant. "Perhaps. It certainly seemed like that."

"Do you have any memory of what it was like?" said Simon, peering at his friend, and Xiao felt as though he was one of the toads Simon dissected in his biology class.

"Only like I was doing that floating thing."

"But did it *feel* like you were dead?" pressed Simon. "You know, did you see anyone? Ghosts? Or hear voices?"

Xiao shook his head. "I don't remember anything. I have no memory at all. Only this sensation inside me, like I was adrift at sea, but still hooked to something stopping me from drowning or going too far out."

His friends stared. "Woah, Xiao, that sounds totally weird. I think you were going over. You know, to heaven, or something, but, like, something stopped you," said Peter.

Xiao clocked his smug look and laughed. "Going to heaven? No, I don't think so. It didn't feel like I was heading anywhere. Just floating."

"Perhaps you were just waiting until your body got better," suggested Peter.

"Maybe. I don't know. I feel it's changed me though."

"In what way?" asked Simon, staring. Xiao could see his glance run over his body, checking for any physical changes in him.

"I want to be a better person. A kinder person."

Peter and Simon turned to look at each other, mystified by Xiao's announcement.

"But you're great, Xiao," said Peter. "Best friend ever."

"You're smart, funny, and cool to be with," added Simon.

Xiao blushed at the words of support his friend gave him. It was only down to their close friendship, borne of similar experiences, the bullying, the loneliness (all three were only children) that he could talk openly.

"Thanks. But I've been dreadful to my parents. I treated them bad. They love me. They deserve me to be a more thoughtful boy."

"But we all give our parents hell. That's part of being a kid," said Simon, smirking.

"I don't feel I can be that kid anymore."

"So what kind of kid do you want to be?" asked Peter, intrigued.

"I told you. A better one," responded Xiao, and he stared at the floor for a few seconds, suddenly very uncomfortable with the direction of their chat.

He recalled the new game his mum had bought for him in Hamley's.

"I've got the new Crystal Pyramids of Mars game on X-Box. Let's play!" announced Xiao.

He dove down onto the floor, pulled out the game from his cabinet, and shoved it in his X-Box. Peter and Simon leapt out of their chairs and sat down on the floor with Xiao. He fired up his fifty-two-inch, ultra-high-resolution TV, and the Crystal Pyramids of Mars game exploded onto the screen. Xiao flicked on the immersive mode and projectors embedded into the walls brought the action to life around him and his friends.

Strange labyrinths, crystal pyramids, and alien monsters filled his room. Xiao handed out controllers to each of his friends. Taking his own, he focused on the game, becoming his avatar, a tooled-up, elite, fighting Universal Guard, and all thoughts of life after death were forgotten, as he faced-off against the angry monsters in tunnels within the pyramids.

The game progressed amongst the boys' cheers, screams, and yells, and Xiao became more absorbed in the gameplay.

"You're loved."

The voice seemed inside of him, but it was outside as well. Xiao thought Simon or Peter had spoken. He looked at them quizzically, but, engrossed in the game, they didn't notice. Or was it him who'd spoken?

"Her love brought you back."

Xiao turned his head toward Simon. The voice had tinges of his friend's voice. But as he watched him, flicking buttons on the controller and whooping it up as he zapped another monster, he knew his friend hadn't spoken. Had it been him again? Nothing made sense. Confusion ripped through him, as he whizzed his head around to take in Peter's antics.

"You must be good for her."

This time the voice resembled Peter. Younger, immature, out of breath. Like his overweight friend.

"Why are you saying this?" screamed Xiao, standing up and dropping the controller. "Stop talking to me like that! Don't keep telling me what I should do!"

Simon and Peter dragged their attentions from the game, and glared, baffled, at Xiao, as the monster on screen took his chance and pounced on Simon and Peter's avatars, tearing them apart.

Simon noticed, and yelled furiously, "Oh fucking great, Xiao! You've messed up the game! What's wrong with you, man?"

Xiao watched.

"Are you some kind of fucking idiot?"

He could see their failure of purpose.

"I was really into that. Man, I thought you were a friend. You're a selfish little shit!"

How they misread all the signals.

"Xiao, Simon's right. We were playing a game. Why did you interrupt? Are you feeling okay?"

Humans. They couldn't see the truth before them.

Suddenly, Xiao could feel heat. Like his organs were cooking. The room had turned into a microwave and it was on full blast.

He howled, clutching his stomach, and Xiao fell to the ground.

"Get away. You creatures. You burn me with your ignorance." Xiao's voice had deepened. More grown up. But somehow, he sounded right. He felt one with this new timbre. He screamed, "Leave my place. Go! Go!"

Peter and Simon crawled backwards on their backsides to get away from him, their faces awash with fear. Around them, the holographic monsters trawled between the corridors of the crystal pyramid, the game continuing even though they had stopped.

Xiao's insides raged, hotter. The fire within him scorched his skin. Xiao pulled up his t-shirt. His skin was getting redder, darkening in patches. The flames were burning through him.

"Do you see it?" shrieked Xiao, showing his front to his friends. "Do you see what you're doing to me?"

Xiao watched his friends scramble to their feet and hurtle toward the door. It flew open, and his friends leapt back, now skittery and terrified.

"Xiao, what are you doing?"

He turned at the sound of the voice of the one who loved him.

"I burn, Mother. Their ignorance. Their failure to see the truth. It burns me. See the flames on my body?"

Xiao displayed his torso to his mother but couldn't understand her puzzled expression.

"Erm, Xiao, I think your friends had better go home now."

His mother indicated with a backward thumb for Peter and Simon to head out of his bedroom. They nodded and ran out the room. Xiao could hear their feet heavy on the floor as they pelted down the landing and alighted the stairs.

He listened as his mother sighed, and muttered irritably, "Get that crap off!"

She reached down to one of the controllers and pressed the off button. The monsters and weird landscapes of Mars vanished.

The moment his friends departed, Xiao could feel the temperature lessening inside of him. He peered down at his stomach and the dark, maroon patch he'd seen stretching across his skin had paled. The flames within him were going out.

The heat had abated.

"You have saved me, Mother. You save with your love. Always."

Xiao rested back on his heels. He smiled and closed his eyes, and then opened them. The wracking pain of fire inside him had gone.

"Thank you, Mum." Xiao recognized his voice slipping back to a child once more. Inside him, it felt right again.

She reached down to pull him up. Xiao could see that her body shivered.

"You need to rest, Xiao."

She led him gently to the bed and pulled back the covers. Xiao crawled in and slid down under the duvet.

"Thank you, Mum," Xiao repeated, and touched her hand.

But she pulled it away. Her eyes widened in shock.

"What's wrong, Mum?"

His mother shook her head. "Nothing, darling. Absolutely nothing. You rest now."

He reached out toward her for a cuddle, but she backed away, her smiling face no longer smiling.

"Rest, darling," she said, and Xiao thought her voice sounded shaky.

Outside, Lei pulled the door to Xiao's bedroom closed, and lent against it. She'd wanted to imagine her son was better. That he'd recovered. Whatever had befallen him had left him. Whether it had been a visiting spirit or a force, that which blighted him, had departed. He'd shown no signs of possession for weeks.

She truly believed it was all over.

She prayed it was all over.

She raised her head to the heavens, pressing her back against the wood panels, and let sorrow wash over her. Her chin quivered. Tremors of desperation shook through her body. Tears triggered, and they fell down her face.

"Why? Why?" she whispered, and tried to forget. But she couldn't.

That thing she'd sensed as her son's hand touched hers.

A feeling of immeasurable power.

Startling. Shocking. Absorbing.

Its need for her love.

And its need to survive.

Chapter 21

The meeting is well underway when I decide to make an appearance. The wrens have convinced me to give Ashton another chance. Despite my misgivings, I focus on the Manor House in Thurso and parts of my living room interlace with a dark-green-carpeted and wood-paneled hallway. I let my soul force connect with my quantum energies and I am pulled into the hallway just outside the room where the meeting is being held. I wait until the area is clear of people before I lock my shimmer into Earth's plane of reality.

All is clear, devoid of anyone, although I can hear voices clearly approaching. I lock my shimmer into Earth's degree of reality and open the door to the drawing room where the meeting is taking place.

Ashton is in mid-flow when I enter. Heads turn and eyes widen as I walk in. My husband has a wry smile, his typical 'feeling better now?' touched with a condescending attitude.

"Hello, everyone. Have I missed anything?" I ask nonchalantly. I realize almost immediately that it doesn't come over as nonchalant at all. It comes over as flippant.

Ashton takes the chair and speaks, his eyes still laughing at a sick joke only he knows the punchline to. He gives me a glance that barely hides his lascivious thoughts, and I can't get Salim out of my mind. Boy, I must still be seriously scarred by what Al Nadir did to me.

"Ellie Noor, thank you for joining us. No, you haven't missed much. Just the fact that your husband has shattered our understanding of physics and the laws of the universe in general. Other than that, it's been a pretty boring meeting."

His voice is laden with sarcasm and I can't help but feel that, despite Sam and I being the super-humans in the room, he wants to have the supremacy and enjoys belittling us and turning us into sideshow freaks. No matter how much I reconcile it, my thoughts still return back to my original feeling. Ashton makes my Kudamaz skin crawl.

"Yes, Sam tends to do that, but I have a few other areas of interest that he may not have introduced to you. I take it, Ashton, that everyone's signed the 'Eyes Only' forms?"

I deliver my words with the most clipped and powerful tone I can possibly muster.

"Absolutely. We're all locked down here with your secrets. So, Ellie, let's see what you can do. Put on your floorshow for us."

Ashton raises his eyebrow again, so reminiscent of Salim I have to swallow hard to stop from retching.

It has to be a coincidence, the words he is using. Al Nadir's sex torture floorshows are well documented in intelligence files. I had been saved from having to submit to Sabena's bottomless pit of depravity by Aby-od removing me from her clutches just in time. But Ashton can't possibly be intending to hurt me by its reference. Can he?

Ashton stares hard at me, and I take his stare with equal force.

"Floorshow. Interesting turn of phrase." I look at Sam and I know he can read me. He shakes his head. Pelting into my mind are his words, 'Don't go there!' But I have already arrived.

"The last person to use those words ended up in a very disconnected state experiencing a pain previously unimaginable by humans."

A shudder ripples through the gathered guests. My choice of words is specific and focused on deliberately unnerving everyone in the room. If Ashton wants to play games with Sam and me, first he has to understand the rules.

Ashton throws his arms in the air, conceding to my stand-off.

"I'm sorry, Ellie, if I have in some way offended you. I meant no insult."

His lips say one thing, but his eyes another. It is very clear that he used the words to intimidate me. His statement of apology confirms that he knew that those words, for Sam and me, were loaded with backstory.

I glance at the assembled crowd. With the exception of the two intelligence chiefs, few others could know the true meaning of those words.

"Apology accepted, Ashton!" I snap.

Using his surname without a prefix forces the room to appreciate I am defined by a convention beyond their societal structures and political preconceptions. The fact that Ashton is prime minster means nothing to me. And I make sure everyone knows that.

I am Kudamaz. I am the Protector. And it is about damn time I flexed my superhuman muscle to prove it.

Chapter 22

The large, antique table has probably sat there for a hundred years or more. Solid. Sturdy. Real. A perfect target to demonstrate an inkling of what I'm capable of.

"Look at the table," I command.

Those assembled stare at the piece of furniture that holds their papers, pens, and intelligence packs. Their faces are a mixture of wonder and terror. It is a face I've come to recognize. Even Sam held it before he changed. I know he was terrified of me when I rescued him. Beyond the drugs, it was a fear of the unknown, a deep-seated primal fear engendered in humans when facing something for which they have no term of reference. Apart, of course, from that which has been delivered by pop culture, and a heightened sense of fear created by government misinformation and general paranoia of everything that cannot be explained rationally.

I notice Ashton is composed and Redfern appears disinterested. Strange reaction. I'll give them something to ruffle their feathers and make them question their own existence.

"The table," I repeat, my voice now booming with supreme confidence.

The ministers and officials grip the table as if to start a séance.

"Hands off," I yell sharply.

Their fingers jump off the wood like it had conducted a massive heat pulse to their fingertips.

"Look," says Reggie Wellwood, and pints to the center of the table. Movement has started. In my mind, I've connected with the atoms in the wood. Calmly, I ask them to part. Naturally, I assure them I'll merge them back when my display is over.

I'm still not sure how I ask base elements to do things. It's a form of telepathy, but in the instance of communication, I am one with those atoms. I can feel that I'm part of the structure with which I'm communicating. Sometimes it's a gentle, diplomatic engagement, and one that's on an even footing. At other times, I'm dominant, commanding, and I determine the outcome on my terms only. Like the way I disintegrate bullets or guns, there is no negotiation. I just force the atoms to increase their vibration and the heat generated breaks their molecular structure and they split apart.

In the case of the table, however, I take a much more conciliatory stance. On my negotiation, the atoms move apart and the middle of the table begins to disrupt its form. No longer a solid structure, the gasps of surprise come forth as I expect.

The atoms circulate in a clockwise motion, gradually rising as more atoms pull away and join the mini swirling hurricane that has erupted a few inches above the table.

The hole created by the parting atoms clearly shows the dismal, ditch-water-green carpet underneath. Not a sound comes from the assembled party. I watch them but their eyes are fixed on the spectacle I'm creating.

Only Ashton flicks a look back at me. That eyebrow is raised again, and his tongue has emerged from a gently parted mouth to lick his thick lips.

I try hard to overwrite those memories, but they never seem to leave me.

"Everyone, look," I say. "Don't miss this."

Ashton drags his eyes reluctantly back to the table.

Inside the mini hurricane, something is forming. It takes a few seconds for the assembled party to acknowledge I am creating something. The atoms of the wood table coalesce and a shape emerges. I sweep a look outside the window and spy a family of rabbits nosing around on the lawn, completely unaware of the strangeness just a few feet from them.

Excellent models. I concentrate the atoms into forming the shape of the rabbits. I can feel them, their alertness, anxiousness, and, of course, their wonderful playfulness and innocence of being. When I was human, I always enjoyed nature. I loved the sense of peace she gave me when I was amongst her beautiful creations. Nature has a natural calming effect; the colors through the seasons, the gentle sounds she generates, leaves rustling, rushing rivers. They ease human nerves. Now I'm Kudamaz, I hear the beautiful harmonies that the plants send out. Their language is captured in harmonics beyond the range of the human ear. This sound of nature can be quite distracting to me at times, but I've learnt to tune out, the way I used to when I was a human, cutting out the loud voice of some jerk talking incessantly on his phone in a busy cattle truck masquerading as a morning commuter train.

The essence of those fluffy fellows slip through me and into the creation I am forming. Little pointy ears, cotton wool ball of a tail, round beady eyes, and big feet. They all flit through my mind and come together in the wood illustration I am making. Those little animals are blind to how their frolicking on the lawn has attracted me into my current undertaking.

Around me, sighs of disbelief emit from dropped mouths. The method I have fashioned is a form of telepathic stereo-lithography. The image and life force of the rabbit is captured by my mind and reproduced using the wood atoms as raw material

Within five minutes, the carving is finished. It possesses incredible detail, right down to each hair follicle. Resembling more a sculptor's labor of love over many months than a few minutes, the mind-blowing realism gives the impression the rabbit is about to hop off the table.

"This is incredible," says Janice.

I notice that she is always the first to speak. This time, she is the first to stand up and touch the rabbit. I stare at her, amazed, and smile. Undaunted by the unexplainable, she picks up the rabbit statue in her shaking hands.

"Absolutely incredible," she repeats, subconsciously stroking the wooden rabbit, the fluffy hair too irresistible not to touch.

None of the men around us even try to venture near the wooden rabbit.

"So now you can see what I'm capable of. Over the past few months, with Sam, I've been using these and other abilities to destroy the majority of Al Nadir bases around the world. I'm aware that some are still in activation, but it will not be long before Al Nadir are crushed completely."

I stare around the table. My presentation has left all the members mute. I look at Sam, and he smiles at me. I can see he is impressed by my little display. I nod. Time everyone showed some respect. I am not just a woman anymore. I am a force beyond their understanding, and they need to realize it.

"Janice, can you put Bugs down please," I say, and Janice gently places the wooden statue on the part of the table that still has solidity.

"Thank you. As much as I'd like to keep this little fella, I do need to revert the table back to what it was again. I don't think the owners would be too happy if I left that big hole in the center of this lovely table."

Nervous sniggers erupt around the room. They aren't really sure how to react, but the comedic element of my presentation has generated a little sense of ease.

I stare at the wooden animal and start to reverse the process. Quickly, the atoms in the wooden artefact deconstruct and aligned back to form the middle of the table. Eyes widen in amazement by the speed at which I restore the table. Within minutes of it being a beautiful, carved animal, the table is fully reinstated again, resembling the same one it had had for centuries. Nothing indicates that it has been through any metamorphosis.

Janice, still standing, leans over and smooths her hand across the table's surface, which, seconds before, had been a hole.

"Unbelievable," she mutters, and then looks in awe and wonder at me. "How do you do it?"

Ashton jumps in before I can respond. I bristle at his rude interjection, but remain silent.

"I'm sorry, Janice. We can't divulge how Sam can shimmer or how Ellie can manipulate matter. All you need to know is that their abilities are at the disposal of the UK and our allies in Freedom Earth to rid the world of terrorism and evil in any form."

I watch as those assembled nod, still dazed by what they have seen. I can see their notion of reality has been challenged. What they've witnessed in those few moments has been indelibly imprinted on their minds forever. The experience has changed every belief they've ever had.

Only Ashton and Redfern appear to be level-headed. Redfern, in particular, I notice, has taken the presentation very calmly. Ashton mentioned he was a physicist by education, so perhaps his natural logic and scientific attitude has helped him reconcile what he has seen.

Ashton, of course, has been working with Sam and I since March, along with President Hutchinson, so I know nothing will be much of a revelation to him.

I realize Ashton is also taking in the reaction of his colleagues the same way as myself. Cartwright shuffles in his seat, looking somewhat irritated. I know he is due to speak any second.

"Prime Minister, Dr. Sam Noor and Mrs. Ellie Noor have been heavily involved in Operation Pancake to remove Al Nadir, and their effectiveness in doing so is a testament to the fact we have only a small number of Al Nadir terrorists left. The question I have to ask is, why is it only now we're being told of their abilities? I was instructed that Mrs. Noor had the requisite abilities and I had to have her on operations. Having seen her fight first-hand, I was more than assured of her capability in the field. I was given explicit orders by you and the US President to take her on board, and lead with Dr. Noor on Operation Pancake with our Special Forces and Allied parties around the world. Don't you think, sir, it would have been a hell of a lot more beneficial to all concerned if I'd been informed of her other abilities and Dr. Noor's?"

Cartwright looks Ashton squarely in the eye, but the prime minister, I can see, doesn't give a damn about the outburst. He shrugs but says nothing. His arrogance is immediately obvious to all around. Cartwright snorts, annoyed that his delivery has been waved to the side without consideration.

I watch as Gibbs straightens up and edges forward in his chair. Usually, Five and Six are at each other's throats, always playing the game of brinkmanship. But this time, Gibbs is right by his fellow intelligence chief's side.

"Nathan's right. We're head of intelligence in this country. Why was this kept from us? Things could have been done a lot quicker had we known what we were dealing with. We never realized what incredible assets we had."

I hear Gibbs' words. Neither Sam nor I are assets. They speak about us as if we are pieces of high-tech equipment. What is wrong with these humans? Don't they realize with one swipe I could annihilate them all?

"Okat, that's enough! Sam and I aren't assets," I say, staring hard, my unnatural blue eyes burning into Cartwright and Gibbs. "And we aren't at your disposal, Ashton or anyone else." I glare viciously at the PM. "We're here because we want to clean up the mess left by Al Nadir and make the world a better place. But if you fail to respect us or appreciate the true nature of the power we wield, we will go, and you'll never see us again."

I turn to look at Sam seated next to me who is staggered by my outburst. I notice Ashton nod to himself as if recognizing something he hadn't seen before.

"Dr. Noor, is this the way you feel?" asks Ashton to my husband.

Sam stands up. He catches my eye and then looks away.

'Don't you dare go against me,' I scream to him in my mind.

"Yes, Prime Minister. Ellie is quite correct. We're here to make a difference, to help Earth rid itself of evil in its many forms, and enable it to become a place of peace, love, and harmony. Your work with Freedom Earth is wonderful, and both Ellie and I are committed to it. But we won't be regarded as just assets to be used as you see fit. The moment that starts to happen, we will leave you, and Earth can fend for itself."

And so the rules of engagement have been finally defined.

Ashton rises from his chair and walks toward Sam and I. Unexpectedly, he throws his arms around the both of us. His touch still makes me tingle. And not in pleasant way.

"I am so, so sorry for any disrespect or affront that has been caused. Really, Ellie, Sam, you are my friends. More than that, you're my family, now I have lost mine. And you mean the world to me."

He squeezes my shoulder and Sam's. I swing a vexed look at Sam, but he is facing a different way, looking to the top of the table. Ashton is playing the 'friendship' game and reinitiating his power through the fact he is so close to us. It is very simple psychology and Ashton knows how to roll with it.

"I only decided today to tell you all about these fabulous people as we have much to do and you needed to know the powers that they have. Powers that will speed up developments considerably. Everyone around this table will be involved in our new endeavors. You will all be working closely with Sam and Ellie, and I realized nothing should be hidden. Lies do not build trust. Lies build betrayal."

Ashton glances at me, and I notice a thin flickering of a smirk on his face. That line is targeted at me. Why does he persist in this fruitless game of wills? Does he really want a biblical smiting here and now?

"We need to be open with each other, for trust is essential in building our new tomorrow."

Around the table, heads nod in agreement.

They are all like the sheep outside. All are caught up in the PM's fervent belief of a new tomorrow. I can't stand it. It reminds me of mad Treeborne. Only Ashton is sane and calculating to a point of being chilling. As much as I try to put it down to my warped perception, something still gnaws at me.

I know Ashton is not the man Aby-od thinks he is.

Chapter 23

Lei heard the front door open. She thought Peter and Simon were finding their own way out. Then Chen's deep voice resonated to her level on the landing.

"You boys okay?"

She swallowed, wiped the tears away, and raced down to greet her husband before Xiao's friends had an opportunity to disclose his antics.

Chen had been so pleased with Xiao's rapid recovery. His weirdness had vanished. His behavior had completely stabilized. He hadn't had an episode in weeks now.

Chen was known as 'The One' by the world's press. His ability to know what was about to be 'on trend' was legendary. When he'd initially witnessed Xiao's affliction, his first consideration had been the potential damage Xiao could do to his image if it ever got out his only son was dysfunctional.

Lei had been disappointed by this reaction. She'd always believed he'd cared about his family before business. As much as she tried to deny it, Chen's face relayed his selfish obsession with stardom, and being the blessed designer who could do no wrong.

On returning from hospital, the day Xiao had woken from his coma, Chen had gravely stated his position to her.

"I cannot have a son of mine who's screwed up. If he has a relapse, that's it, Lei. I'm going to admit him into a psychiatric clinic for a full mental evaluation. And he'll stay there for as long as it takes to get him better."

Lei had nodded, but as her husband continued to speak with chilling authority, her blood had turned to ice.

"And this time, you will not visit him. You'll have no association with that boy until he's completely well. Remember, any leaks of him being crazy could damage my brand."

Lei recalled flaring up, screaming at Chen, "Your brand! This is our son! I will not abandon him. Neither will you."

"Lei, you'll do what I say."

"I will not!"

Lei had sensed the heat in her face. With muscles tight, eyes fierce, and mouth scowling, she showed her obvious dissention to her bullying husband.

"Lei, I will not have you obsess the way you did before. It damn near killed you and destroyed us. I won't see you go through that level of pain again."

It seemed Chen had taken a considerate stance. He tilted his head to one side and took her arm gently, meaning to pull her into a romantic embrace, but Lei wasn't convinced. She recognized Chen's manipulation tactic to subvert her anger.

Snatching her arm back, she snarled, "Don't you dare put this on me! What you said about your brand was the truth. You care more about what your celebrity friends think than you do about your own son's welfare." Chen reached out again, but Lei stepped back, slapping his hand away. "I see you, Chen, for what you really are. A shallow, fickle bastard!"

Chen's eyes grew large, his cheeks puffed, and he let out an exasperated sigh. "Yes, I fucking well care about them. What they say in those mags, blogs, TV, have bought us all this." Chen waved his arms around the luxurious living room. "Having them on my side, their endorsement, their love of the Chen Chang brand, has given all of us a life seen by the few. I love my son, I'll give him the best treatment money can buy, but I'm not going to sacrifice my life just because you're obsessed with his."

Lei listened, but all she could hear was Chen saying, 'I'm going to survive no matter what'.

Lei sat herself into a plump, Liberty-print-covered armchair, back straight, hands clasped. Chen stood, towering above her, but her deportment and sheer will of spirit made her mighty. She stared ahead, purposely avoiding Chen.

"I know you love Xiao and me, but you love yourself more," she said. "I've always known you carried a darkness within you. I somehow, perhaps foolishly, believed I could balance it with my light. Now I know your need for survival runs deeper than your need for love."

Lei raised her eyes and drilled into Chen. She watched. His Adam's apple bobbed in his neck. He opened his mouth to interject. Lei flicked away his attempt with her hand and let her furious mouth tear into her husband.

"You touch our son and we are over. I will walk out of that door, and out of your life."

A glassy sheen slipped across Chen's eyes.

"I love you, Chen. I love you with my heart, body, mind, and soul. You are embedded within me. Part of me. I cannot imagine life without you. But make no mistake, you do anything to Xiao, if you lock him up, or hurt him in any way, I will leave you."

Lei stared at Chen. His powerful body crumbled underneath the weight of her words.

"Lei, please, darling…"

"I mean it, Chen. No going back. Hurt Xiao. I'm gone."

Chen trembled. Lei remained steadfast. Almost stone. Chen moved forward. Each step a signal to Lei to restore her faith in him.

"I'm sorry, Lei. You know I'd never do anything to hurt Xiao. I love him."

"You threatened to incarcerate him, detain him, and give me no access. That is hurting our son."

Chen shook his head. "I only want him to be a normal, healthy boy. Please, Lei, understand me."

Lei didn't move. Her teachings in the meditative state, keeping mind, body, and soul centered and grounded, served her well. She watched her husband gradually collapse to his knees in desperation, whilst she kept a solid focus. Unwavering. Unaffected by external stimulus.

Her detachment was cold, but only by appearance. Inside, she burned with a flame of love and hope.

Love for her family.

Hope for the future.

Lei returned to the present and the situation in front of her. Chen inside the hallway looking grave. Peter and Simon recounting in spurts what had happened with Xiao. On their faces was etched the terror of their experience. Eyes of saucers. Lips dry and quivering.

"My God, Mr. Chang. I'm not sure what is wrong with Xiao, but he sure as hell scared the bejesus out of us," said Simon, talking confidently ahead of Peter.

Lei could see that her husband intimidated Peter, who didn't have the asserted social positioning that Simon carried. As Simon explained, Peter kept his eyes on the floor.

"What did Xiao do?" asked Chen, almost turning his back on Peter, so that he could fix on Simon's account.

"Mr. Chang, he freaked us out. He went crazy, speaking in a weird voice, telling us we were loved, and then telling us to go. At one point, he flashed his stomach at us saying he was burning. On fire. You know? But there was nothing there. His skin was okay. I think, sir, Xiao's real sick. Needs a doctor. Tell him we'll see him when he gets better. But boy, he scared us real bad."

Simon couldn't hold back. His voice increased in pace and became almost hysterical by the end of his briefing to Chen.

Lei heard and caught Chen's eyes. He kept his face neutral, his voice a steady timbre, but inside his eyes flared a reignited fury.

"Okay, boys. Sorry he scared you. Xiao's been having a tough time of it. He's on new meds and if his adrenalin increases, they can bring on hallucinations. He really should have been resting, not playing games. He'll call you when he feels better. Do you boys need a ride home? I can get Fredericks to drop you off."

Lei listened to her husband spin a yarn of pure fabrication. Apart from his eyes - and that was only what she could read, as she knew him so well - Chen gave nothing away at all.

"Thanks, Mr. Chang, but Jasperson, my driver, is coming. I texted him when Xiao went weird. He's only a few blocks away. I'll drop Peter off on the way home." Simon took control and Chen nodded with approval.

Sweeping her arm out toward the living room's carved archway, Lei ventured forth, to the boys. "Why don't you wait in the living room until Jasperson arrives?"

The boys heeded her instruction and slipped into the living room.

Once they were inside, Lei advanced on Chen. "Don't say a word," she snapped, glaring.

Chen's black eyes hooded and darkened in response. "He should be seen by experts," he growled.

"You said it. He got excited. That's all. He's resting now. He'll be fine after that."

"You're in denial, Lei."

"And you're crossing that line! Remember what I said. You go there, and I'm walking," hissed Lei, and she lasered into Chen's soul, touching his darkness, flipping him to the light through her tremendous will.

Chen struggled before Lei's tenacious spirit and her resolute belief in her son's continued recovery. She watched Chen shake his head. He walked toward her.

"Okay Lei. I'll let you handle this. But the minute he becomes too much-"

"Of course," finished Lei, whipping out her words across Chen's with a dominating deliverance.

A ringing bell cut through their fiery exchange. Lei stared at the door.

"Jasperson's here. I'll get the kids."

Lei felt a gust of air hit her neck as Chen opened the door to Jasperson. She headed for the living room to collect the boys. Emerging again, with Peter and Simon in tow, a shuffling made Lei glance up. Chen and the boys followed suit. Xiao stood above them on the mezzanine landing, holding onto the filigree iron-work railings overhanging the hallway below.

He gripped the railings and yelled out, "Peter, Simon, I'm sorry." Lei could hear deep sorrow in his voice. "I just had a bad headache before you arrived, and meds made me a bit strange. Sorry I scared you. See you at school, okay, guys?"

Lei watched Peter wave, and mutter, "Yeah. Okay, Xiao. No probs. Get well."

Simon, however, was much more reticent in his response. "Huh, yeah. Well, fine, Xiao, whatever. You get well, man. See ya."

Closing the door, Chen revolved to face Lei. "So, darling…" Lei detected the sarcasm in her husband's voice, and she bristled. "Just how long do you think it'll be before our son's condition is broadcast to all the movers and shakers in this town?"

He glanced up at Xiao, and Lei noticed his scowl of derision.

"I don't care, Chen. Let them say whatever they want. Every family has problems. Simon's parents are screwed up. His mother's a junkie, his father's an adulterer. Peter's mother is shopping-obsessed, and God knows what kind of mixed-up man his father is. They all have problems. No one's perfect. Don't worry so much about the look of the thing. You are Chen Chang. Investors come and go. Celebrities wax and wane. But you are constant. You are unique. Keep that conviction, that power I see in you. Don't let stardom become a terrorist. Destroying our future. Let the love of your family define you, not confine you. With us, Xiao and me, you have everything. You need nothing else."

Lei searched deep into Chen's eyes for understanding. Behind her, Xiao descended the stairs. His soft step approached. Chen reached out for her, and she encircled her arms around his massive frame.

"What would I do without you?" whispered Chen.

Xiao walked up to Lei, as she embraced her husband.

"Be strong and you'll never have to know."

"I love you," murmured Chen, and Lei could feel a flooding warmth of his lovelight through her fingers into her body.

She smiled. He'd understood.
Together they would get through whatever was to come.
For their love would show them the way.

Chapter 24

Over the past months I have worked with Ashton, never has he been quite as overt in his innuendo as he has been today. From the moment I met him, I knew something was a little off. No one carries a perfect equilibrium. It is just impossible. But in the light of no evidence and nothing to show wrongdoing, I can't do anything.

He is the architect of Freedom Earth, and that movement has created a wealth of good throughout the world, even to the point of religious unification. The premise is built on 'if you're bad, you're going to have to pay with your life'. After the pain and suffering caused by Al Nadir's vicious reign, no one seems to want to stand in Ashton's way. The very darkness that is created by Al Nadir's terrible tyrannical time gives true cause and just path for Ashton to drive his light into the world. A light that everyone wants to receive.

It seems the world is happy and willing to be subjugated for Ashton's style of freedom. Sign up to Freedom Earth was unprecedented. Only a few countries were dragging their feet, and that wasn't down to politics, more to holiday leave and locating the right people to make the decision. Ashton has secured a global endorsement to his movement. The G8 countries signed up on the day of the Freedom Earth announcement back on March31. Within days, the rest followed.

Freedom Earth is more than a movement; it is an over-arching religion. An ideology everyone believes in. But I know it has been born out of the need for absolute global domination.

I find it difficult to comprehend such blatant manipulation from a human being.

But I cannot fault that people are happy with their lives. They feel secure. Safe.

Terrorism is dead. Dead being the operative word as, between Hutchinson and Ashton, almost every Al Nadir operative, save for the ones waiting to be tracked down by Sam's final analysis, have been executed. I can understand execution at the higher levels, those spies in governments around the world who have caused so much devastation and suffering, but I cannot countenance death for all those poor folk who were caroled into Al Nadir as a way to survive. All those slum dwellers whose only crime had been to be born in poverty. I know they'd been trained to deceive, lie, and kill. But that had been their route to continued existence. If I'd been in their position, would I have refused?

It is a sobering thought.

Salim's millions of acolytes have been nothing more than his slaves, to do with as he pleased. He bought them and, by that purchase, signed their death warrants.

I recall the way they'd been executed.

I'd shimmered to Malaysia to oversee the executions of the armies in Al Nadir's South East Asia camps. The prisoners had been taken from their makeshift prisons that had been created after Al Nadir armies had been rounded up across the world. They were herded in their thousands into large warehouses fitted with large Harmon wave devices, set to kill.

Sam had augmented the Harmon wave device. No longer did it hit a body at the quantum level, shattering internally and viciously a human's cells. His new design meant there was no pain. Having experienced the excruciating agony of Aswa-da's Harmon gun, Sam was absolutely adamant that execution by Harmon wave was to be completely painless and instantaneous. He built upon his benevolent redesign of the Harmon Grid used in those elaborate transatlantic executions of Hans Stein-Muller and Pedro Russo back on April 1 that year. Although I wasn't pleased with our engagement in designing any execution device, my constant pleas for the devices to be agony-free, were embedded into the final design.

For that, I was grateful.

The prisoners huddled in rows as they were told to by the guards. Rows upon rows of men and women, even as young as twelve, stood side by side. Apparently, according to some intelligence, those youngsters had been involved in vicious bombings of schools and shopping malls in KL. As I looked inside, I caught a girl's eye on the end of one of the rows. She was in her late twenties, fragile and deeply frightened. She looked as far from a terrorist as one could look. I tried to smile at her, to give her confidence, encouragement. A sense of 'it's all going to be okay'. But she wasn't buying it. I saw her orange jump suit darken around her upper thigh and watched the line of dark trickle down the inside of her leg. She looked away from me, embarrassed. My empathic shield was on full, preventing me from feeling her pain. But as she turned again to face me, I got everything. Her eyes spoke shame, despair, and hate for herself at being who she was: a poor girl who was about to die.

A guard tapped me on the shoulder, indicating that 'the process', as they termed it, was about to start. It was time I should leave.

The huge, steel doors started to close. The people lined up in their neat rows were silent. No screams. No pleas. Just completely without words.

I turned away as the doors slammed shut and the auto bolts slid into position. The Harmon devices were embedded in the ceilings. I could feel the vibration of energies as they charged up. It was a sensation only a Kudamaz would feel. I knew the people inside would sense nothing.

My body convulsed in time with the blast from the Harmon devices.

It lasted less than a second.

I listened as the auto bolts slid back and the big steel doors jerked themselves open.

I stood there. I was in the doorway as I'd been minutes before in front of those thousands of people in their perfect rows. Silent and waiting.

The cavernous warehouse was empty. Where once was life, there was now nothing.

No bodies to clear up.

The way in which this execution method came about still tears at me. Given the massive numbers being executed, Ashton had appealed to Sam to employ Kudamaz technology as a humane option. He also stressed that he wanted 'as little mess as possible'.

Sam and I argued for many Earth days after Ashton had approached him. My husband claimed that all the people to be executed were killers themselves. They were traitors to their countries and to the world.

Sam said they'd be executed by current Earth means anyway, firing squad, lethal injection, gas. None were as humane as the Harmon wave.

I looked out into the big expanse of nothing and wondered. How humane was genocide?

Chapter 25

Aby-od's focus remained fixed on the Screen in the Observation Room. Time did not pass per se on Kudamun, but his interaction with Earth forced another moment from his life. Earth was not the only planet he oversaw, but it was, unfortunately, the planet with one of the fastest time signatures. Some planets' hours lasted as long as an Earth day, or even an Earth year, and there was one planet at the far edge of the universe, which had the slowest time signature of all; one of their hours was equivalent to one hundred thousand Earth years. Strangely, planets with slower time signatures were the calmest and most peaceful. Those whose signatures raced were turbulent and unpredictable. No matter. I didn't set their time signatures, reasoned Aby-od, I'm just the one to make sure their ticking doesn't stop.

The longer Aby-od spent dealing with the affairs of Earth, the more of his own life force was taken. Ironically, it was also the planet that lately seemed to be the most tumultuous, thus requiring all of his time. After Ellie had become the Protector, the amount of monitoring and interventions had dropped significantly, and Earth, it seemed, was becoming the peaceful planet it was when it had started.

Aby-od stared at the Screen and pondered on developments as they unfurled. Ellie was there, hands flying around, her mouth animated, her eyes blazing with fury. Aby-od looked at Ashton, a man captivated by Ellie's spectacle. Sam watched on, appearing amused.

Aby-od hadn't initiated audio but the conversation was clearly heated. Aby-od waved a hand in front of a crystal protruding from the wall and voices blasted around him.

"Okay, that's enough! Sam and I aren't assets."

Ellie's powerful timbre came through into the room. Aby-od had heard that voice across the years. A force of unmistakable determination. With confidence, but sweetness, it could only lead to whatever success Ellie sought.

Aby-od wasn't a betting man. That concept was an anathema to him. But if he had been, he would have bet Ellie to be the Protector even before she'd been reconstituted. Although he knew who Ellie was, even if he hadn't, it would have been obvious to him. Of all the people on Earth, she was the one whose traits matched the profile of the Protector of Ki.

Aby-od turned back to the Screen, which flashed on again, allowing Aby-od to observe the discourse on Earth. Prime Minister Ashton had annoyed Ellie, and, in her own indomitable way, she was letting rip.

He recalled Ellie's consternation with Ashton's practices. How she believed that he wasn't the man he made out to be. That somehow the good he'd done was for an unknown and ultimately evil goal. The severe lack of any evidence whatsoever to substantiate her claim forced Aby-od to consider that Ellie was searching for conspiracies where none existed.

The world, now calm and peaceful, and, most of all, in balance, did not require her interventions. Her very existence depended on the premise that Earth needed her. But now Al Nadir had been cast into the tattered fragments of distant memory and world peace was an achievable objective via Freedom Earth, Ellie's purpose was unclear.

Aby-od had monitored Ashton and, with the exception of his dubious sexual predilections and his obvious greed, he hadn't displayed intentional evil to the world. Aby-od recognized that the British PM was brutal and cold-hearted where Al Nadir was concerned. That was to be expected. He showed the strength of a leader who'd experienced the infection of home-grown terrorism and whose country had almost paid the ultimate price for such activity. Crushing Al Nadir was a justified response and his delivery of hardline justice was no more than what Aby-od would have expected.

The sudden renewing of capital punishment to be a spectacle of attraction for the public was outlandish and theatrical. Macabre to its core. But Al Nadir had destroyed his people and decimated their lives. It was no less than what the terrorists deserved.

Aby-od could see Ashton had adopted his vicious hardline as a deterrent to any straggling faction that considered themselves worthy of reforming Al Nadir. By blanket branding all of Al Nadir as traitors, Ashton could, without need of any further judicial intervention, apply the death penalty to every Al Nadir operative, large or small.

Reassured by Sam and Ellie, Aby-od knew these executions had been swift and humane. Unlike Al Nadir's modus operandi of suffering, the element of pain had been removed from proceedings completely.

The new and painless Harmon wave technology designed by Sam had made everything immediate. The Al Nadir terrorist wasn't aware of their fate, except when the bolt of harmonic energy had been released and received. Of course, by that point, thought Aby-od, their soul force had already disengaged from their corporeal shell and commenced its journey to a higher level of consciousness, with the on-going reward or punishment meted out during the next-level pathway.

Aby-od rationalized that however terrible state execution was, the benevolent method of the execution demonstrated a level of good, and therefore the light balance was kept in check. Nothing signaled the amount of evil Ellie suggested. It just didn't register. Ashton was doing a difficult, painful job for the greater good.

Ellie had a lesser role to play. She had sacrificed her human side for a calling to protect. With peace now an acknowledged reality, where was Ellie's place?

Manifesting the condition of evil in situations she encountered gave her reason. A purpose. This was a need Ellie had. It was not a representation of fact.

Reconstitution, it seemed, was not without side effects. Aby-od had to tread with caution. Ellie was not as strong as he thought.

Aby-od turned away from the Observation screen and it blinked off, its sentient consciousness aware that the observer's view was no longer upon it.

Aby-od walked through into another chamber.

With his mind on Ellie, he shook his head and muttered, "Oh, my poor, dear Ellie!"

He didn't notice movement at the edge of the Observation Room's entrance. A figure in the shadows looked on. A smile cut across the immutable face of the intruder, caught in semi-darkness.

Under his breath, he whispered, "Oh, poor Ellie indeed."

Chapter 26

I listen. Ashton has mutated his address at the meeting from strong and forthright to caring and beholding his success to Sam and me. It is just a technique, but no one, not even Sam, could see the insincerity of the consummate manipulator before me.

Ashton, arms around both of us, smiles. Or, rather, smirks. That awful jerking causing his top lip to rise gives a flash of perfect enamel. His crowds think it to be coy, but, to me, it drips of salacious intention.

"A wonderful team, I'm sure you'll agree."

Ashton looks at everyone in the room, his power play obvious and sickening. I want to squirm out of his hold, but he squeezes my shoulder and Sam's together in a stance of solidarity.

"So now we're all on the same page, let's talk about energy, and how saving the planet and relinquishing fossil fuels can really be achieved through Quantum Force."

Saving again! Does this man do nothing but offer salvation to mankind? Why does he even need me? He can do it all himself.

I catch Sam's eye.

'Can you believe this?'

Sam's telepathic response is uncharacteristically sluggish. 'Ellie, he's doing good. Don't be so judgmental.'

'Doing good?' Yeah! But for who?'

'The world, of course.'

'Oh, here we go, the changing-the-world-for-good mantra. But you know, Sam, all I see is what he's doing for his good, not the world.'

'Ellie, you're blind. Ashton's just said it. Terrorism is all but dead. Religion is no longer divisive. The world rejoices and unites under Freedom Earth.

Even this new energy, Aby-od said, was part of man's natural evolutionary step. It's bringing them out of a period of great darkness and towards a time of pure enlightenment.'

'I hope you're right.'

'The Balance Shift doesn't lie, Ellie. We'd be beyond the Dark Zone if all he was doing was wrong.'

I can't get away from the facts. It always comes back to the Balance Shift. The universal truth, despite my misgivings and my deep distrust of Ashton, is undeniable. Sam is right. The Balance Shift can't lie. Ashton is doing good and keeping the strong white light balance.

But that didn't mean I can't make him aware of his own human frailty. That innate weakness, for all his wealth and power, will always snap at his heels. The yapping terrier of mortality.

Ashton stares straight across at me, as if he can read my mind argument with Sam. I smile, slip my arm around his back, and grip his waist. I apply hardly any force, as much as I want to, but Ashton still breathes in sharply. He looks down at my hand and then into my face. His expression is plain. Did I really exert such a force to elicit immediate pain? I keep my face free of any display of animosity.

"All okay?" I whisper, just loud enough to reach Ashton's ear but no one else's.

Ashton's habitual smirk slips a little as I apply a fraction more pressure. I watch his eyebrow raise and feel his torso tense beneath my fingers. His smirk descends further as the edges of his mouth tighten downward.

"Ashton is quite the little savior," I tell the room.

Ashton drops his arms from my shoulder and Sam's, and pulls away, clapping his hands together.

"Thank you, Ellie. How lovely of you to think so. But that crown goes to you."

"Oh, really! And here was me thinking you were the one saving planet Earth."

I can't resist the biting sarcasm. I've had my fill of Ashton's perpetual saving complex. The lack of Balance Shift, I cannot explain, although, as any good investigator knows, anomalies need to be explored. Something not chiming with the way things should be signals a clue to what the truth really is.

Sam moves away, shaking his head.

'Stop it!' he screams in my mind. 'Leave him be.'

I have a sudden urge to stick out my tongue to Sam the way I used to when I was human, and he'd said something that I knew was correct but didn't want to accept. But I restrain from protruding my pink member and keep my surge of pseudo-emotion free of any physical manifestation.

"Not saving the Earth, Ellie, my dearest, just giving up on our love affair with fossil fuel. With my-"

"Your?" I snap.

"Our quantum energy, fossil fuel is relegated finally to history. This is the quantum age. An age of cost-efficient, clean, and high-performance fuel accessible to all. The petro-politics of last century is over. The stranglehold over our lives and the reason for so many wars is gone. We can be free, in charge of our own destinies, not following a path decreed by those with oil and gas fields and pipelines, but, instead, able to create a new future with hope and a promise filled with peace."

Around the table, I watch Ashton's hand-picked brethren clap.

I've seen the schematics and the fiercely complex calculations that explain Ashton's new quantum energy. Sam has too. The science appears to be beyond the current capability of humans. Concerned, I have broached the subject with both Sam and Aby-od. After examination of the research papers, they both concluded that although a scientific leap has been made, nothing is out of sequence for a planet about to enter a higher level of consciousness.

Aby-od had been exacting in his put down to me. "Once again, my dear Ellie, you're chasing shadows. You especially should realize that everything is connected. Freedom Earth, the movement that has enabled religious unification, an end to war, terror, and suffering, and the emergence of a new energy source that underpins an independence away from the traditional sources that created instability, dominance, and corruption across the centuries, the congruence of these two things has made Earth a safer, better, and more enlightened planet than ever in its entire short history."

I remember Aby-od touching my shoulder as he spoke. A fatherly gesture, but one in which I could detect veiled condescension.

"Earth is a shining light of hope. A credit to your intervention. All that is needed now is for you to help Prime Minister Ashton and his team guide the planet forward. The evil you knew..." Aby-od stumbled. I knew he was recalling our first meeting after he'd rescued me from Al Nadir. His voice sharpened, compensating for the memory that still affected him. "The evil you knew and experienced is gone. Your role is now redefined as one of caretaker."

"I'm the Protector, not a fucking Caretaker!" I exploded, indignantly.

Aby-od shook his head.

"Times have changed, Ellie. Earth needs something different from you, and you must provide this. If you do not, you will act to the detriment of Earth, and the duty of care you hold under your Kudamaz responsibility will be breached. This can never happen."

Aby-od's voice, stable and even-toned, had ground into my mind as a powerful resonance that, even in recall, causes me to screw up my face and frown as irritation seeps out of me.

Who does Aby-od think I am to infer that I'd willfully breach my duty of care?

Doesn't he realize I was only voicing concern about Ashton and his allegedly benevolent activities because of my inherent need to protect Earth from evil in any shape? My duty of care Aby-od spoke of was front and center in my thoughts always, and never would it be compromised by a need to support a potentially belligerent force in the guise of a national leader.

"And so I'm pleased that some of the country's oldest coal and oil-fired power stations, those that are ramping up pollutants, will experience full-scale conversion to our clean quantum energy within the next few weeks."

I drift back from my confrontation with Aby-od to hear Ashton in full-blown 'bow down to me' mode. I grit my teeth. Help Prime Minister Ashton and his team. Right!

"Our automotive companies across the country have received the production plans to manufacture under license the quantum podule engine. Service stations throughout the land have been installed with new kiosks providing light photons, the basic element to kick start the quantum pod engine. The 'run your car at light speed' national campaign starts tomorrow. We're all set to issue our decree absolute to the black stuff!"

Ashton smirks, enjoying his little quip.

I know speed of operations isn't down to his efficiency, but our involvement. Sam had redesigned the internal combustion engine to accommodate the new science of the quantum energy podule. His intervention had been permitted on the grounds that humans had already demonstrated advanced capabilities in creation of the quantum energy source. Anyway, Ashton had an extremely good take on an initial redesign of the new engine before Sam even contributed. All Sam did was finesse the design. No one on Kudamun could deny that quantum energy was an extraordinary breakthrough and catapulted Earth's technological trajectory forward at least by half a millennium or so.

I'd reviewed the feeds from the Observation Room that showed Ashton's engagement with the quantum energy research. The stream started at Culham Research Labs in Oxford, as Ashton had told us. Queries within the feeds showed quantum energy was an area of research that humans across the world had been involved in, including Culham Research, for many decades. With the back-up data that Ashton had given when he'd requested our help, it showed, or seemed to show, his science team had been working on securing a breakthrough for a very long time. Access to see everything through the Observation Room had showed Ashton to have been a slave driver to his scientists, pushing them hard to get results.

Those results had arrived in early May this year, around the same time that Ashton had banished Al Nadir to just a bitter and twisted memory. A version of scarred humanity soon to be eradicated by Freedom Earth-sanctioned public executions on an unprecedented, global scale. And Ashton iced his peace cake with his achievement of the incredible unification of religion. Although some religions weren't completely satisfied by his prophet-like announcements, the sheer momentum of the unification goal swept up even the undecided to an eventual plain of consensus and integrated thought. I could see, during every meeting, the leaders of each religion feeling that if they didn't comply, they'd be stranded, outside of it all, left in the cold, failing to feel the warmth of true revelation, of true rapture.

As I consider these occurrences, Aby-od's words seemed more likely. The congruence of those elements did suggest a time of new enlightenment. Maybe I am somehow perceiving everything through a distorted lens. The white light balance is strong. Earth is safe. Al Nadir is gone.

Why should I raise alarm about something when, examined in the round, it makes perfect sense?

Ashton stares at me, his eyes sparkling and his mouth grinning as his jokes are accepted by the gathered throng.

A completed picture of perfected good.

Only I still detect a missing piece.

Chapter 27

Sam lingered outside of Aby-od's quarters, his hesitation grounded in the conversation he was about to have. Nevertheless, he knew it was time to broach the subject with Aby-od.

"Hello, Sam. Can I help you?"

Aby-od had caught his shadow in the doorway of his beautiful crystal quarters. Sam stepped inside. "Hi, Aby-od. Got a second to spare?"

Sam stared at Aby-od, attempting to conceal the concern inside him. Aby-od saw through instantly.

"It's Ellie, isn't it?"

On having the heart of his worry pin-pointed so accurately, Sam nodded.

"Come and sit down. I was going to speak to you if you hadn't sought me out. Your timing, as always, Sam, is excellent."

At Aby-od's outstretched arm, Sam dropped down into the fluffy, blue sofa. His body heavily sank into the fabric, and despite its ability to instill calmness in the sitter, Sam didn't feel the sofa's power working too effectively at that moment. He swallowed, rubbed his face, and shook his head, unsure of what he was doing.

"Sam, we have to address this issue." Aby-od sat down, right-angled to him on the end of another sofa.

Sam screwed his face up, annoyed with himself, but he knew he had to continue. "Yes, I know we do," he said finally.

"Ellie's behavior with Ashton is borne from her intrinsic need to be needed. With Ashton driving world peace, her role has changed. I tried to explain this but, Sam, she went crazy. She swore at me. Raging and uncontrolled. That simply can't continue."

"I know. She doesn't want to accept that Ashton has been the catalyst to an incredible change that is occurring on Earth. He's changing the world for good, Aby-od. Despite what he's been, at his heart, he's a good guy."

"Sam, you don't have to tell me. I've monitored him. The High Council has run their own checks. We are all aware of his…certain behaviors."

Sam smirked, knowing Ashton's sexual ambivalence when it came to his night-time escapades. But that didn't make him any less of a peacemaker. What went on behind closed doors was Ashton's own affair and should not be used as a barometer to determine whether what he was doing was good for Earth.

"He's certainly greedy too," continued Aby-od, "and he is ruthless with his enemies. His treatment of Al Nadir has been brutal. But, as all the Senior Elders have confirmed, it was expected given the scourge Al Nadir has been on Earth's development and the role they played in almost taking Earth down a path of pure darkness. I've seen nothing to warrant Ellie's constant insinuation of his veiled evil. Have you?"

Sam shook his head. Aby-od's assessment of Ashton was spot on. He was a tough bastard. Sam had seen that during Operation Snowdrop. He'd had no compunction to send thousands to their deaths just to meet mission objectives. But he was always working for greater good. His anchor was buried in a sea of justice. Ashton's goal had been the same as his: to keep their country safe by any means. Ellie couldn't possibly understand what, as agents, they'd both faced and had to deal with.

Ambiguity refracts perspective.

Clouds clarity.

Nothing was ever the black and white world she'd lived in.

"Ellie's duty has changed due to the amazing and wonderful changes on Earth, and now she must change in relation to this. She must accept what is happening and stop her search to find evil, where there is none, simply to justify her role as Protector.

Aby-od's voice hit Sam in somber waves. It was what he'd thought. Ellie was seeing everything in a bad light as she was floundering. Her assigned role as Protector was lessening and she was struggling to find her purpose.

The reason she lost her humanity.

"What can I do?" asked Sam, imploring Aby-od to find the answers he didn't have.

"Lead her on the path she needs to travel. Demonstrate your own confidence in Ashton. Show her that he's a man to have her trust. She believes in you, doesn't she?"

"Of course she does. We fight, but that's just superficial. At our core we trust and believe in each other absolutely. The power of our love is paramount. Nothing can break that."

"Use that power, Sam. Show her you trust Ashton. She'll learn to trust in him from the conviction she holds in you."

"Trust by proxy," said Sam, smiling and understanding what he had to do. Aby-od's logic was, once again, flawless and precise. He knew it had been a good idea talking things through with Kudamun's sage leader.

Aby-od smiled too, and turned his head to look at Sam. "I see you understand me. I haven't given up on Ellie. She has, so far, been a spectacular Protector, and she has shifted Earth firmly and safely into the white light scale of the Balance Shift. Now all she needs to do is focus on taking care of Earth's current direction."

Sam listened. 'Taking care of'. That had been the explosive term for Ellie. She'd given her all to be the Protector. A Kudamaz being of supreme power, not someone who was just helping and guiding another human leader to great things. Such a role subverted her own power. It demeaned her and made her little more than a celestial mentor to Ashton.

"I think that the 'taking care' bit is even more of a problem for Ellie, more than just her issues of trust with Ashton," said Sam, voicing his feelings.

"Ah!" said Aby-od, but Sam couldn't discern from Aby-od's almost blank expression what he was thinking. His eyes had taken on a vacant look, and his calm, immutable face gave away nothing. A perfect poker player face!

"Ellie became the Protector to save Earth," said Sam. "But now she has nothing to save. She's been told to 'take care' of Earth's path and help Ashton. He's the one with supreme purpose now. It's like she's got a supporting role in Ashton – the movie."

Aby-od grinned at Sam's words. "Quite inciteful, Sam. That positioning which Ellie now has to accept, I know, isn't easy for her. The way she became Protector, the circumstances surrounding her sudden and brutal transformation, has defined the way she's played her role. She accepted that she'd gained so much more as the Protector. That Earth couldn't survive without her and gave her reason for such a rapid acceptance."

Sam heard that Aby-od knew the problem completely. He listened as Aby-od continued his assessment of Ellie's behavior.

"But now she's no longer responsible for Earth's survival. It's survived. She has to take a back seat and let someone else take the steering wheel. That's why she hates Ashton so much. And why she persists on seeing evil where there is none."

"He's taken her crown," responded Sam. "But how can I change that?"

"Again, it's down to you, Sam. Impress upon her that her role is still key to Earth's future. As Protector of Earth's new path, she must support Ashton and oversee this momentous change happening on Earth. But her acceptance of her new role will only come through your understanding of it too. You need to show Ellie her new role as Protector of Earth's new path is just as important as the one she had as Protector of Earth's survival."

Sam nodded. "So what you're saying, Aby-od," confirmed Sam, "is the direction may have changed, but her purpose remains constant. For the good of humanity. That is still at the heart of the Protector's purpose."

"Exactly, Sam. You now see that. Ellie needs to as well."

"Thank you, Aby-od." Sam stood, making ready to leave. "You've made my path to help Ellie, as well as that of Earth's, so much clearer."

Chapter 28

I stand in front of the Screen. What am I hoping to see? What am I trying to find? Ashton is like a god on Earth, and almost worshiped for what he has achieved.

Quantum Force is about to go online with its first major power stations in the UK and US simultaneously. All the religious leaders are meeting for a pre-event get-together before the big show in which Ashton will be presenting to the world unification of all religions under Freedom Earth. Of course, Sam and I have been invited to attend both ceremonies, giving both an undeniable touch of credibility.

Terrorism and crime have been virtually wiped out, owing to the Surv-Motes Sam designed. The requested upgrade to weaponize them, despite my severe misgivings, has gone through swiftly and safely, and, as a result, civilians throughout the UK have benefited from this seemingly fierce surveillance device. Robberies, rapes, and murders have all been foiled due to the interventions of the upgraded Surv-Motes. And the perpetrators? Zapped into the next life by a Harmon beam and obliterated to quantum dust.

So successful have been the Surv-Motes, other world leaders have asked Ashton for the supplier's details. I know it won't be long before Surv-Motes are instigated in every major city across the world.

I'd reviewed the Balance Shift of Earth before entering the Observation Room. It was the way it always was, stuck in the white light area, not too much to cause alarm but just enough to indicate that the Earth was really in a good place.

I stare at the flickering Observation Screen. Just static. I haven't invoked a query or stated a time and date to view.

I move across the crystals, my hand lingering on them. Why am I doing this?

I know my motivation.

Ashton.

I have to confirm something in my mind. Something that I started considering when Ashton's family had died, and then buried when I saw his pain.

"Query. Natasha Ashton. Scenes before her death."

On the Observation Screen, Natasha holding the hand of her daughter pops up. I draw my hand across a crystal embedded in the wall, and I am there, standing on the esplanade watching the two of them buying ice creams and walking along the coastline. I look around three-hundred-and-sixty degrees, and I notice a car on the other side of the road. A black, G-class Merc with darkened windows. It comes up gently, not speeding. Just before it passes Mariella, the window slides down, a silencer pokes out, and the shot is taken. The Merc continues down the road for a short distance.

I move my hand to pause in time with the real-time recording. I walk over to the car.

"Inside." I instruct, and the view changes.

I am inside the Merc staring at the man holding the gun. With dark and intense features, he could be a Turk, Arab, or Israeli. The driver has the same look. Both are well dressed in expensive, casual clothes.

I whip my hand back, and the man holding the gun speaks.

"Around again. Need to get the bitch."

Translation systems are on, and I know the man speaks with a Gulf Arab dialect.

It is all I need. I know the rest. I don't need to see the slaying of Natasha.

"Over," I say, and the Observation Screen turns to static.

I walk back from the Screen, intending to leave the room. But something still niggles at me. I turn back.

"Full query. Richard Ashton. British Prime Minister."

I wait for the view to run on the Screen. First, the most recent images show of Ashton as PM. I turn the air with my hand and the images on screen quicken, going into Ashton's past. Visions of him as a minister and lowly MP. Back farther. Ashton as a Journalist. His activity, however, is strange. It is focused on meeting after meeting in secret places, on planes, and in car parks. A series of liaisons in the shadows. I don't need to hear what Ashton is saying to know it has little to do with the headlines he is supposed to write and more to do with a meatier backstory.

I can see that whatever Ashton was doing, he was always at the heart of some seedy, dubious activity.

I delve further into his past.

A lawyer, brilliant, sharp, and uncompromising. He tears into every opposition and appears to win many cases. He researches, works hard, and his successes in the courtroom validate the fruits of his labor. Again, Ashton always seems to surround himself with people of a questionable nature, receiving or passing on information for a stack of moolah.

Ashton liked to party hard too, and his attraction to both sexes is made clear in the images on screen. I speed up or jump completely sections of his viewing line showing his stream of sexual conquests. I always knew he was a predator, but seeing the actual evidence makes me want to heave.

I flick through views. Ashton was handy with his fists and wasn't slow in delivering his unique 'get out clause' on individuals who chose to linger longer in his bed than he wanted. The look on Ashton's face shows he was also turned on by sexual violence. That abhors me.

I hold my breath. Do I want to go further? Should I go further? I know I have to see for myself what Ashton has been to understand what he potentially could become.

I turn the air backward in a circle, fast. Observations show a younger Ashton. Although very handsome, there is something deeply cruel and cold about him.

Scene after scene depicts an array of brutal and sadistic violence. In some scenes he is seducing, torturing, and killing the same person in the one viewing. Meetings, discussions, liaisons, training on new weapons and technologies, gym workouts, analyzing information, killing, stealing, breaking in, surveilling, exploding, travelling, running, and shooting.

All these things together mean one thing.

Ashton had been a spy. And a good one by the way his seniors appear to value him.

I move further back and notice he'd worked for Six. He was in his mid-twenties. Probably grabbed straight out of university.

I watch Ashton on an exercise. He'd gone through a very tough assault course, and then was suddenly captured. Although it was clear he was still in training mode, he was obviously disoriented. Strapped into a chair, he was beaten, and long thin needles were inserted into his skin. He grimaced and then screamed but didn't speak. The interrogators beat him again then stuck a hose down his throat, flooding him with water. Then they beat him so hard he couldn't stand.

But I can see he hadn't revealed whatever information he had hidden.

Finally, his superior came in accompanied by a medic. The superior shook hands with Ashton, and the medic tended to the injuries his colleagues had inflicted.

I fix on the Screen and wonder about Sam. Had my husband endured such during training?

I look at Ashton, bruised and bloody, but silent, and I realize that he is no cream-puff politician. He never had been. Suffering was his bread and butter. He'd been trained to take it and dish it out.

I forward it again and see Ashton killing and enjoying the thrill of each mission.

Had Sam been like that too?

When he was human, he said he'd done things he wasn't proud of, ME9s to get through policies that were unsavory to the electorate and abused human rights.

I stop viewing Ashton and request the last ten years of Sam Noor MI6 Agent.

I swallow and ignore a voice inside me. Don't do this!

Sam appears, talking to a man. I recognize him from Foreign Office functions as Sir Justin Maide, a Whitehall mandarin with whom Sam dealt. My inherent databanks as the Protector tell a different story. Maide was head honcho in Six. I examine the Screen. Sam is in Whitehall, clearly fed up with his meeting but energized by Maide's discussion. I can see a change in him. He is happy to be challenged.

Fast forward and Sam is on training in Gibraltar. Assault courses, weapons training, self-defense. Sam learned everything so quickly. His superiors, especially Maide, are delighted.

And then I see it. The abduction and capture. The final chapter in the training. Literally a make or break exercise.

It's similar to Ashton's. But instead of needles, they'd used electrodes.

I have to look away.

Sam screams. But he doesn't reveal any intel.

They beat, waterboard, beat, electrocute, and finally beat him again, just to make completely sure he'd endured the correct level of pain.

I shake my head, totally and utterly incredulous.

Why the fuck would anyone go through that and call it a job? I have no answer to that question. Only insanity.

I move the viewing forward. Unfortunately, the way in which the scenes play out are almost identical to Ashton's, and, if anything, they are more violent and raging. I turn my face away, unable to reconcile the man I loved with the actions he does on screen.

"Ellie, don't watch this."

I look up and Sam is in the door arch of the Observation Room.

"I knew you'd done terrible things, but…"

I can't find the words to reflect the horrifying scenes I'd just forced myself to witness.

"Ellie, I was a soldier. No more, no less. I did what I had to do to protect the country I love. I'm not sorry for what I've done. They were all evil. All terrorists. We had to fight fire with fire. Anything less and we'd have been trampled, annihilated. It was a terrible time. Maybe we went too far. I don't know. I was too much inside it all to differentiate right from wrong. All I knew is we had to succeed. We had to win."

Listening to Sam's voice, all the torment rushes back to me. His life of lies. His betrayal.

"Win at any cost." I state finally, and stare at Sam.

"Ellie, don't rake up the past. What is done is done. I'm not that man anymore. I'm not even human anymore. Please, let the past lie in peace."

I don't respond. I can't.

Aswa-da's control of Sam. How easily he fell under the dark lord's influence. Now I understand.

I forward the viewing to one image I'd noticed from about four years ago.

Sam, Ashton, Matthew Kinley and Maide, all in a meeting discussing a mission codenamed 'Snowdrop'. I know Sam is still watching me. He's come up behind me. I look around and Sam is shaking his head. His memory banks press through, making him recall something he doesn't want to.

Sorrow breaks out across his face.

"What was Snowdrop?"

Chapter 29

May 25, 2017

Lei sat by Xiao's side, up right and resolute, as she had done every day since his coma had struck. But something about that day was different. She'd sensed a strength of action within her. In the morning, Chen had called her 'a shining light of positivity'. For Xiao, she must be that now.

Looking down at Xiao's lifelessness, she swallowed. Inside her, a vibration began. A pulsing resonance, soft and warm, caressing her tortured heart.

Take his hand in yours.

Show him how much you love him.

Bring the moments back.

Make them happen again.

Force the connection.

The words of instruction flew into her brain from a place she couldn't fathom.

Within her, the resonance built. Lei was gaining understanding. Her love for Xiao. His love for her. The emotions formed a harmonic pattern. A steady resonating beat, coalescing with her soul.

She took Xiao's hand. Floppy. Almost devoid of life.

Bring the moments back. Make them happen again.

Lei remembered Xiao hand in hers. Fingers tight, holding on. His excitement. When she'd taken him to the zoo – seeing a tiger up close for the first time. He'd been scared but exhilarated; his little fingers had pressed hard around hers. Entering the Science Museum, seeing a piece of real moon rock, Xiao had been amazed. One small hand pressed against the glass display case; the other intertwined with her own. She'd felt his blood pump firmly, quickening the flow with his racing heart rate. Such exhilaration.

Another time.

Going to the US. Seeing Disneyland in Florida. Staring at the famous fairy palace. Xiao's hand pressed into her fingers. Although just a young child, her son's intense hold crushed around her hand. Lei recalled wincing as his nails bit into her skin, such was his excitement. She kept him in her clutches. She didn't let go.

The power of a mother's bond.

Undeniable. Formidable. Potent.

Lei closed her eyes and let the memories wash over her. Moment after moment.

His hand tightening. She embodied it. In her mind, bringing back the energy of the feeling. Making it real.

The joy and happiness of having a son. Xiao's need of love from her. Her need of love from Xiao.

Lei captured the moments. Sensing the energies, the moments bestowed, she pushed those sensations into the steady, strong resonance of love that flowed within her and she felt had, somehow, connected with her soul.

With every gentle pulse, and each memory manifested, reality started to form. Brought together from its indeterminant quantum future.

And a slight, barely noticeable pressure asserted against her soft skin.

Gradually, the pressure pushed, graduating its force. Until Lei knew.

Xiao, her boy, was returning.

The Light of Ki considered the situation before it.

The Earth woman called Lei sat beside the bed. She'd somehow connected with the boy Xiao's consciousness. The Light of Ki knew that Lei was the boy's mother and her motherly love had ascended the levels of universal energy states and breached the level it had placed Xiao in.

Lei had broken through the seemingly impenetrable defenses the Light of Ki had placed around Xiao like an encapsulating bubble. In this place, Xiao's consciousness had been stabilized and light-based nourishment provided through direct connectivity to the pure energies within the universe.

Those same energies that had ebbed and flowed on their constantly moving paths through its crystal formation.

The Light of Ki became dejected.

Now all it had was a human vessel. A fragile, emotionally charged human. Surely, the most inappropriate receptacle for its energy.

And a receptacle that had almost died several times. Had it not been for the Light of Ki's ability to pull Xiao's consciousness quickly out of his body, his brain would have burnt out.

It was for this reason that the Light of Ki struggled to understand how the human mother Lei had been able to pull the boy out of the entranced state from his higher-level consciousness prison of safety.

Several Earth seconds before it had felt the energy pull, the Light of Ki became aware of a pulsing, similar to a human heartbeat. A steady but strong resonance reverberated through the boy's body, flowing its harmonic energy into the microtubules within the neurons inside Xiao's brain, and connecting and weaving its resonance deep into the universal quantum states. Once there, the resonance ascended the levels toward where Xiao's consciousness rested safely.

At the moment, the pulsing resonance hit the seventh level of consciousness, the Light of Ki discerned the tremendous pull of the boy's consciousness back into the reality state.

The resonance increased intensity, flooding the boy's consciousness with need.

A need to be loved. To be wanted by someone who loved her.

With sudden recognition, the Light of Ki knew the resonance pulse was Mother Love.

Lei was using her phenomenal, empathically driven bond she had with Xiao to create powerful thought energy originating from the joy and happiness of past moments when mother and son had been together.

But Lei had added another ingredient into this metaphysical mix, reflected the Light of Ki.

She'd used her own soul force as a booster to power-up her thought energies, and, pondered the Light of Ki, had enveloped those thought energies into an invincible stream of pure love and a desperate need to be wanted.

That delivered energy stream had within it the most perfect union of mind, heart, and soul the Light of Ki had ever seen.

The Light of Ki knew it had witnessed something that the Ancient Ones believed no Earth human could achieve.

It was, by all standards of human behavior, impossible. The mind, heart, and soul combined energy stream powered by sheer motherly love had shot into one of the highest levels of consciousness for humans, broken through the many energy defenses the Light of Ki had established, and pulled Xiao out of his secure consciousness cell back into a reality state within a quantum moment.

At first, the Light of Ki was concerned.

Would such an immediate disassociation and disconnection from the universal energies hurt the boy?

Consciousness had surged into Xiao, and with it coursed the Light of Ki. Back into that delicate human body.

The Light of Ki waited an Earth second to feel the breakdown of the boy's state. He was ready, the second he detected the boy's mind failing, to initiate ascension back into the higher-level consciousness state.

Lei held Xiao's hand and the Light of Ki could feel her motherly love flowing into the boy. The Light of Ki realized that although it wasn't as stable a force as the universal energies that cushioned the boy before, it couldn't deny the boy's mind and internal framework was growing stronger and more resilient, able to contain and align the Light of Ki within his form.

The Light of Ki waited for a few more Earth moments, and as strength grew in Xiao, it became confident of the force of Lei's motherly love supporting the boy's recovery. It was content to allow the boy to remain this way. It would monitor, and at the slightest risk to the boy, it would make the ascension again.

Looking through Xiao's eyes, the Light of Ki could see the desperate need Lei had for her son to return. The Light of Ki took over Xiao's psyche completely as it realigned the boy's consciousness at the quantum level within his neurons, enabling him to function as a human boy again.

Inside Xiao, the Light of Ki could feel his delight at returning. Over and over, it heard the words, 'Thank you. Thank you'.

Such a feeling of gratitude flashed through the Light of Ki; it was pleased of Lei's ability.

The Light of Ki first spoke through the boy. Turning toward the boy's father, a human named Chen, it couldn't help but feel the dark force within the man. A human borne of the soul of Etima.

And a man who could be a dangerous influence on Xiao.

Vitriol slipped out unrestricted from Xiao's lips as the Light of Ki addressed the parents.

The Light of Ki attempted to explain to Lei what the situation really was, but it seemed Chen's darkness made clarity of its delivery disjointed.

Coherency was lost to the Light of Ki.

It focused on Survival. The word that had helped Lei understand.

The Light of Ki could feel itself grow dimmer as Xiao's internal force, bolstered by his mother's pure love, which grew stronger.

It aligned within the force of love flooding Xiao and subsumed itself within the pounding, timeless energies.

And Xiao then took control.

Chapter 30

"Darling, please don't."

Sam places his hand on the Observation Screen main crystal control to shut off the image.

"Wait!" I shout, placing my hand on top of my husband's. "I need to understand what was so special about Snowdrop."

I can access the information in my extensive databanks. But I don't want to. I want Sam to tell me.

From the scenes depicted, this was a mission beyond top secret. Ashton's involvement verified the massive importance of whatever Snowdrop was.

"Snowdrop was an infiltration mission," says Sam. "Matthew Kinley was a double agent working for Six but also inside the higher echelons of Al Nadir. He gave them information we could afford to lose and us vital intelligence we needed to win. But it came at a cost."

Sam stares at his feet, weighing up whether to continue. I watch him. The force of something thunders through him, and he shudders. Slowly, he brings his head up. His eyes lock on to mine.

"Do you remember the Piccadilly bombing, early June four years ago?"

I nod.

That day, hell had taken over London.

I had been in Green Park tube station when the bombs went off. The vibrations had shaken the foundations. Mortar pieces fell from the ceiling and the walls. People screamed. I ran for the exit as fast as I could with the rest of the terrified passengers.

I recall from my data banks that the bombs had been placed on multiple tube carriages going in both directions on the Piccadilly and Bakerloo lines. The entire station had collapsed under the ferocity of the blasts. The ceilings had caved in as four tube trains lit up like firecrackers with carriage after carriage exploding in sequence. The chains of explosions took out thousands of people.

Innocent lives.

I swoosh my hand over the crystal controls and state before Sam could stop me, "Piccadilly bombing."

On screen, the images of the bombings play out in shocking, gruesome detail. I wave a hand, and I am there in the middle of the carnage. And so is Sam.

But he isn't observing anymore.

His eyes are shut and tears stream down his face. The droplets sparkle to nothing, but they come from his eyes in a constant deluge.

"Sam, what the *hell* happened?"

He waves his hand and we are back in the Observation Room. He turns his back on the images and faces me.

"We knew."

"You knew what?"

"About Piccadilly."

And finally, that piece of truth that had so evaded me slots into the jigsaw of my final days.

Snowdrop was the missing link.

Sam's knowledge of Snowdrop and what they'd done could've brought the whole government to its knees. It gave reason to Maide's insane paranoia and his off-the-books actions.

"Kinley gave us the intel two days before the hit."

"So why didn't you evacuate and check for bombs?"

"It was a test. For Snowdrop to work, Al Nadir had to believe Kinley had turned and trust him completely. If we'd intervened, Kinley would've been burned."

"So you willfully let all those people die just so Kinley could be accepted into the Al Nadir elite club!"

I struggle with my words. I hold down my anger, but I can feel it rising.

I cannot comprehend any mission brief that authorizes humans to die.

"Sam, there must have been another way to convince Al Nadir. I can't believe you couldn't have found another way."

"Darling, we were up against it. Kinley was on a knife edge. One slip, one show of his own humanity, and that would have been it, the mission blown. But Kinley got close. Al Douri was impressed with him and brought him right into the fold. After Piccadilly, we saved so many more lives. We found ways to get ahead of Al Nadir. Ashton, Maide, and I, when we got the intel about the Piccadilly bombing, we wrestled all night with the decision, but in the end, there was no avoiding it. Lives had to be sacrificed. They were collateral damage. We squared away our decision that night against the future lives we'd save, and the chance to bring Al Douri down."

"But, Sam, surely you could see that much death and destruction was wrong? Nothing was worth it."

"Ellie, it wasn't wrong. It was essential."

"A death toll of five thousand eight hundred and twenty is essential? Whatever way you dress it up, it was state sanctioned murder."

Sam doesn't speak. The sorrow has gone deeper, slipping into his darkening eyes as he remembers.

"The way I lived during those years, darling, nothing was black and white. Everything was tainted. The drive to succeed. To destroy Al Nadir. To protect God, Queen, and country. It was all so overpowering. Maybe we were all corrupted by an ideal that could never be. Ashton, Maide, and I agreed together that no sacrifice was too great if it meant toppling Salim Al Douri and his Al Nadir empire."

"Was Ashton always involved with you?"

Sam shakes his head.

"No. He'd just been elected prime minister for a second term. He had an enormous amount to deal with, but his pure hatred of Al Nadir motivated him to get involved. His background experience in Six came to the fore whenever Al Nadir was discussed, and I could always see he wanted to get his hands dirty."

"He certainly has done that," I snap, loathing what I've learnt.

Sam stares back at me, realization erupting in his eyes. "And, really, is what I've done that much different to the ruthless way you took down Al Nadir after you became the Protector? Your duty to protect turned you into a soldier as well. And you didn't flinch when ridding Earth of evil, did you?"

"Don't put what I did in March on the same page as your actions. No innocents suffered."

Suddenly, Sam flips back at me sternly, his sorrow vanished. "Ellie, don't judge what you don't know. Yes, you're the Protector and the kind of things I used to do is probably now described as evil. But every day I did whatever I had to do. Whatever shit I was faced with, I got through it. And you know why?"

I shrug, but then notice Sam's eyes glistened with tears.

"Because I had you."

Sam walks over and drapes his arms around me, pulling me close to him.

"You have always been my anchor, steadying me in the ebb and flow of the river of immorality and deceit that I had to submerge myself in every single day. I couldn't live without you."

I reach up and kiss Sam. "That's why Ashton brings you into the frame," I say. "Like Sam, I've done terrible things. That's what he said."

Sam nods. "And that's why he's so impassioned to bring about peace, to stop all war, unify religion, and give us energy security. You know, you've got Ashton all wrong. He may not be a good guy but, darling, neither was I. It doesn't mean we can't try to rebalance the sins of our past."

I listen to Sam. His perspective is clearer than mine. I can't get past Ashton's smirking, patronizing attitude. But I have to.

I have to give Ashton a chance.

I have to let go of the past that still defines me and learn to embrace a future where mankind's evolutionary path to enlightenment is just on the cusp of being realized.

Chapter 31

I stare at the Reality Gap flickering above me. Something fades. Subtle, but I can see it. The vibrancy of color is washed out. The zaps of silver, so oft observed, are tainted with a drawling burst instead of a leaping spark. Lethargy is caught in their movement. The orange is dulled and resigned. Though due to what, I cannot tell. Even the purple, so bright, so vivid, appears bruised. A victim of assault in the throes of recovery? Or still under that assault?

I shake my head. What am I thinking? Am I imagining this vision? Have I become the 'paranoid, insane fool' Sam and Aby-od depicted me to be in their previous conversations in May?

Sam moves next to me and comes out of slumber. I've said before of there being no need for me to sleep. I never get tired. My Kudamaz physiology prevents such energy dissipation. Sleep is a choice not a necessity. Sam, however, despite being Kudamaz, still has the want to sleep buried into his human-Kudamaz psychology, more than his physiology. I lie next to him awake when he's dozing. Or I wake him gently by making love to him. I do this with a regularity that means his real sleep doesn't amass to many Earth hours.

I roll on top of him now and kiss his soft lips. Sam returns the kiss and pushes me onto my back. His smile radiates love and still makes me tingle, as if it was his first look at me.

"Morning, sweetness," he drawls, and rubs my hair.

His words and gestures, they relish the past. They celebrate a time when there were such things as mornings and evenings. A moment when all I knew was flesh and blood. When the world was the only place of existence and Sam was a diplomat in the UK's Foreign and Commonwealth Office. Those bright sunny mornings of ignorance, I would welcome back and would forsake my powers in a blink to have them again.

A tear trickles down my face.

I wipe it away, unthinking. But then I recognize its importance.

A tear.

I am shielded from emotion. I have no water inside me as a human does, but I exhibited a human response to days past. A concentration of energies has built inside me manifesting a reaction. I have brought the tear into being through recalling memories of the past. In short, I have created the tear's reality on my face.

I tense and Sam pulls up to look at me.

"Darling, are you alright?" Sam sees my tear. "What on Earth? Ellie, you're crying. Why?"

Sam, I can see, is deeply confused. We'd just seconds before been in each other's arms and I'd been happy.

"It's okay, sweetness, I'm okay. It's just a physical reaction to a build-up of energies generated by old memories. I'm really alright."

Sam smoothes my shoulders and strokes down my arms, carrying on downward, outlining the contours of my sumptuous body.

"I know something that will take your mind off old memories. The generation of some new ones." Sam's eyes twinkle with seductive playfulness.

Chapter 32

He stood within the obsidian crystals that twinkled around him in Etima's region in Kudamun. A Balance Shift indicator bobbed in front of Temenos. He stared, taking in the iridescent red numbers that floated in the air.

Nothing showed. Not even a glimmer.

Temenos smiled, relieved, and switched off the Balance Shift indicator. He couldn't help but allow a shiver of true amazement to ripple through him. What Lord Aswa-da had achieved was beyond the capabilities of any other Kudamaz Senior Elder that ever graced those hallowed halls of Etima-Si-Sig, the Hall of Dark Silence, where he stood.

He'd redefined the notion of possibility.

In his steps, Temenos now trod, but his print left much still to be filled, and he was unsure as to whether he could rise to such a feat. He couldn't stop the trepidation within him. He knew what would happen if he continued to feel such a way, but nothing could stop the sensations. A fear of a looming disaster, despite the incredible achievements that had already been made, gripped him constantly.

One wrong turn. One foot misplaced.

And everything would collapse.

"Fool!"

The voice, unexpected and sudden, reverberated within his head with such a fierceness he sensed his light cells shaking apart. The sensation was like he'd been hit with a Harmon wave. His quantum self vibrated, and his soul force quivered.

"Fool!" bellowed the voice within him. "You will not think this way!"

Temenos swallowed, placing a hand to his temple in sheer pain at the mental assault.

"I apologize, Revered One, My Lord. Do not think me weak."

"I do not," stormed the disembodied voice, now resounding not just inside his head but in the hall itself. "And I want none of your pathetic apologies. They are not needed. The pieces have been placed. The Chosen One is moving them. The rise is beginning. The transformation has begun. Their Instrument will be ours. Darkness will reign. Together we will change Kudamun for good."

Temenos shook as the words of the dark lord thundered at him.

"I know what I must do," stated Temenos with conviction. His momentary doubt now dissipated, destroyed within the decibels of sheer power that crashed through him. But that power forced him to appreciate what was at stake.

"I know you will. For you do not want to experience how I handle failure."

Temenos heard the voice end its warning with a deep, throaty laugh. There was no humor within the tone.

Only menace, laced with a promise of agonizing vengeance should he not meet the Revered One's expectations.

Chapter 33

June 27, 2017

It was always expected.

From the second Ashton confided in Sam and me about his 'new energy discovery', this moment was just waiting to be pulled into existence.

"It's going to be quite an event, darling," murmurs Sam, touching my shoulder. He kisses my neck softly. We're in our Silent Waters apartment. A place that I still like to spend most of my time in despite the obscenely large quarters I have in Kudamun. I like to feel close to something I know to be true. I know it's a lie. But at least it's a lie of my own making.

I shrug, as I rearrange my dress in front of the mirror. "Yes, perhaps."

Sam has clocked the ambivalence flowing through me. "You're not convinced this is right, are you?"

I turn to my husband. I have tried to keep my face devoid of bias, but I knew he'd pick up on my hesitation. "It's not that I don't think it's right for Earth. It's just I'm unsure about the timing. I'm not sure Earth is ready."

"Aby-od thinks it is."

"Aby-od thinks a lot of things," I snap, remembering his systematic denouncement of all my theories concerning Ashton. "And not all of them are correct." I look away, not wanting Sam to see the spark of anger in my eyes.

Sam pulls me back. He turns my chin to face him and touches my cheek, staring into my eyes.

"Sweetness, has he annoyed you?"

I shake my head. Aby-od hasn't annoyed me exactly. But he hasn't been supportive of me either. "It's just this energy source. I don't know…" I stop talking, unable to figure out what I am trying to say.

Sam steps in front of me, his eyebrow arched, and arms crossed. Irritation ripples across his face.

"What is wrong with you, Ellie? Why can't you see what's in front of you? This is right for Earth. You've seen the research papers, the test data, even the Observation Room views, everything confirms that humans have been working on this for a while. They just happened to have had their breakthrough recently. Why do you still question it?"

"Sam, I just feel everything is too soon for humanity. We know other planets that have this type of quantum spin energy and they are at least an Earth millennium ahead of human capabilities."

Sam nods and seems to be considering my words. Then, unexpectedly, he runs his fingers through his hair, the way he used to when I exasperated him.

"Ellie, you've got to let this go. Yes, Earth may be ahead, even unnaturally ahead from our perception of where they should be technologically-speaking, but, as Aby-od has said before and you never stop saying, everything's connected. Their breakthrough aligns with their peace drive. Petrol, if you excuse the pun, darling, has fueled so many wars. I know. For the past ten years, I've seen the vicious collateral damage caused by obsession with the petrodollar. Even before Al Nadir, terrorism and energy security went hand in hand creating terrible destruction across so many countries, devastating lives, and destroying entire generations of people. This new energy rebalances everything."

I stare at my husband and bite my lip, still worried.

"Are you absolutely certain this new quantum energy source is on the level? That everything you've seen has panned out how you expected?"

Sam ponders.

I see something in his eyes.

"You're not sure, are you?"

Sam looks pensive for a moment, then shakes his head.

"Honestly sweetness, it's nothing. Just chasing ghosts."

I open my mouth, but Sam leaps in, like a second wind has taken hold of him and given him new confidence.

"Darling, it's not a coincidence."

"What isn't?" I scrunch my face up, annoyed by my husband's confusing retort.

"That all these things are happening together. Religious unification, peace, an end to war, and this new energy source. Don't you see, sweetness? The timing is aligned perfectly. And your role as Protector of Earth's new path is critical. You must embrace it. I believe in Ashton, and you know I have the ability to 'read people'. I'd know if he was suspect. I know you think you see bad in him, but although he's an arrogant bastard, he's got Earth's golden future in his sights. All I can see, and all I've ever seen is he's doing right by the world."

"So you think I'm just crazy?" I almost spit the words at Sam.

"No, darling, I don't think that. I never have. But I know you're worried about where you fit in this brave new world. Ellie, you're still the Protector. No one will take that away from you. But now, it's about protecting the path of Earth's future, more than her survival. That's your new role."

I nod, taking comfort in Sam's words. They offer a sense of clarity. They, somehow, make my path clearer. Sam notices my agreement and continues.

"Who knows? Ashton may even be part of a bigger plan for Earth. Perhaps a plan by the Ancient Ones. Something to which not even Kudamun is privy. From our databanks, we know the Ancient Ones have done this kind of thing before on other planets to accelerate evolutionary development."

I can't deny that Sam's suggestion is feasible. It has floated through my mind several times, but something inside me holds back on believing it. Maybe it is my intense dislike of Ashton. His salaciousness. His condescension. Everything he stands for, I can't abide by and I can't accept.

Then a vision of Ashton standing between his wife and daughter's bodies hits me hard. I can feel his pain again. I allow myself to enter the vision. His heart thuds a beat as if it wants to slow to nothing, that, inside, the flat line beckons to him, more a lifeline than an indication of cessation.

He closes his eyes and tears flood his face.

All those mannerisms that I despise have vanished.

Here is a man withstanding agony for his belief but wanting, deep inside, to release himself.

I push myself out of the vision, feeling unsure of what I trust, my earlier view of Ashton, or what he has now become.

"Ashton's a good man, Ellie. I know you think otherwise, but he's always been about the greater good. He's like me, Ellie. We're so similar."

I turn sharply to glare at my husband. Despite the honesty brought out by Ashton's suffering, I can't concede to Sam being like Ashton. Yes, in his job, he'd behaved in a similar way, but that was one part of Sam's life he'd compartmentalized. And surely a man is greater than the actions taken in delivery of his duty.

"You're nothing like him." I hiss, shaking my head.

Sam walks over to me, his face sullen, his beautiful lips thinning, and his dark eyes hooding with an uncomfortable foreboding.

"Oh, I am, Ellie. You saw the viewings. You know what I did. Our lives were driven by a need to protect our country. That sole doctrine defined how our lives were lived. The risks we took, those we killed, the horror of those days, we did it all so that innocent people, like you, could go about their daily lives safe, secure, and protected. Blissfully unaware of the dangers that plagued the country."

"So you're a Protector too!" I retort, and then immediately hate myself for being so crass.

As Protector, I am imbued with powers to protect myself as much as this planet. When I'd gone into all those Al Nadir bases, I'd been fortified with the knowledge that I couldn't die. When Sam and Ashton had gone on their missions, they'd entered with the grim fact that they could be breathing their last breaths.

But still they did it.

They placed the lives of others, 'the innocent ones', ahead of their own. Such conviction was either borne of single-minded patriotism or a blind assessment of their true human worth.

I stare at Sam, who is still smarting from my last words, but he remains quiet.

I know Sam is aware of his worth, as is Ashton. Both have been exceptional in their duty to protect and serve.

Perhaps their selflessness had been the catalyst for peace breaking out across the world, and Ashton has been identified as a messenger to make this peace happen.

I think again about what I've seen. His gruesome exploits. The callous way he extinguished lives. It was his job, I reason. But in the last viewing of Ashton with Ivanov, it showed him relishing Ivanov's death despite knowing he could have allowed him to live.

That is not the disposition of a peacemaker.

My logic, however, forces me to flip again. Ivanov had beaten him and hurt him badly. I remember the feeling of wanting to cause agony to those who had hurt me. I delighted in hearing Salim's howls of pain and seeing the terrified look on Sabena's face as I taunted and cuffed her, stating I'd make her suffer for what she'd done to me.

As Protector I should not feel this seething rage to cause suffering. I should be immune, my focus and my being set as it is at a higher level, impervious to emotional reaction.

But I am not immune. I wanted vengeance for what they'd put Sam and I through.

An uncomfortable dawning rises within me. It brings light of the kind I didn't want to acknowledge. Maybe reconstitution hadn't been without its flaws, as Aby-od had led me to believe.

How can I draw judgment on Ashton when I can't determine my own actions?

And he did tell me he wanted peace, he wanted Freedom Earth to work and for Quantum Force to be a success because of what he'd seen. His background gives him more of an impetus to want peace even more than a man of the cloth. Hadn't he seen the brutality manifested in mankind? The acts of evil wrought by greed, avarice, and the maniacal obsession to dominate.

Every time I think about Ashton, my understanding of him flip-flops. A man with a dark past. A man who has no limits. A man who strives for peace. A man who can change the world for good.

"Are we going?" asks Sam, with a gentle lilt. His attitude has quickly changed. I know he can't read my exact thought energy but, being Kudamaz, he can detect fluctuations in my vibrational resonance. A slightly higher oscillation in wavelength denotes deep thoughtfulness and concentration.

"Yes, okay. Let's go." I sigh and lean over the sofa to pick up my bag.

Sam touches my shoulder and turns me around. I stare at him and he strokes my cheek lovingly. "Something's wrong, isn't it?"

"No. Just a bit confused."

"About Ashton?"

"About everything, sweetness. You see, I never had time…" I stop. Sam looks at me, a questioning stare in his dark-chocolate eyes. "Oh, it doesn't matter," I finish, glancing away to hide the hurt in my face.

But I know Sam realizes what I am feeling.

I had no choice as to what I became. I had been thrust into a role without a moment to think, to consider the consequences. At the time, it had been all about survival and saving Sam. But now, I feel, sometimes, despite my incredible powers and a knowledge that spans a lifetime of universes, so completely and utterly lost.

"Come here, darling."

Sam draws me into his arms. His lips drop down and his tongue probes softly inside my mouth. His touch sends a shiver through me. Sam looks down and into my unnaturally shining azure blue eyes.

"Have we time to…?" he enquires, with a glint of mischievousness in his eye.

"Better not," I admit reluctantly. "Don't want to be late for Ashton's big switch-on."

"Sweetness, there is a big switch-on happening right now," mumbles Sam, with a sexy grin. He ruffles my spiky, platinum blond hair. Bending down, he tries to kiss me again. But I pull away.

"Sam, get a grip."

"That's exactly what I plan to do!"

"Dr. Sam Noor, you and I have a date with Ashton. Be a good boy," I say, my eyes twinkling. "We can play later."

In a break from his alpha-male shimmer, Sam's arms envelope me as our shimmers initiate, and he kisses my forehead and whispers, "I love you, sweetness."

Chapter 34

Eyes searched the crowd, as Ashton stepped out of his Jag. His close protection team held onto him, limpet-like, a guard on either side with two behind and two more in front, walking in a tight diamond formation. His primary bodyguard, placed next to him, took no chances, and carried his Sig in his hand. Ashton strode purposefully toward the elaborate stage that had been constructed in front of the entrance of the newly refitted Drax Power Station in Selby, North Yorkshire.

An area in front of the stage had been cordoned off to prevent the crowd getting any closer. Steel fencing had been erected to keep people in an enclosed area. Around the stage, massive screens had been suspended to give a view of the stage and, intermittently, a view of another power plant in the US with a similar stage set-up.

The refit process had been undertaken very quickly. Sam and Ashton had worked on the redesign together. Ashton took control and used Sam in only an advisory capacity. Ashton glanced at the power station behind the podium and sighed, sad that none of the amazing technology could be seen. The gigantic crystal that had been grown in just under two weeks and was now housed within the massive Gold Plus chamber was hidden, buried deep within the belly of the power station.

For the cameras, a huge red 'switch on' button had been constructed on the podium. In truth, this was just for show. The chief engineer of the power station, concealed from the public's view, within its cavernous innards, would turn on the system. But the illusion made for good television.

Ashton flicked a look around. Where are they? He pushed down his concern and started to walk up the steps.

"Hello, Prime Minister."

Ashton spun around to check out where the owner of the voice and smiled, seeing Sam and Ellie walking over to join him.

"Ashton, you've built up a crowd. All waiting for your big turn on!" Ellie grinned, but Sam looked ready to criticize. Ashton noticed Ellie squeeze his arm, and Sam's mouth refrained from address.

Hearing the poorly-veiled innuendo, Ashton's eyes widened. He licked his full lips, moistening them, and took in a slow glance of Ellie from head to foot.

"Okay, where would you like us?" snapped Sam, staring pointedly at the prime minister, and then at Ellie.

The PM could see his rather lascivious glance at Ellie hadn't gone unnoticed. I know where I'd like your wife, Ashton thought, smirking.

"Over here," stated Dawes, pointing to a place on the floor, as he slid between the VIPs and pulled them into a tableau of players on the podium.

Ellie and Sam maneuvered so that Ellie was on the right and Sam was on the left of Ashton. In front of the PM, the large, red button illuminated and flashed intermittently, awaiting Ashton's touch.

Above the podium, a screen suspended, showing a simultaneous switch-on in one of the largest power stations in America, the John E Amos Power Plant in Winfield, West Virginia.

Ashton swung a look back and forth between Ellie and Sam. He'd wanted them to shimmer to be seen at both locations, but Ellie had counselled him against such a move. Ashton recalled her recalcitrance during a recent meeting.

"Absolutely not, Ashton! Can you imagine what something like us shimmering could do to people? They'll freak out. They're not ready for omnipotent beings yet. We agreed to a select number of people knowing, religious leaders, your inner team, and security chiefs, but that's it. No one else."

Ellie's sharp, dogmatic tone still stung rather than rung in his ears.

Ashton swiped a surreptitious look at Ellie who stared out to the crowd, smiling and waving. They had no idea who she really was, only that she had a strong connection to the PM. And, of course, sweet and caring Ellie wanted to keep it that way. Always the bloody thoughtful one where her precious humans were concerned.

Radiating strength, Ellie stood next to Ashton, and Sam, like his wife, exuded an undeniable energy that simmered just beneath the surface of his wholesome smile.

Between them, Ashton suddenly felt dwarfed. Although his height was the same as Sam's and much higher than Ellie's, he imagined his presence was the size of a mouse. Ellie glanced in his direction and, as if feeling his lack of stature, threw back her shoulders and regarded him with flickers of disdain.

Two can play, sweetheart, thought Ashton. He whispered in Ellie's ear, seconds before the TV cameras switched on, "Time to put on the floorshow for them."

"What did you say?" Ellie's eyes flashed dark, and fury burned within them.

Sam noticed, and looked from Ashton to Ellie. "Something wrong?"

Ashton answered, staring at Sam and ignoring Ellie, "I just said, time to put on a great event for them."

Ashton didn't need to look at Ellie. He could feel her anger searing into his face. As Dawes put up a finger to count down to live transmission, Ashton sneaked a sideways glance at Ellie, eyebrow raised and smirk in place.

"...two, one. We are live. Go, Prime Minster!"

Chapter 35

Xiao stared into the mirror, lifting his t-shirt up, and pondered, worried and confused.

The view of his bedroom surrounded him. He loved Marvel superheroes. He'd nagged his parents to buy him everything. All the merchandise kicked out by those studio execs, he'd lapped up. He even got his mother to take him to Comic Con in LA, where he met some of his screen idols and bought his Iron Man fist chair.

He remembered the charity auction he'd dragged his mother to. She'd not protested. All items on display had been one-offs in design. He'd seen the chair and begged his mum to buy it. Despite its price tag in tens of thousands of dollars, his mum had dutifully bid higher and higher, and eventually secured the prize article for him.

In times past, he'd imagined himself as a kind of superbeing, given powers by accident or design, but able to use those powers to help mankind. Xiao had often wondered what he would do if humanity's future rested on his shoulders.

Would he be strong enough to take that weight?

Or would he crumble under the pressure of such great responsibility?

The eyes that stared back at Xiao wondered that question still.

He dropped his t-shirt down, tore himself away from the reflection, and thought about what had happened with Peter and Simon.

As they'd played on the computer games, the waves of love had washed through him. Unable to hold in the feeling, he'd cried out to his friends. Verbalizing the adoration that coursed through him, he'd expected to receive kindness in return from his friends, but they'd greeted it with fury. As Simon spoke his furious words, Xiao had looked down and, in the center of his stomach, angry redness had erupted. The tips of the flames that licked his insides poked through his charred, split skin. The room had vibrated with a dark resonance. Like the air had charged up, filled with lethal molecules attacking him. Burning him alive.

He couldn't stand being in his friends' proximity. Their selfishness. Their bitterness. Their ignorance. Each of their feelings fanned the flames within him.

Xiao knew he'd die if they didn't leave.

Then his mother had appeared. Xiao showed her his fiery torso, but she'd done nothing. He couldn't understand why she couldn't see the flames leaping through his skin. With such a spectacle, he'd thought she would have shown fright or concern for his safety. Made a dash to get water or a towel to put out the fire. She'd just stood looking confused.

His friends had run out on her instruction to leave.

With her arms outstretched, she touched him, and immediately, upon that soft alighting on his young skin, he sensed quietness inside him regain its hold again.

The pain subsided. The flames dimmed. The heat dulled.

She'd placed him in bed. Around him the resonance of love. He fell into its gentle rhythm, closed his eyes, and rested.

Although he knew the sleep had been just a few minutes, he'd awoken completely different.

Xiao raised his t-shirt again, peered at his perfectly smooth stomach, and struggled to understand why he had no scar from the burn he remembered so vividly.

Behind him, he heard the door to his bedroom open.

"Xiao, darling, I thought you'd like to see the big switch on of Quantum Force with Prime Minister Ashton. I know you love all that weird quantum stuff, and he's going to be live in a minute. Your dad and I are watching too. Come down and we can watch it as a family."

Xiao turned around to face his mother. Inside, he wanted to ask her why she hadn't worried about the flames on his stomach. But his mind had fixed on her mention of Quantum Force. The name triggered a reverberation of disquiet deep within him.

"Of course, mother," Xiao answered, but his voice trembled.

"Are you okay, Xiao?"

His mother's dark eyes were again wide with concern.

Xiao nodded and forced an air of calm.

Descending the stairs, he could hear the prime minister's voice booming from his father's surround sound speakers in the living room. He breathed, pushing the serenity he was so desperate to feel.

But inside him rose that feeling of foreboding.

Nearing the living room, as the prime minister's words ascended into the air, and into his ears, Xiao could no longer hold back. He accepted the tightening in his throat, the burning in his heart, and the blackening of his soul.

And understood what it meant for humanity.

Chapter 36

Our eyes meet for a second. That arched eyebrow and smirk. They had departed after his family had been ripped from him, but now they have returned like a disease that can't be treated.

I know what I heard, and it wasn't 'great event'. Sam heard it too, of that I was sure, but chose not to engage. Ashton stares out into the crowds, waving. He loves the attention. He is in the present, not the past. And I hate how just a word can transport me back. Am I so weak that not even the Protector's shield can stop that word from penetrating into my mind?

The cameras come up close to Ashton and he smiles, turns on the charm, and works them like an old pro in a late-night bar.

"Today is the dawn of a new age in energy security. For too long, we have been held captive by the demands of nations rich in fossil fuels, forced to turn a blind eye to their acts of inhumanity, their staged pomposity, their bullying of others, and their state-funded terrorism. But not anymore. Those days are over. From today, we shall no longer bow down to those countries rich in oil and gas but poor in understanding of human rights. We shall no longer be accepting of any acts by another country that does not serve Freedom Earth."

At that moment, the big screen zaps into activity, showing the US president in a similar mock-up with a red button in front of him.

"And I'm sure my good buddy, President Hutchinson, would agree."

I hear the president's voice shouting out, "Absolutely right, Prime Minister. Together, on this day, we put an end to being tied into an uncomfortable marriage of oil and gas. A marriage that has cost us all dearly over the years. Unnecessary wars and crippling economic power plays will be in the past. We have a new future that gives us clean, limitless energy on our terms. As a country under Freedom Earth, we have the opportunity to embrace this energy security."

I hear, in unison, both Ashton and Hutchinson call out across the airwaves, "Today, my friends, we shall witness the power and the glory that is Quantum Force!"

Simultaneously, the two world leaders smash their curled fists onto the red button, and, inside their respective power stations, I know the huge photon guns have fired off into the massive crystal structures. The crystal will refract the photonic light at specific angle, sending it deep into the quantum field. On emerging out from the field, the Gold Plus chamber will capture and magnify the quark spin energy. The collector pod will suck the magnified energy and finally push it into the generator to create the electricity.

All of which happens in less than a blink.

When it reaches fully operational mode, which will be in less than ten minutes, the power station will kick out almost four gigawatts of power for the country.

Two neon panels on either side of us light up as the button is pressed. One says, 'We are One. We are Freedom Earth'. The other shouts the words, 'Quantum Force. Clean and Safe Energy Forever'.

Both statements are bold and typically overt, in keeping with Ashton's driving ambition for a new world of peace and security.

Sam looks at me, half smiling, but I sense that same hint of doubt again that I'd faced before. I wrinkle my nose as if smelling something unpleasant.

'All okay, darling?' I ask in Sam's mind.

'Yes.'

The tone is hard and clipped. It's far from okay.

As Ashton links arms with Sam and me in his usual show of solidarity, I call out in my mind to Sam, 'Well, they've done it. Him and Hutchinson. Real quantum energy forever. Quite a thing to achieve. Don't you think, darling?'

'Yes, a truly incredible feat for humans.' In Sam's telepathic response, something wavers. And I now recognize a stronger reluctance in his mind voice to believe what he has seen.

'You do believe they have achieved this? It's not just some Ashton play with smoke and mirrors?'

'Of course they've achieved this. There's no question about that.'

'Then what?' I snap in my husband's mind.

'It's just, well…' I wait for Sam to finish the thought. But his speech drifts, a little incoherently. 'I mean, the energy really is from the quark spin. It couldn't come from anywhere else. Could it?'

Sam's rhetorical question piques me. I struggle to comprehend why Sam has chosen this moment to raise his suspicions. He has, after all, been working with Ashton and his team of scientists since May this year. If there was anything suspect, why didn't he speak out sooner?

'They couldn't have falsified the data?' asks Sam.

'Sam,' I yell in his mind, 'I don't know what they could have done. It's you who's been working with Ashton on this, not me!'

My voice inside Sam's head is icy and disdainful.

I am now concerned. I've just watched Ashton go headlong into an energy revolution believing everything was water-tight. There was no question as to the source of the energy. And the experimental data backed everything up. Now, going by Sam's sudden outburst, it seems that things may not have been so certain.

'Sam, what is it?'

'No, nothing's wrong.'

My eyes narrow. 'What do you mean, wrong?' I ping-pong back into Sam's mind.

'I must have been mistaken.' Sam's voice in my mind has become more uncertain.

'What could you have mistaken about?'

'The depth level of the penetration at quantum level. In the last calculation I reviewed yesterday with Ashton, it seemed for a moment to look wrong.' Sam's voice sounded sheepish. Like he'd done something he wasn't proud of. 'Well, I mean, too deep.'

'Too deep?' I repeat, and note I sound like a parrot.

'Ellie, do you have to repeat everything I bloody well say!'

'Well, darling, so far you've said nothing other than create a bunch of suspicions and bad feeling within me.' I glare at Sam. 'Is the data you're worried about available? Can I see it?'

'Nothing's available. It was just an anomaly. I spoke to Ashton about it. The fact the depth level was deeper than could possibly be achieved without breaking natural law. But Ashton just laughed and said I'd misread the calculations. He brought up the calculations on his tablet in seconds, and they all looked almost the same, but with a subtle difference in quantum depth to the numbers I saw.'

I listen. An artic glacier melts down my back.

Making an accusation against techno-structures that are bound by the Order of Kudamun could be lethal. I understand Sam's reticence to confide, even to me.

'Have you spoken to Aby-od about this?'

'Yes, and he took one look at Ashton's calculations and told me I was mistaken. We looked at the playback in the Observation Room. There was nothing to note. The depth level wasn't anything like I thought I saw. And the Observation Screen captures live recall as it happens on Earth. There's no hiding from that.'

I remember my assertion to Aby-od that the reliability of the Observation Screen was under question when it produced anomalous responses when I'd queried Al Hutchinson's involvement with Ashton in Quantum Force. I recall with a shudder how Aby-od, as kind as he is, had almost instituted proceedings, which in lieu of any firm evidence from my side to back up my case, would have meant me being faced with summary execution.

I look at Ashton smiling and enjoying the attention. Is there more to this energy than even the Kudamaz can see? If that's true, where does Ashton get his knowledge from?

'Are you sure of what you saw?'

'No. No, I'm not sure. I'm not sure at all. That's why I wasn't going to mention anything. As Aby-od couldn't corroborate, I knew I was wrong. I quickly left investigating further and bluffed my way out from under Aby-od's bureaucratic, accusative eye.'

Inside me, I can feel that pulling uneasiness again. Ashton and Hutchinson have both gone live having spent just over a month refitting their largest plants with the Quantum Force technology. If this energy came from somewhere other than quantum spin, it could be unstable, dangerous even, for Earth.

I then consider what Sam has said. He's already discussed this anomaly with Aby-od. If the powerful technology and Kudamun's all-seeing ability through the Observation Room didn't show Aby-od anything of concern, what does it mean? There isn't anything? That Sam had been wrong? That he'd read the calculation incorrectly – something I doubted severely – or was there another reason? A reason so far undiscovered?

Could this new energy, Freedom Earth, religious unification, and even Ashton's constant equilibrium be happening beyond the control of Kudamun? Could the Ancient Ones, or another force unknown to Kudamun's phenomenal comprehension, have placed Earth on her current trajectory?

If Kudamun can't see any wrong, I can't detect anything, and Sam is unsure of his doubts, am I just snatching at shadows?

If I truly believe Quantum Force is bad for mankind, why don't I just stop all of this? I could shimmer into the Gold Plus chamber and obliterate the gigantic crystal to dust.

But, of course, I know I can't.

I have no indefatigable proof that it is wrong for mankind. By taking such a step, I risk destroying the chance of mankind's evolutionary leap in development. Such a disastrous action wouldn't be lost on the Kudamaz, nor the Ancient Ones, who would discover my misdemeanor. The repercussions would be so severe as to perhaps even warrant a reassessment of Kudamun's ability to oversee a planet's path, resulting in a ruling to reassign the task elsewhere. Such a position has never come to pass before. Kudamun has no precedent. The weighing up of facts through constant observations substantiated by Balance Shift counter analysis determines the actions that we, the Kudamaz, take. Pushing a planet's development backward instead of forward has never happened.

Ever.

I cast a glance at Sam. He's done his reflecting on his moment of confusion and put his doubt back to bed, concealed it under the covers and switched off the light.

Now he smiles and absorbs the merriment of the crowds. Thousands have descended upon the power station. People who'd never even recognized the enormous construction as a power plant now line up to see Ashton and celebrate this amazing thing they'd heard so much about in the media. Quantum Force. It is as if science fact and science fiction has melded together. And the people are living in a fantasy. The future, laid down by sci-fi movies of old, has finally arrived.

Picking up the humans' vibrations, I feel their wanting of hope, to really believe something wonderful is happening.

I try to float on the crowd's great optimism. I scan across for their Balance Shifts and discover many are veering toward the dark energy despite the projected joy and happiness of the event.

In their souls is a festering jealously of those who'd held the energy crown, and any current happiness is borne out of darkness, joy at the UK finally wiping out those energy giant countries with her own new power. A real retribution against those giants for decades of energy dominance.

"Today we have freed ourselves of the obsession in oil and gas. An obsession that had us bowing down to countries who would do us harm."

Incredulous, I listen to Ashton. He seems tuned into the vibrations of the people, knowing what to say.

"Countries that *did* do us harm."

As Ashton delivers the line, he looks out at the crowds. They boo and hiss. Some members of the crowd fire-up Ashton's notorious 'straight to camera' video after Ivanov's attack. More start to play the video. Others lift their phones up whilst running it on their screens in the same way concert-goers raise and wave their lighters.

Suddenly, the crowd is a sea of mobiles running Ashton's video on a loop, broadcasting it from different points in the timeline so that the prime minister's voice is drowned out by his own voice on video.

I watch Ashton shake his head, smile, and flick up an eyebrow at Sam and me. Ashton appears to look awkward, but I know he is happy with the adulation. Dawes touches his chin and stares at the PM, worried about the unscheduled intrusion by the crowd's antics.

Ashton rests back a little from the podium. I watch him turn to Sam.

"Can you believe this?" Ashton whispers, sotto voce.

Sam taps the PM on the back and states, equally low, but I can still hear, "They love you, sir. Just ride it!"

Ashton smirks that awful, arrogance-infested gesture that I hate.

I gaze out into the crowd. Thousands are running the video. I can feel a building energy within the mass of people. Something is rising.

Chapter 37

The vibrational energy dips into a darker harmonic. I have a sense of something within the crowds, but I cannot discern what it is.

People with HoloTabs start to project pictures of Ashton and Natasha and his family. The holograms pop up across the sea of heads, making a weird kaleidoscope of faces and places.

Then the voices begin to chant.

The crowd demands the downfall of the two countries that had been involved in the attacks and assassinations on Ashton and his family. I listen to the chanting and its raw anger chill me. The crowd's Balance Shifts show a homogenous glut of darkness. This isn't just a crowd coming to watch their prime minister turn on a new power plant. This is a baying mob.

As the energies become darker still, a new intonation from the crowds sound. Their statement is clear. They demanded war.

I stare at Ashton. He loves the adulation. I watch as he sends the crowd into a total frenzy as he sheds carefully released tears. The big screens give a close-up of Ashton's crying face and the crowd begins to cry too.

Ahead of him, his people ring out the death chant to his enemies.

Ashton turns to the people, wiping his tears away with his sleeve for greater effect.

"Thank you, everyone. But I will not stoop to the level of those who have wronged my family and I. War and death is not the way."

I recall the brutality of Ashton's past. Believe me, the irony is not lost on me. It is, however, lost on his adoring fans.

"Peace is the only way. We are one. We are Freedom Earth."

The crowds repeat the words of the PM like a set of automatons. They believe not in the words spoken, only in the person who speaks them.

"Those who stand with me, with Freedom Earth, have nothing to fear. But those who stand against me, against peace and goodness…"

The boos emanate loudly from the unruly crowd. Ashton waits for them to subside, nodding his head in agreement to the mood of the people.

"Will suffer the consequences of such a decision."

The people cheer as Ashton states his hardline stance. On each word from Ashton, I can see the crowd descend further into a pit of intolerant, racist hatred.

To the right of me, Dawes holds up his tablet. All social media channels have picked up on Ashton's performance, and, predictably, Facebook, Twitter, and Instagram are going wild with comments, videos, and hashtags a plenty.

At one point, when the people are waiting for Ashton's response, deep in the crowds, an exquisite sixteen-year-old girl screams out, "Ashton is peace. Ashton is love!"

The TV cameras snap their attention toward her, and across the area, the screens light up with young girl's beautiful, innocent face aglow with an almost fanatical adoration for Ashton. In her eyes, I see an absolute assurance that she would do anything the PM told her to do.

Ashton turns his head casually in the girl's direction. He waves at her, winks, and lightly smacks his full lips in anticipation of their meeting. The girl, I think, looks as if she might faint as the interest upon her mounts. Ashton points to his security to bring the girl out of the crowds.

A burly security guard pushes into the crowd and pulls the girl, somewhat indelicately, by her arm through the thong of shouting and staring Ashton acolytes. The girl's eyes widen with a mix of fear and wonderment, as the guard runs a series of devices across her body, ensuring she is clean of any weapons. The guard pats down the pretty, young thing, just for good measure. He can't help himself lingering a moment longer than necessary on her breasts and hips.

I watch him sneer. He definitely learnt that from the Ashton guidebook. He gives a thumbs up to the head of security and allows her to proceed toward the stage. Her legs tremble and she points hesitantly toward the steps then looks back at the security team, checking if it is okay to walk up. The head of security nods.

As she ascends, I take in the girl. Statuesquely tall, honey-blond hair, and green eyes with flecks of olive, high cheekbones, and a wide mouth housed in a sculptured jaw and softly-pointed chin. Generous breasts and a curved, pert bottom are perfectly accentuated by her trim waist and flat stomach. As girls of sixteen go, this mystery miss is a drop-dead stunner.

Her foot is nearing the top when another security guy holds his hand out to her, pulling her gently up the final step, and leads her over to Ashton. I move back to allow the girl to slip in beside Ashton and me.

Every sense, however, is screaming at me to tell the girl to run far, far away from this man. I know such a warning, if I made it, would tumble upon unhearing ears. From the gleam in her eye, I can tell she worships Ashton and holds the PM in the same mind space as a rock god.

The girl stares out at the crowd that, seconds before, she'd been a part of, with a clash of reverence and shock.

"Come this way, my dear," ushers Ashton in his silky, smooth voice of seduction. He angles himself just behind the gorgeous girl. It gives him a good opportunity to leer at her. He catches me looking, arches his eyebrow, and slips the top of his tongue out to moisten his bottom lip.

I think, at that moment, I could vomit!

With hands on the girl's shoulders, Ashton whispers into her ear, "What's your name sweetheart?"

The girl shivers and her eyes enlarge. She clearly questions what she is experiencing and whether she has fallen into some weird daydream.

Through trembling lips, she murmurs, "Lizzie."

"Lizzie, would you like to say something to the world?"

Ashton brushes down her hair in a fatherly gesture as Lizzie, star-struck, nods. At her acknowledgement, Ashton beckons for a microphone, and one is immediately thrust into Lizzie's shaking hands.

"There you go. Say hello to the world!"

The cameras zoom in tight on Lizzie's face. She looks to Ashton and then to me. I try to force a smile of encouragement, but the building nausea Ashton generates in me means it's only half formed.

Lizzie stares back at Ashton, who licks his lips, smoothly purring in the girl's ear, "Go on then, sweetheart. Go for it!"

Lizzie brings her face back to the cameras. The crowd has dropped to silence both here and in the US. Everyone waits for Lizzie to speak.

Lizzie opens her mouth, her huge, green eyes searching for an explanation as to why she is there.

"I just want to say..." starts Lizzie, and then she stops, flushed with embarrassment.

"Go on," encourages Ashton gently.

"I just want to say that Prime Minister Ashton is the most wonderful person in this world. He has dedicated his life to peace. To bringing us all together. To helping everyone. Through Freedom Earth, there is no war. Everyone is safe. I can walk home knowing that I can never be attacked. I lost my brother to terrorism four years ago in the Westfield bombing in London. Prime Minister Ashton has ended terrorism. He destroyed Al Nadir. And now, today, we are receiving yet another fabulous gift from him. Cheap, clean, and never-ending energy. Prime Minister, we love you. We all love you so much."

I stare at Lizzie, dumbstruck. I know she worships Ashton, it is obvious in her eyes, but her words sound like a script. It sounds too perfect. But I look into the sea of people and they are soaring on Lizzie's words, high on the atmosphere of the weird Ashton-love cult.

"What do you say?" shouts Lizzie, suddenly taking full control and regarding the crowd. "We love him, don't we? We love you. We love you." Lizzie turns back to Ashton and flutters her eyelashes. "We love you."

The crowd strikes up the new chant. Ashton just smiles.

I think about what Lizzie has said. In many ways, it makes sense. Ashton has made everything safer and better. But it is all on his terms. No one else seems to see it like that.

I feel the vibration of the power plant behind me as it goes into maximum operational mode.

"Thank you, my dear. Thank you all. I am only here to do a duty, to bring true peace on earth, and to change the world for good."

I jerk back as Ashton hands slip around my waist and Lizzie's. His staged camaraderie in full swing, he grins in front of the cameras.

"Everyone, today, the twenty seventh of June, will hence be known as Quantum Force Day, and throughout every Freedom Earth country, it will be a day of holiday and celebration. What do you say, Mr. President?"

I can hear the whoop-whoop noises coming from the US contingent, and Al Hutchinson's comfortable Southern tones as he agrees with Ashton.

Across the land, and across the Earth, Quantum Force has been initiated. Two of the largest power plants are kicking out virtually seven gigawatts of power, and that energy is coming from somewhere.

Staring out across the crowd, feeling Ashton's snake fingers touching my body, having doubts about all of this, Freedom Earth, the constant light Balance Shift on Earth, religious unification, and this weird energy, I do the one thing I haven't done since reconstitution.

I pray.

Chapter 38

Alone in the Observation Room, Temenos watched the behavior of the humans with growing interest. From the pocket of his robes, he drew out a tiny, oval object. The Perception Shield device. With the appearance of a pebble, it wouldn't have garnered a second glance on Earth. Temenos' predecessor designed its inconspicuous exterior for Earth use. Temenos smoothed his hand across the pebble's surface and it glowed rosy pink from the center. An iridescent sparkle emitted from the pebble and travelled up Temenos' arm. It took over Temenos' entire body, giving the impression he was about to shimmer.

Temenos walked over to the crystal control for the Observation Room to invoke Immersive Mode. This was a state in which he could not only observe the Earth moment but exist within the moment to experience it as it happened. The Order of Kudamun forbid any changes to be made, but then, Temenos was never a great believer in those antediluvian laws. And with his predecessor having shown him ways to avoid detection and, thus, the Kudamaz alarms, he knew he could do anything he pleased on Earth.

He swiped his hand down across the crystal embedded in the wall, and the crowd was all around him. One by one, the people raised their phones, playing out Ashton's video.

In front of Temenos, a young man, full of hatred for foreigners, swung his phone above his head, loudly playing the video. Temenos felt the anger inside of him. He was easily malleable, just like so many other humans. With their selfish ways, their envy of all around them, and their loathing of anyone not like them, from a different culture or creed, humans were open for complete manipulation. And their blindness to the world, to their understanding of the energies that flowed through them, made such manipulation an act of effortlessness. Temenos delved into the young man's mind and placed a thought there in the same way he'd done before.

'What about the prime minister's family? Those Saudi bastards took them away. Murdering monsters!'

Temenos formed the thought energy, and the young man captured the thought. In parallel, Temenos forced him to look on his phone for web pictures of Natasha and Ashton and broadcast them through the HoloTab application. Temenos raised his arm and, in synch, the young man raised his as well, and suddenly the phone spat out hologram images of Ashton and Natasha, together and smiling.

Temenos spoke words into the ear of the young man, and he yelled seething with rage, "Look at them! So in love. Those Saudi bastards stole that love! Murdering monsters!"

The crowd pointed at the images, and more of them tried to find other HoloTab images of Ashton's family. Ashton watched the images pop up across the sea of turning heads. He shook his head and turned his face away. Temenos recognized his torment and anguish.

He was also mindful of Sam and Ellie, but their lack of action, not even turning in his direction, confirmed the Perception Shield he used, designed by his predecessor, was still in place.

Temenos smiled, satisfied, and focused further words into the young man's mind, who called out, "Down with Saudi Arabia! Down with Russia!"

The young man repeated the chant and indicated for others around him to join in, and then several more people took up the xenophobic chorus. Then more followed suit.

Temenos weaved between people, touching them, and on his tap, they chanted, "Down with Saudi Arabia. Down with Russia."

As more people contributed to the chant, their vibrational energy became darker. On tapping a middle-aged man, the mantra turned into, "Death to Saudi Arabia, Death to Russia!"

Intertwining between the humans, Temenos conducted the crowd in their fury and rage, creating a great crescendo of hatred. And their souls burned black.

Temenos looked up at Ashton who stood, overwhelmed, on the podium. The PM tried to pat down the crowd's effusive, emotive responses, but no one took any notice. Too absorbed were they in their recognition that Ashton, their great leader, had suffered at the hands of those countries. From the vibrational energies, Temenos knew that, had there been Russian or Saudi nationals within the hoard, they'd have been ripped apart limb from limb.

Temenos could feel the swelling bloodlust, the need for them to avenge the pain that had been caused to their leader.

Temenos sneered.

And so, the pieces were falling into place.

Although within the crowds, Temenos was still aware of what was happening in the Observation Room in Kudamun. He sensed a Kudamaz resonance approaching, and knew it was a Senior Elder, most likely Aby-od.

He withdrew the pebble, smoothed it again, and the iridescent sparkle vanished, and he flashed his hand across the crystal panel, switching the Screen to quantum static.

In the archway, Aby-od came into view.

Temenos walked past Aby-od, and each gave the other a polite, perfunctory nod. He made his way to his quarters and permitted himself a small smirk.

From the shadows, within his quarters, a voice came.

"You have done well. All is as it should be."

Chapter 39

June 28, 2017

Proof, undisputable by any other means, that Earth is not alone.

That had been the verbal mechanism by which religious unification had been achieved for Ashton. He'd dangled Ellie and Sam in front of all the religious leaders like a cosmic couple of carrots. And, with a few well-chosen, loaded sentences, the religious leaders folded into line, agreeing to virtually anything demanded of them by Ashton.

Almost two months had transpired since Ashton's unification brain-child. The birth had been without incident. Religious leaders had been told they were part of something greater than what they could ever understand. That they were the chosen few, and to them, a form of enlightenment had been revealed.

The next stage of their involvement required their pledge of allegiance recognizing Freedom Earth as the overarching sociological theology over and above their own religion. And that humanity and peace on Earth was the first and last goal.

Ashton stared at the room that had been exquisitely prepared for his guests.

Across the decades, the sumptuous dining hall in Downing Street had played host to the great and the good. Its ornate, handwoven silk pink and light, jade rugs had received the tread of many a statesperson and senior diplomat. Chandeliers of crystal and gold were suspended high above the long antique table. Paneled wood walls were adorned with paintings of distant prime ministers, old masters depicting a time of pomp and pageantry. Elaborate, huge, gold mirrors reflected scenes of inane chatter, political gameplay, brinkmanship, and, of course, extreme peacocking.

His visitors in attendance that evening would be no different, each coming with egos the size of a palace, excruciating grandiosity, and a singular wisdom that their way was the only way.

Getting them in one room was one thing. Ashton knew that them agreeing to unification under his new sociological theology of Freedom Earth was very much another.

Ashton watched them file in one by one like school kids returning to a classroom from break time in the playground. In a way, his analogy was fitting. A lesson was about to learnt. Perhaps the only lesson that those religious leaders would ever truly need to learn.

A lesson in the meaning of humanity. A lesson in the power of Freedom Earth as decreed by God himself.

The Most Reverend Gregory Forster entered first. In his posture, Ashton noticed, was command. In his stride, an announcement that he had the right to push ahead of his peers. Ashton smirked. Nothing like a touch of dominance within the devout. He watched as Reverend Gregory marched in. His looming, gangly body, that Ashton recalled, usually headed in different directions, seemingly at odds with itself, was now coherent and followed a clearly defined trajectory. The PM realized the experience with Ellie and Sam had had an irrevocable effect on the religious leader.

Ashton grabbed champagne off a passing tray bearer. In the same instant, Reverend Gregory headed toward a pretty, young Asian man who carried the champagne held in intricately carved, crystal flutes.

Ashton nodded his head as Reverend Gregory smiled warmly, swiped a flute, raised it high to him, and then quaffed it quickly.

"Excellent champagne, Prime Minister."

"Naturally," stated Ashton, as if it was the most obvious thing in the world.

Ashton clocked the other religious leaders walking in with stout assurance. Ashton found it amusing, observing them, as each leader passed on their pleasantries, but he could see all were cautious and acutely aware they needed to be one better than their peers.

They had to find a way to become closer to him.

The Most Reverend Matthew Knightly chatted intermittently with Chief Rabbi Jacob Newton. Their engagement appeared genial, but Knightly was on point and wary of the rabbi. Especially following their last discussion.

"Matthew, have you heard about this Freedom Earth religious unification?"

Knightly had sat heavily into the green, leather armchair in the Members

Lounge at The Athenaeum Club. He had regarded the portly gentleman in the chair next to him with narrowing, dark-brown eyes.

"Oh, yes, Jacob. Gregory told me about it initially. Absolutely incredible. I met with these beings. They call themselves Ellie and Sam, but I'm sure that's just for our benefit."

Rabbi Jacob had smiled with a supercilious air, moved his portly bulk forward, bent his head down conspiratorially, and aligned it with Knightly's pudgy ear.

"Oh, so you weren't invited directly by the PM? Only got to hear of it from Gregory then?"

Knightly had glared and pursed his mouth in bitter annoyance. "Of course I was invited directly," Knightly snapped, his anger sparking visibly to the rabbi.

Rabbi Jacob nodded. "Good. Good. When the PM contacted me, I wondered what was really going on."

"Yes," muttered Knightly, recalling his first engagement with Gregory, the original messenger of Ashton's unification plan.

Perhaps he'd been given more time to consider his response. He should take his double notification as a positive, and not as a snub.

Back in the Downing Street dining hall, Knightly seated himself at the table along with his fellow peers and smiled amiably. Inside, however, it still gnawed at him that he'd heard it all first from a third party.

Knightly tried to camouflage his unsettled attitude, but the PM had picked up on it. "Is all well, Your Grace?"

Knightly looked in Ashton's direction, pleased that although his unsettled feelings had been borne of a slight inequality, he'd been singled out for the PM's attention.

"Yes, Prime Minister. All is well. And may I say on behalf of my fellow peers here, we are very excited and enthused to hear more about the religious unification initiative under Freedom Earth."

Knightly raised his voice so that it carried with a dominant authority across the table. Knightly smiled slyly as he was aware of voices dropping to a mere hush, as the words 'Prime Minister' filtered into their conversations. All attending, Knightly knew, were desperate to hear what he had to say, and if they could, contrive something to say of a more prolific nature in front of the PM.

Ashton eyed those congregated before him. And so the game of bluff and bluster had begun, he thought and sneered

Irrespective of their religious leanings, Ashton recognized, those assembled around him carried more Machiavellian maneuvers than the average senior politician.

"Delighted to hear that," announced Ashton, swaying his head from side to side and taking in the full length of guests at his table.

"I do hope you all feel the same way as His Grace?"

Ashton's glacial stare brought mutterings of, "Of course, Prime Minister," and "Naturally, Prime Minister."

A Mexican wave of verbal agreement.

Ashton had arranged the table placements to afford him eye contact with everyone, and he didn't dial back on the intimidation. It was his party. His Freedom Earth. They were either with him or against him. No subtle shades of indecision would he permit.

"So, if I may," declared Ashton, as if he cared at all about anyone's feelings, "I'd like to invite you all to open the document in the gold-leaf envelope that has just been placed in front of you."

He couldn't help but grin as heads dropped simultaneously like feeding sheep. Their eyes widened in surprise as they noticed the DL-sized envelopes that had been slipped with considerable stealth underneath their noses. Ashton knew by catching the religious leaders with his intense stare, each had suffered unintentional blindness, or, from his perspective, intentional blindness.

The envelope had materialized, like a trick from a magician, from nowhere.

Dumbly, each religious leader picked up their handwritten envelopes and opened them gingerly. Inside was a simple one-page letter on Freedom Earth official headed paper.

Ashton looked on as his guests read the words contained therein.

The prime minister watched, interest building on his face, and a slight sneer erupted, as his guests started to fidget uncomfortably. They turned to talk to the guest next to them. Some shook their heads. Others chose not to talk, just stare at the paper, inert.

Ashton considered he'd observed enough and raised his hand to quell any dissention.

"Honored guests, when we last met, you were all introduced individually to Sam and Ellie, God's emissaries. Through them, you were informed of the need to unify religion and agree that there was only one way. The way of

Freedom Earth. One voice that spoke the truth. One power that unified all. The light of humanity giving peace on Earth. Today, we are here together to recognize the commitment you made to Ellie, Sam, and me to unify religion under the overarching ideology of Freedom Earth. In doing so, you will put aside your differences of other faiths. Any conflict that you have had in the past will, henceforth, be banished to the past and forgotten. No one religion will presume its right of purpose over another. No one religion will be forced onto another of a different faith.

"We are now living in a new time. A time when knowledge of something greater is unquestionably understood by all of you. It is not in scripture or in a religious book. But there is absolute proof that powers oversee us, judge us, and are actively preparing us for the next stage in our evolution.

"Therefore, all wars borne of religion must, from this day and henceforth, cease. Failure to do so will enrage those who are waiting for Earth to embrace full enlightenment. Ramifications of such a refusal cannot be quantified, but it can be assumed, given the powers wielded by those that constantly observe us, such a direction would not be perspicacious in the advancement of our future development."

Ashton paused and examined the table's reaction. Leaders looked to each of their peers as if waiting for the other to make a comment first, but in the face of Ashton's silent glowering, and the implied threat of something akin to annihilation, no one dared to speak.

"Your silence concerns me," stated Ashton, his voice reverberating with slow menace. "Do you not want to be bathed in the light of peace?"

Ashton's guests made little incoherent murmurs like ripples across a sea as the wind gently tickles it. A tidal wave of movement, however, was afoot. In front of Ashton, the air vibrated as if leaping to attention, its purpose finally initiated, and the molecules electrified with awaited anticipation.

Ashton smirked. *Right on time, guys.*

"Please give welcome to our last guests."

His hand flew out across the table and in the direction of the shimmering air.

Everyone stared.

Ashton followed Rabbi Newton's eyeline. His gentle nod, Ashton knew in recognition of who was returning. The PM recalled how Ellie had cured Rabbi Newton's affliction, and knew why the Rabbi had begun to smile smugly. It was obvious to Ashton, Rabbi Newton felt he had a greater connection than most in the room with the superbeings.

Around us, the plush, opulent dining hall at Number 10 comes into reality. I stare at everyone, smiling. Each table guest has seen us before, but amazement still reigns across their faces.

"Hello, everyone, again," Sam and I say in perfect unison.

As I scan the room for familiar faces. I notice, in sadness, that the Dalai Lama isn't present, but his deputy, Lama Bodhidharma, is. The new Buddhist wasn't introduced to us on our previous trip to Dharamshala and he's now open-mouthed, in complete shock, witnessing our mind-blowing entrance.

Chapter 40

I smile at the gawking Lama Bodhidharma and walk over to shake his hand. Sam, his hand still clasped in mine, steps up beside me.

"I don't believe we've been introduced. I'm Ellie and this is Sam. We're pleased to meet you, Lama Bodhidharma."

The Buddhist priest looks at me, amazed by the fact I know who he is. He places his hand out tentatively, and I can see in his eyes, he is judging whether I am real or not.

"I am pleased to meet you, Ellie and Sam. His Holiness the Dalai Lama told me about you, but I was not sure what to expect. His Holiness sends his profound apologies for not being able to be with you tonight, but he will be at the celebrations tomorrow."

I nod magnanimously and catch in my peripheral vision an irritable Ashton at my side. Our entrance, although auspicious in its timing, has led to all the table focusing on us rather than him. I turn back and issue my thanks directly to the PM. Inside, however, I feel like saying 'There, there, you petulant prick!'

"Ashton, you've done a fabulous job again. Hasn't he, Sam? Almost like he doesn't need us at all."

I swing a look at my husband, and his stern eyes flash back. 'Behave!'

'As if!' I shout in my mind, grinning with my characteristic naughtiness.

'Just saying, darling. You know what you're like,' Sam retorts in my mind.

I stay telepathically silent, not wanting to provoke Sam further.

"Of course he needs us. But you're right, he's done a marvelous job," answers Sam, back in Earth tempo.

Our mind discourse, delivered in less than a human blink, ensures that no one around the table knows a thing. Ashton smirks his usual, lips-curled-back, resinous smirk, clearly pleased at the reference we've made to his achievement.

"Thank you both. But without you, I'm nothing."

Ashton's soft-spoken humility startles me. His self-deprecation, although refreshing amidst his customary demeanor steeped in piles of hubris and piety, throws me off-key. I look at him and he smiles openly, and an unexpected tingle flashes through me.

What the hell was that?

Ashton's smile ignites something I definitely don't want to acknowledge. Sam glares at me, not annoyed, more troubled. My unnatural, azure-blue eyes cement onto Ashton's, and embedded within my stare is a deep question.

Ashton tilts his head toward me. In his eyes, a similar question is forming. I pull away, too disgusted. But deep inside, I am intrigued. I glance down the table, keeping my eyes firmly averted from Ashton. I realize I am suddenly too scared to return back to Ashton in case the answer I receive in his eyes taps into that which should never be unleashed.

An obsidian awakening that I fear has an inevitability wrapped around it.

Like a destiny awaiting me still.

Sam senses my sudden negative vibe and instinctively holds my hand tight. I grip it, wanting desperately to leave the dinner and return to Kudamun.

Something within the room affects my inner energies.

Maybe Ashton. But I can't understand how. He is human, as Aby-od has so enjoyed telling me a million times. And all those in the room I've met previously, and none have caused me to feel uneasy before. I look at Lama Bodhidharma. He is the exception. This is our first meeting. I scan his Balance Shift, which edges toward the light scale. But he is most definitely human and not the source of my discomfort.

It takes me a few seconds to register Ashton speaking, and Sam leads me to a seat beside the PM and the Archbishop of Canterbury.

Dazed, I sit down. Internally, I battle to re-center my energies. Despite my tremendous powers, at times I feel fragile. Now is one of those times.

Aware of the religious leaders staring at me, I force my energies to build rapidly in defense of whatever is causing my imbalance. With a swift sweep up and down the table, I read each leader's Balance Shift. For religious leaders, I'd have expected more bias toward the light side. But this isn't the case with all. Obviously, being a religious leader is not concomitant to having an abundance of white light energy.

I flick a look at Ashton, who is staring the other way. Unsurprisingly, he is in almost a perfect Equilibrium. Whatever Sam, Aby-od, and the whole bloody High Council of Kudamun says, that has to mean something. I wish someone in Kudamun had the balls to investigate it besides me.

'He's in fucking Equilibrium again!' I scream at Sam in my mind. I have to vent. I just have to. And telepathic ranting is the best way right now.

Sam retorts, 'Please, Ellie, not now, sweetness!'

'But why? There has to be a reason. Surely you think it's weird?'

'I don't dare to think. You're the Protector. You're the one with all the answers.'

I detect Sam's snapping sarcasm. 'Okay, I know that's how it comes over, but some things still puzzle me.'

'Sweetness, Aby-od has checked him. The High Council verified his actions and they cleared the way for us to engage with him in the manner we have. If there was anything suspect, after all those investigations, it would have been picked up.'

'I suppose you're right,' I confirm with reluctance.

"Ellie, Sam, could you explain again for all, your rationale behind the faiths unifying under Freedom Earth?"

I slip back into Earth time. Ashton's request forces me to regard him again. I take a beat before speaking. With Ashton beside me, I can feel that strange tingle. I choose to ignore it.

I stand, firm and strong, walk around the table to the front, and stare at all assembled.

"As we all are aware, Earth went through a period of great darkness with the rise of Al Nadir. But now that darkness is over. Al Nadir is no more. Terrorism has been defeated in all its forms. Earth is now firmly in the light. Through increased goodness, hope, and charity to others, mankind has moved quickly on a trajectory toward its next stage, evolutionary enlightenment. Freedom Earth, originally the idea of Prime Minister Richard Ashton, has been approved and is supported completely by us. But for Freedom Earth to be realized, and the next stage of mankind's evolution achieved, all the faiths on Earth must unite in agreeing to the overarching ideology that encompasses them all, and that is Freedom Earth. Once agreed, all wars of any kind, or any conflict borne of religious separatism, must end immediately. You must all extend an olive branch of peace to your neighbor, despite whether that neighbor days before brandished a knife or gun to kill you. All animosity between religions must cease. Any prisoners held on religious grounds must be released. All subjugation of any religious individuals by another religion will stop. In signing up to Freedom Earth and agreeing to religious unification, you agree to love your fellow man and fellow woman as you love yourself, whatever color, culture, or creed, and you decree that your one goal, over all other, is driving peace on Earth."

I pause to glance at Sam. He nods, proud and pleased by what we had been able to instigate.

"You have all been selected to represent your respective religions. If you wish to continue on this path of Freedom Earth. Please pick up your document and sign where indicated. Your signature will then place into motion a series of events to enable unification to be realized throughout the world."

Across the table, a pondering stillness takes over. No one moves. I sweep a look at Ashton. That tingle has thankfully vanished. He bows his head in respect of my proclamation.

Suddenly, the room erupts into movement. Pens are searched for and plates are moved around to make room for the Freedom Earth letter. The sound of nib scraped on paper resounds in the air.

I watch religious unification in action.

Centuries of hatred vanish with a swift flurry of a signature.

Can it all be that simple? Has Ashton, through our intervention, achieved something truly meteoric? Something no one had ever tried to achieve as the goal was too great to even comprehend?

Is this why his Equilibrium is always in perfect balance?

I stare at Ashton, as he rises from his seat and starts to collect the signed declarations. He folds each one and places it into a white, leather, zip-up pocket. His composure, quiet, bordering on peaceful, strikes me as counter to his habitual showmanship. With polite gratitude delivered to each leader, he slips softly back into his seat. He settles back and lifts his head.

His eyes catch mine.

Within his hazel orbs, a flickering admission of what is to come.

I try to discern. Try to determine.

But his cryptic gaze eludes me.

I tear myself away.

Without answers.

So, like the rest of the world, all I can do is watch and wait.

Chapter 41

June 29, 2017

Religion in its many forms has been a tool of mankind. A way of controlling the populace, instituting loyalty, and maintaining societal thresholds. In virtually all religions, there is an inference of man being observed, judged and/or tested. It's a common denominator stretching through many theological prophecies. In Ashton's unification plan, it has become the super-glue to stick the religions together.

Through our judicious involvement, we give this singular view validity. More than that, we have shown ourselves as proof that everyone on Earth is part of a much bigger picture.

In revealing ourselves to those religious leaders, Ashton has asserted a position of the one having the greater knowledge. He has already made the universal connection; those religious leaders are only playing catch up. His understanding presents a completely new canvas. A world beyond their limited perceptions.

In the instant they saw Sam and me shimmer, their perspective on life was shattered and redefined. Through that definition, a weakness has been generated in them, and this has been focused on by Ashton to manipulate the leaders into accepting his will and the way of Freedom Earth.

Without our engagement, Ashton could never have achieved a millimeter toward religious unification. Of course, he knows that. And I believe that insight has tempered his arrogance and diluted his hubris.

Certainly, over the past twenty-four hours, I've noticed a significant change in Ashton. Humility seemed to embody his every action. I know it is still just an act. Always on point. Always the showman. But at least it's made my interactions with him that much more bearable. I don't have to endure his salacious quips, snide comments, and patronizing patter.

Perhaps, he is coming to appreciate just how powerful Sam and I are.

I stare out from the wings of the Freedom Earth stage erected at Wembley Stadium. Every single one of the ninety thousand seats has been snapped up by religious officials across many faiths. The members of the public who couldn't secure a seat will watch the celebrations live online, streamed simultaneously via TV satellites across the globe. In other cities, similar celebrations are taking place, and the TV transmission is arranged to intersect with reports from Freedom Earth Live commentators at different venues, showing the celebrations and discussions. All these venues hold the same Freedom Earth stage with the words 'Peace on Earth' dangling above the stage. Across the world, the unification celebrations feature frontline attendance by prime ministers, presidents and royalty. Reporters from international news stations, as well as Freedom Earth Live commentators, are also situated outside jails and holding centers, awaiting the release of all religious prisoners held within them.

It seems the world has been primed for this day.

I recall Chequers on April 2 and that moment when Ashton had divulged to Sam and I his religious unification mission, stating it was only possible because of Al Nadir. The terrorist collective had been the lynchpin to the whole plan. Through their organizational mopping up of all the religious terrorist factions under their banner, Al Nadir made those fundamentalist factions and religious extremists targets to receive the same state execution treatment when their collective started to crumble.

In cleansing the world of Al Nadir, all those religious factions were also disposed of. They could have been the stumbling block to religious unification, but through Al Douri's genius in branding them Al Nadir, fundamentalist extremism in all religions had been systematically, and most effectively, wiped out.

What remained were individuals still incarcerated by unscrupulous governments who deemed they were a threat to their political position, citing their distribution of subversive religious doctrines as the rationale for locking up such individuals. These people, often jailed and tortured for upholding the right to believe what they felt in their hearts, were branded terrorists by their governments. But not by the rest of the world.

I have read the Freedom Earth Religious Unification Statute Paper, which sets out the requirements with regard to such governments.

'Under religious unification, those countries holding religious prisoners will be commanded to release them. Failure to do so will reflect treason against

Freedom Earth and swift retribution will follow'.

I shudder. The words are nothing more than an incitement to war. Warring with your neighboring country is one thing. But no country can risk going to war with Freedom Earth, aka the world.

Ashton has created a set of conditions that mean religious unification, however incredible a notion, cannot fail.

I stare at Ashton standing in the wings. A make-up girl touches up powder to his nose and cheeks before he faces the world. Looking at him, I wonder whether he's also been the real architect of Al Nadir. A crazy thought, but one that has some traction considering the huge effect Al Nadir has had on the success of religious unification.

'Love is in the air' booms out, and people begin to cheer. I can hear and see in my mind a massive gathering outside the stadium. People have travelled just to be close to Ashton. To hear what he has to say. I look at the screens depicting the stadiums in different countries, and the same cheesy song resounds, triggering a similar boisterous reaction from the crowds.

It seems very welcoming and positive, until I glance around. Above, encircling the stadium perimeter, is the darker face of Freedom Earth, the Surv-Motes. Tennis-ball-sized devices with millions of multi-dimensional nano hawk eyes are automatically scanning for signs of aggression, subversion, and dissention. Thanks to Sam, the Surv-Motes have been weaponized with shoot to stun or kill Harmon wave guns.

Across the media, the effect of the Surv-Motes has been publicized. Saving women from rape and murder. Saving homes from being burgled. Saving the people of Earth from crimes against themselves and their possessions.

Although ruthless in its execution, and so typical of everything Ashton has instigated, I can't deny the Surv-Mote surveillance civil defense program, now incorporated into so many Freedom Earth countries, has delivered a form of true freedom to the people of Earth.

Whichever way I turn, Ashton has initiated a saving pattern. I know that he really does see himself as some kind of divine savior.

As the cheesy song mutates into 'One Vision', Ashton psyches himself, ready for the off. He glances around at me and nods, smiling, and I gave him the thumbs up. Ashton, suited up in all-over Gucci, walks quickly into the center of the stage. On his entry, the footlights illuminate, and cameras zoom in. Across the stadium, people stand, clap, and cheer. Outside, the gathered hoards raise their voices. 'Go Ashton!' is screamed from all directions.

Someone backstage turns the music down, and Ashton slips into gear. He steps across the stage to the very front and, without an introduction, that monotonous typical spiel espoused by former PMs, Ashton launches into a simple delivery.

"I had a dream when I was young. A dream of sweet illusion. A glimpse of hope and unity. A vision of one sweet union."

I watch as people remain standing, enchanted, not returning to their seats for fear they will miss a second of his performance.

Sam stands next to me, amazed at the crowd's reaction. Ashton is, after all, just citing the words from a rock song.

Staring out into the tens of thousands amassed in the stadium, Ashton continues.

"And with Freedom Earth, that vision of one sweet union has become a reality. But today, that vision has been elevated to the next level. Indeed, mankind is now on the path to enlightenment. For today we see the true light of humanity shine. Today we witness the unification of all religions under the single ideology of Freedom Earth."

At Ashton's words, I watch across the stadium, high above the heads of the people, holographic images float of the signed declarations from all the religious leaders present at the banquet at Number 10 yesterday. The names of the religious affiliations are highlighted and made to sparkle in case anyone should miss the commitment that has been made by their own religious leaders.

"These great leaders..."

Ashton flings out his arms in the direction of both sides of the stage and beckons the religious leaders waiting to join him. Cautiously, they step onto the stage. The Most Reverend Gregory once again strides forward, as if he has the God-given right to approach the PM first. The Most Reverend Knightly joins Ashton from the other side of the stage. The Dalai Lama, having arrived that morning, smiles broadly, waving at everyone as he shuffles forward. Chief Rabbi Newton marches onto the stage, tall and proud, alongside Dr. Al Shirawi, who gazes, thunderstruck, into the stadium. Leader after leader piles in from all denominations and all kinds of faiths. Some stroll on, appearing to be nonchalant, but, seeing the mass of people, then shrink back, staggered. Others tentatively move onto the stage, and then, caught in the lights, suddenly lap up the attention, calling and waving wildly.

All this time, Ashton stays relatively quiet. He goads the leaders to enter with the odd, "Yeah! Welcome to these great leaders. Show your appreciation." And he claps. In unison, the moment the PM claps, the entire stadium puts their one hundred and eighty thousand sweaty palms together. The applause is truly thunderous.

"The wonderful leaders here today have recognized that, above all, one goal unifies all of us: Peace on Earth."

I hear the crowd roar.

"Freedom Earth is the overarching ideology of humanity, and all these fabulous leaders behind me have signed up to this, placing all their religions underneath Freedom Earth. In doing so, each leader here has subscribed to a complete abolition of all wars borne of religion, the cessation of all religious persecution of any kind, and the immediate and unconditional release of every single prisoner held on religious grounds. No one religion must force itself onto any person, place, or nation. Every religion is equal and worthy of existence on Earth as any other, and no one religion must assume they have the right to take a greater place on Earth than any other.

"From today, the twenty-ninth of June, all religions on Earth have agreed to unification under Freedom Earth. In making this leap of true faith, a new world of peace, hope, and unity can now abound across the Earth."

The music phases in again and Ashton takes to the front of the stage.

Showman-like again, he rings out the words, "One voice, one hope, one real decision. That decision's been made today. The future now awaits us with a glorious opportunity to unleash the true potential of mankind. To be the best we can be. To love, to care, to share and show kindness, even in our darkest moments. For that is humanity's light. And that is Freedom Earth!"

Ashton raises his fist up high as the music phases out on 'Gimme one hope', and the crowd whips into a frenzy, thrusting their arms high in solidarity with Ashton.

I cannot believe what I am seeing. An entire stadium of apparently conservative religious individuals are delirious with adoration.

Ashton turns around and beckons Sam and me onto the stage. I look hesitantly at Sam, who shrugs, indicating an ambiguous stance to his agreement to proceed.

'He wants us on stage?' I state in my mind to Sam. 'What do you think? Good idea?'

'Can't hurt. I mean he's not going to force us to do anything, is he?'

'No, but he may say we're Kudamaz, God's emissaries, or some such thing, you know, and back us into a corner. I don't want our presence to be revealed to the public. They wouldn't cope with it.'

'The religious leaders coped okay. Why not the world?'

I glare at Sam, infuriated by his suddenly tactless view. 'Why not the world? Are you insane? Us doing any of our Kudamaz stuff would frighten the shit out of everyone. They'd think we'd come to take over Earth. You know how Earth has been indoctrinated into believing aliens are bad news. It would be immensely dangerous and would damage all the work we've done.'

Sam stays silent. His failure to retaliate signals I'd thrust some sense back into him.

Music blares out again from the stadium. I flick my head in the direction of the stage, and Ashton, his smiling face showing signs of strain, gesticulates for Sam and me to join him. I shake my head and hold onto Sam's hand tightly.

Ashton's eyebrows pinch together in frustration, and his face wrinkles with displeasure. He mouths at me, "Why?"

Then he sprints over to where I am in the wings.

"What's wrong with you, folks?" he asks as amiably as he can muster. But I can see the veiled annoyance in the wrinkled downturn at the sides of his mouth.

"We don't feel you need us," Sam says, gripping my hand tighter, and he eyes Ashton with icy defiance.

"Of course I fucking need you. You're the whole reason any of this is possible," Ashton hisses and yanks my hand hard, pulling me and Sam out onto the stage.

I know within a millisecond what Ashton's move is but, by then, I can't pull back. The force of my pulling against him would fling him into the back of the stage and most probably kill him.

As I stand with the lights burning bright around me, with cameras pointed, and microphones driven into my face, with ninety thousand people waiting and a further four billion watching, I consider that maybe I shouldn't have hesitated in pulling back and showing Ashton what my strength can actually do.

Chapter 42

Ashton fumed.

His big day. The most important day of his entire life, and she refused to play ball.

'Hello, world.' Hello *fucking* world? What was she trying to do? Make him look a fool?

All he needed was a little shimmer or a word or two to imply the power she had. The power they both had. Even Sam, usually the one to acquiesce to him, didn't want to know. It wasn't much to ask, thought Ashton. But it wasn't to be. All he got was Ellie's stoic recalcitrance and nothing more exciting than smile, the briefest of greetings to the world and then she sauntered casually, hand in hand with Sam, back off the stage.

Ashton, left astounded and po-faced by the unexpected departure of the Kudamaz couple, stared out at the audience. They watched him, patiently expecting something unbelievable was going to happen. But as the seconds ticked by, they looked at each other, puzzled and visibly nonplussed when it didn't.

Everyone present picked up on the vibes. The enormous downer the woman on stage had placed on the celebrations filtered through the world.

Ever the professional player, Ashton papered over their cracks of confusion.

"Thank you, my best friends, Sam and Ellie Noor!"

He clapped in a bid to raise the energies in the stadium. Deeply humiliated and angry, but with the world literally watching his every move, Ashton could only smile and cheer. He signaled for more upbeat music, and 'Time of my Life' belted across the stadium.

He turned to the assembled religious leaders who, like the audience and the world, had expected something amazing from Sam and Ellie, and now, from their obvious shunning of the PM, harbored feelings of perplexity. Ashton recognized it in their eyes, a single question.

Were the super couple really behind the unification plan?

That was the killer look sent to Ashton and he knew he had to bury it, and quick.

"We've heard what religious unification means to Earth, but what does it mean to you?"

Giving the stage over to the religious leaders to encapsulate in their own words why religious unification under Freedom Earth was so important to them, provided Ashton time to cool down and gain back his composure. He flashed a glance back into the wings. Ellie smiled and raised an eyebrow in an irksome manner. Clearly, she was enjoying the irony of the predicament she'd put him in.

Ashton seethed. How dare she do this!

He glared again but the Kudamaz couple had sunk further into the wings, and he couldn't discern their outlines. Ashton held back a deep sigh that was forming and clapped as Most Reverend Knightly took the stand.

Ashton stood to the side, a little away from the archbishop, and listened, nodding his approval and every so often swinging a glance toward the audience and the cameras, initiating their admiration for the words the archbishop was speaking through an applause.

In his earpiece, Dawes suddenly screamed, "Prime Minister, we've got the Pope, live, now!"

Whilst Most Reverend Knightly continued to proclaim his mission, on behalf of the Catholic Church, the screens above him flashed up a view of The Vatican.

Ashton stared with the rest of the audience and the world as the cameras zoomed in on the balcony where the Papal Father could be seen emerging through the heavy brocade drapes. Had it only been four weeks ago when he'd first seen that heavy brocade? His mind drifted back.

As he'd expected, the Catholic archbishop, upon his experience of enlightenment with Sam and Ellie, had met with Rome.

Cumberford had received a call from a cardinal and an invitation proffered with a degree of urgency. Ashton had Cumberford clear his diary and headed out to Northolt to his waiting plane. On the way, he gave a heads up to Ellie and Sam to be in The Vatican at five.

A few hours later, Ashton sat in the lounge awaiting Pope Paul VII. He sipped at the tea he'd been given and snatched a quick glance at his watch. Five to five. Almost show time!

A door pushed open and a black robed individual walked into the room, followed by a small, gently-stooping gentleman with soft, blue eyes dressed in white with the customary shawl at the shoulders.

Ashton jumped up.

"Prime Minister, I am pleased to meet you. Cardinal Carlo Nuzzi, secretary of state to The Vatican. We are delighted by your swift attendance."

"Thank you, Cardinal Nuzzi. I apologize, but I must ask you now to depart. The message I bring is for His Holiness."

Ashton stared at the sudden exasperation flaring up in the cardinal. His portly body wobbling, jello-like, and his lips trembled, ready to announce that the request was quite impossible.

The prime minister seared the air with a final, "And *only* His Holiness. Otherwise I'm leaving!"

Clocking Ashton's steadfast, cold gaze, Cardinal Nuzzi swallowed deeply. Ashton noticed concern as he conferred an almost silent whisper to the pontiff. Pope Paul VII nodded, his head kept close to the cardinal. Finally, he raised his face to Ashton, put his hand in the air and, with a fluttering butterfly of soft Italian, dismissed Cardinal Nuzzi and the entourage that trailed behind.

With bemusement still radiating in his face, Cardinal Nuzzi bowed low to the Pope and the PM, and made his exit swiftly.

"Prime Minister Richard Ashton, you seem to be causing quite a stir in ecumenical circle," the Pope spoke softly, but with firm authority. Ashton caught the determinedness within the outwardly kind eyes of His Holiness. "And I'd like to know why."

Ashton smirked with his usual smugness and nodded toward the clearing between the quadrant of antique arm chairs and sofas.

"Your Holiness, that's why I'm here," admitted Ashton, taking a surreptitious glance at his watch. *Dead on five o'clock. Action stations!* "If you care to look behind you, Your Holiness, all will be revealed."

Ashton made a further gesture, pointing to the space behind the pontiff.

The Pope turned, following the PM's instruction, and watched as the air sparkled between the seventeenth-century seating. Ashton could see the Pope's eyes widen in sheer disbelief and his jaw seemed to slacken.

He held onto the pectoral cross hung around his neck and whispered, "Dear God, what is this?"

"The truth, Your Holiness," answered Ashton, and watched with the pontiff as the twinkling air molecules seemed to coalesce to manifest a shape.

With more molecules, more detail was added until, within seconds, the shape became two people, standing and smiling amidst the fading sparkles.

Ashton grinned, immensely pleased by the entrance.

Sam walked forward, his hand outstretched. "Good afternoon, Your Holiness, Prime Minister."

Ellie, fast on her husband's heels, added, "It's an honor to meet you, Your Holiness. I do hope we didn't scare you."

Ashton moved in on the Pope. "Your Holiness, this is why I'm causing a 'stir', as you put it. May I introduce God's emissaries? Sam and Ellie."

Ashton read the Pope's colliding acknowledgements of wonder and fear in his face. In his mid-eighties, the Pope was wearing very well and displayed little evidence of his aging years. However, after Sam and Ellie's materialization, the Pope gripped tightly to the carved back of the sofa to support himself in case his legs gave way.

It was obvious to Ashton that the pontiff was questioning what he'd seen with his own eyes. The apparent wonder and fear grew in degrees across his features.

Ellie stepped forward. Reaching the Pope, she touched his arm and gently guided him around to the front of the sofa, where he could sit down and regain the strength that had dissipated from him.

Entering the seating quadrant, Ashton sat next to Sam in a high-backed, embroidered chair. The pontiff settled onto the sofa opposite Ashton and Sam, and Ellie, still standing, maneuvered herself beside the Pope on a three-seater sofa. Wiggling back and forth to get comfy, Ellie issued a wide, welcoming grin.

Ashton eyed the Pope's body language. His back had curvature due to a lifetime of bending and bowing during his religious considerations. He turned back to Ellie who, like Ashton, was watching the pontiff intently.

The Pope's body stiffened, frightened and unsure of what was happening. But, giving over to the fact he was a servant of God, he sought to mask his anxiety within a humble smile.

Ellie turned around on the sofa cushion and faced the Pope. "You're in pain."

Without a further word, Ellie laid her hands upon his curved back and closed her eyes.

Ashton noticed the pontiff jumped slightly, twitch, and grimace. But slowly, his body relaxed under Ellie's touch. The Pope pushed back against her hand, and then pulled his back upright.

Ashton examined Ellie's deft handiwork, and he knew from watching what she'd done to mend the Rabbi's ankle that she was realigning the Pope's spine. Having scanned through the Pope's private medical file, Ashton realized that Ellie was healing the loss of tissue in the facet joints and intervertebral discs that had naturally worn down over the decades. Gently, Ellie placed her hand in the Pope's trembling palm and pulled him to stand up with her.

As the pontiff stood straight, revelation and exaltation radiated from his face.

Ashton nodded to Ellie. *Job done!*

Returning to the present, Ashton stared with the audience and the world at the screens and listened as the Pope spoke of an amazing revelation that had been given to him, and a wonderful gift that had been bestowed within the bones of his being.

He then gave his absolute blessing to religious unification under Freedom Earth.

"This development is being witnessed by God, and under his instruction a new age of enlightenment and peace is fast approaching. It is down to us, as leaders of religion, to unconditionally recognize this global way forward and state our commitment in encouraging peace on Earth to prevail."

The energies had lifted. Ellie's deadpan address was suddenly forgotten.

Here was the Pope speaking live, directly from Rome, telling his global congregation of 1.8 billion people that Freedom Earth was the only way forward for mankind.

Ashton couldn't get a better endorsement than that.

Chapter 43

June 30, 2017

Sunlight streamed in through the arched windows mounted high in the courtroom. Frosted glass prevented any viewing from either side, and thick iron grills across the panes held the inhabitants ensconced in a filigree cage of metal protection.

Ashton sat at the back on the very last seat. He watched as the jury and others filtered in. Old, young, men, and women of all nationalities and creeds packed the courtroom. Ashton examined the court bailiff as he eyed the people fussing and fretting before they seated themselves. Ashton read immediately that his sullen expression masked a wariness in his sweeping surveillance. He was on point and ready. He knew these Al Nadir trials drew in the crowds. Their glamorous lifestyles and movie-star good looks made them famous. The media had coined the phrase 'terrorist celebrities', which was most apt. The public, morbidly fascinated by their hideous exploits and amazing 'beyond reach' wealth, came in their droves to such trials in a bid to know more.

Ashton hated Al Nadir. As prime minister, he'd sanctioned any action and agreed on any measure if it meant the downfall of that vicious terrorist collective.

A young woman in her late twenties, pert bottom and full breasts, suddenly squeezed past Ashton, and he instantly allowed himself to be sidetracked from his thoughts by her standout features. The woman didn't acknowledge the PM at all. She pushed roughly past without a thank you or even a glance or smile in his direction. Her knees scraped against his own, but still the woman didn't make conversation, brief or otherwise. She sat herself down almost on top of Ashton, who would have enjoyed such an occurrence had she not have been so very ill-mannered and rude as to have ignored him.

Ashton coughed, attempting to attract her awareness of his presence. The woman dug into her bag and pulled out her phone. Ashton glanced at it. *She probably wants a selfie with me.* He lurched forward as if to place an arm around her shoulder, but she dropped down to place her bag on the ground.

"Well, come on then," muttered Ashton, annoyed.

His statement was left unheeded. Ashton snorted with contempt. He was the prime minister, and they were all treating him like any ordinary man. In fact, correction, affirmed Ashton, they weren't treating him like anyone at all.

Ashton looked around him. The woman who'd almost squashed him stared out to the front, her eyes like saucers, her lips moistening slightly. Ashton knew she was anticipating the arrival of the defendant. He swung his head to the right. A young man, tall and blond, definitely good-looking but with a tough 'bottle-in-yer-face' attitude, fidgeted in his seat. An elderly man a few rows forward peered around the courtroom, and Ashton caught a sense of jumpiness, like he sat on an anthill and the ants were coming out to explore.

From the side, the defendant was brought in. Ashton watched the man swagger, full of cocksure confidence. He wore his suave good looks like an accessory to his crimes, a mask to shield the world from who he really was. The man looked up at the courtroom visitors. His attention fixed on the female contingent, and he licked his lips and blew kisses across the room before he took his seat. Ashton noticed the women and their reactions, pupils dilated, cheeks flushed, lips full and rosy as estrogen surged through them, their arousal peaked.

Knowing the crimes that the terrorist had allegedly perpetrated, Ashton found the women's reactions deeply perverse. It seemed they chose to overlook his sins in favor of his body and the primal lust possessing them.

Staring at the terrorist, Ashton became even more livid. Attention was all on him, and he was being ignored completely.

Ashton couldn't take the ignominy of the moment. He stood up, stepped into the aisle of the courtroom, and yelled, "I'm here. I'm your prime minister! Look at me instead of that murdering evil bastard!"

Ashton's childish and self-indulgent outburst was met with nothing. No action. No one turned. No one spoke. No one looked at Ashton at all.

Complete apathy to his appearance.

Ashton seethed, unable to understand the public's total lack of attention. Walking down the aisle, he flicked his head back and forth, fixing on everyone in the room. An elderly man pursed his lips and looked pensive as the judge entered and seated himself. A middle-aged woman, clearly not won over by the terrorist's charm and raw sensuality, glowered with deep hatred.

Given the size of the main courtroom and the public gallery above, Ashton surmised there had to be about two hundred people. Unlike most of the women, swooning over the defendant, the men's expressions declared they were expectant of final justice.

"Hello, everyone," called out Ashton, making his way to the front of the court. He waved his arms around, as if conducting a code in semaphore, and then called louder and a little more anxiously, "I'm Richard Ashton, the prime minister. Hello! Hello?"

Ashton flapped his hands and stuck his face up close in front of the seated crowds, but no one conceded to his presence.

He stepped over to the prosecutor and tapped him on the shoulder.

No reaction.

Ashton ran over to the terrorist in the dock and shouted, "Burn that fucker!"

He was sure that such a line coming from the UK prime minister would herald a response. But the terrorist didn't stir from pushing out his blatant carnal vibes, and the judge didn't regard him with a 'contempt of court' rebuke.

Ashton reached the elevated section of the courtroom. Climbing up, Ashton pushed past a court official to stand very close to the judge. The man didn't look around or tell him he couldn't be there.

The judge continued to speak, unaware of Ashton virtually sitting in his lap.

Ashton breathed in and out, forcing calm, and tried to rationalize exactly why the hell no one was saying anything to him.

And then he saw them.

Natasha, Mariella, and Abigail seated two rows behind the chief prosecutor. Ashton blinked, uncertain of whether to trust his own vision. He knocked the judge's elbow.

"Can you see them?" Ashton asked, but the judge rattled on, declaring the alleged offenses of the defendant, oblivious to Ashton's attempts to interrupt him. Ashton huffed, angry. But, deeper than that, he had a sense of concern.

He left the judge's side and made his way down toward the chief prosecutor and the strange visitation of his family.

The three of them in unison twisted their heads with marked precision, like automatons, and glared at Ashton. Their stares punctured his heart. Pierced his soul.

Mariella was the first. Opening her small mouth, she asked, "Why is my hair red, Daddy?"

Abigail followed, "You let them drug me, Daddy. Why didn't you protect me?"

Natasha finished, "Darling, you never were much of a loving husband."

Watching them, Ashton could feel a sob building in his throat. He ran toward his family. "I'm so sorry I wasn't there for you."

As he reached them, they all started to scream like banshees, listing his trail of inadequacies.

"Uncaring Daddy"

"Selfish Daddy."

"Useless lover."

"Bad Daddy."

"Heartless husband."

"Callous Daddy."

The sound of their vitriol grew louder, reverberating in Ashton's head, omnipotent in range and capacity. With his hands clasped over his ears, still he couldn't shut out their demented shrieking fury. Ashton was sure their caterwauling would have attracted someone's attention, but no one within the court looked in Ashton's direction. The prime minister gazed into the courtroom, and people gawped back but didn't respond. They didn't acknowledge he was even there. They seemed to stare straight through him.

Ashton turned away, intending to leave. And then he stopped.

Hadn't he left them before? He couldn't leave them again. He turned back.

The judge spoke, still failing to reference the visit of the PM or his spectral family. Instead, he steadily handed over the court to the prosecuting counsel to continue proceedings.

Ashton shook his head. What was this? Why was this happening?

Abruptly, the screaming ceased. The stark vacation of their screams left Ashton momentarily disoriented. He whipped around on his toes to face his family.

They stood staring but said nothing.

Ashton reached out to his wife. Her eyes were round and glassy as tears filled them. Her lips trembled.

"Why did you leave us?"

Such a small, frightened voice. Its tone struck Ashton. He swallowed, wrought with shaking sadness, and touched her face. Her lips. He just wanted to feel those soft lips on his one more time.

Natasha pushed up to greet him. Ashton closed his eyes, and he was carried back to the moment when they'd first met.

Those lips, wrapped in vivid cerise, pouting, pronouncing displeasure to the Maitre'd on a meal that hadn't met with her satisfaction. She gazed up from her scolding attack straight into Ashton's eyes. A flicker of a smile flashed across her lips, and she dropped her eyelids demurely. Then she opened them full and wide and buried deep into him a single message of absolute want. He answered her message with a vow of ultimate ecstasy. Ashton grabbed her hand, threw a fifty down for the meal she hadn't eaten, and snatched her away to make good on the promise he'd delivered in his eyes.

Remembering, he encircled her in his arms and pulled her tight. Beneath his lips, he detected something wet. He licked them, and a coppery metallic taste touched his tongue.

Instantly, he recognized the substance.

He snapped open his eyes.

Natasha's lips dripped with blood that pooled in the soft valley between her upper lip.

Ashton tried to pull away, but Natasha gripped him.

"You made me this!" Natasha hissed, her eyes now accusing and hate-filled, and her face starting to rupture and crack.

Ashton howled with sudden shock and thrust Natasha away from him. Stepping backward, he watched as Mariella and Abigail's faces started to break apart like their mother's. Their flesh fell away in strips like an invisible potato peeler was working its way down their faces.

Ashton heaved, bile rising fast within him, but his training, embedded and ground into his cellular memory, responded and forced him to reprocess the scene with complete dispassion. He dragged his gaze away to take in the court's reaction.

The prosecuting counsel droned on with a monotonic address of the cocky, suave terrorist's crimes. The devastating disintegration of his loved ones was still unnoticed by the assembled mass in the court. He stared across the room and at the jury, who watched the prosecutor with avid interest.

And then something triggered a recall in him.

He stared again at the jury. The Foreman, a small, weaselly guy in his late forties with a receding hair line and currants for eyes, appeared to be getting redder. At once, the descriptions tumbled into Ashton's mind as he realized the man had a nano-bomb inside him.

He had to warn the court. Get them to evacuate. Oh God! Why was all this happening again? He thought the days of the nano-bomb were over. Sam had fixed it. Made sure it was in the past.

So why now? What was this? Was he in the past?

"You're going to die, darling. The way we did."

Natasha's voice trapped him into looking back at her, and, in that second, he wished he hadn't. With her skin flailed away, he was left staring at the interlacing configuration of muscle strands around her lips, nose, and eyes, still wet with blood.

He held back on the urge to puke and ran over to the judge.

"You've got to get out," Ashton screamed. But no one replied.

He turned around to check on the foreman. His face had turned a shade of violet, and his eyes were bulbous and bloodshot.

"For fuck's sake, everyone, you've got to get out. He's got a bomb."

Ashton ran over to the prosecutor and shook him hard. But he just kept on with his debilitating diatribe as if someone had pressed play on him and he couldn't stop.

Ashton flicked another look at the foreman. His face was now purple, and his eyes were stalking. His body was quaking in a rhythmic way. He'd placed his hands between his thighs like he had an urge to urinate.

"Please! Please, can you not hear me? He's going to fucking explode. Stop this!" yelled Ashton. But he was ignored.

"You're going to die, sweetheart. Accept it."

He heard Natasha's voice but, this time, he didn't look at her or his daughters.

If no one listened to him, he had to go. He had to find his own way out.

He had to save himself.

Ashton sped down the aisle to the doors at the end. He grabbed them and pulled. But they were locked. He tugged at the doors, and screamed out. But no one came.

He turned to look at the court. The foreman was now dark purple, and his face seemed to vibrate. His eyeballs were huge, with pupils taking over his whites almost completely, and they burst upward as if an internal force was pushing them out of their sockets.

Ashton backed up against the door. He pushed his hands into his pockets. He had to find something to pick the lock. His hand touched something. A paperclip. With his back to the court, he shoved it into the lock and attempted to pick it, reminding himself of his training.

"Always trying to save yourself. Fuck everyone else. But you're too late, darling. You were always too fucking late. For everything."

Natasha was upon him, her gruesome face bearing down, blood dripping onto him.

From the corner of his eye, Ashton watched as the foreman's face enlarged, a helium balloon instead of a head.

"You're fucked, darling! Welcome to hell!"

And Natasha leapt upon Ashton, pressing her blood sodden lips on him as the courtroom exploded in a flash of white, oblivion-greeting light.

Ashton sat bolt upright in bed. Thankful to be alone. Sweat dripped down him, soaking the sheets. His body shivered. He focused with words of inner meditation and centered himself. The positive energies quelled his body's shaking.

He picked up his phone and dialed.

Cumberford answered.

"I need the Lord Chief Justice and the Lord Chancellor in my office at noon today. I don't care where they are, they must be there. Make it happen, Cumberford."

Ashton listened to his PPS's fawning agreement and slammed the phone down.

He'd decided on what had to be done and nothing on Earth would dare to overturn his final decree on it.

Chapter 44

It's that snuggling close underneath your loved one's arm, feeling their strength of protection around you. The sensual musk of their body. The gentle teasing touch of their hands against your skin. A glance of a kiss on your hair as you rest your head on their chest and track slowly the contours of their body with your exploring fingers.

These little things define what it means to love and be loved.

Whether Kudamaz or human, I have found the difference is indistinguishable. The power of love remains unchanged. It is a universal constant that flows through all species, wherever they call home.

It was love that saved Sam.

And love that saved the universe.

Some say that hate is more powerful than love. That dark overpowers light. Having witnessed both, I have to disagree vehemently.

Hate is an emotion that is singular in its construct. And of a single mind, the holder becomes. Hate bestows upon a person a weight that they carry, forcing their heart to be heavy and their soul to be chained down. It creates a self-fulfilling notion and a self-perpetuating circle that eventually reasserts a person's perception so that their only view on life is tinged with bitterness, envy, and regret. In anger fueled by hate, a person is left weak.

Love, conversely, is the emotion of openness. Of expression. Of freedom. A person who experiences love feels their heart is soaring. That lightness of being, and connection to the one who is loved, it feeds and rejuvenates the soul. Love makes a person glow from the inside out. Love courts gratitude. Love makes a person strong.

And with that strength comes the promise that everything is achievable. Nothing is impossible. Life is limitless.

I nestle into Sam as he sleeps and think about what is happening on Earth. From the Balance Shift status, the planet is holding strong, and an abundance of light energy is being generated.

I recall the events of late, the switching on of Quantum Force, unification of religion under Freedom Earth, and the proliferation of those awful Surv-Motes delivering instant justice. It seems that a considerable amount of this activity, although represented as good, is, to me, more synonymous with Ashton's need to control and dominate. A state outlined with a considerably darker hue.

I've spoken to Aby-od, and to Sam, but nothing shows in the databanks in the Observation Room. And, more to the point, nothing shows in my internal databanks either. All I have is a feeling. Old Sam would have said 'woman's intuition'. I can't pin-point the reason, and thus it is useless to even open the subject with the High Council. They have reviewed Ashton and everyone around him in detail. Sam has made the joke that Ashton has now received the highest clearance level of any prime minister.

Perhaps it is just me. That feeling that I am soon going to be superfluous to requirements. Earth is peaceful. More peaceful than it has ever been. But I remember the death chants against Russia and Saudi Arabia. The baying for blood. That certainly hadn't been peaceful. And are the Surv-Motes keeping down crime at the expense of human civil rights?

I can't, however, refute the evidence that religion is in a better place. No more persecution, wars, or indoctrination. Just everyone living together under Freedom Earth in harmony. Even if that harmony is somewhat forced.

Sam stirs beneath my head and rubs my back.

"Baby, are you awake?" he asks with sleepy eyes.

I am always surprised by Sam's need to sleep. As Kudamaz, we have no real need to sleep at all, especially when we are in Kudamun. Our time on Earth will fractionally drop our energy, but a quick hop and shimmer to Kudamun and those sentient crystals quickly provide the nourishing top-up to our energy reserves. But Sam just enjoys the act of being in a bed and sleeping. I figure it has to be down to his human-Kudamaz hybrid bodily structure, some whisper of his former human needs caught within the energy particles that make up his brain.

"Yep. I've been awake for a while. I don't sleep much. You know that."

Sam looks down at me on his chest. A touch of sadness drifts over him. He knows the reason for my not wanting to sleep. Those nightmares still plague me, forcing my databanks into overdrive and replaying the last days of my human existence.

"It's okay. I don't get them so much anymore, darling."

Sam doesn't say anything but reaches down, takes my face in his hands, and lowers his lips to mine.

"I love you, sweetness. You'll forever be mine, won't you?"

I stare into Sam's eyes and notice a flicker of fear.

"Of course I will. I've already been yours forever."

Sam smiles and kisses me again, and I feel a desperation in his lingering embrace.

I pull away. "Sam, what's wrong?"

"Nothing." But his eyes say differently.

"Not buying. Tell me?"

"I just had a weird feeling whilst I was sleeping that you were fading away from me. That I was losing you."

I screw up my face, incredulous. "Losing me, baby? I'm here for eternity with you, whether you like it or not!" I jab Sam in the ribs and tickle him to get a smile rather than the worriedness creeping over his face.

Sam laughs and grabs me, flips me over onto my back, and kisses me. His hands tip-toe down my body and rest on my stomach. A sigh of deep want slips from me, and Sam leaves my lips and traces the line of my neck with soft kisses. His little pecks continue down the valley between my breasts until he rests his lips on my stomach. He glances up at me, smiling, and then, gradually, his kisses travel farther down. I close my eyes and arch my back in parallel with Sam turning his attention to…

Buzzzzz.

The phone on the bedside cabinet rings out, delivering an immediate distraction.

"Tell him to fuck off!" I scream, unable to believe that we've been interrupted by him. I know it is Ashton. He is the only one who has that number.

Ignoring me, Sam leans over and picks up the phone.

"Yes, Richard? What is it?"

Sam's tone and the lack of 'Prime Minister' or 'sir' in his address advises that this was definitely the wrong time to be calling. I bloody well hope that dickhead Ashton gets the message.

Sam flicks on the speaker so I can hear.

Ashton doesn't apologize for interrupting, nor does he make a salacious comment, as is his usual modus operandi. I listen as the PM says each word, and his wavering nuance indicates fear and anger. Like he is about to shout or even scream but is frantically holding back the urge. But most of all, his voice has lost its quietly commanding tone of absolute authority.

Something has disturbed Ashton greatly.

I remain silent, instructing Sam telepathically to 'keep him talking'. I focus on Ashton, SearchSighting him and he leaps into my mind. I am there in his bedroom. Ashton is still in bed with sheets wrapped around him, sweat dripping down his face and naked upper body, his hair, always so immaculate, now disheveled, sticking out in tufts like small pinecones. Every facet of his being appears to be shaking.

I know that Ashton, like Sam, has been trained to withstand anything. To be truly fearless. To take command and own every situation so that he can determine the outcome.

In his eyes is the glimmer of a terror even he can't believe he's witnessed.

I watch Ashton push up on the bed to try and get comfortable whilst talking to Sam. He runs his hand through his hair, down his creased forehead, and across his sweat-soaked face to grip his chin and breathe heavily into his palm. Agitation surges through him. He wants to act but seems afraid to do so at the same time.

"Sam, I need you and Ellie to come and see me this morning. I need your urgent support."

I stare at Ashton as he speaks to Sam.

Here is a man with control at his fingertips, who only discloses emotions needed to further his own goal. When his family were assassinated, he'd used grief to assert a position of ultimate strength, and, in return, he'd received almost god-like adoration from the public. The incarceration and assaults that he'd suffered, he used to manipulate and, thus, promote a train of thought to underpin and bolster his future actions.

Everything Ashton does has a defined purpose. Like a chess master, he moves each piece on his board to gain strategic advantage. The suffering, the beatings, the death of his family, all the plays with religious leaders, heads of state, and energy moguls are part of a greater scene that Ashton alone directs. Chance doesn't enter into proceedings. I've even started to believe that Ashton controls fate.

Examining his eyes darting back and forth with a touch of inner frenzy, as if waiting for someone or something to arrive, I conclude that, whatever happened, it has affected Ashton mentally and rocked his very soul.

"What is it, Richard? You don't sound quite yourself."

Sam, even without SearchSight, picks up immediately on Ashton's tinge of uncertainty couched within his determined voice.

Ashton pushes his hand back through his hair again, making more pine cones, and fear ripples across his face. He sighs, scrunches up his lips, clearly at odds with himself and exasperated by his sudden lack of resolve.

"I'm not myself, Sam. That's why I need you guys. I really need you this morning. Can you get here for eleven thirty? I don't want to say anymore on it until I see you."

Ashton's face creases up again, annoyed to be virtually begging Sam for help. He reaches over toward his bedside cabinet and snatches at a bottle of Jack Daniels sitting on the edge. Without tipping it into the crystal highball glass next to it, he tosses back his head and takes a massive swig. He holds the bottle to his lips for a good few seconds, gulping down the contents, before resting it down on the bedsheets against the outline of his thigh.

He breathes out and sighs, appearing to gain back his mettle. Dutch courage working before my eyes, it seems.

Sam looks at me, ponderous and questioning. I circle my finger, signaling for him to carry on talking.

"Okay, Richard. I understand. We'll be there. In your office or lounge?"

"Private lounge."

In front of me, Ashton raises the bottle and takes another long swig, swallowing a copious amount of alcohol that, especially in the morning, I know wasn't good for anyone. Let alone the prime minister of the UK.

"Right. Well, see you then," Sam answers, still puzzled.

"Yes, and thank you, Sam."

Sam raises an eyebrow at me, surprised by the PM's delivery of gratitude.

I watch Ashton switch off the phone and settle back into his cushioned, opulent headboard. For the third time, he picks up the bottle and gulps back the equivalent of a four-finger measure, draining the bottle. He holds it up and wrinkles break out across his forehead, creasing into a line above his nose as he scowls, irritated that the bottle is finished. With a lurch upward, he drops the empty bottle to the floor, leaving it to nestle in the thick Axminster carpet.

Ashton then pushes across the bed to get out from the other side. I know at once that he will be completely naked, and I have no wish to SearchSight that view, thank you very much. I skip out of SearchSight mode and Ashton and his bedroom vanish from my mind's eye.

I look at Sam, who still stares ahead, confused by the interaction he's had with the PM.

"Learn anything?" Sam asks.

I shake my head, moving closer to my husband.

"Only that whatever's happened to him, it's freaked him out enough to knock back almost half a bottle of JD in the time you were talking to him."

"That bad, eh?"

"Yep! And he looks like shit warmed up too."

Sam's eyes widen. "Now that's unusual."

"You're telling me." I respond.

"And you couldn't glean anything from your SearchSight?" Sam enquires, slipping an arm around my shoulders and pulling me into him.

"No, I couldn't, but we'll know soon enough."

"Could go and check the Observation Room?" suggests Sam, as he rubs my back.

I move against him and a small moan escapes from my lips. "I could but, as you say, we'll know soon enough. And anyway, I've got a better way to spend our time."

And I pull Sam back down to the bed, smiling.

"Whatever you say, Mrs. Noor. You're the boss," Sam responds, grinning, and he focuses back his attention on finishing what Ashton had so rudely interrupted.

Chapter 45

Ashton waited.

He drummed his fingers on the coffee table whilst he stared into the air with growing impatience. The air in front of the ornately carved sixteenth century white fireplace started to thicken, slide, and sparkle. Ashton breathed out a sigh, muttering, "At last!"

He stood up, patted down his suit, ensuring he was pristine, and stepped toward the figures emerging from the ether into his private lounge.

Ellie fixed on Ashton. Sam smiled and, in unison, called into Ellie's mind, 'He cleaned up a bit from your last description of him.'

'Yep, he has,' answered Ellie. 'I wonder what this is all about.'

'We'll soon find out,' responded Sam telepathically, walking over to the PM.

"Richard, what's happening?"

Ashton recognized Sam had taken his earlier advice given in Thurso and dropped the use of his title completely. In retrospect, Ashton thought, perhaps I shouldn't have been so rash. Having superbeings like Sam call him 'sir' and 'Prime Minister' gave him even more stature, affording him greater leverage with other world leaders.

But he couldn't return back after what he'd said. That would do nothing but undermine his own position and place doubt in the Kudamaz couple's mind as to the level of his inherent confidence.

Ashton knew his desperate phone call that morning had been sufficient to reveal a sense of weakness in him to Ellie and Sam, and that was a situation he wouldn't allow to be perpetuated any further.

Above all, he was Richard Ashton, Leader of Freedom Earth, and Prime Minister of the United Kingdom. Strength was at his core. He must ensure power and force were his only displays from now on.

He moved over to the credenza housing an impressive array of drinks.

"What are you having?" Ashton enquired, his back to Sam and Ellie.

"That's okay, just an orange juice. Bit early for a tipple," called Sam.

In his mind, Ellie returned laughing, 'Hasn't he had enough already?'

Sam jabbed Ellie in the side and told her in his mind to 'Be a good girl!"

Ellie didn't indicate she'd received his admonishment and sauntered over to the PM.

"Actually, Ashton, I'll have a JD and ginger."

Ashton glared at Ellie. Did she do that remote viewing thing on him that morning? If so, did she tell Sam? Was he now just another pathetic human in their eyes?

He stared at Ellie. He noticed she carried a feather-light smile with a waft of smugness.

Ashton pushed down his anger and leered at Ellie, licking his lips, and imagined her naked, helpless, and at his total mercy. At that moment, he didn't give a fuck if she could read his mind or not.

"Good choice, Ellie. I always like a few shots to kickstart the 'ole Ashton engine in the morning."

"So I've heard," mumbled Ellie into her glass, and snatched a sideways glance at Sam.

But her movement was caught in Ashton's 'always surveilling' peripheral vision. He pursed his lips. The sides of his mouth dropped down and a flicker of agitation flared in his face. In Ashton's mind, he was on top, pinning her down, taking her ruthlessly, violently. Forcing her to scream as she came in shameful ecstasy.

"Richard, can you tell us why you needed us here? We are very busy."

Ashton twitched. The tone of Sam's voice was no longer respectful nor subservient. A seismic change had occurred, and he was sure that his raw fear that morning had been its instigator.

"I've made a decision," stated Ashton, beckoning the Kudamaz couple to take a seat on his white Regency sofa. He slid into his armchair and continued.

As he spoke, Ashton felt his strength returning. His imagined ravaging of Ellie helped restore his energy flow and, within minutes, he'd generated total command over himself and the situation before him.

"I'm removing the jury from court proceedings. There will be no more trial by jury."

Chapter 46

Xiao could hear their voices. Soft and intimate. Discussing something only meant for their ears. He pressed against the doorway and listened.

"When you told me, when you faced your past, Chen, that gave you strength. You set yourself free from those chains of sorrow. But you know you've made so much more of your life since then. That incident didn't define your life."

His mother had a gentle tone of tolerance and understanding. Whatever she faced, Xiao knew his mother, like those towering oak trees near his school in Hyde Park, could stand strong and resolute in the face of emotional wind and rain. Her compassion gave her the flexibility to sway with them, like the branches of the oak in the fiercesome wind, and lead them to believe that she was moved by their argument. But Xiao knew his mother carried an almost unassailable level of determination, and a courage to maintain her principles.

At any cost.

His mother was his hero.

And he loved her.

Xiao moved forward, waiting on his father's response. A growl sounded, and it registered a dark anxiety in him. His father, a man who had not played a role in his life, except to give him material things, and punish him, if his mother had allowed, for his disobedience, was still a mystery.

Now he could hear his mother speak of an incident. A thing his father had recently faced. Xiao wanted to get closer, but didn't, afraid his presence would be revealed.

"Darling Lei, you and I both know that incident did define my life for a while. As an instrument of the mob, suffering and death were all I knew. The things I've done, Lei, I wonder whether I should even be alive."

"Shush, my darling. Do not speak of such a thing. You were used. You didn't choose that path. You had no choice. You were a victim, Chen."

Xiao shivered. *An instrument of the mob. Suffering and death.* Those were the words his father had said. The shiver morphed into a more violent shudder. Xiao peered through the crack in the door at his parents. His father sat on the sofa facing Xiao. His mother was on the same sofa, but she'd turned her body a little away from the door, giving her full attention to his father. She clasped his shaking, massive hands in hers.

His father shook his head. Xiao noticed more wrinkles on his father's face. On his forehead, under his eyes, around his mouth. And they seemed to be moving.

Xiao watched as the skin on his father's face started to slide down like it was just a mask of glutinous liquid. It dripped down, a watercolor painting blasted by water, revealing a different image underneath.

A different face.

Upon sight, unable to take the trauma before him, Xiao collapsed heavily, banging the door and alerting his parents as he hit the floor.

Chapter 47

For a second, I think Ashton had said he is going to remove trial by jury, a legal process that has been in situ in the courts of England since the twelfth century.

'Is he mad?' I shout in my mind to my husband.

Sam deigns not to respond. Instead, he asks Ashton, "Why?"

"Remember, back at the end of January this year, Sierra Corazone, the high-level Spanish Al Nadir terrorist whose trial literally blew up, taking the Old Bailey and hundreds of innocent people with it?"

I recall the terrible attack.

From my databanks, I can see it was later concluded a nano-bomb had been inserted into one of the Jurors, a Mr. Albert Kipper. His family had been taken as 'motivational assets', which was an Al Nadir term used to ensure Kipper didn't talk. In usual Al Nadir fashion of no ties and no loose ends, Kipper's family were assassinated the moment the bomb exploded.

"Yes, Ashton. We remember it," I answer.

My somber tone clearly projects Ashton back into the past. "Those were bad times," he says.

"Don't I know it," adds Sam, recollection of the scourge of the nano-bomb attacks evident in his haunted eyes. "We lost too many good people then."

I cast my gaze at Sam and then Ashton. I can see the bond between fellow agents become visible before me. I've seen the horrors they'd gone through in speeded-up form in the Observation Room, but as much as the immersive, connected ability of the Observation Room provides, I still cannot comprehend the terror that Ashton and human Sam had faced. Not knowing whether a terrorist you had captured or an agent who made it back from a mission would suddenly explode, taking you with them.

"Ashton, we've solved the nano-bomb. What's that got to do with changing the judicial process?"

I really can't understand where his mind is heading.

Ashton sits back, sips at his drink considerably slower than the ones he'd had that morning, nods, and sneers, as if I am a green intern still learning the ropes of government.

"My dearest Ellie." *Well he can cut that condescending shit out for a start.* "I would have thought my logic is stunningly clear. The jury is the weak link in delivering the justice we need to ensure. I appreciate that, before, we needed something to provide balance and an equitable examination of the law. But, as you know, much has changed in the past few months. With the Surv-Motes, juries offer no additional value. In fact, they are now a liability, an area which still remains open to corruption and intimidation.

"As you're aware, Surv-Motes stream every occurrence they encounter, criminal or otherwise, directly back to the AI servers in Freedom Earth HQ, where they are cross-correlated with data streams from other surveillance devices, including other Surv-Motes across the world. Using the quantum computing and your brilliant command of harnessing quantum entanglement, intelligence can be instantaneously brought up and final decisions made to stun and incarcerate or execute. If the Surv-Mote disturbs an actual serious crime, its orders are to stun, detain, review, and then execute.

"There is no question as to whether a person has committed a crime. It's captured on a live feed. The only issue is the degree of severity denoting the need to imprison or execute. And this of course is liable to change as things go on."

Ashton has been talking a while. All the time, Sam listens but is gearing up to launch his tirade. "I know how the Surv-Mote works. I helped you build the bloody thing! What I want to know is why now?"

An uncomfortableness resonates in my mind as Ashton's words tumble back to me. I crash through Ashton's response to my husband.

"What did you mean when you said the degree of severity is liable to change?"

Ashton, hacked off at me for interrupting his delivery, runs his eyes up and down my body, making an unashamed push at being lascivious, and I sense he doesn't give a damn whether Sam picks up on it.

It is as though Ashton is taunting me to play his game.

I choose to glance away rather than glower or quip at him.

He wants attention. The little boy in the nursery, always acting naughty, wanting all eyes on him, and he laps up being the focus of everyone.

I am not going to give him that satisfaction.

Ashton pushes down on the chair cushion and moves himself closer to Sam and me.

"Okay, picture this. All rapists and murderers have been disposed of and anyone thinking of doing these crimes will be deterred from the fact it's an immediate death when caught. Murder and rape are crimes that have been officially stamped out of society."

"Great place to be in."

I glare at Sam for agreeing.

"Exactly, Sam. A great place to be in. But then what happens? If rapes were marked at two and first-degree murder as one on the severity scale, lesser crimes move up in severity, as in the absence of murder and rape, they are now seen as the worst kind or crime in society, and thus warranting of a higher severity level."

"Right," I exclaim, not liking at all where the PM's logic path is going.

"Therefore, a longer-term sentence or even the death penalty would ultimately be delivered to something that currently warrants a custodial sentence."

I can feel my eyes widening in disbelief as Ashton gives his ludicrous rationale for bringing back the death penalty for stealing a loaf of bread.

"You basically want to kill everyone who's a criminal, don't you?" I spit the words out and don't look at Sam. I know he'll disapprove of my outburst, but it has to be said.

Ashton sits back and regards me with a quizzical stare, as if I am the crazy one in the room.

"Ellie, I'm surprised at your hostility. Don't you want a world that is free of crime? Where people can return to leaving their doors unlocked, and allowing their children to play in the playground, knowing they are completely safe? Crime in all its many heinous forms has tipped Earth's balance toward darkness for too long."

I listen. Now he is talking like the fucking Kudamaz. Next, he's going to say he's first cousins with the Ancient Ones.

"With this wonderful Surv-Mote technology, we have a real opportunity to restore light. To eradicate crime forever, and really make Elysium here on Earth. I'm sure that's something, as Protector, you want too."

Ashton's eyebrows rise on the statement.

Sam turns around and stares at me. His telepathic response hits my mind,

"He's got a very good point, sweetness. I think you should hear him out."

I don't engage.

It isn't the outcome of a crime-free nation, or a crime-free world, that I rally against. It is the way in which all of this is being achieved. Ashton instills fear in people and has projected a path of uncompromising righteousness as the only way to goodness. He's dipped into Al Nadir's time, drawing examples of how truly horrendous those days were and showing how far and how fast mankind has travelled under his expert leadership.

Ashton eyes me. His tongue slips out and wets his bottom lip with a hurried sweep, like a lizard snatching a fly. I recoil inwardly and Ashton smirks, seemingly taking pleasure from my moment of discomfort. I pull my shoulders back and lazer him with my unnatural, azure eyes radiating absolute zero.

"I want peace, Ashton, but I want it the right way. Not by making people terrified of their own existence."

Ashton doesn't counter with any knee-jerk reaction. He smiles with a sugary calmness that makes me squirm. Finally, he shakes his head. The gesture shows dismay for my lack of intelligence.

I grip down on the cushion and feel my fingers penetrating through to the foam inside it.

"Oh, Ellie, Ellie. How wrongly you have interpreted what I've said. Law abiding citizens have nothing to fear. Only those who break the law will be held accountable for their actions. Nothing's changed for the everyday man or woman on the street. In fact, no, scratch that, something *has* changed. People will be safer and more secure in their homes and lives, and they'll know that we value their upholding of the law and unreservedly punish those who don't. There won't be any exceptions. Surv-Mote technology won't allow for it. No one will slip through the net.

"The cost of lengthy trials and prison sentences that, in the past, lawful taxpayers footed the bill for will instead be redirected into healthcare and education. That's a much more deserving destination of their contributed, hard-earned crust than lining the pockets of wealthy lawyers and barristers and prison upkeep. Surely you must agree, Ellie?"

I sit, my mouth opened a fraction, as I know I want to say something. What he's said isn't the point. People are being coerced into a strict behavioral pattern of subservience through fear and total subjugation. But I have to admit, Ashton's rationale is damn near perfect.

"What happens if the wrong person gets imprisoned, or worse, executed?"

My argument is weak, and I know it. So does Ashton. He smiles, victorious.

"Ellie, darling, you know with Sam's amazing Surv-Motes that's never going to happen."

He smirks, arrogance dripping off of him. I can't believe I actually thought he'd gained some humility. The Ashton of old, pre-family massacre and healer of faiths, is back, storming through dissention and tearing apart anyone who doesn't comply with his wishes.

Before I can retaliate, a knock comes at the door behind me.

Ashton issues a terse, "Come in," and Cumberford enters with two men.

Chapter 48

I recognize the Saville Row cut, sophisticated and timeless. The men that walk in are money. The man to the left of Cumberford comes into full view, and I rise from my seat. Tall, broad-shouldered, and big boned, he has a military air about him and a cunning gleam in his eye. Despite his polished appearance, he looks like the kind of guy you'd want on your side in a bar fight. The man on the other side of Ashton's PPS is short and tubby with a grey, receding hairline and creepy, dead eyes. He carries a pinched expression on his face like he's just been force-fed limes.

Both men possess a strong, purposeful gait, striding forward with intense assurance.

"Sam and Ellie, may I introduce Lord Martin Merle, my Lord Chief Justice, and Lord David Geddam, the Lord Chancellor?"

The tall man, who I now know is the Lord Chancellor, Lord Geddam, pushes his hand out to shake Sam's hand and mine. The short, creepy fellow, Lord Merle, Lord Chief Justice, then proffers his hand out to be shaken.

From their questioning stares, it is obvious they don't know anything about Sam and me.

Lord Geddam speaks first. Although polite, I detect a flavor of irritation on the periphery of his address. "Prime Minister, how can we help you? Your PPS called and commanded that we cleared our diaries and make this appointment at noon today. But apart from the theatrics of your staff, we have received no papers on this to determine the focus of discussion."

"It's all a bit of mystery," adds Lord Merle.

"Please, gentlemen, take a seat. What would you like to drink?" Ashton smoothes over Cumberford's bullying approach with charming aplomb and heads to the drinks credenza to prepare their drinks personally.

"Well, yes, thank you. Scotch on the rocks for me," answers Lord Geddam.

"I'll have a G and T, Bombay Sapphire if you have it," instructs Lord Merle.

"Of course," answers Ashton, smiling broadly, and I watch him start to make the drinks.

"What is your role in all of this?" questions Lord Geddam, staring at me pointedly.

So, not one to mince his words, I see.

"We're here in an advisory capacity," states Sam, and shoots a glare at me. In parallel, in my mind, I hear, 'Whatever you feel, keep it in.'

"Yes. They're my personal advisors on Freedom Earth and all its constituent parts," interrupts Ashton, as he returned with drinks.

When we stood up, the seating changed, and I find myself now sitting on the sofa with Ashton as Sam takes the armchair. The law lords face opposite us on another sofa.

"They're my inner circle. Practically family, aren't you?" Ashton looks around at me, smiling, and pats my knee. It takes all my power to resist ripping his hand apart.

I nod, and Sam says, "We're close," in a non-committal tone.

The law lords, I can see are getting agitated, as they are none the wiser as to why they are here.

"Right, well, that's good. But that doesn't really answer our former question. Why did you command us to be here?" Lord Merle shoots Ashton a menacing glare, and I can see there is definitely a past between the two men.

Ashton doesn't take Lord Merle's bait. "What's your view on the Surv-Mote performance to date?" Ashton throws the question out to both law lords and waits on their response.

Lord Merle wrinkles his blobby nose and I'm reminded of the French bulldog that used to live in the flat downstairs when I first moved in with Sam. He coughs and takes a drink of his gin and tonic to lubricate his chords, and then moves a little way back from Ashton. It appears he is simultaneously distancing himself from the PM whilst giving himself more height.

"I think the Surv-Mote is an extraordinary device. You can't seem to go anywhere without one popping up. I don't know how many there are in service, but there must be at least a million. I was up in Livingston yesterday and one loomed up as I walked out my hotel. As for their performance, well, as they say, proof is in the pudding. Crime has dropped by thirty-two percent across the UK, and violent crime has dropped by over half. No-go areas in South East and East London, where gun and knife crime rates were at their highest in January this year, have seen a complete overhaul and are now safe again. Crime rates across the region have plummeted. I think the extensive executions of gang members by the Surv-Motes certainly helped enable this outcome."

Ashton beams as Lord Merle gave his positive review of Surv-Mote technology. He shoots a self-satisfied glance at me. I remain silent but watch the palpable intensity rising in law lords' responses.

"What do you think, Lord Geddam?" enquires Sam, focusing on the Lord Chancellor.

"I have to absolutely agree with my colleague here. Surv-Mote technology has done what no amount of CCTV surveillance and pavement policing could do. It has embedded fear of the law sufficient enough to drastically reduce violent crime. I don't fully understand its operation, but I can wholeheartedly confirm that without it we certainly wouldn't be in the safe place we are currently."

Ashton slithers efficiently into the conversation, and my skin crawls. "So you'd say it has significantly changed the way in which the rule of law is delivered?"

"Complete game-changer, I'd say," admits Lord Geddam. "What's your take, Martin?"

"Totally shaken up the rule of law. Made those occurrences where killers and rapists get away on a technicality through the skillfulness of their quick-tongued, sharp-suited, overpaid lawyers finally a thing of the past. Something I'm pleased to see the back of, quite frankly. Justice was shackled. The Surv-Mote has seen its emancipation. It's the law delivered with teeth!"

"Would you say that, with Surv-Mote capability, the speed of the decision-making and, excuse the pun, execution of command…" sneers Ashton. I note he waits for the little guffaws that filter out of the law lords' mouths to subside before he continues. "Has made some parts of the legal system…obsolete?"

I stare at the law lords' reaction to Ashton's blatantly incendiary words.

Chapter 49

Lord Merle frowned, narrowing his target on the prime minister. Ashton recognized it. An intimidating stare that had been earned through a lifetime of bullying and domination. Ashton's old house head boy hovered into view. That same pitiless, piercing glare that looked on as Ashton was thrashed by the other prefects, and then left naked with the head boy to finish his initiation. Ashton held in a shudder and pushed the memory down, buried it beneath his years of countless conquests and cruel examination of a human's soul.

"Obsolete?" questioned Lord Merle. "Elucidate further, Prime Minister."

Ashton noted the lack of courtesy from Merle, and it pricked at his personal sensibilities. Ashton recalled when the animosity started, and then he remembered everything. Ashton had been a new lawyer, and Merle a judge. They'd crossed their legal swords on a very nasty murder case. Ashton was on the defense's side. Through his intel network, Ashton has smashed the case open with a plea for an acquittal due to contamination of evidence. Merle had, in fact, been coerced by parties unknown into making the acquittal stick. Ashton never found exactly what was known about Merle, or what leverage had been discovered. In his intel networks, everything was conducted through a number of nodes and sensitive intel was coded. No one in the network had the full picture or information. Ashton likened the operation to early blockchain, but using people as blocks instead of code.

Whatever the nodes discovered; it was damaging enough to Merle to warrant his granting an acquittal. Maybe, mused Ashton, Merle's absence of politeness reflective of his discovery that Ashton had been behind that 'coercion exercise'.

Ashton decided to flip the tables. Sharply, he requested, "You elucidate,

Lord Merle. What side of the legal system offers no value now that with Surv-Mote technology we know, without doubt, who has committed a crime?"

Lord Geddam's eyes flashed with recognition. "Trial by jury," he exclaimed, and Ashton smirked with utter complacency at Ellie. The Lord Chancellor had unwittingly validated Ashton's next move. But Merle wasn't quite so approving of the suggestion. "Trials have been around for centuries, Prime Minister. Can't just abolish something so ingrained into society's fabric. The legal system has to be seen as being equitable. Jury is not just a legal construct; it is one integrated at the heart of our democratic constitution. Impartial judgement reached at by an assessment of pure facts by a body of twelve men and women. And remember, Prime Minister, a person is innocent until proven guilty."

Delighted, Ashton listened, and threw Lord Merle completely off-base by smiling. Merle hadn't realized but by making the play for the jury, he'd actually stated, using his pure logic, the reason why trial by jury was outdated and superseded by Surv-Mote capabilities.

"How right you are, Lord Merle. Innocent until *proven* guilty." Seeing Merle and Geddam remain quiet and intrigued as to the discourse's trajectory, Ashton continued, "An assessment of the pure facts. That is exactly what Surv-Mote technology delivers. The pure facts. A live data stream of the actual crime, completely cross-correlated and AI interrogated to determine a person's guilty status and the sentence concomitant to level of severity of the crime."

"But how equitable is it?" snapped Merle, standing fast to his principled argument.

"It's equitable in so far as it can interrogate, in a millisecond, five hundred thousand terabytes of data and cross-correlate other intel from other sources, such as police records, victims files, health records, transport data, the list is endless, and would have already been completed several times over during the time I've spent here talking about it. Show me any jury who can do that. A Surv-Mote cannot be bought, harassed, or intimidated. A Surv-Mote's integrity is pure and cannot be manipulated. It cannot be hacked as it uses advanced quantum encryption processes and protections systems. You know as well as any that, in the law industry, despite the changes brought in following the Old Bailey attack, every jury could still become the target for unscrupulous 'money's no object' criminals. The jury is the weak link, gentlemen, and, by your faces, I can see that you recognize this."

The law lords exchanged glances and looked at Sam and Ellie.

"You're the PM's advisors. What's your position on all this?" asked Geddam. From his expression, Ashton could see the Lord Chancellor had already bought in to what he'd proposed, but he sought to win over his colleague Merle, who still scowled, unconvinced by his decision.

"The truth, gentlemen," interrupted Ashton, angling his delivery at Merle, ensuring he appreciated the inference, "is that Surv-Motes can find out anything on anyone. They are part of the constitutional framework making up Freedom Earth. We no longer look to our decisions with the insight of being one, isolated, marginally-significant country in the shadow of US. We are now a leader on the world stage. Freedom Earth was born in the UK. The countries that signed up to it now beat to our tune, not their own. Some have trial by jury, some do not. But all those Freedom Earth countries now have Surv-Mote technology. That is the common factor that joins us all. The basic fact is that, through our Surv-Mote technology, a person is guilty until they can unequivocally prove their innocence. If a Surv-Mote catches them engaging in a crime, they're guilty. Basic cold assessment of the facts. No room for misinterpretation or facts taken down incorrectly. Just justice delivered where and when it needs to be to, to keep our country, our people, and the world that is Freedom Earth safe, secure, and free from any tyranny or crime of any kind. Surely, that's the very reason you went into the law business in the first place."

Faced with Ashton's clear and plain logic that indeed, touched at the reason for their being in the legal profession, the law lords issued small nods of agreement.

"The case you have stated is flawless, Prime Minister," exclaimed Merle, somewhat begrudgingly. "These are indeed transformational times that require a rethink in how the legal system operates. I believe that a pilot of say six months should be entered into, whereby all trial by jury is stopped, and judgement is delivered through the Surv-Mote system. This should be monitored, and any issues or areas that this discussion didn't highlight or haven't come into being at this time should be reported on, and a final assessment made at the end of the six months as to whether it will serve the interests of the public of the UK to have trial by jury permanently removed from the legal system. Do you agree, David?"

Ashton held a smirk. He took in Ellie's incredulous face. She looked at the Lord Chancellor, but then stared at her husband, shadows of dismay flitting across her beautiful face.

"Totally agree. Excellent way forward. How do you feel, Prime Minister?"

"I think your suggestion will suit all parties' needs," stated Ashton. "What do you think, Sam, Ellie?"

"I agree that it's time for change," admitted, Sam glaring at the PM. Ashton noticed he looked a little uncomfortable, as if Ellie was shouting or poking him, but her mouth was silent, and her hands were clearly visible. Puzzled, Ashton turned his attention to Ellie.

"And so, my dear, your thoughts?" requested Ashton, smiling, showing how incredibly accommodating he was to hear all views.

"A decision has been made," said Ellie, "and it will change the world for good. Excuse me, gentlemen, I have another appointment I have to attend. Ashton, good day!"

I barely manage to deliver my line before rising off the sofa. The vitriol I'd been spitting in Sam's mind had gone unheeded. I could do nothing more. In disgust at how compliant both law lords have been to Ashton's wishes, I vacate the room. In my mind, I have one place to go. Kudamun. To see Abyod and hear his response to Ashton's new take on the balance of justice.

Chapter 50

That growing unease has finally taken over me. Creation of the execution stages saw its genesis. Presiding over the multitude of global executions with the Harmon wave has seen this inner uncomfortableness persist inside me. Yet every time I'm in Kudamun, and I express my concern, my deep anxiety to Aby-od, he dismisses it. He says it's down to me searching for a reason to exist. That if good is the overpowering factor on Earth, my role is uncertain. I know that isn't true, but the logic of it seems immaculate.

I've stared at the Balance Shift data for many Earth hours, trying to discern some anomaly. But it's shown me nothing. Only that light is prevailing, and the dark energy is firmly in check.

A state I should exalt in, not question.

But Ashton's removal of the jury system and his instigation of Surv-Motes as being the final legal say demonstrates how poisoned the law has become.

I am still shaking by the time I shimmer into Kudamun.

"Aby-od, he's fucking insane! He's abolished the rule of law. The jury system, it's been around for centuries, and in one go he's wiped it. The law lords just bent over and took it. Too terrified to do anything else. I've got to do something about him. He's taking over everything."

"Ellie, you have to stop this constant analysis of something that is simply not there. He must have had a good reason to remove the jury system. Perhaps it was no longer a requirement in this new social order that is based on peace and non-conflict."

Aby-od's voice turns brittle with annoyance. The scowl on his face deepens as I shake my head, disagreeing with his advice.

"No, it's about his total control. Those bloody Surv-Motes give him absolute rule, and no one can question him. He has the data to back up any execution, and if not execution, the data to prosecute without the need of a jury."

Aby-od shrugs. "It seems an efficient way to engage in legal matters. Execution is brutal, I cannot deny, Ellie. But I have viewed in the Observation Room the workings of these Surv-Motes and they are as much a deterrent as they are a weapon. I have seen people who would have been victims of heinous crimes still alive, still unharmed, as a result of these Surv-Motes intervening. The people across Earth have welcomed their introduction, and those that haven't are most probably criminals themselves. I still see no wrong in anything Ashton has done."

I shake my head.

"Aby-od, something isn't right. I've looked through Shift data since March 27 until now and there has barely been any differential at all. It may be that the Therab changed the Shift, but I have to tell you what I sense."

Aby-od frowns. "But there has been some. The counter isn't fixed on the same number continuously?"

"No, that's true. There has been some Shift activity. But, Aby-od, it's so nominal as to be inconsequential. Earth is showing too much goodness in its Shift position. I can't believe that all those Surv-Mote executions, and the millions of people who were coerced into terrorism through their own wretched backgrounds and who were obliterated in one go hasn't somehow reflected some pain, some suffering, and, therefore, a dark energy to manifest."

"But, Ellie, those people, although trapped into terrorism by their poverty, were responsible for appalling evil as the tools of Al Douri and Al Nadir. Their very existence created such darkness as to place Earth on its perilous path of self-destruction. Surely you can see that, by their death, a white light rebalance will occur and indeed has. Al Nadir is no more. Earth is free of tyranny. It is moving toward greater harmony. The faiths that humans follow are united. This is unprecedented. A step of considerable courage. It shows mankind's acceptance of others, a benevolence on a global scale, and, in its wake, a denouncement of war and removal of inequality and hostility. A single voice of humanity now speaks. Ashton is an incredible man creating Freedom Earth. I cannot understand why you can't see that."

"And I can't see why everyone bows down to Ashton. I know he lost his family, but he's milked that for everything it's worth. I can't see why even you admire him. He's constantly using his powers to manipulate others. No one questions him anymore. They just accept. Everyone accepts Ashton. Accepts what he's doing is right. Accepts his Freedom Earth. Accepts his Quantum

Force. Accepts his way to unite the religions. Accepts his way to deliver justice. Well, *I don't fucking accept it, Aby-od*! I still believe there is something terrible yet to happen. We don't know about it and Ashton is at the very center of it."

Aby-od stares at me. He shakes his head. His eyes display pity for me. He softens his expression, and speaks down, not in a condescending tone, more in a voice one would use for a small child still learning to grow, to understand.

"Oh, Ellie, if what you say is true, why hasn't the Shift tipped more to the dark energy? If Ashton really is as evil as you make out, the Balance Shift counter would recognize this and react accordingly. But, Ellie, it hasn't. White light imbues the world. There is a sense of peace and calm. Earth is in the midst of taking its evolutionary leap. It's embracing universal connectedness, ascending to a higher level of consciousness that we expect to see in a planet's inhabitants that have moved their positioning from war to peace. What is happening on Earth is natural. Al Nadir was a trigger point of darkness and destruction, but, in its demise, a new positioning had been brought forth. Ashton is just a catalyst creating a reaction. It's down to the people to choose their direction. Their way to peace, love, and harmony. And, Ellie, I've watched Ashton. I've watched the people around him. They indicate no untoward behavior, no evil wrongdoings of any kind. Despite what you may think of Ashton, he has changed the world for good."

Aby-od speaks Ashton's words and I shiver. Is Aby-od somehow under the PM's spell too?

"Aby-od, I told you before I'd find proof. As it stands, I've found nothing. But it doesn't mean there isn't any. It just means I must search harder and go deeper to find the truth. And I will. I won't stop until I reveal Ashton to be the evil, sick bastard I know he is."

I see Aby-od's glare, so full of sympathy for me. Sadness in his eyes, he holds his hand out. His fingers graze against my face.

"Ellie, oh my child, you are so damaged, and I have made you so. I know the reconstitution has affected you, somehow warped your view of what is right. You search for evil where there is none. You manifest darkness where there is light. You must stop this insanity, this lunacy that has overcome you. As Protector, you're tainted. Your perception cannot be a guide in which to establish your future engagement on Earth. My dear Ellie, why don't you stay here in Kudamun? Get yourself better and regain your focus. Have a clarity on who is dark and who is light. You're no use to Earth or yourself in the state you are in."

I hear his words. The disappointment in his voice now has a hard-edged denouncement. A categorical statement of my ineptitude. Had I blood inside me it would be boiling over.

Damaged goods.

Aby-od has said it, clear and plain, and confirming, beyond any hesitation of doubt, that lingering moment when he could have revolved his thinking and given me a worthy chance of my hypothesis being considered on sturdier ground. But no, it is lost.

I am lost to Aby-od.

In his eyes, I have embraced insanity in my constant questioning of a man I know is leading the world down a dark alley. I stare back at Aby-od. The hurt cannot be shielded.

I give myself into the pain and scream, "Aby-od enough! I will come back with what you need. Inestimable proof of Ashton's evil trickery. Proof of how he has blinded you along with all the sheep on planet Earth. Know this, Lord Aby-od, I am not mad. I am probably the sanest of all in this world of dark villainy and shadow."

I shimmer into my quarters and look around. I love my Kudamaz home, but I can't just swan around doing nothing. I have a mission to prove my sanity and Ashton's machinations of evil.

I return to Silent Waters and I don't say a word to Sam on the subject. He, like Aby-od, believes me to be mad. I will keep my duties and work with Ashton on his quest to unite the world under Freedom Earth. But all the time I will be continuously listening, watching, and assessing.

The knowing of his 'soon to slip' urges me forward, pledges energy to my fractured soul, and gives me hope of restoration, back to a time when I am believed and trusted. To where eyes observe me with pride, not pity.

And where I can release myself from this self-imposed cell of denial.

Chapter 51

Lei smothered him. Cosseted his every moment. She couldn't help herself. When she'd seen him in a huddle, unconscious on the floor outside the living room, all her fears of him landing in another dreadful coma surfaced.

Chen had picked Xiao up in his burly arms. Planting a kiss on his forehead, he'd carried him upstairs to his bedroom. Lei had trailed behind, watching. Xiao hadn't moved. He hadn't raised an eyelid to acknowledge their presence.

Lei swallowed, not wanting to confront what the truth may be. She sat with Xiao. Her attention, seen by Chen as obsessive bordering on fanatical, had never wavered. She stayed, glued, by Xiao's side.

Chen swiped a look at her. "For God's sake, Lei, surely you can see he isn't normal. We have to do something about our son."

Chen spoke softly to her. Not his usual arrogant, commanding growl. Lei smiled. She knew her husband was tiptoeing between her emotions, terrified of waking that Lei who would walk and take their son, and probably half his fortune, with her.

Lei looked into her husband's soulful eyes, as he perched like a mythical giant on the edge of Xiao's bed. Shuffling under her caustic inspection, he added, "Wouldn't it be better to get someone with an expert eye? I'm sure it would ease your mind."

"No, Chen. No doctors. They can't tell me what I already know. Xiao's condition isn't biological. He's recovering from a temporary metaphysical possession. But Chen, he is improving."

"Improving, Lei!" She watched her husband chew his bottom lip to control himself. Lei realized his sudden pull back. On the brink of broadcasting his true feelings about Xiao, Chen shook his head. "Okay. If you truly believe he's improving, I'll take no action. But remember, this is your choice, Lei. I'm surrendering to your wishes. But I want you to know they're not mine."

Lei caught Chen's dark glare.

She nodded. "So be it," she whispered, a knowing glint in her eye, a slight smirk on her immaculate face.

Chen stood up to leave. He murmured to Lei, "If you need me, I'm in my study. Those recent runway visits showed me there's more talent out there. I'm going to put together a target acquisition list and discuss with HR when to move on them. I've got to strike before the competition does."

"Of course. I'll be here," stated Lei, and settled into the seat beside her son.

In the hours that followed, Lei held tight to Xiao's hand, and he eventually woke. Lei noticed that her son displayed a miraculous level of defiance to mend himself. A single-minded objective to regain his body and mind, and reclaim the right to be a trusted, normal boy.

"Mum, I'm fine. I really am."

Next morning, at the breakfast bar, Lei heard her son whine his assurance of his condition. Chen stared, eyebrows raised in disbelief, but he stayed silent and munched on his toast.

"Mum, Dad, I want to go to school on my own today on the tube. The other kids have been saying I'm a mummy's boy, that I'm weird. Taking the piss out of me."

"Xiao! Don't swear," admonished Lei, but she was delighted to hear him talking like a young boy again. She just wanted to throw her arms around him with joy at this sudden step-change shift in recovery.

"Piss isn't swearing. Everybody says it. Now Simon, he really swears."

"Nothing to be proud of, son. A clean mouth leads to a clean mind," interrupted Chen, reaching for a yogurt pot. Lei swung a look that said 'hypocrite', but she didn't embellish the look with a comment. Chen harrumphed and stuck his spoon into the pot.

"So, can I?" pressed Xiao, and Lei, smirked, detecting her son's smooth and learned ability to detract from the current subject matter, namely his potty mouth.

"It's a bit too early for that, darling. You had a bit of a funny turn yesterday. Don't you remember?"

"Mum, I said, I tripped and fell over the rug. I'm okay. I'm fit. I'm well," Xiao pleaded with her, his big, saucer-like eyes doleful and beseeching.

"And what about that *other* episode a few weeks ago with Simon and Peter?

That wasn't a trip, was it?" snapped Chen, staring hard at Lei, his mouth turned down in displeasure, his face vehemently against Xiao's suggestion of going it alone.

"It was, of sorts," mumbled Xiao. "I tripped out on the meds."

"Xiao Chang, that was an excuse I gave to your friends," said Chen. "It wasn't the cause of your episode."

"How do you know? You're not a doctor. You've not got qualifications to confirm one way or the other. In the light of lack of evidence to the contrary, I'm going to say the meds screwed me up and caused that episode."

"In the light of evidence…where in God's name did you learn to speak like that?" shouted Chen. "Probably the bloody internet!"

Lei sniggered, as Chen looked at her, dumbfounded.

"Don't swear, Dad, not at the breakfast table!" chided Xiao, laughing.

Chen shook his head. Lei knocked his elbow, her snigger turning quickly into a chortle.

"So, guys, can I go to school on my own? I'm absolutely fine. And the fresh air will do me good. Cooped up all the time in the back of that car can't be good for my development."

Lei stared at Chen. Her husband shrugged. "Xiao, son, you sound like you should be a spokesperson for something on TV. Want to study politics? You've got certainly got a handle for manipulation."

Xiao grinned. "Is that a yes, Dad?"

Lei inspected her son. His posture of a self-entitled brat was back. It wasn't what she particularly liked to see her son displaying, but she was a realist. With his cushioned, charmed life, it reflected what she expected to see. The way he stood up and twisted the words around his father resembled the old Xiao, the one prior to Sharm-El-Sheikh and all that followed. She'd not seen him like that in a while.

In one glance, she knew her Xiao had finally returned.

Without waiting for her husband's approval, she blurted out, "Yes, Xiao. You may travel on the tube today. But if you feel uncomfortable or unwell, call Fredericks immediately. Don't wait. You promise me?"

Xiao beamed. "Of course, Mum. I promise."

Chen huffed, annoyed by her lack of recalcitrance to her son's wishes. Xiao noticed.

"Dad, are you okay about this?"

Chen glared at Lei, but she pushed her back up straight against the breakfast stool. In her slender fingers was a piece of rosemary-encrusted focaccia bread. She dipped it in the baba ghanoush and held it, as she met Chen's eyeline. *Defy me, and you'll know it.*

Chen swallowed, clocking her stare. He looked at Xiao who hadn't dropped his ear to ear smile.

Chen nodded. Lei let a flutter of a grin sweep her face, as she watched Xiao fling his arms around his father and kiss him. He then turned and kissed her too.

"Thank you, Mum. Thank you, Dad. I promise you I will take care of myself."

Xiao slipped down from the breakfast bar and ran out of the kitchen.

"I hope you know what you're doing, darling," murmured Chen, moving forward to touch Lei's hand.

"I always know what I'm doing," said Lei arrogantly. "You can see the way he twisted you into knots. He's not the same Xiao as a few days ago. Maybe that fall knocked him back into shape. I don't know. But what I do know is our Xiao is back. I can see that. You can too. We have given him a chance to be himself again."

Chen didn't say anything.

Lei searched within her husband's face for agreement. After a pause of several minutes, Chen grabbed her hand and kissed her fingers.

"You're right. We can't hold the boy back. He has to face life. Whatever that means. He now has to face it head on and prove he can take it."

Hearing Chen's sharp words, the reality of the decision she'd made came into focus.

I pray to God I haven't been too rash, thought Lei, as a little vibration of doubt rose within her.

Chapter 52

I flop onto the sofa.

Will this need to fight never cease? Aby-od cannot see the truth in front of him. Sam is too indoctrinated by his own past to see what is happening.

Ashton is a parasite. Sucking the blood of humanity. Draining it dry. Leaving it as just an empty husk, flimsy in his wind of change, taking his direction only, as no strength to take an alternative remains.

His last action, removing the jury from the judicial process and gaining supreme right of law, should have shown his hand. People somewhere should have said, 'Whoa, this guy's going too far.'

But no one did.

And now his law is final. He has suppressed free speech if it isn't in line with Freedom Earth. To speak out is now deemed as treason and punishable by death.

I take out the Balance Shift counter and pressed the button. The numbers of the Shift illuminate in the air and bob contentedly in front of me. Any difference is barely noticeable.

I can hear Aby-od in my head.

'If Ashton really is as evil as you make out, the Balance Shift counter would recognize this and react accordingly.'

I stare at the numbers and my frustration builds. Deep inside me, something is erupting. Am I going mad? Maybe Ashton is right and I'm wrong. Aby-od says I'm damaged. Maybe I am?

As my mind whirrs through possibilities, I notice my hands tightening, my fingers pressing harder into my palms. I look down and see blood trickling from my closed fingers. I feel nothing. No pain. Opening my fingers, the blood sparkles and vanishes.

I lost my human life to be like *this*?

The Shift numbers float, goading me to oppose them.

'The Balance Shift doesn't lie.'

Sam creeps into my head, delivering his final judgement.

Confused and infuriated, I scream and throw the Balance Shift counter with force against the wall. I watch as it flies through the lounge wall into the bedroom and lands on the bed.

Nothing gets around the fact that the Shift is right, and I am wrong.

I've given up my humanity to be wrong.

Unexpectedly, exhaustion washes over my whole being. I am tired of fighting. Tired of confrontation with Ashton, Aby-od, and Sam.

Tired of all the expectations put upon me.

I stand up, saunter over to the bar, and pour a shot of whiskey. I haven't touched drink at all since my reconstitution. In fact, I barely ever eat. My internal energies continue whether I consume food or not. And in Kudamun the sentient crystals give their light nourishment to me.

But now, I need something more substantial.

A flicker of a memory from days of a life past.

I savor the smooth malt and smoky flavors on my tongue before it slips down my throat into a sparkling nothingness.

I knock it back and pour another. I can't get drunk, but I can get myself intoxicated on the feeling of being drunk. Running the memory and going through the motions.

I have to let go.

I click the music app on my phone and the Bluetooth connection with the massive speaker springs to life blaring out whatever tune I listened to last.

I pour more whiskey, take the bottle, and start to dance. I let the music caress me and engulf me within its notes.

As I move, I notice my bracelet that I adore so much is shining. The mauve and violet crystals are twinkling with greater illumination.

I smile, enjoying the colors.

"Twinkle, twinkle little star."

I laugh. The intoxicated memory recall is working, and I love it.

Finally, I am letting go. I whirl around, dancing with a freedom I dare to acknowledge.

I am the Protector. I can do anything. Go anywhere. Why don't I just enjoy that power?

Why be obsessed with Ashton? He isn't the issue. I am the issue.

I need to enjoy who I am. I have no boundaries. No restrictions. Everything can be mine.

I notice my bracelet twinkling brighter. It is as if my soul is finally recognizing its worth.

The air starts to slip a little and I can see a shimmer. Sam.

"Hello, darling," I begin to say. But the air abruptly stops vibrating, and Sam doesn't appear. "Anyone there?" I call out, and giggle as I sound like a B-movie horror actress minutes before she is slashed to pieces.

The air is still and silent, but the room thunders with the mix playing from my phone. I gaze at the air, alarmed, but, as my intoxication mode takes greater hold, my concern is overlaid with a feeling of lightness. I shrug, uninterested in even pursuing my databanks to investigate further, and tip the rest of the whiskey bottle into my glass.

I sway back and forth, singing the words and drinking the whiskey. The song comes to its crescendo and I lift my glass high in the air, singing raucously.

"We are the champions of the world!"

That is it. I *have* the world. My ability to shimmer gives me the world, and I'd never bothered to use it for me, only for duty.

I clock the seventeenth-century globe we'd been given as a wedding present from Sam's parents. Apparently worth a fortune, I remember Sam saying.

I lightly touch the surface and it spins.

"Where shall I go today?"

I place my finger on the location that fate has decided for me.

Australia.

I've only been there on missions with Special Forces and spent most of the time in Australia's untamed center and deserts that had become the homes of Al Nadir's Australasian cells. I've seen hardly anything of its beautiful cities. Especially not the most stunning one, Sydney. It is morning now over there. I can take Sam and we could be tourists. No one would know any different.

I scan my connected databanks and discover that my favorite opera, La Traviata, is playing at the Opera House.

I concentrate my energies and two box-seat tickets appear in my hand. I've never manifested something that I want before, but, as they say, there's always a first time.

My bracelet shines, seemingly agreeing with my decision.

Around the room, music pelts out.

'I want to break free'.

"Yes, I do," I call out, laughing louder, and take a deep swig of my whiskey. Closing my eyes, I allow myself to be taken over by the waves of self-induced intoxication and the thudding beat of the music.

I am finished fighting. Finished analyzing. Finished watching, waiting, and assessing.

If the world is good, so be it, the world is good. Who am I to say otherwise?

All I am doing is causing myself and others pain. From now on, they'll see a new Ellie.

I wander over to the mirror. My face gleams brighter. My eyes sparkle like sunlight is within them.

The new me is already in the making.

Chapter 53

The end of Al Nadir.

The words tingled inside Sam with a joyous flutter.

He'd been in MI6 HQ the day Al Douri emerged from his fabled hermit-like existence bringing with him concurrent bombing in thirty cities across the globe.

Devastation reigned.

As he'd watched the carnage take over the world, with Sir Justin Maide, his former boss in the Secret Intelligence Service, Sam had made a vow, there and then, to do whatever it took to defeat those bastards.

Ironically, days before, he'd been ready to resign. In the job for four years, Sam hadn't been comfortable lying to Ellie. He'd stated to Maide that his time was up in Six, and he was interested in working in the Foreign and Commonwealth Office as a diplomat. Maide had been resentful and annoyed, but he'd agreed reluctantly to make appropriate introductions.

Thinking back, if he'd just walked out on the job before Al Douri made his entrance, would any of this have happened? Would he even be alive now? Would Ellie? Sam shook his head.

'Stupid Sam.' He could hear Ellie scolding him. 'Our lives are written. More than fate. Everything is connected. We couldn't change what had to be.'

She'd said it so many times, but even as Kudamaz, with the boundless knowledge he now possessed, knowing his human life had followed a predefined path was a bitter pill to swallow.

In his dressing room in Silent Waters, Sam took in his reflection in the floor-to-ceiling mirrors that made up one side of the room. He'd chosen his faithful Armani dove-grey suit, a crisp, white shirt, topped off with startling azure-blue crystal cufflinks in the design of an integrated chip. Ellie had bought them years back for one of their wedding anniversaries. He always wore them for luck. The color of the crystal reminded him of Ellie's eyes, watching over him wherever he was. As a human, her eyes hadn't been so blue; they'd had tinges of gray, making them alluring and seductive. As the Protector, Ellie's eyes had changed. They were now almost the same shade as that astonishing blue of his cufflinks. But their intensity was deeper, and they shone, radiating the incredible energies she had inside her.

He'd asked her if she'd like to join him today, but Ellie declined, stating, "Today should be about honoring those who've died in the struggle against Al Nadir. I only took out the trash. It was you, and those like you, who fought the real fight."

Sam had understood her reasoning. And he valued it.

He initiated shimmer and focused on Downing Street, and Ashton's private office.

"Hello, Sam," said Ashton within a second of Sam coming out of shimmer. "Such a wonderful day. I'm sure none of us believed this day would ever arrive."

"Oh, Richard, I'm sure some of us did." Sam stared, his eyes hooding over, remembering. "Otherwise we wouldn't have taken all those risks, made all those sacrifices, would we?"

Ashton nodded with reflective knowing. "Very true."

Sam realized both of them were caught up in the past. A past, according to Ellie, they had been destined to experience.

The creak of Ashton's office door brought Sam back, and Cartwright marched in.

"Morning, Prime Minister, Sam."

Sam watched as Ashton welcomed the MI6 Chief, smiling broadly. "So, today, the official end to Al Nadir," said Ashton. "A great day indeed."

"Yes, sir. A truly great day." Cartwright searched the room. "Where's Gibbs?"

Ashton smirked. "On domestic duties, I believe. Wife's birthday. Took her off on holiday."

"Pity. He'd have loved to have hit the final nail in Al Nadir's coffin," said Cartwright. "Are the president, Downer, and Greene going to HoloVid in?"

Sam could see him sweep a look over to the table to check if the HoloVid screen had been set up for transmission.

"No, Cartwright. I've got another way planned, if Sam doesn't mind."

Sam clocked Ashton's raised eyebrows and knew he wanted to use what Ellie termed their 'celestial taxi service'.

"Richard, I'm not sure that's really appropriate. I mean-" started Sam.

But Ashton's effusive tone, laden with authority and enthusiasm, stole his argument. "Nonsense, Sam. This is the perfect time for you to share your abilities so that all of us can celebrate the death of Al Nadir together. An objective you've been working on for so long and lost so much to achieve."

Sam shuffled, and glanced swiftly at Cartwright who appeared to be completely confused by his discourse with the PM.

"He's talking about me shimmering you guys out to the president."

"Huh?" said Cartwright, and then Sam noticed as understanding dawned on his face. "That teleportation thing you did in Thurso?" Cartwright looked suddenly disturbed as the PM nodded. "Oh goodness, you don't mean you could…you could take us with you?"

"That's exactly what he means. It's perfectly harmless. I've done it a few times. Haven't I, Sam?" interjected Ashton with smug assurance.

"Yes," said Sam, cautiously. "But I wouldn't say it's totally harmless. It does make you feel quite nauseous and disoriented."

Concern erupted across Cartwright's face and Ashton laughed.

"No more than a high-speed fairground ride! Come on, Cartwright. Where's your balls, man?"

"Between my legs, and that's where I'd like them to stay," muttered Cartwright, alarmed. "I've seen the result of some of those teleportation experiments DARPA did with rats, and my God, it wasn't pretty."

"Right, so I'll head off with Sam and I'll tell the president and the CIA you couldn't join us, as you didn't want to end up an unfinished jigsaw puzzle." Ashton stared, hard, the smirk full on his face, his eyes laughing, jeering at Cartwright's fear.

"It's Cartwright's choice, Richard. I'm not pressing."

"I'll join you!" whipped out Cartwright, his face scarlet with embarrassment at the PM's blatant ridicule.

"Good man!" responded Ashton, slapping Cartwright heavily on the back.

Sam could read Cartwright still wasn't a hundred percent certain of the choice he'd made, but he'd wanted to face off against Ashton's bullying.

"Okay, this is a bit awkward, but I need you both to put your arms around me."

Cartwright's eyebrows raised and he sneered, "Around you? What, as in hug you?"

"Erm, yes," stated Sam. "I need to ensure you, erm, have contact with my body at all times." Sam cast a glance at Ashton. The amusement on his face was obvious.

"You know me, Sam. Always happy to follow exact instructions," quipped Ashton with a saucy tone, and he slipped his arms quickly around Sam's waist, pulling him close.

Sam swallowed uneasily. Somehow, having Ellie as the buffer to Ashton's touch made things less uncomfortable when they'd all shimmered to Dharamshala a few months before.

"Come on, Cartwright. Lose those prom queen jitters," said Ashton.

Flushing red, Cartwright paced forward and tentatively put his arms out toward Sam. Ashton grabbed his hands and wrapped them around Sam's body, just above his waist.

"Ready?" muttered Sam, as Ashton pressed closer to him.

"As I'll ever be," said Ashton, smirking and licking his lips.

"Okay, Cartwright?" asked Sam, flicking his eyes towards the ill at ease MI6 chief.

"Uh, huh," said Cartwright, but couldn't look Sam nor Ashton in the eye.

"Here we go."

Sam initiated shimmer, locking onto his quantum self in the Oval Office, Washington DC.

Ashton announced to a clearly terrified Cartwright, "Get ready to feel the rush!"

And around Sam, Ashton's office vanished in a vibrating array of iridescent twinkling lights, and between the sparkles, Sam could make out the sturdy, curved, white walls, navy carpet, and convex window of the world's most famous round room.

Chapter 54

"Wow, what an ability."

Cartwright's thunderstruck exclamation rang in Sam's mind. The MI6 chief had made the stunned statement when Sam had encased him and Ashton in his shimmer field and headed to the Oval Office in Washington DC. Ashton, who was now used to shimmering, hadn't made much of the in-a-blink journey, but Cartwright had been completely awestruck.

Leaving Cartwright back in River House, Sam had shimmered to Downing Street to drop off Ashton, and then headed to Silent Waters to catch up on time with Ellie.

Music slammed into him, coming out of shimmer, and Sam looked around for his wife.

"Woah, Ellie, turn it down. At that rate, they'll hear it in Kudamun."

Ellie slinked forward, swaying. "Appropriate song, isn't it? It's a kind of magic, magic, magic!" sang Ellie, and she giggled.

Sam sniffed his wife. Jack Daniels. "Have you been drinking?"

"So what if I have? We're due a bit of fun!"

Sam slipped forward and grabbed Ellie in his arms. "We're Kudamaz. We can't get drunk!"

"No, but we can manifest the feeling by running our memory databanks. It's virtually the same thing. Try it." Ellie leant back, swept the JD bottle from the bar, and took a slug. Her bright, azure-blue eyes lit up and she thrust the bottle into Sam's chest. But he pushed Ellie's hand away.

"We really shouldn't. We have a responsibilities now," said Sam, caution flickering across his stern face.

"Fuck it, Sam. We've given our all over the past months. Al Nadir's gone. Crime is over. Ashton's got world peace sewn up. Religious division is no more. Limitless energy rules. What role is there for me? I've got all this power, but I've never had a chance to really enjoy it. Well now I bloody well intend to. Fancy going to the opera?"

Sam did a doubletake. "The opera? Now?"

"Yeah." Ellie knocked more JD back and smiled. "Right now."

"Operas in London start at nineteen hundred. The performance would have already started."

Ellie laughed, and sneaked her arms back around Sam. "Who said anything about London?"

Sam turned his head at an angle, puzzled. Ellie took his hand and led him toward the bedroom, dropping off the JD bottle on the shelf unit on the way. With her hand free, she grasped Sam's other hand and pulled him down onto the bed.

Falling on top of Ellie, he clocked the clothes laid out. Casual but smart. Quizzically, he stared at his wife. With eyes sparkling, he brushed his lips against her face and grasped her head softly.

"What are you planning, sweetness?"

Ellie licked her lips and pulled Sam into a deep kiss. "Oh, darling, I have a surprise for you."

Sam felt Ellie push her hand out and withdraw something from underneath the clothes.

"These!"

Sam looked at the small, white cards Ellie waved, and knew instantly they were theatre tickets. He snatched them and stared.

"Verdi's La Traviata, Opera House, Sydney!" read Sam, amazed.

"It's for tonight, but tonight in Sydney. The whole day is before us. Come on, Sam. Let's go. Have that fun we're deserved."

Sam turned back on the clothes spread out. "But they're not exactly for the opera."

"Distance is irrelevant to us. We'll pop back and change. I've got an amazing number I designed myself and made in the Pod earlier. Darling, please, let's go. You know how La Traviata's my favorite."

Sam could see Ellie was searching for approval from him. Although desperate to go, she still needed his acceptance. He held back. Flitting to a place for sheer fun wasn't something they'd done before. Sam felt Ellie's close inspection of him, and she shook her head, still smiling, spilling out an effervescence that seemed infectious.

"Come on, Sam. We must stop living within the confines of these humans.

We can do so much more. We can do anything we want. We mustn't let ourselves be shackled by their conventions. Nothing holds us. We are free!"

Sam moved up on one elbow and took in Ellie. Her face fervent and excited. Eyes gleaming and radiant. Even more super-charged than she'd ever been.

Without warning, Ellie pressed Sam back down and kissed him, hard. Sam breathed back surprise and returned her advances with similar passion.

"So, Sam, what do you say? Good idea?"

Sam looked back at the clothes, and then to Ellie's beaming features.

"Good idea," agreed Sam, smiling, and he returned his mouth back to the happy lips below him.

Chapter 55

Ashton sat up in bed, alive with a single feeling.

He'd *changed the world for good.*

In just four months, everything that had been in place, that had been a solid fixture of what the world should be had been scratched away and what remained was a place of his own design.

He'd not just obliterated Al Nadir, but also any form of criminal activity at all. With those amazing Surv-Motes, people could walk the streets, free of the threat of being robbed, raped, or murdered.

Abundant, cheap energy was a reality for power-hungry nations, and Ashton had made sure the UK led the energy revolution with Quantum Force. Of course, he'd also made sure his pockets had been well and truly lined. Not just with the swindled five billion pounds from the late Prince Khalifa of Saudi Arabia, but also the lucrative deals he'd instigated with countries through his own shell companies, handled by Stalbridge, and his legion of off-the-books cronies.

Peace throughout the globe was emerging through his Freedom Earth drive, an ingenious peace movement that forced all the former UN countries of the world to sign up to a number of key tenets:

1. Unify all religions in Freedom Earth countries under the single ideology of humanity to all and world peace.
2. Halt all wars borne of religion in all Freedom Earth countries and immediately free all prisoners held on religious grounds.
3. Execute all Al Nadir terrorists in Freedom Earth countries.

4. Agree to take action against, and, if necessary, execute anyone who harmed another Freedom Earth country, as such an act would be deemed an act of terrorism.
5. Forsake the right of sovereign soil in favor of a greater and more powerful allegiance under all Freedom Earth.
6. Accept the introduction of Freedom Earth's Surv-Mote technology to abolish criminal activity completely.
7. Remove the jury from their legal system as it was archaic and prone to manipulation of justice, and, with the Surv-Mote technology, an unnecessary liability.

Ashton knew Freedom Earth would never have had a chance without those Kudamaz superbeings, Ellie and Sam Noor. Salim Al Douri had also paved his path too, bringing forth his totally evil domination and destroying Malta in a blink. Such actions had shaken the world. In its blind panic, society had accepted Ashton's show of lethal goodness. A new morality carved from the hellish coals that Al Nadir had forced the world to burn in for so long.

He thought for a second, considering all that had passed. His victories had not come without pain. As his mind drifted back to the morgue in Exeter, he shivered. Poor Natasha. Little Mariella. Mixed up Abigail. His family ripped from him. Tears pricked, and he breathed deep.

Don't let them touch you.

Don't let them weaken you.

Embrace the pain.

Turn it to your strength.

Inside, he heard the instructions. Not originating from any indoctrinated compartmentalization process. These directives were deeper.

He remembered Katzy. His gorgeous, sexy, vivacious lover who had been murdered for no other reason but to gain access to him and torture him afterwards.

That was when the demands had started. Long before his family's demise. And with the demands came the darkness.

Flooding him.

Taking him over with a surging power. A resonance of righteousness. He knew he could not fail.

It was like, each day, he'd just been waiting. Treading water until his final moment.

He was so close.

Utter power of the entire world was in his grasp. Soon, he would reveal the Kudamaz couple. Whether they liked it or not. He'd trick them into revelation.

Then there would be no holding back.

The world would know what he'd known for so long. Everyone would fall in line. The president of the US or president of China, it made no difference. All would fall to their knees.

The people of the world were behind him. They loved him. Worshiped him. He would take the role they'd forced upon him. He would be their new god. And he would deliver his word to all.

Ashton closed his eyes, absorbed in the wondrous sensation of what the future held. A blond-haired woman, azure-blue eyes shining unnaturally bright cut brutally across his thoughts. Her sweet smile turned to a derisive sneer.

"You don't need us!"

Ellie Noor, the Protector of Earth. He'd been dizzy with the number of times she'd said that line. Her instinct to keep her powers in the shadows. To never reveal who she was. It plagued him. If he was to take control, he had to get her to show her Kudamaz self. But what then?

Ellie didn't like him. She'd made that feeling abundantly clear countless times. He'd faced her, and she'd shown her stoic duty to protect and serve the people of Earth, but she didn't serve him.

Sam was different. He demonstrated loyalty. Maybe something of a flicker of his former self remained within him. Ashton didn't know how Kudamaz physiology worked. But he did know Sam leaned more toward him in arguments than Ellie did.

Recalling their last confrontation, the day before, Ashton had seen Sam immediately support his decision to abolish the jury. Bolstered by the incredible efficiency and ruthless effectiveness of the Surv-Motes in detecting and stopping crimes, the law lords had agreed to the jury's removal. Sam had seconded the decision, but Ellie had not stated her view for or against. She'd stayed neutral, accepting the state of play in the room. But her voice, a chillingly cold tone of hatred, had told Ashton her true feelings.

Whatever way he turned the situation, Ellie was the problem. If he really tricked her into revelation, what would she do? Kill him? Leave forever? Or fall into his fold?

A sheep like the rest of the population on Earth.

She was the unknown variable.

The sum of all his successes.

Or the sum of his failure.

There had to be some way to swing the balance. Tip the odds in his favor.

Thinking heavily, Ashton got out of bed. He stretched, and then leant over to his bedside cabinet, snatched his ever-present bottle of JD, and poured a finger full into his Swarovski crystal tumbler.

Lately, his habit of morning imbibing he'd slipped into after Katzy and his family had died had lessened a little. But that morning, he felt the need to fortify himself with a bit of Dutch courage.

He lifted the glass to his lips and closed his eyes to savor the smoky taste, and heard a faint rustling beside his bed.

Instantly, Ashton's eyes sprung open, alert and searching. His bedroom was empty. No one was there. Ashton sighed and brought the glass again upward toward his lips. But then he stopped.

Within the finely cut crystal facets of the glass, a mistiness was building up. Ashton's eyes bulged wider. Slowly, he brought the glass closer, inspecting it. Places within the mistiness darkened, making a formation of something.

A face.

Ashton shook his head. His logical, agent-trained mind stated it could not be.

The thudding, pounding, cold resonance in his soul stated otherwise.

In shock, Ashton dropped the glass onto the floor. It shattered into pieces, but he didn't react.

Despite the weird apparition Ashton had seen, it wasn't the reason for letting the glass fall.

Inside his mind, someone spoke, as if standing in the room with him.

Clear and distinct.

"Ellie Noor will no longer be a problem for you."

Chapter 56

I clasp hold of Sam's hand. Being Kudamaz, neither of us are affected by Earth temperatures nor mediums. I can, if I want, walk around the Arctic Circle in my bikini and feel no change to my internal energy than if I stride through the Sahara Desert.

If I had the inclination to follow Jules Verne's idea and shimmer '20,000 leagues under the sea', nothing would happen to me. I wouldn't be crushed by external pressures. A stroll around the seabed would take place without incident.

Sam, in his abilities, is, of course, the same as me.

But for the look of the thing, we always must dress appropriately. That's why the attire I selected for our Aussie jaunt was suitable for a spring climate. My choice of light jeans, t-shirts, and cotton jumpers works well.

One look and it's plain to see we're just holidaymakers.

Sam swings his arm back and forth as we stride along the boardwalk in front of Bondi Beach. I look around. People are stretched out on the grassy hill in front of the beach, and many are making their way down to the sands. Boards in their hands, excitement in their eyes, ready to face off the waves with gusto. I anticipated it would be cooler, but the sun beats down, despite it just being a few minutes past nine.

Sam rests me against the metal railing and drops his lips to mine. For a fleeting moment, I recall when he'd kissed me like that against railings before.

It was the day I discovered everything.

His lies, his life as a spy, that dreadful surveillance. My world had split apart. I'd shivered, wracked with fear, not knowing who the hell I'd married.

Sam had chosen to eat out that evening. He'd kissed me hard, out in the open, against the railings in Chelsea. Just like now. His consuming passion engulfs me.

I close my eyes, push back the memories, and hold Sam in my arms. I don't want this wonderful feeling to be awash with the horrors of those things I bury. Those recollections of my time in Al Nadir's clutches. The things I force to stay dormant.

I feel Sam's fingers against my face, lightly stroking. I open my eyes and look up at him. Sam smiles.

"You're right, sweetness. We did need this."

I nod at Sam's confirmation. I knew he needed this break away.

It was something my soul force told me I had to do.

People around us, laughing, chatting, having fun, they're oblivious to Kudamun. Have no idea about how close they came to total obliteration.

These humans. Enjoying their lives. No responsibility. Not the kind I carry, anyway. No sense of duty to anyone except themselves. Without knowing, a vibe of jealously and shaded sorrow shudders through me. I shake my head, pushing down the feelings. But Sam, ever the one to see the micro-tells of others, still notices.

"Everything alright, darling?"

In his dark chocolate eyes, Sam's immediate concern registers. He holds me close, his strong arms encasing my body, slipping around my waist, pressing his muscular frame into me.

I kiss Sam, and skillfully attempt to obviate his inquiry with determined pressure on his lips. My tongue slides into his hot mouth, dancing with his.

I believe I've detracted Sam's inspection of my feelings, but he unexpectedly pulls out of the kiss and stares at me. That jealous streak and shaded sorrow floats just beneath the surface of my being. I try to shake it. I know it's irrational for me to be envious of these frail, weak humans, but the feeling persists. And Sam is on the verge of detecting it.

He tips his head sideways, looking quizzical. "There *is* something wrong."

He ruffles my spiky, blond hair. A gesture that is done to reassure me. He's telling me to reveal what it is I harbor within me.

But I can't.

I don't even understand what it is myself. Only that it's forcing me to sense a deep regret. I breathe out and force a smile to blossom across my face.

"Really, darling, I'm okay. Just savoring this time. Something to treasure."

I realize I talk with a hint, inevitability. Again, I have no reason as to why. I shake my head. In my mind, I cancel out the sudden bout of negativity washing through me. I snatch hold of Sam's hand and yank him around so he's facing the pathway down to the sea.

"Come on, sweetness. Race you to the shoreline."

I let go of Sam's hand and, with a playful leap, I run down the concrete path toward the beach.

"Okay, okay," Sam calls back, pretending to be puffed out. I swing my head around, and he bounds down the path after me.

Both of us have to mask our powers and restrain our ability. We can move lightning fast if we have to. In the battles with Al Nadir, we certainly did, but this is different. It's our leisure time. Around us are innocents, not hostiles. They'd be terrified, and their psyches would be shattered if they witnessed what Sam and I could really do in the way of running.

Sam reaches me and together we run hand in hand along the shoreline. I pull him back, stop, and drop to the sand, sitting down to remove my trainers, and I pull off my jumper. Sam joins me, and then jumps up. We dash into the waves and kick up the water. Although we're clothed, we still play like kids, splashing each other and laughing.

Earlier thoughts that made me so disquiet and confused vanish in the rising surf.

With our t-shirts and jeans drenched, we stride out from the sea. I keep my hand in Sam's. We walk along the beach, and then flop onto the sand. I lay my head against Sam's shoulder. He rubs my back and pulls me into him. He rolls on top of me, our legs entwining, and he kisses me, deep and strong. I hear some lads pass us higher up on the beach, laughing raucously.

"Give her one!"

Sam looks up, daggers in his eyes, and the young guys run off, terrified, jostling each other in a bid to get away from Sam's menacing stare.

I laugh. My badass husband. Who knew!

"So, you going to give me one then?" I ask with a saucy glint.

Sam presses against me. "May get us arrested," he growls, but I sense he's warming up to the naughty idea.

"If we are, we can always shimmer out of our cells," I counter, giggling.

"Ellie Noor, you are a bad influence, my girl. You're supposed to be a shining example of everything that is good."

"Aw, sweet of you to say. But don't bad girls have more fun?" My lips tremble, and my hands bounce down Sam's body and cup his ass.

"You're not a bad girl."

"I could be." With my hands on his perfect buttocks, I give him a hard squeeze. "How would you know?"

Sam moans. "Oh, baby, I'd know."

His lips encase mine, and I fall into the kiss. I push up and roll Sam onto his back, looking into his eyes.

"I always want to remember life can be like this. I'm so pleased we came."

As I speak, Sam stares at me. He's reading me. Can he detect the wonder that's in my heart? I'm sure he can. He gently strokes my arm.

"We've got the whole day. Let's explore this place."

"Okay," I say with some reluctance. I just want to rest in Sam's arms, kiss him with a languid obsession, and let the Australian sun beat its rays of joy down on me.

Sam maneuvers underneath me. I dig my elbows and press up. "Where do you want to go?"

"Anywhere, sweetness. The world is our oyster."

I smile, and that wonder rolls up within me. I feel it burst through, making my eyes shine brighter than they ever have. A shroud that shielded me from understanding who I really am slips away.

"Oh, I know that now, darling."

Chapter 57

Ashton noticed the air slip and slide in his private office. He smirked. *Here they come.*

But it wasn't the Kudamaz couple. Only one half. Sam Noor. His wife wasn't gracing Ashton's table with her presence.

That strange message still resounded in his mind, as crisp in delivery as when he'd heard it that morning.

Ellie Noor will no longer be a problem.

"Ellie not joining us then?" said Ashton with a raised eyebrow.

Sam glared back at him, but Ashton could see he bit back on making a retort. "Ellie, for now, has other business. But she promised to join us later," Sam clipped.

"Good, good," said Ashton. "So pleased that she deigns me worthy of her engagement."

Sam's head jerked up and anger shot out of his eyes. Ashton swallowed, and stepped back, knowing well what Sam had been capable of as an agent, and what he could now do as a Kudamaz superbeing to a mortal, breakable human body.

"Richard, you and her need to sort things out soon," Sam growled. "I'm not prepared to continue with your snide quips, sideways looks, and dodgy innuendos." Ashton looked surprised, but Sam continued. "And I told Ellie to get her act together too. She's now realized the error of her ways and has agreed to support you completely. But now you have to show her much more respect than you have. The way things are, the two of you are behaving like children. No more. Otherwise I will walk away, and I'll take Ellie with me, and your Quantum Force and Freedom *fucking* Earth can take a hike! Got it?"

Ashton did get it.

Ellie 'agreed to support him completely'. Whatever Sam had said to his wayward wife, he was finally getting her in line. Could he really believe that all her hostility toward him was over? Was she now falling into the fold? Like a good little sheep.

Ashton permitted himself a sly smirk, and nodded in acceptance of Sam's terms.

"But, Sam, I am surprised and hurt by your outburst. All those times in the past, I really thought Ellie and I were just having a bit of a game. You know, like sparring partners, jibing each other for fun. I never believed she genuinely didn't like me, nor that I really offended her, or you. I would never, never do anything to hurt you. I love you guys. You are my family. My *only* family."

Ashton forced his eyes to slick over with wetness, and his lip quivered. He stared at Sam. His head dipped down sadly, and he could see that Sam immediately looked uncomfortable.

"Yeah, Richard, I know", said Sam, a softer tone entering his voice. "Look. Whatever you thought you were doing with Ellie, she's been really pissed off with you. I'm pretty sure that wasn't your intention, but that's what's happened. So when she arrives later, I want you both to shake hands and call a truce. Agreed?"

Ashton stared back at Sam. "Agreed," he said. "Now, Sam, let's get that great mind of yours back to Quantum Force," said Ashton, flicking into professional mode. "Janice will be arriving in a minute. We need to run through those designs for the podule engine."

Ashton watched Sam flip open his tablet that wasn't a tablet, and a holographic schematic of the podule engine floated in the air. Sam pressed something on the screen and the schematic took solid form, building up its substance in front of Ashton's amazed eyes. This wasn't like the HoloTab app, although that was holographic too; this application made the engine solid, but then produced it as something that could be held and touched. A physical object out of light particles.

"Wow, Sam. Can I get that technology? It's like a HoloTab and 3-D printer in one," whispered Ashton, in awe of what he was witnessing.

"Not in a million years, Richard. And it can do much more than what I'm showing you, but I have to be cognizant of your level of technological development. I don't want to give too much away too soon."

"Like that crystal cube that makes things, eh?" muttered Ashton, remembering how the Kudamaz couple had created the enormous stages for both the US and UK public executions of those vicious Al Nadir super-terrorists.

"Yeah. Something like that," mumbled Sam, not giving up anything to Ashton. "Anyway, by using this process, we can see how the podule will operate inside a car."

Ashton watched as Sam manifested, through his tablet, an everyday car. Sam sliced the car down the middle, to show a cutaway of the engine compartment. With a swoosh of his hand, Sam removed the existing internal combustion engine components and inserted the Quantum Force podule. It was an unusual device and not really a podule at all, thought Ashton, as he moved closer.

It resembled more the head of a snake with a bit off its body. At the front was the photon injector pack, and, through a special pipeline, it connected to the existing gasoline inflow at the side of the car. This was the entry point that would be used to pull in the light photon. The bulbous end of the snake's head housed the Gold Plus chamber containing the weird maroon crystal. Behind the chamber was a thick tunnel. This, Ashton recalled, was the energy collection traction tunnel. The transmission connected to the traction tunnel and delivered the energy collected through the quantum reactions to power the front and rear drive shafts.

Caught up in staring at the halved car now boasting the Quantum Force podule, Ashton didn't notice Janice Perkins had been shown into his office by Redfern.

"Prime Minister, Janice Perkins to see you, sir."

Ashton swiped his head around to welcome his Energy Minister. "Janice, hello, my dear. Look at this. Isn't it marvelous? You remember Sam Noor, don't you?"

Ashton watched Perkins' face redden as she looked at Sam's handsome face. Ashton held down a smirk. *Getting your panties in a pickle, Miss Perkins!*

"Oh yes. Yes, I do remember Sam. That vanishing trick. And your wife, Ellie. She did that thing with the rabbit out of the table. Incredible. I didn't think I'd see you so soon."

Perkins gushed. Sam just smiled. Ashton patted Perkins on the arm.

"Yes, yes, it's all so very exciting. But, Janice, we can't take up Sam's invaluable time. I'm sure he's got somewhere else he needs to be. So, down to business."

Janice nodded, and sat down in an armchair looking intently at the solid model of the car suspended above the coffee table. Ashton noticed she didn't want to sit next to him or Sam. Too much testosterone (or whatever the hell hormone Sam had inside him) for her liking! Her hands slipped onto her thighs and she moved forward.

"Yes, quite, Prime Minister. Sorry. But all this, it is quite literally..." Ashton saw her switch a look between him, Sam, and then the floating model, "Taking my breath away!"

"Understandable, Janice. No need for apologies. So, Sam, please explain how this Quantum Force podule can be fitted or retrofitted to cars so we can make the UK absolutely carbon-free."

Sam lent in, touched the air in front of him, and began a detailed demo of how Quantum Force worked. Watching Sam, Ashton detected he was going at a slower pace, clearly for Janice's benefit, the poor girl. The PM sneered, observing Janice, who had launched into asking more questions. Sam took each with patience and compassion. Janice stole glances at Sam and flushed up again, but Ashton knew she was trying to contain her feelings.

"I'm going to turn on the AC. Room's getting a bit stuffy in here. A lot of heat being generated by your device, Sam."

Ashton arched an eyebrow, and Sam rolled his eyes to the ceiling and tutted.

Janice, Ashton noted, didn't seem to understand consciously their inference, but at a subliminal level she must have, concluded Ashton, as her face had suddenly turned an even deeper shade of pink.

Chapter 58

Today, I would reconcile my differences with Aby-od. It grates on me, the way I've made him my enemy. I've made a vow to end animosity with Aby-od, and with Ashton. I will build the bridges and put out the fires I've started.

Back in our London apartment after our gorgeous trip to Sydney, I relax between the covers. La Traviata still playing in my databanks. Such a wonderful experience. After waking, and making ever so gentle love to me, Sam reluctantly left earlier to visit Ashton and Energy Minister Janice Perkins.

He was due to discuss the crucial roll-out of Quantum Force's car podules, and a cost-effective method for retrofitting the secondhand car market. I agreed that, after I've made up with Aby-od, I'd join and support him in the discussions. I'd slipped on a t-shirt and got out of bed to make him some coffee, and whilst he'd dressed for the meeting, I told him of my plans.

Sam had been so pleased by my change of heart.

Once he'd shimmered to Downing Street, I'd played La Traviata on my phone and blasted it through the speakers, so that every note rang out through the apartment.

I now shrug off the t-shirt and slouch back into bed and drift off to sleep to the sounds of Verdi's operatic epic.

I suddenly awake, with a start, slightly amazed by the fact I'd gone to sleep at all. The music has finished playing. Goodness, have I been asleep for that long?

I move around in the bed, although I know I should get out, but strangely, the softness of the covers is too inviting. Come on, you lazy cow, shake a tail feather, I scold myself sternly, and lurch out of bed.

I walk naked over to the bathroom, turn on the shower, and douse my body in warm droplets. Refreshed, I wrap my wet frame in my fluffy robe and wander into my dressing room to decide on the clothes to wear for confronting Aby-od and throwing down the olive branch to Ashton.

I choose a demure cream blouse and blush pink hip-skimming trousers. A perfect balance of prettiness and professionalism on such a bright sunny day.

I saunter back into the bedroom and something whips the strength from under me.

I cannot stand.

I grip the side of the bed and crawl on top of it on my hands and knees. I fall down, face first, and then summon enough energy to just about roll over onto my back. Shaking, vibrations pour through me.

I lie above the duvet and try to determine what the hell is happening. Around me, reality flickers. Wall-to-ceiling glass windows are suddenly replaced by the glistening crystals of Kudamun. A resonance seems to scream inside me. The frequency increases, flickering realities between the universal plane and Kudamun at a rapid rate.

Dizzy with these oscillations, I close my eyes. The screaming ceases. I venture to think all has calmed inside me.

And then the stabbing starts. Within me, a spiritual scythe rips into me, its point coring me out, leaving a hole where once I was complete.

I double in pain. Exhaustion soaks me. I am the Protector; I don't get exhausted.

I try to rise but cannot. Strength vanishes from me. As if I am losing my existence.

Panicked, I attempt to shimmer. I focus on my home in Kudamun. But there is no pull. My soul force cannot connect with my quantum self.

I try again to shimmer at least three more times, but the actions drain me. I fall back onto the pillow and remain immobile.

A hum. Low and reverberating.

Where does it originate? Inside my head or outside? Or in another plane of reality?

I grimace as the hum grows louder. The reverberation ripples through me, like a human experiencing an electric shock.

My body arches, raising off the duvet. The energy jangles my body up and down like a perverse form of the Mexican wave.

Then I still. I stare down as my body fades out. The duvet's pattern of wild roses is now prominent through my legs and lower torso. What is happening? For the first time since becoming the Protector, I am scared.

Something is pulling me out of the universal plane, but I know no destination awaits. It is a shimmer to nothingness. I am being rubbed out.

Extinguished.

Oh, where is Sam? I need him. How can this be? I can't die. I am Kudamaz. We are almost immortal. We have existed for millions of years. We cannot die.

Sam, I need you. I love you. I don't want to leave you.

I reach out to touch his mind, but I can't connect. I can't reach him. His image dissolves. I can't formulate his face. I cry.

The energy resonance bounces me hard on the bed, like I am possessed by some malevolent spirit. On each movement, I filter out.

Please don't let me die, I try to say. No words form. Don't let me die, I shout in my mind.

Aswa-da. He is responsible for this thing that is happening. But I can do nothing. Reality continues to flash back and forth between Kudamun and Earth. I am being torn apart by the velocity of these reality fluctuations.

I burn. An agony of such intensity, tears pour from my eyes. I focus but can't hold on. My Kudamaz quarters interlock with my Earth-based bedroom in a bizarre confusion of structures, textures, and solid formations.

I shudder. An invisible hand snatches at my throat, strangling with a savage force.

I can feel an energy inside me rise up. Out of my body seeps a dark, sparling aura. I watch, almost removed from myself, as the aura envelopes me.

Then darkness.

No Earth. No Kudamun. No universe.

Is this death?

My body still vibrates. Energy surges with persistence through me.

I feel forces tugging at me on either side. Splitting me. And I can't stop it. My consciousness fades. All I am, my total being, is but a vicious vibration. I struggle to think. Little strength remains to focus.

What am I thinking? What is thought? What am I?

A particle.

A fragment.

A whisper of existence…

Gone!

Then a rushing of something inside me. Raw and untamed.

I open my eyes. I'm in my London apartment, lying on my bed.

I can feel it. Liberation.

I swing my legs over the side of the bed and stand. Strong and firm. I know something has happened to me. Like a form of reconstitution. But my formidable mind cannot inform any further on the experience.

I feel free of the responsibility that has weighed me down. And with that responsibility has come their betrayal. I can feel it. Feel it all. How they've betrayed me. Those who acted for good.

My life has been eviscerated, my humanity stolen, by Aby-od for good. But what good did it do me? My powers are my monsters, constantly torturing far worse than Al Nadir or MI6 ever could. For each time I use them, they define my superhuman status, and the loss of my own human self.

I was sacrificed.

Aby-od told me nothing. Just lies to coerce and manipulate. Thinking back to that second before I was killed, Aby-od had said, 'Trust me. No harm will come to you'.

I had believed him, but it was all lies. He knew my humanity was to be shattered to oblivion. He didn't care. His obsession for good to prevail, for light to be restored, that was his singular focus. I meant nothing to him.

And I still don't.

Everyone has lied to me. They have used me for their own gain. Sam. Aby-od. Both liars of the light.

Now it stops. That thing, raw and untamed. I can feel it rising and with it comes a veiling. A shrouding of the light.

I succumb. I let the pain ascend, dragging with it all the hate that has been trapped.

Aby-od, I hate him.

Sam, I hate him.

Still the surging, raw energy rises. I embrace the dark and let it flow through me, welcoming the clarity through its ascendance. That suffocating, stifling scarf that had wrapped around me, throttling me in a good of a design beyond my control, tears away.

I scream. Letting go of the pain. The sorrow. The injustice of my life. The hurt by the lies. It all empties out of me. My emotions tip, I feel my stability slide, and I smile as the difference immerses me.

An overwhelming freedom. Finally.

To be what I really want to be. Good has deprived me. Left me barren.

My association with it is over.

Chapter 59

I sense the shimmer behind me. I turn. Sam is there.

Thundering with hurt, he stares at me.

"I thought you were going to be there today! You promised you and Ashton were going to sort out your differences. We waited for you to arrive all morning. I felt like a bloody idiot, sitting there with Ashton. He snapped at me that he had to attend the Cabinet and left in a huff. Where the hell were you?"

"Had other things to do. More important. Sorry!" I quip, and grin.

But Sam does not reciprocate. He interrogates me with his eyes. It's a practice he's adept at. The pain gnaws my insides. My guts would be awash with blood, if, of course, I had my old physiology.

A shadow encases me, and I feel the urge to strike.

"But let's not worry about that. There's better things to take our interest than Ashton."

I look at Sam and lick my lips. I stare hard at his groin and then his face. I unbutton my silk blouse and the let the edges fall apart to reveal my glistening skin. I shrug off the blouse. It falls. I unzip my trousers and let them slide down my smooth, contoured legs.

They pool at my feet, accompanying the blouse. Air touches my skin. I tingle. My bra, front fixed, I pull at the catch. My pert breasts pop up, ready for Sam's touch. I shimmy my panties down over my hips and they flop to the ground. I step out of them and stand. Poised. Ready to be devoured.

Sam is emotionless. By this time, he would usually have been all over me. Not now. Caution registers in his ebony eyes. He just stares. His action confirms an acknowledgement of my change.

Rage inside me burns. He is asserting himself, taking control, as always.

Forcing his will upon me to concede a withdrawal.

I look at Sam. I don't smile. I move toward him, but he doesn't step forward or back. He remains stationary.

"What's wrong? Not hungry?"

Sam turns his head away from me and starts to leave the bedroom. He hasn't said a word. I'm in front of him before his foot drops to the floor.

"Do you have a problem?"

I know my eyes are blazing wildly. I catch a glimpse of myself in the wall mirrors at the side. I like the view. A tall body, naked and glistening, contoured by subtle but strong muscles and a sculptured face with shining, azure eyes. I am mouth-watering. But Sam still hasn't grabbed me.

"Do *I* have a problem? Look who's talking! You're the one who's *fucking* unstable."

"What do you mean?" I snap back.

"One minute you're for Ashton and want to reconcile with him; next you leave us high and dry and ignore him totally. You know I had to cover for you," responds Sam. His clipped, precise tone rattles me.

"So? Is that a big deal?"

"Ellie, you keep switching. I can't stand it. Something's wrong. You're not right." Sam steps away. But I reach out and hold his head firmly. I reach up and kiss him. I suck out his mouth and bite his bottom lip sharply.

And then I sneer, "I'm more right than I've ever been! I am who I want to be. Not what you want me to be. Not what Aby-od wants me to be. What I want. And that's how I shall live my life from now. I take what I want when I want. And, right now, I want you."

The rage inside me delivers a new level of strength I can't believe. I push against Sam, locking my leg around his, and force him to the ground. He doesn't protest. His face is shocked, but he says nothing. I straddle him, kissing and licking his face. He doesn't return the kisses. It is as if I am kissing a corpse. I persist. Sam pushes me away. His recalcitrance to sex flips a switch within me.

I claw at him, his shirt, trousers, boxers, all removed in seconds. Beneath me, naked, I feel his muscles, firm and bulging. I move down his body and grasp him tight. I stare, and he turns his head to one side. He can't face me. He closes his eyes. He doesn't want to admit he can't help himself. Around my hands, Sam is titanium, hard and huge. I sigh, rise, and lower myself on top of him. He sinks deep into me. Exquisite and full. Although not human, as Kudamaz, I have a sensory system of light energy that connects and seems to replicate a human's nervous system, delivering both pleasurable sensations, and, should an adversary ever be powerful enough, considerable pain.

I can see Sam is ashamed of his inability to refuse me. I press down and ride him hard. I let the fury of his betrayal whip me up into a frenzy of angry passion. My hands lock onto his shoulders, pinning him to the floor as I use him, my movements raging faster as I push him further up into me.

Sam tries to disengage, but I force myself down. Holding him, I dig my nails into his skin. I draw blood. His human-Kudamaz hybrid blood that sparkles and vanishes.

He turns to face me. His eyes are sad and pitying. He pities me. The bastard pities me. For everything that he's done. And he pities *me*!

The pain surges through me. I grasp his head and slam it to the floor. He makes no reaction. I reach down and bite, drawing blood from his lips. I clutch around his thighs, pull him off the floor, and, in response, he thrusts up. I scream. Climax is close.

To explain, the Kudamaz do not climax in a messy, human way. It is just a surge of incredible energy alighting our sensory system of light. But the feeling is more wonderful, more stimulating, more powerful than anything a human climax could produce. And I am heading to that nirvana. On my terms…

Sam grips me, arching his body, and I cry out as we come in unison. Energy explodes inside me as a million tiny fingers stimulate me simultaneously from within.

I stop and smile down at Sam, but my husband is catatonic. His face is drained. I can see he's numb. In trauma. I continue to smile, and then dive down to kiss his face. I snip at his lips with my teeth. I giggle like a playful schoolgirl who's just lost her virginity behind the bike sheds.

In his eyes, the sadness returns. And the pity. How dare he pity *me*?

The pain rises again inside me. No one pities me. I hold his head. At first with a softness, to confuse, I kiss his lips and smooth his face. And then I grip his head and whack it hard against the floor, again and again. The thumping sounds funny. I laugh and continue bashing Sam until I feel him go limp underneath me.

I release his head and it rolls back; his eyes shut.

I rise and stand, legs apart over my immobile husband.

"Pathetic!"

He didn't even try to fight or resist. He isn't the man I'd believed he was. I need more. I need someone to match my power. I need someone who can be my equal.

And I know just who that person is.

Chapter 60

I stand in the changing room in Harvey Nicks. It would have been easy to shimmer to Kudamun and create an outfit through the Pod-generator as I usually do, but this way is much more fun.

I've picked out a few garments: a black and silver brocade skirt (indecently short), a silver bra top by Dolce and Gabbana, a jade-green, tight-fitting leather catsuit with a plunging neckline by Missoni, and a sleek wraparound dress in black and silver satin by Valentino. A good few thousand pounds of fabric lies in my hands.

I can hear the assistant outside the door.

"Everything alright, madam? Do the clothes fit you? Do you need anything else?"

I call back, trying to hide the giggle in my voice, "Yes, they're lovely. Just coming out."

I go to unlock the door, can't hold myself, and start laughing loudly.

The assistant calls out, concerned, "Anything wrong, madam?"

Seconds before she opens the door, I shimmer, still laughing hard. My destination is my house in Winchester. In my bedroom, the stolen three garments are still in my arms. I can sense a shiver of exhilaration flow through my body. I think about the assistant and what she'll say when she opens that door to find an empty changing room. What will she say to her boss? I can't help laughing again. She'll probably get the sack. Stupid human.

I pick up the sleek wraparound. I smooth the satin between my thumb and forefinger and purr, enjoying the feel of it. Yes, that is the one I will wear. I remove my clothes and encase my naked body in the gorgeous, satin luxury. I slip my toes into a pair of steel-tipped Manolos and place a mauve, diamond-studded collar around my neck. I walk over to the mirror and admire the view.

I am ready. In my mind, the place has burst in. I watch. A sardonic smile flits across my face, and I shimmer.

I love shimmering. Coming out of my travels to see opened mouths and shocked eyes, it's such fun. My entrance into Number 10 is much the same. There was a time when I used to wait just out of reality until no observers were around. I cared not to harm human sensibilities. Nowadays, I don't care. Fuck it! I'm the Protector. I can do anything I want, and all those humans had better get used to it.

I laugh at Jensen's startled expression as I lock into reality. His jaw, like in the cartoons, almost drops on seeing me. I can't discern whether it is my unique transportation ability or my new wardrobe that causes his awestruck silence.

Ashton has his back to me, whittling on about his Freedom bloody Earth. His usual blah blah blah. He turns, perplexed, when Jensen, his puppy dog, fails to respond.

And he sees me.

His eyes widen, and they take me in from head to toe. His tongue slips out, making an involuntarily lick of his full lips, and he sneers, unable to conceal his outright salacious want.

"Ellie, goodness. You've finally arrived. Sam's gone now. I wasn't expecting you'd have the time to visit me today. Is there something I can help you with?"

I sashay toward the PM, past Jensen like he doesn't exist. My eyes are on Ashton only.

I could have shimmered over to Ashton but the walk over to him is much more rewarding, More pronounced. As I walk, the sensual satin material parts, delivering a delicious view of my sculptured legs and firm thighs to Ashton. The satin rubs against my alert breasts, stimulating my glistening skin and jaunty nipples. They pop up, straining against the material.

I flick a look down at them, and back to Ashton, and smile. He still hasn't moved, but plenty of action is happening in his groin.

He stares at me, salivating slightly, and asks again, "Why are you here? Is there something..."

Oh, how I love robbing men of their capacity to speak.

Playfully, I bite my bottom lip. He can see I'm wanton.

"Ashton, I know you are one sick fucking bastard who's got the world eating from his hand. Freedom Earth is just a power roll, and all that energy shit. All you're doing is taking control of what humans need the most. Easy equation. And it's making you richer than Croesus. Am I right?"

Ashton is dumbstruck. My outburst is not what he expected. Although, in his private office, with Jensen in toe, I'm not sure what he was expecting. Perhaps a little more horizontal maneuvering.

Well, he'd better get used to the new me.

Ashton was careful. His body couldn't help but jump to attention. The stiffness between his legs caused some discomfort, but he remained still. He made no attempt to move in Ellie's direction. If this was indeed Ellie. For this wasn't the fierce but diplomatic and gently interrogative attitude of a few days ago. This Ellie was wild, unabashed and unstoppable. Like a human volcano spewing out pure sexual desire.

Ashton regarded this new Ellie. Should he be worried by her ultra-confrontational approach? Could she damage him? His plans? He cast a glance at Jensen, who shrugged, unsure of what was transpiring. His face, pensive and pinched, gave no confidence to Ashton.

The PM swallowed. It was down to him. Back up from Jensen wasn't forthcoming. He opened his mouth to speak and the vision before him chewed up his opportunity.

"I really don't give a fuck what you're up to. But the one who's going to have the power is me, not you."

It had begun. He knew this moment would arrive. Ellie Noor recognizing the true worth of her abilities. Recognizing just how insignificant humans were. How, like ants, their lives could be stamped out. He wondered, with all her powers, why this day hadn't come sooner.

He suddenly noticed it. The flicker attracted him. A touch of darkness in her stunning, unnatural blue eyes. He'd never seen it before. Her eyes had radiated with light. He took in her features. Her mouth, gorgeous though it was, downturned slightly, in a cruel way at the sides. Her cheek bones jutted just a fraction sharper than before. Something about her poise, her deportment, shouted a dissonance with the world around her. As if she was now master of everything, and by her tiniest of movements, she reassembled the world the way she wanted it. Dominance defined in deft delivery.

But how had such a change occurred?

"Ashton, you can keep your money. It's a human foible anyway. If I need money, I'll just shimmer into a bank vault, take what I need, and shimmer out. That simple. No elaborate plan. Go in, take the money, and go out. My way."

Still speechless, Ashton listened. Caution flooded him. He was dealing with someone who has unbelievable power, but who had, up to that moment, applied her powers for good. He knew she was ruthless when it came to taking down Al Nadir, but that was to eradicate evil and do what was right for the planet. This Ellie in front of him wasn't the same. Of that he was certain. This Ellie had embraced evil. He could feel the air tangibly darken in degrees around her.

Diplomacy was the only route. Complete with that old political chestnut: plausible denial.

"Ellie, my dear, I have no idea what you're talking about. I told you yesterday that everything I do, everything I have ever done, has been to make the world a better place. The 'energy shit' you reference has helped to redefine the geopolitical map and given a much-needed redistribution of power back to the West, and especially the UK, after the East having dominated for so long. We have the energy security we've always craved for. It's changed the way international politics is done. And it's good for all, Ellie. Everybody wins!"

Ellie's head shook, and she sneered in a way Ashton recognized as mimicking him. Files were pushed off his desk. They clattered noisily to the floor. Up onto the mahogany desk Ellie jumped and sat, smiling, with legs dangling disgracefully open. Enough to distract.

"Yeah, yeah, whatever. Save it for your political puppets and gullible public. In this room, we both know what you are."

Ashton shot a glare at a terrified Jensen. The PM motioned with his eyes, dropping down to rest on the panic button underneath the desk. Jensen walked silently over to the button. Ashton didn't realize the actions of his confidante were being observed.

Chapter 61

Silence. Cold.

These two sensations assert that she has gone. Before, the shouting, the heat of tumultuous rage. Underneath his fingers the woven rug that bore witness to the assault. Not just his body, more so his soul.

She had invaded him. Her dominance an instrument used to ensure his degradation. Sam pushed down and propped himself against the sofa, his body weak from the ferocity of her anger. It all came back, in his face, her lips, eyes, hands. And her snarling, unrestrained wildness. He'd tried, but he couldn't control her. She was like a hurricane, sweeping up all around her; he couldn't match the force of her fury.

When was the moment of change?

Sam tried to establish her timescale of transformation. But he couldn't. She'd been in a rage about Ashton's decision to abolish the jury system. Ashton had explained his reasons, but she'd been too angry to listen, and left to moan to Aby-od in Kudamun.

He'd arrived at the apartment around eight o'clock following his joint MI6/CIA celebratory meeting with their respective heads of state, Ashton and Hutchinson, on the end of Al Nadir.

On his return, Ellie had been happy and quite spirited and playful. She'd suggested a quick flit to Sydney to spend the day there, walk along the beach, and then take in an opera in the evening.

Sam realized it had been the first time since Ellie had been imbued with her powers that she'd chosen to use them for her own enjoyment. Up until that time, Ellie's powers had been focused on the sole discharge of her duties as the Protector. She used them when she needed to, but not to excess, nor for entertainment. It was as though the powers were ring-fenced, boxed up and latched down tight until the world required her to apply them.

Sam could see her method was a subtle form of rejection. She handled her powers with caution, as a cop handles a gun; she kept them at a distance. As if she knew too much engagement of her powers would make them intrinsic to her being, and this, Sam could now see, was not what she wanted. She didn't want to acknowledge her own acceptance of them, for then she would relinquish her grip on what was left of her. Her humanity.

Sam cursed himself for not seeing this before. He'd been so busy with Ashton, Hutchinson, the Freedom Earth movement, Quantum Force, and the unification of religion, he'd not seen the deep pain that Ellie was drowning in.

If her powers were her demons, Sam thought, why did she suddenly turn and want to embrace the very thing she hated?

Why did she want to shimmer to Sydney?

Sam closed his eyes. He could still feel the warmth of the sun on his face. Ellie's hand in his. They'd walked like tourists along the sand, taking in the sights and watching the sea lap with solid regularity against the shore. He'd been so pleased to be Kudamaz. To be able to go anywhere at any time. And Ellie had welcomed this freedom. He saw, in her eyes, an unveiled wonder.

They lay on the sand, their arms and legs entwined, and kissed. Observers thought them to be new lovers. The freshness of their love shone from them.

He recalled that they had shimmered back to the apartment to change before going to the opera. In the apartment, a shower had been run. Ellie beckoned him in. They'd made love, although their movements, like a ballet, were almost choreographed. Smooth, subtle, and tender, their energies connected and exploded with a velveteen magnificence.

Ellie had absorbed the operatic delights. Immersed herself in the tragedy of Violetta and her destructive love for Alfredo. During the final act, Sam had touched her arm. Her emotions had flowed, open and unrestricted. He'd not acknowledged it at the time, but for a Protector to demonstrate emotions was almost anathema, and she'd cried twice in less than three days. Something inside her was breaking down.

On the floor, the musk of her gorgeous but violent body still on him, he forced himself to recall each moment in the theatre box, and then each second back in their London apartment.

He remembered, after the performance, as they sauntered out of Sydney Opera House, Ellie's face was so free. He'd be gloriously happy, as it seemed his wife had finally discovered inner peace. An acceptance of her destiny. A oneness with herself. And an unpolluted regard for what she now was.

Back in London, drained from the exuberance of the opera, they'd fallen asleep in each other's arms. He'd stroked her forehead in the night, and she awoke and grinned playfully. Her Kudamaz persona had not precluded her naughty streak, and it had never left her. They made love, luxuriating in the act, and lessening the hours between that inkiness that surrounded them and daybreak.

Together, still wrapped up in each other's love, they'd woken.

Out of slumber, Ellie mentioned she'd make things right with Aby-od as 'it wasn't healthy to have such poor feeling between them'. Aby-od had been like a father to Ellie, and recent arguments with him had created unnecessary and unwarranted animosity. Ellie stated she'd been 'rash in her judgement, and Aby-od was right, she did need a rest and to move her mind back to a happier space'.

Such a turnabout, Sam considered, had been fueled by Ellie's new acceptance. Experiences of the night before, the opera especially, seemed to have touched his wife, and even softened her hardline stance against Ashton.

In his mind, as he dressed, he could hear the coffee machine gurgling, as Ellie called over, "You know, Sam, Freedom Earth is a good thing. I've thought about it, and I realize what I've been saying has been crazy. I've had enough of fighting Ashton. Although I'm not sure about his methods, there's no denying he's achieved what we've always wanted. Peace, harmony, and global goodness. Why should I continue to question when everyone around me, including you and Aby-od, agrees he's a good guy? Everybody is happy with the situation. I may as well join in and be part of this worldwide happiness."

Sam recalled he had searched Ellie's face for cynicism or doubt, but her face matched her words. A vision of sincerity.

"I can't tell you how pleased I am to hear you say this. It pained me to see you in a constant state of conflict. Peace is so close, Ellie. Come into the fold and enjoy it."

Ellie had confirmed she would drop by at the meeting he had with Ashton and Energy Minister Perkins, and focus on mending her fractured relationship with the PM, as soon as she was finished reconciling with Aby-od.

Sam had waited. And waited.

The Quantum Force meeting with Perkins came and went. Sam hung around, chatting to Ashton about times past, when they'd both been agents.

Regaling stories. Laughing about circumstances, people, places. A little camaraderie shared.

Ashton delved into a discussion about the direction Freedom Earth should take in the future. Sam had given his solid assurance to support him. He'd noticed Ashton's eyes flick down to look at his watch.

Then, out of the blue, he'd snarled, "Not coming, is she?"

Sam had felt so ashamed, sitting next to the PM. He'd made such a big speech. Telling Ashton how to play it. Giving his word Ellie was proffering an olive branch too. After their initial discourse and agents-down-memory-lane episode, Ashton had wriggled around, staring at his watch. After he'd made his brittle comment, the air had become frosty.

"I don't understand it, Prime Minister. This isn't like Ellie. I do apologize."

"Sam, it *is* like Ellie. It's exactly like Ellie. She's done it to me before. Remember Thurso? Just before the big reveal, she fucked off then, didn't she? It's all part of her thing. Land me in the shit. Embarrass me. But really, Sam, don't take it badly. It doesn't matter. She obviously had something more important to attend to. Clearly, I'm not high enough on her pecking order. Anyway, I'm not hanging around here anymore. I've got a Cabinet meeting to attend. Sam, if you excuse me. Good day."

Ashton snipped his words sharply and pointedly, and left without even turning around. Sam had flushed with embarrassment at being spoken to like that. He'd not even tried to counter the argument Ashton had put forth, for he knew the PM spoke the truth.

In a rage, he'd shimmered back to Silent Waters, and what then happened had turned his world inside out.

How could she do that? To him? To the man she claimed to love?

Sam had no answers, only questions. Like before. Déjà vu plied at him, and he was back in that smelly, petrol-soaked garage with a whining, sniffling Quentin Ludlow, and a firelighter that flicked on and off until Quentin's words of state-sanctioned indifference pushed him over the edge and the man's calf barbecued gently beneath Sam's wrath.

With Ellie, there were always unanswered questions.

Sam pulled himself off the floor and focused on shimmering to Kudamun, to the one who could perhaps remove the growing questions marks over the enigma that was his wife.

Chapter 62

I'm already in front of Jensen.

I rise in my Manolos, towering over the pitiable human. His screams arouse me. I breathe, fast and deep, and stare at Ashton, savoring Jensen's agony. I bend his fingers back away from the button and hear the tell-tale crack. Jensen howls. Ashton drops his eyelids, not wanting to watch. Strange. I never took him to be squeamish.

The remaining fingers snap like those awful twiglets at eighties parties. Jensen buckles under me. His sobbing wracks through him. Good job he never met Salim or Sabena.

"Okay, guys, here it is. The bottom line. You either play things my way or it's going to get very messy in here."

I release Jensen to shake in the corner, nursing his broken fingers, and turn my attention to Ashton. I notice he hasn't moved or said another word after I shut him up. He's weighing me up. Analyzing me. Trying to figure out what I've become, now that I'm not 'good old, trusting Ellie'. Good luck with that one, sweetheart!

I virtually glide over to him. I grab his face, holding his chin tight. I capture his eyes in mine.

"Did I ever tell you what I did to make Salim talk?"

I smile, a fake disarmed one. Ashton appears afraid. I walk around him, a tigress circling her prey.

"I severed his arm."

I reach out and snatch Jensen, still shaking uncontrollably, from the floor by his shoulders. He yelps like the puppy dog I always envisioned him to be. I ignore him and point to his arm and shoulder connection.

"About here." I smile, luxuriating in my sinful citing. "Right through, with my mind."

I look at Ashton. Nothing shows. His eyes are impassive and calm. It rattles me that I'm not shocking him. I'll have to up the ante on this.

Jensen is the opposite. Staring at me, guppy fish effect intact, he mutters, "You didn't?"

Ashton seals his eyes shut. It is as if he can read my mind. Which, of course, he cannot. But, somehow, he knows I am going to demo it.

"Oh, I did. Would you like to see?"

Ashton leaps into action, jumping in. "Ellie, sweetheart, we believe you. We know you did something appropriate to get his confession. You don't have to hit replay."

Ashton looks scared and pained now. I've got his attention.

"No. No, I don't have to." I force a solemn, genteel expression. He believes me. Idiot. "But I want to."

Ashton is stunned. He attempts to say something. But I'm focused. His right hand is in my mind. I can see the atoms. Move faster, I command them. Faster. Faster. And move away. Right away. The atoms follow my instruction.

I smile, knowing the heat in Ashton's hand has started. His face is astonished. His eyes stare at his hand as it disconnects smoothly from his wrist and floats a few inches from his face. Just like with Salim, the blood vessels are packed tight and caught in suspended animation.

Ashton shudders and breathes in and out, fast. I can see he's using every ounce of his reserve and every second of The Firm's training to hold back the screams and keep himself upright.

Jensen, unfortunately, doesn't have any training and he's already started shrieking.

"Silence," I hiss, glowering at the risible human. "Otherwise I'll rip out your tongue. One blink is all it takes."

At my threat, Jensen clamps his mouth physically shut with his good hand.

"So, Ashton, now you understand my party tricks extend a little way beyond making rabbits out of antique tables, disappearing into thin air, and seeing everything you do when I'm nowhere near you. This last skill set is particularly useful. Don't you think?"

Ashton nods coolly, but I can see he's confused. He expected pain, but there isn't any. Well, not yet.

"I had to be sure we understand each other. You're thinking 'why aren't I in agony?' Pain shield is on full blast, blocking those nerve endings that pick up pain signals. Nothing's getting to that ol' brain of yours. But if I was to turn the shield off..."

Ashton jumps. "Please, Ellie, don't. You can have anything."

I listen. He's but a child, for all his announcements of power. He's lacking comprehension, a context in which to appreciate what I can do.

"Oh, I know I can have anything. I don't need your approval to give it to me."

Ashton is glued to my eyes. Locked into that look is all the taunting, belittling, and sordid innuendo he's plagued me with over the past months.

That darkness, that anger, blood red and saturating me, it rises up. I can feel it in my throat. The words erupt out of me. A pressured valve suddenly cut, I explode, but with exacting precision.

"You *knew* what they planned to do."

Ashton appears befuddled before me. All an act. I can see through his meagre disguise.

I press again.

"Sabena. Her floorshow. You knew."

Ashton had read the intel reports of Sabena's floorshows. Horrifically detailed, the reports held a certain fascination for him. Such a way to die. Gang-raped to within an inch of her life and then split through, piece by piece, whilst alive, from head to toe. Just the words seemed to entice him. Tease him to demean a woman who, although powerful, had been irrevocably affected by the wait, the knowing how she was going to die. Such knowledge would undermine the strongest. Ellie, he knew, was no different. Even in her superhuman state, careful application of selective words still weakened her.

He was paying the price for his temptation.

"Yes, I did," Ashton answered, deadpan and staring at Ellie. He'd lost his habitual smirk.

Jensen held his broken fingers and looked between Ellie and Ashton. He hadn't a clue what was being discussed. He was Ashton's confidante, but he didn't have the facts on what occurred on March 27. He did know that whatever they were talking about, Ellie was raging, but her manner remained measured and chilling. She looked like a woman about to bring down Armageddon.

"And you used your knowledge to hurt me, undermine me, recently?"

"Yes."

Ashton watched Ellie's eyes flicker.

His world shattered in pain. Torn apart. Total obliteration. A bomb? Was he caught in ground zero? Eyes blind. Awash with excruciating agony. Torture took his concentration. Focus. Try to think.

Pain shield. Oh God. She'd turned it off!

He kept his eyes shut and regulated his breathing. But on every breath, the white hacking heat of pain lacerated through him. He succumbed to the miasma of suffering and fell down, screaming.

"Shut up and open them," requested Ellie. "Or I'll tear off your eyelids. Don't think I won't."

Ashton snapped his orbs open, but small shrieks slipped out of his mouth. His hand that had detached from his wrist floated as before, only now the full force of the severing hit him in relentless waves of piercing, scythe-sharp agony.

On the PM's screams, Ashton's close protection tried to bash the door down. Ellie sneered. In a flash, the door vanished, leaving just a wall.

Jensen huddled shaking in the corner, too terrified to engage in the scene further. He closed his eyes and prayed for it all to be a nightmare caused by eating cheese before bed.

Ashton stared at Ellie. Without a door, his close protection would need to use alternative means to gain access to the room. By that time, it may be too late. There may be nothing of him left to rescue.

"Always knew, Ashton. Every time you said it, I knew."

Ellie's face, a victory served by the oldest method of inquiry. Pain immemorial.

She blinked. Ashton breathed. His anguish evaporated. His hand drifted back to his wrist, slotted inside, and connected. His blood flowed into his fingers. Nerves twitched, signaling impulses racing back and forth. As if nothing had happened. He couldn't see a tear. The cells joined perfectly.

With a tentative jerk, Ashton moved his hand up and down. Nothing fell apart. It worked. Normal. Even better than normal. The joints were much more flexible.

Dumbfounded, Ashton looked at Ellie and then Jensen, his confidante. Ellie picked up on the look. She nodded.

"Now you, Jensen."

Jensen gawked as his fingers straightened and bones mended, returning to their physiological formation. Like Ashton, he moved his fingers cautiously and realized they were all back to normal.

"Good as new again. You'd better let your people in."

Ellie flicked a look towards the wall, and the door was restored.

Ashton yelled abruptly for his close protection to enter.

Off the floor, Jensen jumped up and took a seat next Ashton, and the now-seated Ellie crossed her legs in a soft, demure fashion, as the PM's protection squad surged in.

"Prime Minister, sir, we heard screams. What's happening, sir?"

The close protection looked around the room at Ashton, Jensen, and then Ellie. His primary bodyguard's eyes fell onto Ellie's gorgeous body, and then looked away. But Ashton recognized his primary bodyguard returned his view in a bid to snatch a further furtive glance at Ellie's luscious legs. He swallowed heavily, a tad confused.

"Erm, sir, we really did hear-"

"What on earth is wrong with you? We're in a private and highly confidential meeting. Eyes only. And ears only. So get out!" Ashton swung his arm out to the door.

His close protection swept a glance around the room.

"Security is never tighter here. We're all one happy family. Aren't we, Ashton?" Ellie smiled; her beguiling lightness camouflaged her rage.

The close protection acknowledged Ellie as having security clearance at the highest level possible. They knew she was very close to the prime minister, and that alone was enough to stop them from asking further.

Ashton recalled Ellie's debrief report and Sabena's words that Ellie had just recited.

"Yes, one happy family," responded Ashton.

One happy, totally dysfunctional, fucked-up family!

Clocking the wry look on Ellie's face, Ashton could almost believe she could hear his thoughts as well.

Chapter 63

Sam shimmered into Aby-od's quarters inside his massive entrance hall. The crystal surroundings that he loved were now cold and inhospitable. Around him, a world opened up that had stolen his sweetness away. Sam knew Aby-od would detect his shimmer. He entered the hall almost immediately. Sam's face displayed his anguish to Kudamun's leader.

"I don't know what I'm going to do. She's everything to me."

"Sam, what happened?" Aby-od ran over and held Sam's shoulders.

"It's Ellie. She's changed." Sam turned away, ashamed, as he realized he'd have to explain what had happened. Her face was in front of him again, snarling and laughing. Eyes sparkling with enjoyment at his degradation. He swallowed and composed his response to Aby-od.

"She assaulted me." Sam stared at the crystal walls. He couldn't meet Aby-od's concerned stare.

"Assaulted you? What do you mean, Sam?"

"Aby-od, I mean *exactly* what I said."

Sam couldn't hold back on the horror resounding within his voice. He glanced at Aby-od. He knew the sage leader recognized that something terrible had been awoken. Within his eyes, Sam knew the leader would discern a flicker of raw incredulity at having to cope with something Sam believed he'd never have to confront.

"When did this happen?" asked Aby-od.

Sam was grateful for Aby-od not pursuing further on the details of the assault. He knew Aby-od recognized he was distraught and mortified, and the experience had psychologically scarred him.

"Hours ago. After the...the assault, she knocked me out cold and left. There was no warning. I arrived back to our apartment and she raged at me like a hurricane. I couldn't control her. I've never seen her like that. Even in the midst of fighting Al Nadir, she always kept something back. She delivered, if you will, a reserved anger. But in the flat, she was an unleashed force. I was nothing against her. Aby-od, she wanted to hurt me."

Sam trembled, and then held himself straight, and turned to stare at Aby-od. There wasn't any point in hiding the facts. If Aby-od was to help him, he had to know the truth. Aby-od nodded but his face remained impassive. He said nothing, but guided Sam to a large, ice-blue, fluffy sofa, and sat down with him. Aby-od turned his hand for Sam to continue.

"She knew I couldn't resist her. Aby-od, she used me violently, just for her twisted satisfaction. She enjoyed feeling my pain, seeing my degradation at her hands. In her eyes, I saw evil. Ellie, the woman I married, the woman I've loved for what is an eternity, she'd vanished. In front of me was just a laughing banshee, a wild succubus that was happy to drain my life away. How can this be, Aby-od? Has reconstitution caused this terrible change? Or has something taken possession of my darling?"

Aby-od listened to Sam's outpouring of pain, and his mind ran through possible permutations of what had caused Ellie's behavioral change.

"Did Ellie say anything to you that sounded odd before the change?"

"Well, she wanted to go to Sydney when I arrived back last night and spend the day there, and then go to the Opera House in the evening."

"Why was that odd?"

"Aby-od, Ellie's never shimmered for enjoyment anywhere before. Just the idea of her wanting to go somewhere struck me as strange. But she was so happy, so free. I could see she'd accepted who she was."

Aby-od coughed, interrupting Sam's flow, as a puzzled look took over him. "Accepted who she was? What do you mean? Ellie always accepted that was the Protector."

"No, Aby-od, I don't think she did. I was like you. I believed she was all okay with her new self. That she enjoyed being Kudamaz. But then I thought about how she used her powers. She handled them with respect and care, but only used them when there was cause to. Never for her pleasure. It was as if she was keeping them hidden away from her own self, for she knew excessive use would make them intrinsic to her being, and that's what she didn't want. It was as if they were an 'add-on', like a gun, that she could use, and then relegate to a place far removed from herself. Last night, that changed. She openly requested that we go to Sydney to have some fun. It wasn't a mission; it was for pure pleasure."

Aby-od's features had drawn tight with worry and his mouth had descended into a deep frown. Sam's description of Ellie was what he'd always feared. His calling to her had been so badly misjudged, and Aswa-da's interference had caused her psyche immeasurable damage. He'd never had enough time to prepare her. He'd told her nothing. What had happened to human Ellie was nothing less than a sacrifice, and now the grief of that demise had been targeted to create a change in her. But who would do this? Aswa-da? Someone else on Kudamun? He'd have to investigate.

"Did Ellie talk during the assault?" Aby-od phrased his words with carefully intoned consideration.

Sam nodded. "Yes, she did. She kept talking about 'being who she wanted to be, and not who I or you wanted her to be'. She was so angry with me. Viciously so. It was as if I'd taken something from her. But I don't know what that could be. Is there any way we can see what, if anything, happened to her that morning through the Observation Room? Would it allow us to go to a specified point in time and change what that thing was?"

Aby-od stood up. The review function of the Observation Room would be able to show, perhaps, what had happened, but not how to change it. From what Sam had told him already, he'd arrived at the only conclusion. Her internal resonance frequency had been realigned, using the pain of losing her humanity as the trigger, and all the white light energies within her had been reversed. Ellie, one of the whitest of white hearts, had now a black coal in the soul of her being.

Inside the Observation Room, Aby-od cued up the viewing of Sam and Ellie's apartment. He fast-forwarded sections not relevant and arrived at the part where Ellie had collapsed. She crawled, out of breath, onto the bed and lay. Her body still. Her eyes closed. She appeared to be asleep. The bracelet that he'd given her to control and train her SearchSight ability suddenly started to shine. It was made of a strange but beautiful silver material that featured two crystals embedded in its fabric, one violet and the other mauve.

Sam watched, and the crystals flashed quickly, and their hue darkened, until the crystals were the color of midnight. Ellie hadn't moved during the crystal's pigment transfiguration. Her body was prone and the room silent.

"What the hell is happening to that bracelet?" Sam glared at Aby-od, knowing he'd given it to Ellie.

Aby-od merely stared forlornly at Sam, unable to speak, and beckoned for him to watch the Screen. Fuming, desperately wanting to launch a tirade on Aby-od, but knowing it wouldn't help Ellie, Sam turned back to the inactivity on the Screen. Then it began.

He watched as Ellie woke, eyes bright, wild, and afraid. Something had taken over her body and it shook her with vehemence. The surroundings of their bedroom were indistinct, like in a fogged state. He couldn't make out any of the other furniture, the walls, windows, or doors. Just the bed. Ellie screamed and doubled up in a fetus position, her face showing ripping pain. He could see she tried to shimmer but couldn't get a fix. She tried again and again. Her body moved, undulating like a furious, never-ending sine wave. And on each ascendance, her body faded. The wild roses of the duvet cover erupted through his beloved's body as she slipped out of existence. Sam looked down and cried, his tears sparkling to nothing as they dripped down his face.

Sam recalled another time, another place, where he'd watched his wife on screen. She'd been in agony then too. Was there no way to keep his sweetness safe? Why were they plagued with this misery? Forced to witness each other's suffering. Even as Protector, she wasn't shielded from this torment.

Sam felt Aby-od touch his arm in a comforting gesture, but he jerked back, with ire burning inside him. Sam clenched his fists and looked back up at the Screen. The remaining flicker of Ellie grasped at her throat and tugged at it, as if she was trying to pull invisible hands that strangled away from her. Then she appeared to release the pressure, and her hands fell by her sides. Under Sam's eye, a dark, sparkling aura rose out of the faint outline of Ellie. It took Ellie's form, filling into the outline of her body, like how a child colors in a shape in a book. On the bed, just a black form that slightly resembled his wife, but her features, the beautiful contoured body, was gone.

"What the fuck is this, Aby-od? What cursed magic has been played on my darling?" shouted Sam.

"Sam, there's more," said Aby-od, and Sam, scowling, turned back to the Screen.

Ellie had returned. Her features, her form, everything about her was the same. Almost.

"Zoom in," commanded Sam coldly.

The system focused on her face. Into her eyes. And Sam could see it. The darkness. Lodged there.

Sam watched her stand. Her posture was powerful, with more inner strength than before. She surveyed the room, distaste reflected in her scornful sneer. She moved around, slowly and pointedly. She touched her body, as if she didn't know herself. Something flickered on her sneering mouth, and then she let forth a scream that engulfed her.

A scream that changed her.

Sam turned to Aby-od, and he could see the Kudamun leader's face pale. Sam knew he remembered. A scream had started it all. Would a scream now finish it too?

"Sam, I fear she is lost."

Sam heard the words. He couldn't bear to hear them.

"No. No."

"You were right. That pain she harboured inside her at how her humanity was taken from her has festered over these months. It has gnawed away at her like a virus, but her white heart kept it in check. That's why she only used her powers when she had to. When it was her responsibility to do so. It kept her from the brutal acknowledgement of what she was. The being she had become, and her dreadful loss at not being part of the race for which she'd given up her human life to protect and save."

Sam hated to hear the validation of his own theory. How could someone do this to his beloved one?

"Aby-od, it started with her bracelet. That bloody thing you gave her. How? Didn't you hide the frequencies?" yelled Sam, angrily turning on Aby-od.

"I'm sorry, Sam. It seems the frequency I locked into the crystals to guide and support Ellie in her management of SearchSighting has been used to access her own personal frequency."

"How is this even possible?" spat Sam, his fury taking over, making him shake.

"All us Kudamaz carry an internal resonance and, somehow, someone has used that resonance to flip her polarity from light to dark. They've used her internal pain as the catalyst, that is the origin of her darkness, and caused a reaction that generated a body of dark energy. It's that energy source aligned to the Protector's resonance that has created the Ellie who attacked you."

"Is it like she's been reconstituted again?"

"Very similar. I am sorry."

"Can you please stop apologizing and do something!" Sam's diamond-cut delivery attempted to mask the sob inside him, welling up.

"I will try, my friend. I will try. But right now, you cannot approach Ellie again. You must leave this to me." Aby-od's sternness impressed upon Sam the need to stay removed.

"I can't," growled Sam.

"You must. In her current state, she will kill you if you try to stop her. I promise I will do everything to get your Ellie back. But you must, Sam, leave her alone!"

Sam nodded, speechless.

But how could he remain removed from the one he loved? Once again, it seemed, he was praying for a miracle to save his sweetness.

Chapter 64

I left Ashton and Jensen a few minutes in from my realignment of their perception of power. Both were sitting in semi-shock from what they'd endured, only feigning stability for the duration of the security team storming in to identify why the PM was screaming. Of course, I played the demure maiden. But I made sure my legs were caught in the sights of the close protection officers. I could see, although embarrassed, they lusted after me. They made their exits swiftly.

One big happy family. That's where I left things.

Ashton, there on the sofa, considering his next move. Jensen still too terrified to move.

It did amuse me, seeing them reduced to shaking, shivering pieces of meat. How stupid Ashton had been to think he could affect me. Maybe if I hadn't gained my new power, words like 'floorshow' could have flipped me, undermined my position of strength. But not now.

By each Earth second, I recognize the surging power that is accruing within me. I don't know what has happened to me. A strange kind of metamorphosis. But the energy I possess is a million-fold greater than the Protector's powers. I still have all that connectedness with everything and the ability for atoms to build or destroy themselves at my telepathic command. I can still shimmer anywhere in the universe. Still obliterate with my rainbow light. I can review Balance Shifts and move faster than the human eye can detect.

Alongside all of this, I have a raw energy not doctored by Kudamaz convention, not beholding to responsibility or what is expected. I am free to do what I want when I want.

Inside me, I know Aby-od cannot reach me. Sam cannot touch me. Kudamun cannot hold me.

That inter-dimensional world has made me what I am. What they ripped from me, my humanity, that loss has made me what I now am. I can't deny it. I have a seething inside me. A need to dominate and the power to annihilate anyone who stands in my way.

Acknowledgement of the power I wield is refreshing for me.

All the while I've been in Kudamun as the Protector, I've been reserved in my usage of power.

Not anymore.

Humans only responded to power. I've seen how wars had been fought.

Weakness is there to be crushed.

These primates only understand one action: a foot on the back of their neck and their face in the mud.

Subjugation and submission. My new definition for the use of humans.

The sea, expansive and shining, stretches out before me as I stand on the balcony of the presidential suite in the Burj Al Arab Hotel in Jumeriah, Dubai.

The previous occupants are now scattered across the universe. Those self-entitled, obnoxious, designer-loving imbeciles have acquired their wealth through shady deals anyway. Disgusting whores that they were, they believed they were untouchable.

Well, I certainly wouldn't have touched them. But then, I didn't need to. One blast from my rainbow light, which has become rather more like an obsidian black twinkle, and it was au revoir to their super yachts, Ferraris, and private planes, and bonjour oblivion.

Out on the waters, ripples erupt.

I smile, recalling their horrified faces when I'd shimmered directly in front of them.

Yes, I could probably have incapacitated them, put them into stasis, or suspended animation, or even shimmered them out to somewhere else on earth.

A raft of options I'd had.

It's true. I expect Ellie the Protector would have tip-toed around, considering her actions.

I took one look at them, and thought, 'Fuck it! They're toast!'

It didn't help their future existence when their tough guy staggered out and tried to fire his gun at me.

But what really sealed the deal was when the wife/girlfriend/prostitute* (*delete as applicable) made her coked up comment. "Darlin', that gear is so last season. No one wears wraparounds now!"

Obliteration was the only call.

Probably all Al Nadir sympathizers, already down for execution somewhere. I just took the more direct approach.

The champagne bottle in my hand is almost finished. I pour the remains down my throat. I have nothing but light and energy inside me, but on contact with my lips, the champagne gives me a tingle. It makes me feel light-headed and frivolous.

I look out to sea. Sunlight touches me. A soft caress down my throat and between my breasts. Heat rises within me, and I am aware of a need that hasn't been sated.

Ashton is at his desk as I shimmer in. Just over five hours have passed since our last confrontation. I'd spent that time drinking, sunbathing, and wiping out scumbags.

Jensen is nowhere to be seen.

From Ashton's face, he hasn't been quite so relaxed as me.

He leaps up on seeing my entry.

"Hey, Ashton, sweetheart, don't be so jumpy. You'll give yourself a heart attack."

I laugh and flash my unnatural blue eyes at Ashton. I know that look is wanton and dangerous, and it is a look that a man like Ashton can't resist.

I stare. Despite increasing years, he is fifty-six and no spring chicken, Ashton is still an incredibly sexually charged being, oozing charisma and charm. Despite him wearing a suit, one can't fail to see what kind of fit body he has underneath.

Ashton's eyebrows rise. He is getting the picture, fast.

"Is there something you want?"

Ashton shifts his weight, pushing his shoulders forward, but he remains seated. I fix hard on those hazel eyes. Ashton takes my stare and holds it. His presence is formidable. Like he's forgotten what I'd put him through earlier. He tilts his head back, wordlessly questioning my intention.

I move forward. I don't shimmer. I just saunter casually. The fabric of my 'last-year' wraparound parts to unveil perfect, rock-hard thighs, and just a glimpse of a little more. Ashton pushes his chair back and stands up, his eyes glued to where the dress parts.

"I've been thinking," I begin.

"Yes?"

"I put you through a lot of pain earlier."

"Yes, you did. Regret it?"

"No."

"Oh."

"But I thought that, since you've experienced pain, you need to experience some pleasure. You know, to balance things out. You know what a stickler I am about having everything balanced."

I smile and touch the desk, gradually knocking files and papers to the floor.

Ashton's eyes twinkle, and his gaze travels across my body, head to foot and back again. His full lips moisten, and he moves right away from the desk and stands in front of me.

I face Ashton, not three feet away. His hair is curled against his temple and, as he moves closer, it knocks against his skin. Deep inside me, memories fire up and a heat burns, fierce.

"What about Sam?" asks Ashton cautiously.

"What about him?" I answer, and copy Ashton's head-to-toe inspection of his body with my interrogative eyes.

"Well, he is your husband."

"So?"

"He may not approve."

"Of course he won't approve. But, as I've already said, those days of searching for anybody's approval, including his, are gone. I take what I want when I want it."

"Very liberated."

"Ashton, you have no fucking idea!"

"No. But I'm getting a good feel."

"How can you? You're still three feet away."

Ashton laughs at my little joke. His eyes sparkle, playful and lusting. I can see in his eyes that he is experiencing a reality he'd never thought possible.

"Oh, Ellie, I like this new makeover."

"Yes, and there's still more to see."

Ashton smirks, and his skin flushes with anticipation. "I hoped you'd say that."

Without a second to warn, I leap on Ashton, clawing at him, my hands ripping at his back as he struggles to take off his jacket.

"Let me," I whisper, and blink hard.

"Oh my God!" exclaims Ashton.

On opening my eyes, my command to the atoms that made up the fabrics that clothed Ashton have been heeded. The British PM stands clasped to me without a stitch on. Panic and thrill explode inside him as he tries to second guess my game and comprehend just where the hell his suit is.

I step out of his arms and admire his body like he is my new toy.

He catches my wave of mischievousness. Full of exuberance and exhibitionism, he poses without a shred of shyness. His manhood stands erect and ready, and totally undeterred by the sudden and unexpected de-clothing.

I grasp Ashton's member and glare coldly into his eyes that are now hooded with a little fear.

"Do you feel comfortable right now?"

"Erm, what do you mean?" Ashton's voice falters.

"Just knowing what I could do to your little friend here."

"Well, I was hoping for one particular thing you could do." Ashton grins, trying to lighten the moment, but I continue to twist his mind.

"But how do you know? I mean, I may just decide now's the moment to disconnect it and obliterate it completely. Leaving a little mound where he once stood so proud!"

Ashton gulps, his face drained, and between my strong fingers he goes flaccid. A wilting flower.

"Or I could just stick it on your forehead. A new take on dickhead, eh?"

I laugh loudly, but Ashton sniggers nervously. He fools no one. I can see he is terrified, contemplating the impact of my implied action.

"Would make those sensitive negotiations for Freedom Earth somewhat awkward. I mean, how could you influence anyone with a prick sticking out your head? You'd be a human unicorn."

That vision I am describing blasts into my mind, and I shriek with laughter. Maybe I should do just that.

Scared eyes search for but find no further revelation. Ashton always knew I had power. Now he knows I revel in using it. I lap up Ashton's inadequate position. I can see his acknowledgement. He understands the fearsome reality that faces him. That I could destroy, in just a few seconds, everything he's spent time on building so meticulously.

"But…but… you wouldn't?" mutters Ashton, and he tries to pull my hands away.

"Wouldn't I?" I exclaim, and knock his hand down sharply, like he is a child who has touched something he shouldn't. "I could do anything. You know, the weirdest, most perverse stuff ever imagined. I could even give a completely new meaning to 'go fuck yourself'. Literally!"

Ashton shakes his head. It is an involuntary gesture. He just can't help himself.

"Please," Ashton whines, and massive dinner-plate eyes of hazel plead with me.

"I could do all that, but I'd rather do this."

I move forward, my left hand still gripping his frightened fellow, whilst my right snakes around his neck, pulling him down to me. My lips drop onto Ashton, and I push my tongue hard into his mouth, exploring and discovering.

Underneath my touch, Ashton grows like granite, and he returns my kisses with ferocious passion. My little mind-fuck exercise has worked wonders on teaching him how to behave. A great foreplay, but I've had enough of playing around.

With lips still locked frozen, I push Ashton onto the leather sofa and climb on top of him. I untie the satin cord that hangs lazily around my slim waist. The soft material slips apart, and I shrug off the dress.

Ashton's gaze is drilling and constant. I realize he's not had an opportunity to devour my body with his eyes as I had done to his. His stare eats up what he can see, my perfect, pert breasts that graze across his chest and my flat, hard stomach.

I slide back off him and stand up, poised and statuesque. He literally salivates.

I recall moments when Ashton's lascivious glances had filled me with abhorrence and disgust. Taking in the beautiful man that lounges before me, I wonder why. Probably Kudamaz conditioning, or Aby-od, or Sam, or something inside me that had blackened my vision, forced me to see their view and not my own. I was their prisoner. Held in the bars of convention. Responsibility.

Trapped.

Not anymore.

Ashton's consuming gaze brings me alive. He strokes his hardness leisurely and pats the sofa.

"I know you like to look, don't you?"

I climb back onto the sofa and slide back up his body, straddling him again.

Ashton nods and licks his lips. "I do, but I prefer to sample what's on offer."

"Well, tonight, you feast," I purr, moving upward to position Ashton beneath me. Ashton smiles and strokes my arms. I tingle and, without a word, I thrust down onto him.

"*Oh my God!*" screams Ashton, as I grasp his thighs and push him further into me.

He grabs out at my neck, pulling my face downward to his, and he kisses my lips, revealing his hunger.

I smother his mouth, biting with my teeth and prodding with my searching tongue.

Above him, I pump, piston-like, with rhythmic precision, whilst my breasts dangle in front of his face, teasing him to taste. He leaves my mouth and gorges on my rigid left nipple, sucking with savageness to such an extent that, if I were human, I'd have cried out in pain. As Kudamaz, or whatever the hell I am now, the sensation sparks a deeper want inside me. Unleashing something darker. I scream, sink my fingers into his shoulder blades, and lift him off the sofa. I fasten my mouth over his, vise-tight, and stick my tongue down his throat, choking him.

His face whitens and he struggles beneath me. Only then I realize the strength of my kiss is actually suffocating him.

I withdraw my attack on his mouth, and he breathes shallowly.

"Okay?" I ask, with a wry smirk.

My care for Ashton, however, goes as far as the fact I haven't climaxed yet. I still need to use him and don't want him to pass out until I've been satisfied.

"Just about."

As he speaks, I can feel the rush of energies. Internally, I grip Ashton with a savage clench. He shakes and screws his eyes tight shut. His mouth opens, lopsided and wordless, seeming to want to gasp. It is as if he's been stabbed, and such is the shock, he's been robbed of speech. He shudders, and carries on shuddering, and with a disturbed, tortured expression, he comes.

My inner energies clamp down on Ashton and don't release him until my own surging force has ignited and exploded my sensory system of light with that feeling of ultimate stimulation from within, taking me to blissful paradise.

Ashton slumps underneath me. The intensity of our sexual union is too much for his human frame. Unconsciousness has resulted far quicker than I'd considered.

Peeved by his abrupt fall out, especially as things were just getting interesting, I take his lackluster body in my arms and shimmer to the Burj again.

Well, it is the least I can do. Recharge him and give him some sunshine. Stock him up on some vitamin D. After all, he is going to need some energy to cope with what I have planned for him for the rest of the day.

Chapter 65

Ashton woke. Sunlight streamed in. He opened a lazy eye and scanned the room. Floor-to-ceiling windows, a massive bed covered in red satin, marble pillars, and Arabic wooden fascia's everywhere. Where the hell was he?

Ashton flicked open the other eye and sat bolt upright, taking in more of the room around him. It was suspended above another room, and a glass balcony ran around the edge, giving a frosted view of an equally exotic room below. He could hear the gentle, chugging sound of an air conditioner, which meant he was abroad, and by the aesthetic design, probably the Middle East. He rose from the bed and looked down. He was naked, and his genitals ached with deep stabbing pain inside him. It felt like his body had been ravaged in a sex marathon. Ashton perched himself on the edge of the bed, rubbed his hair, and tried to piece together what had happened. The champagne bottles on the floor indicated he'd been partying. But with who?

Movement through the frosted glass caught his attention, and slowly, he descended the spiral staircase.

"Oh, you're alive! Thought I'd screwed the life out of you."

An absolutely stunning blond woman in a gossamer, thin gown that accentuated every curve stood in front of Ashton, laughing. Her eyebrows arched as she took in his naked body, and she licked her lips.

Ashton struggled to remember. Tiny bits of recollection hit his frazzled brain from all directions.

"Ellie?" he suggested, not really sure.

"Yep! That's me. Good that you remembered."

Ashton padded onto a sumptuous, thick pile rug toward the gorgeous woman he now recognized as Ellie.

"Did we…?" enquired Ashton with much more coyness than Ellie would have given him credit for.

"Oh yeah, we did. Many, many times." Ellie smiled with salacious mischief, greatly enjoying Ashton's awkwardness, and sashayed over to the sofa. She sat down and stared at Ashton. He looked puzzled.

"But aren't you with Sam?" Ashton, exclaimed, as more memories filtered through.

"Let's say I've…" Ellie moved her legs apart slightly. "Expanded my options."

Ashton sighed, feeling lightheaded, and walked over to the bar in the corner, poured a double scotch on the rocks, and downed it in one. He turned to look at Ellie. She tilted her head, an inquisitive twinkle in her eye.

"You going to stay like that?"

Ashton shrugged. "Maybe."

Ellie lifted herself off the sofa and moved toward him, arms outstretched. Ashton stepped backward until his back was against the bar.

I look at Ashton, whose confusion and wanton desire collide.

"Where are we?" he asks.

"Dubai."

"Dubai! How the fuck did we get here?"

How the fuck indeed!

"I shimmered us here. I thought you'd like it. Thought it would rejuvenate you after our little session."

"Our little session?"

"Aw, Ashton, baby, don't you recall? Do you want a replay?"

Ashton's face screwed up in pain, and he pulled away. "No!"

"Okay, okay, darling. Only asking. I just thought, as you're wandering around like that, you were looking for round…" I stop and count on my fingers. "Ten, I believe we're up to! Knocked out on the first round, but then you came through. You've got quite an insatiable fellow, I must say." I giggle, ogling his dick.

The worried frown on Ashton's face only makes me laugh more.

"I don't remember much."

"I know you don't, babes. It's the intensity of our commune. It literally blows your mind. But you'll get used to it. It just gets better from now."

My arms encircle Ashton, and I hold him close. Ashton writhes a little under my touch. My lips land on his, and I pull him into the kiss.

"That's better. We're going to be a great partnership, you and me. The new face of Freedom Earth."

"Ellie, darling, I love doing what we do, but I am bit…sore. Could we just take a breather? Have a chat, a drink, relax. And could I have some clothes?"

I step out of our embrace and walk over to one of the wardrobes. Whilst Ashton was sleeping, I'd been shopping for some new wares. I select a cool, crisp Armani suit in cream linen and present it to Ashton. He nods his approval and dresses. I slip off my gossamer gown, pick up a short, cream and gold Missoni slinky number and show it to Ashton.

I notice that Ashton's eyes go straight to my breasts, rather than the dress I am holding up. I shoot Ashton a meaningful glance, and my eyes go upward to the bedroom. I smirk as Ashton declines my offer and turns away to sort out his disheveled appearance into something that doesn't scream bed-head.

A few minutes later, we are out in the brilliant sunshine that has enticed millions to spend their winter days basking. I sweep a long, sideways glance at Ashton and moisten my lips. The suit, the shades, his presence, the whole package, boy, he really has it.

Unsurprisingly, heads turn as we stroll into the bar.

Ashton slips into a plush, leather sofa, orders two glasses of champagne, and pulls me back into him. I can feel his heart beating, steady and strong.

"You know it's going to change. You'll answer to me."

As I say the words, with such gentility, smiling and pawing him, anyone watching could think we are whispering sweet nothings to each other. Not negotiating over the world.

Ashton's eyes narrow, and I can feel the darkness in him surface. His hand wanders down to my thigh and he squeezes a little. Not threatening. He wouldn't dare. Just a touch of sensuality, enough to make me shiver with anticipation.

"I know that, but at least I have you now."

Sorry, Ashton, I think. No one has me. But I'll let your meagre, little human mind believe that you have.

Until it's time to let you go, when I take control completely.

Chapter 66

People everywhere.

False emotions stuffed inside vehicles of dark. Xiao could feel them. Squashed against him. Their negative energies sucked him in – their wanting, their needing. All their envy and jealousy. Their deep-seated hatred of anything they didn't understand, anything that was new or different. It throbbed a low, doleful vibration in all of them. Xiao picked up on it. He could feel his blood thudding with the same vibration in his veins. His heart knocked within his ribcage, like a prisoner unjustly locked up, desperate to be free.

Xiao looked around the tube carriage. The passengers, unaware of him, continued their plotting, scheming, and exercises in evil. Their faces changed with their bodies. Xiao could see inside them. Their hearts of black, their eyes red, the whites obliterated by the raging flames of hell.

Terrified as he watched, Xiao tried to move away, but the bodies, hot, sweaty, and stale, pushed against him tightly. His heart knocked harder, the vibration ascending to his throat and into his head. His ears rushed, and then suddenly blocked, the way they did when he was on a landing plane. It was as though he was caught in a bubble. Sound had been syringed out of reality.

The mute creatures around him distended their jaws, making the mouths cavernous maws, like boa constrictors did when they were about to gorge on a small mammal. Xiao could see into those gaping holes. Those funnels that fabricated lies. Creating the notion of all being well.

Only Xiao knew it wasn't.

He shivered. The hideous monsters turned toward him. It didn't matter on age; the effect remained the same. A boy of seven or so who'd nagged his mother earlier now displayed the same distorted, hate-filled features.

Xiao stared, observing all the passengers. With the exception of a handful of people who seemed to shine internally, radiating a whiteness of heart and a soul of love, the majority of the people around him had mutated.

From their crimson orbs dripped blood. Xiao knew it was the blood of the innocent ones. Those who'd fallen by the distorted ones' hands. Their greed so defining the fate of others.

Suddenly, the creatures lurched toward Xiao.

His back against the wall of the tube train, with creatures to the left, right, and in front of him, he had nowhere to run.

Xiao thrust his arms out and screamed, "Let my light shine. You creatures of darkness. You who have changed the Equilibrium. Shifted the Balance and stolen the truth. Stay away from me. I know your evil. I know your souls are a starless night. Your lies you speak a thousand-fold, but the light will tip you, overpower you, in its ultimate oblivion, and Equilibrium will be restored again."

The creatures moved closer, reaching out to him, their mouths opening wider, spindly, skeletal fingers touching his hair, his clothes, his body.

"Stay back, Etima's acolytes. Giznu will hold the light. Stay back. I am the light, and I will burn...you...burn...you."

Xiao wheezed, catching his breath, as he yelled his promise to the carriage of creatures who now turned to stare at him.

Xiao thrust himself in the direction of the door as it opened, pushing through the sea of gaping maws and blood-filled chasms where there used to be eyes and out onto the platform.

But there was no sanctuary. The creatures infested the platform too. They grabbed at him. Pawing at his tiny frame. Xiao breathed deep, battering away the outstretched arms. The exit was in front of him. He forced down his fear, and slapped, pushed, and hit back at the cloying, spindly fingers that tried to stop his path.

"Away from me, away from Giznu's light, Etima's vehicles of dark. Spawns of deception and hate."

Xiao delivered his diatribe like a mad, evangelical minister, but could hear nothing. Only the rushing sound of blood in his ears, and that heavy knocking of his heart in his throat.

He sensed the words. He knew he was sending meaning to those dark forces.

Xiao ascended the escalator two steps at a time, but the creatures sped after him. Now breathless, Xiao pushed his frightened but determined body forward. He thrust upward and leapt onto the last step on the escalator. Too scared to look behind him, Xiao headed toward the barrier.

He slammed his Oyster card down on the reader and pelted out of Green Park Station. With the bright sunshine, Xiao hoped, like vampires, the dark creatures would sizzle into nothingness. Looking around him, the hideous creatures with abysses for mouths were literally everywhere.

Xiao stared, shocked, unsure of what to do.

Inside him, a single voice said, 'Run'.

Xiao took the heeding and ran between them, maneuvering his waif-thin frame between the creatures and their outstretched arms. He sprinted across New Piccadilly straight into the path of oncoming cars heading out to Hyde Park and in toward New Piccadilly Plaza (formerly known as Piccadilly Circus). Xiao didn't know this area very well. His home was near Marble Arch, and Bond Street had been his destination. Leaving the tube prematurely had caused uncertainty as to where his home was.

In his silent bubble, Xiao never heard the screeching of brakes and the honking of horns. He failed to hear the stream of cusses or the screams of 'that mad kid's gonna kill himself'.

The cacophony of near-misses and angry drivers was lost to Xiao who kept on running, never once looking back.

And still his heart in his throat knocked harder and harder.

Chapter 67

Sam stared out across London from his Silent Waters apartment. People living their lives. Happy and content. In ignorance. A state he hadn't had the pleasure of living in for a very long time. Intelligence, he considered, brought its own curse.

If he'd just been an average Joe, on an average wage, with an average wife and two kids, would life have been better?

If he closed his eyes, perhaps he could picture a simple existence.

Sam dropped his lids, but nothing came. Only a cold darkness. Alone and isolated.

He'd lost the one thing that mattered to him. The one thing that made his life have any meaning at all.

Ellie's love.

Sam acknowledged inside him Dumuzi's lament of his lost love Selema. Dumuzi had been the Kudamaz life force Sam melded with during reconstitution. Selema, Dumuzi's lover, was the Kudamaz life force used to create the Protector and enable reconstitution in Ellie. Both weren't sentient as another being inside of Sam or Ellie. Dumuzi's presence was more of a sensation, a knowing and an understanding. Sometimes an occurrence with Ellie had triggered a sudden flash of memories of Selema and Dumuzi, but they were almost like Sam was remembering things that had happened to him. There wasn't a demarcation line of personalities. Through reconstitution, Dumuzi's life force molded into the energy particles as Sam came together again, and the two lives became one.

What had become of Selema? Dark Ellie who'd attacked him carried a different resonance. The Protector had transmuted into something else. Sam didn't know if Selema had even survived the transformation.

So many questions.

Sam turned back from the window and caught the rug still crumpled up from the ferocious attack. He couldn't accept Ellie was gone. Whatever Aby-od said, he couldn't just leave her. That was abandoning what he loved. Giving up on her.

He couldn't do it, even if she tried to kill him, he couldn't submit to just accepting her fate. He loved her too much to let her go.

Sam focused on Downing Street, hoping that Ellie may head there to turn her dark energy on Ashton, a man whom she hated as Protector. And perhaps she held that hatred still.

In the midst of the shimmer, Sam recalled Aby-od stating Ellie's frequency state had been polarized, and her ultimate goodness had flipped to complete bad. Those she loved, she now hated, and vice versa. If this is true, thought Sam, feeling suddenly sickened, what would be the nature of her engagement with Ashton?

The shimmer brought Sam into Ashton's private office. He sighed, pleased by the emptiness of the room.

A phone rang out in the other office, but no one answered it. Sam wandered through the door to the PPS's office, but Cumberford wasn't around. Sam opened the door into the Cabinet office. No sign of Redfern either.

Sam was about to leave when the sound of voices quickly approaching the door made him halt. Cumberford stepped in with Redfern and other officials from the Cabinet office.

"Sam, hello. We weren't expecting you. Is Ellie with you? We can't seem to find the PM. He left a voicemail stating he's with Ellie discussing Freedom Earth matters but preferred to have the meeting outside of London."

Sam listened to Redfern speak, and that sickening feeling hit him again, as it did earlier.

"No. Ellie isn't with me."

Sam toned down his alarm, masking it within his usual powerful voice.

"When you see her, let her know I'd like to chat over some things with her regarding removal of the jury," said Redfern. "I know she wasn't happy about it and I just wanted to assure her all was absolutely above board." He eyed Sam. A faint smirk emerged and vanished like starburst from fireworks.

"I'll tell her," snapped Sam, annoyed and worried about Ellie and the PM's whereabouts.

Cumberford ambled into his office, and Sam followed on his heels, with Redfern behind.

"So you don't know where the PM is?" asked Sam.

"No, I don't. But since his family's assassination, we give him breathing room to do what he needs to. He always has security with him, unless he's with you or Ellie, in which case he's expressly requested that security isn't needed."

Sam nodded and turned, distracted, as Cumberford let forth a little exclamation of delight. Sam noticed Cumberford glued to his phone, as an alert had just come in. Sam watched Cumberford slyly invoke the video and lay the phone down on his desk, his eyes staring at the small screen. The volume was very low, but Sam's Kudamaz hearing detected every word. His ears instantly homed in on the words 'Etima' and 'Giznu'.

Sam didn't think; he just snatched up Cumberford's phone amidst comments of, "Hey, Dr. Noor, I was watching that!"

Redfern, rustling papers, looked up. "Something happening? Everything okay, Sam?"

Sam ignored the Cabinet secretary and reran the video, a little louder this time.

As Cumberford muttered underneath his breath, "You could have asked," Sam shot him a dark scowl, and the PPS immediately refrained from any further protests.

Sam stood staring at the screen, amazed and unsure what he was watching. The camera zoomed in on a small Chinese kid appearing to lose his marbles completely. The video carried the tags #ApeShitOnTube #CrazyChineseKid, and from the large number of viewings, over nine million and increasing, the video had gone viral. This worried Sam even more. Sam ran the video again and observed it intently, catching every nuance. The boy in the video was terrified. His voice sounded weird. Too deep and too adult. Like something had possessed him. People around the boy moved away, freaked that an adult man's voice was coming out of a small boy. Some others took their phones out and started to record the mad kid's antics.

The boy threw his arms out and screamed, "Let my light shine. You creatures of darkness. You who have changed the Equilibrium. Shifted the Balance and stolen the truth. Stay away from me. I know your evil. I know your souls are a starless night. Your lies you speak a thousand-fold, but the light will tip you, overpower you, in its ultimate oblivion, and Equilibrium will be restored again."

The boy then shook, his eyes rolled back, and he appeared to have a kind of fit. People in the carriage reached out to help him, but he yelled in the weird adult voice, now booming through the phone speakers although the volume was virtually at minimum.

"Stay back, Etima's acolytes. Giznu will hold the light. Stay back. I am the light, and I will burn...you...burn...you."

Sam listened and reran the piece of video to be absolutely sure he had heard correctly. Etima and Giznu. No mistaking those words.

"When did this alert come in?"

Cumberford shrugged, pretending to type emails, but he was annoyed that Sam was hogging the viewing of his video. "Not sure. I received the alert just a few minutes ago. That's streamed live, so it must've happened around the same time. Why?"

"Doesn't matter," barked Sam, and he turned up the volume and reloaded the video for a third time.

Cumberford sniggered, hearing the boy's strange words.

"That kid must have had magic mushrooms for his school lunch. He's a complete schizo! I mean, who the hell is Etima? Not another new bloody terrorist. And Giznu, what kind of bloody name is that? Sounds Tibetan. Maybe his Shaolin monk, all shaved heads and tambourines."

Sam wasn't listening to Cumberford's drivel. His mind was on the fact a human was talking about the Kudamaz. Ellie, in her great wisdom, always instilled in him 'everything happens for a reason and everything's connected'.

This kid, whoever this kid was, had knowledge no human on Earth should know. Sam had to locate the boy and understand how he had such secret, sacred knowledge. Sam threw the phone back onto Cumberford's desk. "Finally," exclaimed Cumberford, and Sam snorted, pushed past him, and ducked into the corridor, out of the eye of officials or cameras, and shimmered directly into the Observation Room in Kudamun.

Arriving in front of the Screen, Sam queried on the boy, using as much of the information he'd discovered as possible. The Kudamaz databanks hit Sam with an unending reel of data directly to the light circuitry that made up his brain.

Mr. Chen Chang (48), Mrs. Lei Huan Huan Chang (41), Xiao Chang (son, aged 11), 25 Berkeley Square, London, W1J 6BR, UK.

Sam shimmered to the address. Just like Ellie, he stayed one degree out of reality whilst he searched for the best, most shielded place to materialize. An alley with no cameras or people proved the best bet.

The data stream gave no indication to Sam as to why Xiao would be referencing Kudamun. His history showed him as a normal boy, a bit on the boisterous side, who enjoyed challenging authority, very confrontational, with very wealthy parents. Sam sighed. A precocious brat. Great!

Ascending the stairs, Sam felt a strange vibration, as if a floating wave had smacked into his shoulder. Instinctively, he moved back, unsure of what it was. He placed his hand ahead to ensure there wasn't any more roaming energy vibrations ready to slap into him, and assured of the path being clear, he continued to the front door and pressed the bell.

A beautiful, petite Chinese woman opened the door a few inches. Her eyes took Sam in top to toe, and she grasped the side of the door, allowing her the opportunity to push it shut if she needed to. Sam noted her calm, calculating exterior, but her eyes reflected an anguish he picked up immediately.

"Mrs. Lei Huan Huan Chang?"

Sam spoke in English rather than Cantonese, her mother tongue, in case she became scared of a stranger wandering up to her door and rattling off Cantonese to her. The woman nodded but refused to open the door any farther.

A voice from inside boomed in Cantonese, "Who's at the door?"

Sam knew the voice must be Chen. He decided against his better judgment to switch to Cantonese. Using his MI6 persona, he flashed his badge.

"Mrs. Chang, I'm from British Intelligence. We need to speak to your son urgently. We believe him to be in possession of information that could affect National Security."

Sam had barely finished as a massive mound of a man came up behind Lei. He opened the door wider, one huge hand gripping the door frame and the other placed around his wife's shoulder. His face was angry, his eyes black and bulging like charred hazelnuts, his weight pushing forward with menacing intent.

Sam treaded carefully. Chen displayed no pleasantries whatsoever, but Sam knew he was a caring man who demonstrated a natural urge to protect his wife from a doorstep stranger. Sam recognized that instinct in himself and decided on diplomacy rather than direct action being the best route for him.

"Mr. Chen Chang." Sam took out his MI6 ID badge again and flicked it up in front of Chen.

Unexpectedly, Chen snatched the card, his eyes narrowing, and he glared suspiciously at Sam. "British Intelligence? Aren't you about overseas stuff? Not usually working on domestic soil?"

Not wanting to enter into an argument regarding Five and Six demarcation lines and rules of engagement, Sam ignored the comment and stated with cold efficiency, "Mr. Chang, British Intelligence believes your son, Xiao, to be in possession of information that could have ramifications on National Security. It is vital that I speak to him now."

Sam pushed past the couple and entered into a hallway that widened and lead to a sweeping double staircase in the middle. As Sam moved, Chen stuck out his hand to try and stop him, but Chen's fingers bent upward and back suddenly. Sam tried not to, but he had to exert a minuscule amount of force to enter the house, and that small energy almost broke big Chen's sausage-thick fingers.

Chen glared, in pain and shock, and spluttered, "Get the hell out of my house!"

Sam turned around, his expression grave. "No, Mr. Chang. I cannot leave. I must see your son Xiao. He's been acting strangely, yes?"

Lei glanced at Chen, a look of resignation forming in her fragile features. Sam could see, despite Chen's machismo posturing, Lei was very much the boss. Sam pressed forward, working on Lei to gain her eventual submission.

"Xiao's not been himself, has he? He's been saying things out of keeping for a boy his age. I know all about it, Mrs. Chang, and I can help your son. Please let me talk to him, and I promise I'll help him get better."

Lei didn't move. Sam realized his words were the lifeline she needed. In her eyes was a trauma that she couldn't disguise.

Lei pulled away from her husband, and walked forward to join Sam.

"Xiao is upstairs. He won't come out of his room. He arrived a few minutes ago and he was out of breath, as if he'd run non-stop for miles, and then this…"

Lei took out her phone. Sam saw the video was loaded. He noticed her hand was shaking.

"What is this? Why is our son behaving like this?"

Lei burst into tears. Chen joined her; his eyes flickered as if a storm was about to break. He enshrouded her in his massive arms.

"You've upset my wife!"

"I'm sorry, but this is National Security. I must speak to your son."

"I'm sorry too. But I must ask you to leave. This is not a good time."

"Mr. Chang, it's vital I speak to your son."

"I don't know who you are, but you're not British Intelligence. Now get the hell out of my house before I call the real police!"

Sam couldn't make any play. If he pushed forward, he'd hurt Chen and disturb Lei. He had to leave and decide on his options.

"Mummy, who is that?"

Sam looked up to the ornate balcony above the hall. The small boy he recognized from the video stood in a t-shirt and shorts. He caught a glimpse of Sam and started to shake. His voice flipped from child to aged male adult. The timbre of his voice gave even Sam goosebumps.

"Giznu is the light. Etima is the dark. The world is a lie. We all are going to die."

Then Xiao screamed a loud, shrill pitch that deafened all around.

Lei left Sam's side and ran to her son. Chen turned around and grabbed Sam, holding him by the shoulders. Sam controlled his instincts to retaliate and did nothing to defend himself.

"Get out and don't ever return. You cannot help us," Chen yelled, his ire burning.

Wordlessly, Sam turned around and left.

As his foot passed the threshold, he heard Xiao call out to him, but in his mind.

'Save me!'

Chapter 68

I cannot sleep. I don't need to. Energy burns inside me like I have my own private sun at my core. A surging demand to dominate and obliterate those who block my path.

It's a different force to that of the Protector's. Her power was borne of requirement, soaked in protocol and doing the right thing.

My power now is borne of desire.

An unrelenting desire to fulfill what I want with no restrictions, no caveats, and no conditions.

Unconditional power to do literally anything I want.

And what do I want?

I sit on the luxurious, cream sofa while Ashton sleeps above me, and I open my hands. As a human, I'd often stared at my palms, tracing the lines with my fore finger and wondering on my destiny. Staring at my palms now, those lines and creases have vanished. My skin is a biosynthetic covering hiding my true energy form. Looking at my hand and its absence of little veins and indentions serves as a deeper reminder of what Aby-od has tricked me into sacrificing.

That pain of loss rises up, dragging a consuming darkness with which I have claimed my affinity. I enjoy its enveloping as it takes away my responsibility.

That constant need to do the right thing, say the right thing, always for someone else, but never for me.

I concentrate on the center of my palm and remember how I'd manifested La Traviata box seats. Manipulating existing molecules to create something else like the rabbit from the table, that was a power bestowed to the Protector.

Manifesting matter from nothing, effectively transferring a fraction of my own energy into the quantum field making up the universal reality to build something completely new is a power I thought was only possessed by the Ancient Ones.

My databanks tell me the Kudamaz do not have the power of absolute creation.

But, it seems, I do.

So what am I? Beyond Kudamaz? A new, improved version? Or a completely new power, as yet unknown?

If I have the power of creation, can I go farther? Can I suspend life and death? Schrodinger's cat experiment in action.

The thought tickles at my dark intrigue and I shimmer to the bedroom above. I stand at the foot of the bed. I hold my hand out, close my eyes, and focus on Ashton snoring gently on the pillow.

A low thump immediately resonates within me. Strong and firm and steady.

I target its source. Such a complex mechanism giving life.

I sway a little back and forth on the balls of my feet as the thumping flow courses through me.

I open my eyes to observe Ashton.

He stirs, suddenly agitated, but doesn't wake. His eyebrows knit together, and he touches his chest absently.

His movement enthralls me, and I focus with greater force on the thumping flow. This time, my eyes train on Ashton's upper body.

I push my hand out and move it toward Ashton's torso.

The thumping intensifies within me, and I channel the energies generated into my hovering hand. I watch the air thicken and darken. In parallel, Ashton wakes with a shudder, thrusting up from the bed cloths and grabbing his chest, his eyes wide open and startled.

We stare together as the air that has thickened and darkened takes shape. A well-known and much-needed shape.

Much needed, that is, for Ashton.

For, in my hand, beating that soft, soulful, and purposeful thump, nestles a human heart.

More precisely, Ashton's heart.

I look into Ashton's shocked eyes and smirk.

"It seems, darling, I've totally stolen your heart!"

Ashton claws at the skin still intact on his chest, frightened and confused. His face is tinged with a bluish hue, his gaze fixed, horrified, on the organ in my palm, as greasy blood slips between the gaps in my fingers. Ashton opens his mouth, gasping and trying to find the words. His lips tremble, and they wear a thin vein of murky white across them.

Finally, Ashton finds his voice. "How…am… I…"

"Alive?" I finished, smiling.

Ashton nods dumbly.

"The energies in me have created a symbiotic connection from your body and back to your heart. It is as if you are one, but in fact, you exist, in reality, as two parts."

I watch Ashton take in my explanation. As he listens, his face is still and thoughtful. I notice he doesn't shake or become hysterical, which should be any human's reaction.

The look on his face is strangely more one of fascination. An intrigue, like I have, of the human condition. The frailty of humanity. Yet I've found a way to extend it, make it more flexible.

Ashton glares at me. "You're going to put it back in, aren't you?"

I detect the cold, hard edge of Ashton's voice. Even in that position, he shows tremendous courage and stamina.

"Of course, babes. It was just a little experiment. Seeing if I could suspend life and death. Shift your body into an altered state."

"But why?" asks Ashton, and I can see worry drifting in behind his determined glare.

"To see if I could. That's all."

Ashton's face turns from bluish pink to grey, and color fades from his eyes.

"How long can you keep me in this altered state?"

Ashton's enquiring, calm tone prickles at me. In a way, I want him to be begging, screaming for me to give him back his heart. But he doesn't. His attitude seems clinical, as if he's disassociated himself with his own being, and now regards my experiment with an analytical eye.

It isn't the reaction I'd expect of a human. Perhaps it's because of his training in Six. Or maybe something else. That 'always in Equilibrium' mystery I'd never resolved. Not that I care to now. Caring about the Balance is the last thing on my mind.

I am not concerned about Ashton. I already know his role. For, as the architect, I draw it.

"So, how long?" presses Ashton, and I notice a sprinkling of irritation that I didn't answer his question immediately.

"Not long," I respond icily. "The way in which humans have been designed invests a requirement within them, a need for them to be whole. Their life force is an integration of the whole within the fabric of the universe. Changing the coherency of the quantum state in the universe creates an imbalance, and thus a fighting state ensues, which is what is happening right now."

Ashton nods. In his eyes is immediate comprehension.

"So it's your will against the will of the universe?"

For a human, he is quite exceptional. "Yes, exactly. But it's quite a battle, and you've probably got a few more minutes before the universe's will breaks through and claims you. Then you die."

"Well, you better put it back in then," states Ashton, and, unbelievably, he smirks. "This body has still got a lot of living to do yet!"

I focus on the heart thumping peacefully in my palm, and it gradually begins to fade.

With its vanishing, Ashton breathes, deep and long, and the color of pink flushes into his cheeks, and his full lips plump up as blood rushes into them.

Ashton moves forward on all fours toward me, his eyes, now strong hazel, flash darkly.

"I'm going to teach you a fucking lesson, my girl!" he growls, and grabs my waist, pulling me onto the bed.

I fall back onto the covers, laughing. I don't resist. I can't be mean, taking the upper hand as I always do. I lie back and enjoy his attentions and watch as he relishes in his second chance at life.

After all, I'd given it back to him for that one reason.

Chapter 69

I lounge on the sofa in Ashton's private office. I'd shimmered us back after my heart-stopping experiment. I realize I've probably pushed my powers, in terms of breaking those universal laws I despise, as far as I can with that last stunt.

I also want to have fun on a global scale, and as nice as sitting in the plush luxury of a top Dubai hotel is, it isn't ever going to give me the buzz I crave.

Ashton sits at his desk, catching up on correspondence and trying to hide the sneaky side looks he keeps giving me. Although I'd dragged Ashton through all kinds of mind-bending shit and essentially fucked his brains out over the past forty-eight hours, he appears to be happier and more lascivious than ever. It's like our liaisons charge him up. Instead of making him afraid, he laps up every experience, wallowing in the dark perversities I put him through. The flash of naughtiness in his eyes and the faint lick of his lips signaling his need to place those lips somewhere upon my body describes a passion that only grows in strength and intensity with every salacious second that passes.

"That's odd."

I look up, hearing the sudden concern in Ashton's voice. "What's wrong?"

"My media channel isn't loading."

I swing my legs down from the sofa and sashay my way to Ashton's side. "Fuck!"

I stare at the screen, immediately discerning what had caused the PM's expletive. A group of dissidents calling themselves SAFE – Society Against Freedom Earth – have hijacked Ashton's own media channel and posted subversive material branding Ashton as a new dictator responsible for bringing back state-sanctioned genocide through the mass executions of all those AI

Nadir acolytes who had previously been slum dwellers.

As I watch, a video invokes depicting Ashton as a bloodthirsty wolf ripping off people's heads, including those of his dead family.

Ashton grips the desk so hard his knuckles whiten.

"Fuckers!" he hisses.

Anger, I can see, flares within him. I touch his shoulder and he twitches, jerking away. His hands leave the desk, he picks up the screen, which still displays his head on top of a wolf killing people, wrenches it up from the desk, and throws it with a snarl against the wall. On impact, the screen sparks and flashes to black.

"I'm not standing for this shit! Those fuckers will be put down as terrorists and traitors."

I slip my arms around Ashton's neck and pull him to me.

"Of course, babes," I whisper, placating him with my gentle tone.

"This is the first inkling of dissension and I'll not let it fester. Freedom Earth is the new way and anyone not agreeing can welcome oblivion. I'll wipe out the lot of those sick fucking bastards!"

"Babes, I think the world needs to see who you have behind you."

I can see the hurt in Ashton's face. Involving Ashton's dead family has crossed the lines of decency. Whatever their politics, no one will support such sick antics. In the UK, the populace has been horrified by the triple assassination, and has made a special place in their hearts for Ashton.

I SearchSight people talking about SAFE. The majority are appalled by their behavior against the PM. Then I single out a group talking in an ultra-modern office, laughing about Ashton. In their jesting, they suggest putting Ashton's head on a ram and show it shagging 'that Perkins woman'. The young hackers joke, their hands working quickly to create new revolting graphics.

"He's such a tosser! Thinks he's some kind of chosen one, setting a new path for mankind. He's a whacko. We should run a campaign of no confidence, suggesting that turd is incompetent, reckless, and unfit for office."

I watch the SearchSighted individuals laugh at Ashton's expense. I count ten in the office, and one who mainly makes coffee and hangs around the water cooler.

Humans, apart from Ashton, mean little to me, and these loathsome insects mean even less. I recall, as a human, stamping on ants and crushing flies and other bugs that annoyed me. These hacker low-lifes have pissed me off and incensed a man who I enjoy being with, and who gives me enormous pleasure.

I stroke Ashton's cheek and shift myself up onto the desk.

"Ashton, darling, it's time for us to have another celebration event for Freedom Earth. We're gonna show what happens to those who incite treason and turn against you. Today, we are going to Wembley Stadium and all will be revealed. And believe me, babes, after that, no one on Earth will dare stand against you. And those fuckers, I'll eviscerate them. I'll give them a death that will stay emblazoned on the psyche of the world. Everyone will bow down to you and me. They will not take your name or mine in vain. For they will know I am watching, and I will act. I will crush them with their own bones. I'll turn their organs on them. Their bodies will be their killers. Their blood, a poison to an agonizing death. Even their tear glands, when they cry in pain, will be acid, so their sight be burned from them. And I will do all this for you, Ashton, because you are the only way for this pathetic world. The strength you have shown, I stand in awe of you. I will be by your side throughout this time and forever more!"

As I say the words, I realize I really mean them. I've consistently put Ashton through a hellish ordeal, and he hasn't flinched. Now he is deserving of my full support.

Ashton pulls me over to him. I slide sideways across the desk, knocking the keyboard to the floor with other files and papers until my body is opposite him, still on the chair.

He moves forward, grabbing my neck, and places his lips tight on mine. I respond, kissing him ferociously, with a totally unabashed passion. His hands leave my neck and wander down to my shoulders. I still have the cream and gold crochet Missoni number, and Ashton tugs at the halter-neck tie, letting the material fall away. The front of my dress slips down, and Ashton eases its path with a hefty tug, giving freedom to my bouncy breasts. I sigh, satisfied as his lips fasten onto my right nipple, sucking hard, his teeth nipping around my skin.

I lie back on the desk.

I don't hear the door open. Even if I had, I wouldn't have given a damn. I choose what I want. I choose the life I lead.

No one charts an invisible destiny for me anymore. My future, I create myself.

Ashton suddenly tenses on top of me, and I notice his eyebrows rise as he issues a sardonic smile.

"Hello, Sam. How are you?"

I pull my top back up and tie the halter neck behind me. Gently, I slip off the desk and drape myself against Ashton.

Sam stares at me, holding his composure and compartmentalizing emotions. I glare at him, unashamed and defiant.

I haven't seen him since our last 'liaison'.

He looks from me to Ashton. I cast a sideways glance at Ashton, who instinctively refrains from touching me in Sam's presence.

I can see Sam try to hide the build-up of sorrow inside him, but his eyes reflect a despondency. A sad acknowledgment of the facts before him.

His shoulders slump and, as I look between the two men, Ashton realizes the flowing dynamics of change. He slips his arm confidently around my waist and pulls me closer.

I look at Sam with expectancy, willing him to challenge, to step up to Ashton and snatch his woman back. If he shows the brutal force, a sense of the real savagery I'd seen in those viewings in the Observation Room, I might return to him. Even though he betrayed me, lied to me, allowed others to abuse, torture, and destroy me, I may return back to him. If only he will reveal his dark side. That side giving him the edge I love. Maybe Dumuzi's life force has watered down the ferocity he'd carried within him. That wonderful intensity to deliver intolerable agony to others. If he demonstrates that capability and attacks Ashton, here and now, I'll give myself back to him. For I will know his darkness and be assured of his path with me. Together, we can rule over these squabbling, needy parasites called humans.

But Sam does nothing.

He just continues to stare at me. His unblinking eyes drill into me, asking why. He can ask telepathically, but both channels, mouth and mind, remain silent.

My only conjecture to his response is his psyche is so disturbed, his reactionary faculties have been suspended, and what confidence he'd possessed has been stolen from him.

His body droops, his mouth scowls, and his eyes deaden, as if the light that had been illuminated within them for more than six millennia has now been forcibly extinguished.

Originating from his admission of my rejection, and from every angle, implosion within Sam has started.

He cannot turn his face away. Like a teenager watching a banned NC-17 film, his sight stays glued. Although his laser stare targets me, his heat seeking missile has lost its payload.

Defenseless.

A toothless tiger unwilling to fight. Completely broken by the vision before him. I can feel the moment has sucked everything out of Sam.

He is now a vacuum, empty and ice-cold.

I notice his body quavers. As I observe, his great strength appears to crumble. His knees weaken. Barely able to withstand his own weight, I witness it is an effort for Sam to remain upright.

His shattering pain is obvious, but I can see in his eyes a desperate need to remain immutable to the situation. Torment inevitably inveigles its way in, and tears well up in his dark, doleful eyes.

I watch impassively as they pool around the ridges of his eyes and drip down his face, sparkling to nothingness, as our Kudamaz tears, just like our blood, always does.

I find myself drawing dark power from his agony. I smile, knowing this, and brush my fingers deftly down Ashton's cheek. He grasps my fingers, brings them to his lips, and kisses them. Throughout this gesture, Ashton's eyes never leave Sam's. At the sides of his mouth, a group of tightening wrinkles turn into one of Ashton's customary sexy smirks.

"Is there something you want?"

I look in Sam's direction for his response and lurch closer to Ashton, slipping softly into his lap. My arms fold around his neck. I swing my leg over his and turn back to Sam, sneering.

His sparkling tears take over his face, making his cheeks iridescent. He trembles and shakes his head.

"There…is…nothing…I want…anymore!" whispers Sam, his voice breaking.

Without further indication, Sam shimmers out of view.

"Well, there's something I certainly want!" growls Ashton, thrusting me down on the desk.

My arms fall back behind me and I close my eyes. I feel Ashton's hands skim across my thighs as he raises my dress higher.

And I luxuriate in his vicious domination.

Chapter 70

Sam arrived in Kudamun in his private quarters he used to share with Ellie. He stared at the huge bed and his body wouldn't stop shaking. Their bodies entwined like vines, symbiotic and connected. He remembered the moments so well. The love they'd made was embedded into the crystals around him. He could feel Ellie, smell her vanilla-scented musk, her glorious body against him. Her lips against his. Eyes only for him.

He couldn't imagine life without her.

Their lives had been created for them together.

Before entering Ashton's office, Sam knew what he'd see. The polarity flipping within her.

Loving the dark. Hating the light.

That sickening feeling within him. A prescient flicker of what would befall him in front of his eyes. He pushed it all back. Away from him. He couldn't allow himself to wallow in the seeping sorrow that filled his body like an unseen virus.

His first thought had to be with Xiao. The boy's weird behavior and Ellie's transformation were undoubtedly connected. Focus on Xiao and he'd find a way to return Ellie to the wondrous woman he loved.

Sam started to call out to Aby-od. However, the Kudamaz leader had already homed in on Sam's need and shimmered into the room.

Aby-od stared at him and Sam, from the sadness reflected in Aby-od's ebony eyes, knew his pain was visible.

"Sam, are you okay?"

"Yes, I am!" answered Sam with cutting abruptness. "I have a situation with a human."

"A situation?"

"With a human called Xiao. He's been talking about Giznu and Etima, referencing the Shift, Equilibrium, stuff about the light, dark, and the Balance."

Aby-od's face hardened with concern. "Who is this man?"

"It's not a man, it's a young boy, no more than eleven. His voice becomes adult when he talks about the Kudamaz things. Can you explain it?"

Aby-od shook his head. "I've never heard of such an occurrence before. Where is this boy?"

"London, with his parents who believe he's possessed with a spirit."

"The boy is not possessed with a spirit, but certainly the boy has come into contact with a Kudamaz force. Has he always been like this or did it happen recently?"

"No idea," answered Sam, annoyed that he couldn't get anything out of the Changs. "Do you think the Observation Room will show anything?"

"Everything is recorded. It must," stated Aby-od, with amazement that Sam would think otherwise.

Sam and Aby-od entered the Observation Room.

"Query: Xiao Chang, eleven, Berkeley Square, London, UK, Earth," requested Sam, and the Screen in the room flashed up images across Xiao's short life.

Aby-od watched Xiao have fun in Sharm El Sheikh, and his face drained. "Oh no!"

Sam flipped around, zooming in on Aby-od's trepidation. "What is it?"

"Sharm El Sheikh. It's where the white crystal power block is housed containing the white light energy of Earth."

"But, Aby-od, it's hidden by a Dimension Lapse Field, isn't it?"

"It is. But…"

"But what, Aby-od? No human can access the block," questioned Sam, watching Xiao splashing in the water. The POV of the Observation Room playback switched to Xiao staring at his mother, Lei, on a lounger. Love was in her eyes.

As Sam looked at the Screen, an infinitesimal judder appeared, and Xiao was suddenly stepping out of the water. The POV switched again to Lei watching Xiao emerge from the sea. His body seemed to be completely dry.

"Did you see that?" asked Sam.

"Sorry, what was it?"

"It seemed like a vibrational judder. Surely you saw it?" said Sam, a little exasperated by Aby-od's lack of surveillance.

"I didn't. Play it back."

Sam invoked the Observation Screen playback and pointed out the area where Xiao emerged from the sea, and when the vibrational shudder had caught his attention.

"There it is. Do you see it?"

Aby-od gazed intently at where Sam pointed. "Yes, I do see it."

Sam listened to Aby-od's slow drawl as he grasped the facts. Sam knew he still retained Six's training. His Kudamaz abilities enabled him to be lightning-quick at surveillance. Sam realized Aby-od didn't have that ability. However, it didn't alter the fact that he seemed to have a constant failure to recognize the truth when it was in front of him. That lack of opening his eyes, of everything being by the book and hiding behind antediluvian laws, grated on Sam. He recalled the total mess Aby-od made of Ellie's reconstitution. Giving her that bloody bracelet, providing a route in for someone to manipulate and change her. That someone, Sam concluded, could well be Aswa-da. He didn't believe the bastard was dead for a minute. Sam thought about what had happened. How that person, whoever they were, corrupted his Ellie. Ripped her love of him away.

Changed his love.

Her sneering face, full of defiance as she sat in Ashton's lap, as he lay on top of her, her body responding to his lips, his touch.

Sam shivered. He had to stop this recall. He couldn't keep torturing himself. His Ellie was gone.

"I'm sorry, Sam," ventured Aby-od.

Sam snarled unexpectedly, losing himself, venting the pent-up pain, "I'm fucked off with your incompetence! If you hadn't have given her that bloody bracelet, this would never have happened."

Aby-od kept his eyes to the ground. His shoulders gently shook, and Sam recognized that Kudamun's leader was wracked with guilt. "Yes, Sam. Again, you're right. As you say, I made a misjudgment."

Sam quelled his fury. "That kid Xiao's been possessed by a Kudamaz energy. We need to return back to him and find out what it is and how it connects to Ellie's transformation."

Aby-od looked surprised. "How do we really know it does connect to Ellie at all?"

Sam heard Aby-od. But then he tried to unhear the words.

Connection. It was his lifeline. If these two occurrences were isolated, discrete situations with no influence on the other, he truly was lost.

"Aby-od, they have to be connected."

"Not necessarily," answered Aby-od unthinkingly. "We have no proof of their connection."

Sam's anger rose again. "What is wrong with you, Aby-od? Are you some kind of fucking idiot! I'm here trying to grab at something to believe that I can get Ellie back, and you throw it in my face. I love her and I want her. Do you understand what it feels like seeing her with Ashton, watching her in his arms? A man just a day ago she physically abhorred. I feel like I'm dying. But, somehow, I have to carry on. I have to save her. I just can't believe, after all we've gone through, this is our destiny."

Aby-od pushed his hand out to hold onto Sam. A gentle, comforting hand encircled Sam's arm. "I'm an old fool, Sam. I've been in Kudamun too long. Not gone planet-side for a very long time. My emotional frameworks are poor. I'm emotionally barren. Ellie has been the only person in at least a millennium who brought out any emotion out in me. The Kudamaz are supposed to be almost devoid of the ability to show emotions. But I know you're different, you're hurting about her. I don't understand why this happened and, Sam, I'm truly sorry for any contributing part I unsuspectingly played in it."

"I think it's Aswa-da!"

Aby-od shook his head. "It can't be. He's dead."

"He's missing. He's only *presumed* dead. But how do we know? Have you bothered to check up on anything?"

Sam slipped into attack mode on Aby-od, and the leader just took it. Sam could feel a momentum inside him building, taking him forward. Ellie, his gorgeous, beautiful wife belonged to another. And she enjoyed how that fact made him suffer.

Maybe this was indeed his future. Maybe this was his punishment for all the people he'd killed as a human.

He'd been saved only to endure this living hell.

"We'll get her back. She's not lost to you. A love like the one you have with Ellie has withstood the passing of time. She saved you through love, and love will save her. You just have to believe, Sam."

"You know, you sound like her. Just believe. Have faith. Well, Aby-od, they're just words. If you saw her. The way she hates me. Tell me how she is going to come back from that!"

"Sam, she will. Somehow, you'll find a way to save her."

Sam looked away from Aby-od, suddenly infuriated with himself by his lack of action against Ashton.

"Perhaps I should just go back and rip Ashton's head off. That may bring her back to me!"

Horror rippled across Aby-od's face as he knew Sam wasn't just speaking idle words. "Sam, you couldn't do that."

"Why not? I've done similar when I was a human. And now I'm Kudamaz, his head would tear away just like tearing off a piece of garlic bread. And for what that bastard has done, he deserves it."

Aby-od saw the eager bloodlust in Sam's eyes. "No, Sam. Violence is not the way. You may think you'd win back Ellie, but it would be dark Ellie who would return to you. Not your Ellie. The Ellie that you truly love. We must find out why things are happening the way they are."

"Xiao's the key."

"He could be. Will his parents speak to you?"

Sam glared with concrete determination. "They're not going to be given a choice. If their son holds the key to getting back my Ellie, they're going to have to listen to me. Even if I have to tie them up and force them to tell me. I'm not leaving again with questions unanswered."

Sam started to invoke a shimmer. Sensing his quantum self at Berkley Square in London, he connected his soul force with it. Just before the full shimmer took his energies hurtling through the Reality Gap, Aby-od called out, "It may be worthwhile if I joined you."

Sam halted his shimmer and looked, amazed, at Aby-od. "Seeing you might just tip them over the edge. We have to be sensible and gentle in our dealings with them."

"Of course," remarked Aby-od, and he produced a small prism encased in a silvery metal that appeared to move like liquid mercury. Aby-od ran the device across his body, and the leader of Kudamun started to shrink. His distinctive corrugated beard and jet-black, silky ringlets vanished, as did his incredibly muscular frame. His robes were replaced with jeans, a t-shirt, and sneakers.

Sam did a doubletake and Aby-od grinned.

"There. Aren't I much more presentable to the Changs?"

"You are, but I think Xiao will know who you are. He knew I was Kudamaz, and even if you're disguised, Xiao will see through you. I don't know how Xiao will react to you. I really think it's better if it's just me."

Aby-od turned his mouth downward, exhibiting displeasure. "I really thought I could help."

Aby-od fluttered his hand down his body, holding the metallic prism device, and his appearance reverted back to that of the Kudamaz.

Sam, relieved, tapped Aby-od's arm. "Don't take it personally. I'm just trying to control the number of possible outcomes. His parents see me as some kind of government agent, and although they may not like me, they're not going to screw around with the government. I believe I'm part way through convincing Lei, Xiao's mother, that I can help him. Chen is a much more difficult nut to crack, but Lei has great influence on her husband. If she's on board and is absolute in her conviction that I can definitely help Xiao, I'll be able to flip him easily."

"I understand." Aby-od's acceptance belied the sadness he harbored over Sam's rejection of his contribution. "But if you need me…"

Sam nodded, acknowledging Aby-od's worth in his forthcoming engagement with the family Chang. "Of course. I won't hold back in getting you over if I feel things are heading southwards."

A few Earth seconds later, Sam stood, once again, on the steps of the Chang's residence. He rang the doorbell and waited. Sam knew he'd be faced with opposition by Chen, but he still felt Lei was his in-road to Xiao.

"I told you before, I'm not talking to you, and neither is my wife or son. So fuck off, and don't grace my steps with your presence again."

Chen's tirade commenced the moment he opened the door. Sam flashed up his MI6 card, but as Chen attempted to knock it out of his hand, Sam thought 'What the hell!' and broke his own cardinal rule in revealing who he was. He shimmered directly in front of Chen's amazed and suddenly terrified cycs.

Materializing alongside a cherrywood hallway table replete with inlaid marble cranes, Sam announced that he'd had enough, and it was time for the Changs to face facts.

"Chen, Lei, your son, Xiao, has a power inside of him. It seems like he may have encountered the power in Sharm El Sheikh."

Chen snatched up his umbrella from the hall stand and gripped it in the air, swishing it back and forth like a rapier.

"What the hell are you?" roared Chen, his eyes bulging.

Sam turned calmly. It had been a calculated bet to shimmer. It held risks, but Sam knew Lei had to be brought on board quickly. Sam detected in Lei a spiritual person, but more than that, she'd physically witnessed Xiao's moments of transformation, his emergence from the sea completely dry. Although Sam appreciated that she'd probably relegated it to being just a dream, his own reassertion of that scene would awaken a willingness in her to give him a higher level of trust.

"Chen, Lei, I'm not here to harm you. Please put that umbrella down. I know how to fix your boy, Xiao, but you must let me speak to him. If you don't, he will never recover."

Sam aimed his last words at Lei. His stare bore deep into her confused and frightened eyes.

"You want your son to be normal, don't you?"

Lei's small, auburn head moved virtually imperceptibly up and down, too nervous to move even a fraction more. Sam swung a sidelong glance at Chen, who threw down his umbrella.

Sam detected the hope that had been caught within Chen's heart and that he failed to hide by his gruff "Yes".

"Get your son, let me talk to him, and I promise you, all will be well with him once again."

Lei ascended the stairs to fetch Xiao from his bedroom, whilst Chen cast a surly, analyzing eye over Sam.

He finally spoke. "Please get my son back. Along with Lei, Xiao is all I love and all I care about in this wicked, fractured world."

Sam placed his hand out to Chen in a token of solidarity. Chen took it and grasped it tight.

"I *will* bring him back to you."

Chen's glimmer of a smile was the only signal of gratitude to Sam. But with that smile came the trust Sam sought to ensure his mission was a success.

Chapter 71

Sam sat on the sofa Chen pointed to after showing him into the ornate ivory and silver drawing room. Sam looked around him. The house exhibited the typical Georgian grandiosity he'd expect. A high coved and elaborately decorated ceiling, large bayed windows with stained glass in the top depicting birds and flowers, and bright and airy living spaces.

Chen seated himself opposite and stared at Sam. His eyebrows pinched together as he studied him. Sam knew Chen still regarded him with cagey acceptance. As he watched the Chinese millionaire, Sam noticed that Chen moved his buttocks around on the cushion, obviously trying to find his favorite groove.

As Sam watched, mildly amused by Chen's movements, it all came back, human Ellie's joke about him 'rearranging his balls when he sat in the car seat'.

Ellie. Would he ever get her back?

Tears surfaced inside him, and he could sense his eyes turning watery. He looked to the side, toward the door, like he'd heard something, and hoped Chen hadn't seen.

But Chen had.

"Dr. Noor, do you really work for MI6?"

Sam breathed deeply and concentrated on pulling back the water filling his eyes.

"Erm, well, I used to," said Sam, not making eye contact with Chen and preferring to keep his sight centered on the door.

"But you're not now?" persisted Chen.

"I sort of am," answered Sam, concentrating still on using his energies to sparkle away the tears before he faced Chen.

"Sort of? That's a bit ambiguous for a government agent. So, Dr. Noor-"

"Call me Sam."

"Alright, Sam, is it usual for MI6 agents to be trained to teleport?" Chen's quizzical expression and the slight upturn of his mouth into the merest glimmer of a grin told Sam that Chen didn't believe a word he'd told him previously.

Sam stared at the floor with a wry smirk and shrugged, as he resigned himself to tell Chen the truth. "I'm here to help your son. He unintentionally absorbed a Kudamaz force when he was in Egypt."

Chen examined him, his glare interrogative, taking him in, piece by piece. Then he sneered, realization dawning.

"You're Ku...da...maz, aren't you?" Chen peered at Sam, like he was inspecting a newly discovered insect. It made Sam feel deeply uncomfortable, "That's why you can do that weird vanishing act. You're not human. You're an alien. Are you here to invade? Did my son interrupt your plans? Are you here really to help him, or hurt him?"

Suddenly, Chen rose off the chair, and stood in front of Sam, his eyes glared, a dangerous fire of fury burned within. He reached out to grab Sam's shoulder, but Sam flipped to the side and held his hand up against Chen, holding back on exerting any of his powerful Kudamaz force.

"Chen, I can't tell you anymore than I'm allowed to. But I'm definitely *not* here to cause anyone harm, and I'm *not* here to invade Earth. I'm here, like I said before, to help your son."

Chen's anger and intrigue halted abruptly as Xiao entered the drawing room on the arm of his mother. Sam smiled at the young boy, and Xiao made a beeline directly to him and sat next to Sam on the sofa. He looked up at Sam and beamed a full, innocent smile. Sam summoned up a grin and ruffled the little boy's fluffy, dark hair. Sam noticed the boy was much calmer than before.

Lei seated herself beside her husband who'd sat the moment Xiao came in. Apprehension still showed in her face. Sam smiled, sending a signal of comfort, and Lei held Sam's gaze. In her eyes, Sam could see she finally dared to believe he could save Xiao.

"Right, well, shall we find out what Xiao knows?"

"I am here, you know, not a figment of your imaginations," piped up Xiao, looking indignantly between Sam and Lei. His reaction brought a smile to Lei's trembling lips. Quite a precocious little kid, thought Sam.

"Of course, Xiao. My apologies."

Xiao settled forward and held onto Sam's thigh. Xiao turned toward Sam but did not speak. His grip around Sam's thigh tightened, and his eyes closed. As Xiao's lids dropped, Sam heard a deep harmonic. A vibrating, almost sentient sound. The sensation absorbed him. Within his own energies, he could sense the vibration. As he sensed it, the vibrational pattern changed. Sam focused his energies, attempting to align and connect with the vibrational frequency. At the point of matching the pattern, Sam's internal energies surged as a massive force pelted violently through him.

"Dr. Sam Noor and Honorable Elder Dumuzi, I have been everywhere, across time, across space. I touch the lives of many. Embody their passions. Their loves. Their joys. The wonders of their being. I am there, always and forever."

Sam could feel the words buried within the energy surge. It was telepathic transference, but it wasn't the same method he'd shared with Ellie. This communication was primal, dominant. A force stronger than anything he'd encountered in Kudamun.

"Who are you?" questioned Sam, struggling to keep his energies aligned with the incredible force that had touched him.

"I am the Light of Ki, the one that is forever, and I…"

Sam sensed the Light increasing its vibrational energy, and Sam knew he'd lose the connection if he couldn't keep the alignment stable. With one last ditch effort, Sam pushed his energies forward and felt them align in perfect balance with the Light. The words oscillated through him.

"…am held within this Earth boy."

Sam was pulled into the vehement fury of the words from the Light of Ki. Anger rose inside the Light and, as it tried to explain what had happened, the words lost their clarity and white noise vibrated through Sam. The Light's energy lines fluctuated wildly and to such an extent that they caused Sam immediate, ripping pain. It was a strange, shredding sensation, synonymous with the tearing within his cells he'd felt when, as a human, he'd been hit by Aswa-da's Harmon wave.

Sam's soul force held on. The tremendous power tore into him in a bid to just connect.

From Lei and Chen's perspective, Sam was sure they couldn't see nor hear anything of the raging war of energies. Their only observation would be that their child had held a strange man's thigh and closed his eyes.

Internally, Sam fought to maintain the connection, but it was already too devastating to his Kudamaz structure. He could sense his own energies were being cleaved in two just by making the alignment. Sam wondered how Xiao, just a human, and a young child at that, could withstand such an intense, ferocious force within such a small, fragile frame.

Xiao loosened his grip and opened his eyes. He let his mouth fall open and his jaw extended downward like he was awaiting a dentist's examination.

A low hum emerged from Xiao's mouth. Lei stared, aghast, and made to go to her son. Chen glared at Sam, enraged that he'd caused some new affliction rather than making his son well.

Within the hum, a deep, sonorous voice filled the room.

"I have to rest now. Mother, Father, Dr. Sam Noor, and Honorable Elder Dumuzi, we will meet soon. But this life force is weak and must rest. It must not extinguish before the work is done."

Suddenly, Xiao collapsed back onto Sam. His body shuddered, and his eyelids flickered. It appeared to be a seizure, but from his Kudamaz databanks, Sam recognized it as a reassignment of consciousness. The Light of Ki had somehow put Xiao into a higher-level of consciousness, enabling it to align using universal energy states that could then flow through Xiao. Taking this step had so far stopped corporeal breakdown, but Sam, like the Light, sensed that Xiao's fragility wouldn't last long if such communion continued.

Lei leapt up to her son's aid, and Chen grabbed hold of Sam's arm.

"What have you done to my boy?" he growled.

Sam shook away Chen's touch. "I have not harmed your boy. He is in a protective higher consciousness state for his own good. He will be released from this when the force inside Xiao feels it is safe to do so."

"Released? That doesn't sound like a benign force." Lei slipped the words sharply out of her mouth, staring hard at Sam. "It sounds evil."

"Believe me, Lei, that's the farthest from the truth. Your boy has light within him. Pure goodness, pure love, but this is very, very powerful, and the light has to protect him. And I have to protect him too. That light is very precious to the future of mankind."

Lei and Chen were dumbstruck. Lei, a high society Chinese debutante, and Chen, a millionaire fashion king, did not know how to deal with the information Sam imparted.

"What do we do?" Lei asked ahead of her husband, who appeared to want to say the same but couldn't find his voice.

"Trust me," whispered Sam, wrapping Xiao tightly in his arms, as he invoked a shimmer to Kudamun.

Chapter 72

Around Sam, the crystal walls of Kudamun slipped into view as he shimmered into his quarters.

"Aby-od," Sam called in his mind, and the air wavered instantly.

Aby-od appeared and stared at Xiao in Sam's arms. "Is this the boy you spoke of? The one who mentioned Giznu, Etima, and Balance Shift?"

Sam nodded.

"Place him on the sofa. Let me examine him."

Aby-od's hand lightly passed over Xiao, and suddenly the young boy's eyes flicked open and he screamed.

"Oh fuck!" said Sam. "The transference between the universal plane and the Reality Gap must have triggered an expulsion out from the higher state of consciousness plane the Light of Ki had placed him in."

Aby-od stepped back, horrified. "Sam, did you say the Light of Ki?"

"Yeah, sorry. Things have gone on so fast. The Light of Ki has been somehow pushed out of its place in the white crystal and is residing within Xiao. But it doesn't think the boy will last long despite its measures to control the energy within his fragile frame."

Aby-od sat down heavily, his eyes scared and fearful. "This…this is impossible," began Aby-od. "As Leader of Kudamun, for as long as I remember, this has never happened."

"Well, it's sure as hell happening now, Aby-od, and we've got to find a way to help Xiao."

Sam tried to soothe the boy, but his eyes were still terror-struck. His tiny lips yelped with pain and confusion. Sam brought his hand up to Xiao's forehead and lightly touched his brow, as it furrowed in fear.

Aby-od stayed motionless. Sam realized he was thinking deeply. Then

Aby-od stood up and walked to a light blue panel embedded into the side of the crystal wall in his hallway. Sam watched as Kudamun's leader moved his hand in front of the panel and in front of Sam a holographic visual of the Earth popped up. Inside the Earth bobbed two crystal blocks. The dark crystal was positioned off the coast of Mexico and the light crystal in the waters off Sharm El-Sheikh. Both showed energy connections directly back into the Balance Shift counter. The white light crystal showed a point of strength bobbing above the Equilibrium. The Equilibrium was a line that decreed native behaviors on a planet were meeting acceptable universal rules, therefore not too dark and not too light, but balanced and supportive of the development of the planet in question.

Sam stared at the visual with Aby-od.

"The Light of Ki is still connected to the Balance Shift counter. You can see the white light crystal is still in situ."

Sam shook his head. "But it told me," he said, confused.

"How do you know the energy you spoke to really is the Light of Ki and not some wandering interdimensional malevolent force trying to gain access to Kudamun?"

"Has that happened before?" snapped Sam.

"No, never. But there's always a first time."

Sam felt annoyed, as if he'd been played. It wasn't the first time in his life. But he thought now, as Kudamaz, those days were over.

"It told me what it was," spat Sam, his anger rising. "I communicated with it directly, but it damn near ripped me apart just to connect."

"Sam, that doesn't sound like the actions of a benevolent force."

Sam looked away. Aby-od seemed to know more about the white crystal energy and it spiked him. He was always the one who had the knowledge. His finger on the intelligence at all times. He felt he was on the back foot trying to catch up. Just like when Ellie had mocked him about travelling in a flying saucer after she'd been reconstituted in that cavern in Ur, Iraq.

It all flooded back to him. His inadequacies. His vulnerabilities.

Had he really read Xiao wrong? Was the force that said it was the Light of Ki lying to him? Could it be Aswa-da in a different form? Was he a pawn in the dark lord's machinations?

Again!

"Sam, I know you think you connected with the Light of Ki, but if you did, why is the energy still pouring out of the light crystal in Sharm El-Sheikh?"

Sam didn't have an answer. He stared at the hologram of Earth and the light crystal bobbing gently. He could see the energy flows coming out of the light crystal. Everything told him what he thought he knew couldn't be true.

"Why did it say it had been evicted from its place? Why was Xiao in Sharm El-Sheikh when all this happened? Why doesn't it just kill Xiao and take over his body? Why is it trying to keep Xiao alive? Why did I feel its pain in being pushed out of the crystal when I connected with it? Nothing makes sense. Help me, Aby-od. What do we have here?"

Sam couldn't stop asking questions as he realized his mind was going into overdrive.

Aby-od shook his head with solemn sadness. "I don't have answers to any of these questions. I really don't know what's going on."

"You know, Ellie…"

Aby-od's eyes flickered with pity. Sam swallowed, delivering a daggering stare back to Aby-od that screamed, 'I don't need your pity'.

"Yes," said Aby-od, dialing down the consolation in his eyes.

"Well, she always said, 'Everything's connected'. If there's one thing I still believe, it's that. This kid and Ellie's transformation are connected. I've got to do what I've always done. Play this thing out. Wait and see where it goes, gather intelligence, and find a way to bring my Ellie back."

A sorrowful moan from Xiao cut through their talk, making both Kudamaz Elders stare at him. The moan then mutated into a deep, sonorous vibration, and Xiao's jaw slackened, and his mouth dropped open wide.

"Take me away from here. My presence is dangerous to Kudamun. You must return me back to Ki."

"Who are you?" said Aby-od forcefully, his eyes flashing darkly.

"I…am…Light of Ki…Get me out of Kudamun!" responded the Light of Ki, ignoring the opportunity for discourse with the Leader of Kudamun.

"But how? We can see your white light energy connected to the Balance Shift counter. How can you be the Light of Ki? Explain!"

Aby-od pressed hard, but Xiao's body couldn't take the engagement. Xiao shook, and his eyes rolled back as a vicious seizure took over his fragile body.

Sam held him.

"Aby-od, his vital signs are dropping like a stone. Something isn't right. I know you want answers, but this kid isn't going to make it if you keep him here any longer."

"But, Sam, I need to understand. I need to know what is going on. And I need to tell the High Council about this."

Sam knew Aby-od was in shock and wasn't thinking properly. "That's the last thing you should do. All that's happened, and still is happening, is being done by some person or persons in Kudamun. Until we know more, you stay silent."

Sam's stern, dark eyes drilled into Aby-od. The leader nodded, realizing his previous knee-jerk reaction had been foolhardy.

"I'm taking the boy away."

"Where will you take him?" asked Aby-od, reluctantly conceding that Sam's judgement to remove Xiao fast was the best option for the boy, despite the fact he wanted to discover who was behind the Light of Ki's eviction, if indeed it really was an eviction.

"Back to his parents. You need to check and analyze your knowledge banks. Check the light flows from the crystal. Delve into past planet files. Find out if anything like this has happened before. Develop scenarios and possible activities that may have triggered this. Whatever this is. For instance, could the Therab be a catalyst in some way? Fuck, Aby-od, you know what to do, I'm not telling you your job. Just find answers, and I'll work on finding mine. Together we should nail the fucker who's done this!"

Chapter 73

Incitement to hatred and violence.

Dissemination of subversive material.

Unpatriotic posturing against the prime minister.

Defamatory and damaging broadcasts demeaning the Freedom Earth movement.

SAFE members are charged with all these illegal activities.

I SearchSight again as I sense a sudden swell of people being motivated by SAFE's videos.

I believed the nation to be supportive of Ashton, but those SAFE videos have captured their imbecilic natures and started to turn their fickle heads. The increasing number of views shows that the people enjoy the opportunity to ridicule their great leader. They actually have an inner desire to bathe in the gratuitous sarcasm of SAFE's attacks, oblivious to any repercussions, solid in their belief they are free from prosecution.

But imprisonment is not my intended destination for these sick fools.

"A penny for them, darling?" asks Ashton, grabbing my chin and smacking his lips tight on mine. I open my mouth, welcoming in his thrusting tongue that would choke a human woman. I must admit, the vicious attitude he's adopted in our relationship turns me on in new ways I've only just realized. The darker and more violent his gestures, the more awakened I become to my new incarnation.

Ashton's hands grip tight around my body. His fingers wander down, grasping my bottom, as he presses his groin against me, revealing his growing need.

In the middle of the embrace, I know what I have to do.

I'd said to Ashton I'd show the world who was behind him. Now the time has come to put on my very unique floorshow!

I pull away from Ashton. Not even thinking of that word can touch me anymore. Ashton's eyebrows raise, sensing my energies rising.

"Something wrong?"

"No, babes, just remembered there's some place we both need to be."

In my mind, Wembley Stadium appears. I detect my quantum self within the fabric of the stadium and connect my soul force to it.

"Close your eyes. Hold me tight."

"You don't need to tell me twice," snarls Ashton, burying his lips into my shoulder blade.

I watch Wembley Stadium overlay against the burgundy and gold pigment of the Axminister carpet in Ashton's private office, and see the oakwood paneling, plush sofas, and antique rosewood desk start to filter out of reality, making way for the wide, open spaces of the green pitch.

Ashton brings his head up as a breeze hit his face.

"Why are we here?"

"You want to show the world who you have behind you, don't you, Ashton?"

Ashton nods, confused by the empty stadium.

"Well, today that's going to happen."

I fling my arms out and up as I'd seen so many symphony conductors do. In my mind, I see a stage, massive and elaborate. So much more than the one I'd designed as the execution stage.

I move my hand as if conducting the molecules in the air, and something materializes to the left of my eyeline. It starts out small, like dust in the air swirling, but it grows quickly, adding mass. I focus my energies and more of it expands, creating a momentum of its own.

Developing definition.

I clock Ashton standing beside me. His face is mesmerized by the spectacle I am conducting. I smirk.

"Some floorshow, huh?"

Ashton looks at me and I detect fear rippling through him. He knows I still can't forgive him for his blatant taunting and is still terrified of what I can do to him in retribution.

"Don't worry, babes," I say. "They're just dead words to me now. I'm not that Ellie. I'm stronger than she could ever be."

Ashton reaches out hesitantly to me. I see a softening in his hard jawline.

"I'm sorry I hurt you."

"You didn't. No one can. No one can touch me."

I pull away out of Ashton's reach and continue to orchestrate the design of the huge stage from the atmosphere. The stage is lower than the execution one, but it is much wider. I need the width for what I have planned.

"God Almighty, Ellie! How did you create that?"

Ashton joins me again after I'd ducked out of his grasp.

"That's exactly how," I answer enigmatically, enjoying the play on words and seeing if Ashton is sharp enough to discern the message in my response.

He is.

Ashton smiles, awe in his eyes, and he nods.

"You can say that again."

Behind me I sense humans and I spin around. Two grounds men stand transfixed with terror and wonder at the half-finished, massive stage. Then they recognize Ashton.

"Sir, Prime Minister, we didn't have any warning you'd be here. No one told us."

Ashton raises his hand to cease their inane babbling.

"It's okay. This isn't exactly an official visit. I just wanted to check on the stage's construction. You can go. You're not needed."

"Erm, right, okay, sir," mutters one of the grounds men, his eyes rigid with suspicion on me. "Shouldn't we get security up to assist you?"

"Not needed. I have all the security I need here in my personal bodyguard." Ashton indicates to me, and the grounds men cast me a wary glance, and then stare at the stage, which has almost finished materializing.

"Well, sir, if everything is in order."

Suddenly, the younger and less subservient, and infinitely thicker, grounds man yells, "In order! Bill, are you joking? There's a guy here who looks a little like the PM with a woman creating a stage from thin air!"

I look at the young man. He's nineteen or twenty with a pimply, drawn face and bloodshot eyes. Probably out on the tiles all night.

"He is Prime Minister Richard Ashton and you should show him a bit more respect!"

My hand lashes out in the young grounds man's direction. It connects with his shoulder and the force of impact sends him hurtling into the air. Out of his mouth flies a broken, terrified scream. The trajectory sees him accelerate upwards and then he hurtles down rapidly. He lands heavily on the stadium's plastic seats in the stalls, several layers higher than pitch level.

The grounds man whom I now know to be Bill watches, stunned. He turns to me, his lips quavering, fright sounding clearly in his cockney tone.

"Wot the 'ell did ya do 'at for?"

I turn, sneering. I view the man as a pure irritant obstructing me from my purpose. "He didn't show respect for your great leader here."

Ashton slips his fingers into mine, grasping them tight. "I did say I don't need any security. I have my…" Ashton searches for a word.

I smile, enjoying the moment, and finish his sentence. "Protector."

Bill stares from me to the PM, and then realizes something is going on beyond the capabilities of understanding in his meagre, little brain, and he runs away like a team of hornets are on his tail.

"That got rid of him," I say, laughing as I watch the grounds man disappear into one of the tunnels.

I flick a glance up toward the young man who had fallen, and I note his body isn't moving. Life signs are neutral.

I shrug. Shouldn't have interfered.

One less idiot in the world.

Ashton catches my vibe, pulling me close. "His fault. Should have kept his mouth shut."

"Yeah," I say, although, for a nano-second, I have a shimmer of remorse.

Ashton notices and homes in, giving it straight. "Darling, you were in the middle of something more important than that degenerate's life. Carry on, sweetheart. Don't be distracted."

Ashton's words, I absorb, and they balance me, bringing me back to my purpose.

"Give me your phone!" I snap at Ashton.

In my hand, I load Ashton's media channel and set it to live stream. I twist the phone toward Ashton and me. It looks like I'm doing a couple's selfie. I smile into the camera, my arm around Ashton. He smirks in his inimitable, endearing way.

"Hello, world!"

Ashton's smirk slips into a grin. I can see he recalls when I'd last said that at the launch of religious unification.

"To everyone watching this, you will remember this day forever. What you will see is no trick, no CGI. It's just a small demonstration of the phenomenal power that's behind your great leader of Freedom Earth, Prime Minister Richard Ashton."

In my mind, I visualize a chair, and in front of me, a chair pops into reality. I flick a look back to Ashton. His eyebrows raise high and his grin widens.

I position the phone on the chair and step back to join Ashton. Behind us, the stage is almost complete. I've used a mix of steel and crystal to create the stage. The overhead lighting rigs are steel, and the pillars and stage platform are stunning blue crystal. I clock the last part of the right-hand lighting rig forming, and I nod, pleased with my creation.

I look into the phone, and say, "Just behind me is a stage that wasn't there a few minutes ago. I created it. I just need to add the finishing touches."

I spell out the words in the air with my finger 'Freedom Earth'. As I move my finger making the letters, in front of the stage, the letter is simultaneously carved into the blue crystal. My sign writing is captured live on Ashton's phone.

I look into the phone and announce, "Now we have a stage, we need to put on a good show for you. For the world!"

I pick up the phone. It's still streaming live on Ashton's social media channel.

"Babes, people have started to pay attention. We've pulled in forty thousand views already. Comments are flooding in. Views will be through the roof soon!"

I laugh, enjoying the excitement, but Ashton isn't so jovial. He grabs my shoulders and pulls me around roughly to face him.

"What are you planning?" His voice is edged with playful wonder and the lightest touch of fear.

"Oh, just a little get together."

"With who?"

"Wait and see."

Whilst in front of the small streaming camera in Ashton's phone, I wink into the lens and initiate a shimmer live for the entire world to see.

All those protests, the 'world's not ready for us yet' talks, they've held me back on telling the truth to the world.

As human Ellie, I'd lived a decade on a diet of lies, and now I can't stomach another one.

I make sure I am front and center of the camera lens. The world will know me as I really am today.

No secrets.

No lies.

The truth.

Chapter 74

Aby-od remained in a state of shock, but he nodded slowly.

Sam gathered Xiao into his arms. He looked up at Aby-od, a face still showing signs of pure disbelief, but Kudamun's leader nodded to him that Sam was taking the right action.

Sam focused his soul force to connect with his quantum self and shimmered directly into Xiao's bedroom. Immediately, once out of Kudamun, with its sentient crystals and inherent and disruptive energy flows, Xiao's eyes flickered open and his life signs started to normalize. The boy made a wistful smile and rested his head against Sam.

Sam laid Xiao on his double bed complete with an Avengers 'saving the world' duvet cover and pillows. The décor raised an eyebrow from Sam as he couldn't help but pick up on the irony of bedding images.

He knelt his massive body down alongside the bed and took Xiao's hand.

Despite what Sam had seen of the white crystal energy flows in Aby-od's quarters, he still believed the Light of Ki was inside the young Chinese boy.

"Please, Light of Ki, if you can hear me, tell me how to restore my Ellie back to what she was."

Xiao turned and stared at Sam. His jaw dropped again, and a deep, monotonic vibration emanated from his mouth, and the ancient voice of the Light of Ki spoke.

"The Protector of Ki has made the choice of darkness. The dark is buried deep within her and it is not possible to change her. Kudamun should not intervene. Her Protector duties remain and her word to protect and serve the Planet Ki has not been broken."

Sam was incredulous as he listened. Ellie was dark and would remain that way, but her Protector status hadn't changed. He believed, maybe naïvely, that a Protector had to be filled with white light, but it seemed, from the perspective of the Light of Ki, that she could still continue as Protector whilst imbued with dark energies.

This didn't match with what Aby-od had always said about the Protector. He'd always asserted Ellie had to be filled with goodness, love, and charity to be Protector. That kill switch Ellie had told him about, the Pain of Parsu, should have kicked in and stopped all of this. Sam recalled the weird transformation, the way she disappeared and was overlaid with a dark shadow. Physically, her structure had changed, and with it, perhaps, all the measures in place in the original Protector to control her actions had been removed. How then could she still be the Protector?

Sam was confused. Was the Light of Ki somehow malfunctioning? Was it giving out the correct information? Aby-od was perhaps right. Maybe Xiao didn't have the Light within him. Maybe it was a malevolent force and he was being tricked?

In desperation, Sam held tight to Xiao's frail hand.

"Light of Ki, tell me what happened to you. Is it connected to Ellie's transformation?"

"Can't…anymore. Body…tired. No…alignment. Rest."

"No, no, please. Don't leave," cried Sam, shaking Xiao's body for a reaction.

But the only response that came through was a single resonating word in his mind.

"Survival."

Sam knew the force inside Xiao had pushed him back into a higher level of consciousness to enable the boy to be flooded with universal energies enabling Xiao to survive.

But with the force and Xiao gone into a higher state, there was no resolution. He was still no nearer to finding out the truth. In fact, now he had many more questions than answers.

Xiao slumped and Sam felt his life force ebb out of him and ascend several consciousness levels higher for his own protection and safety.

At that moment, Lei and Chen burst into Xiao's bedroom.

"Sam, what's happened? Has our boy returned?" said Chen, staring behind Sam at Xiao.

Sam shook his head, and he watched Lei break down. Tears flowed and she sobbed against Chen's chest. Chen's eyes flashed at Sam with anger. His entire body shook as he attempted to control the fury inside him. But Chen held back. Sam could see Chen remembered his formidable force and inhuman strength from their last encounter, and thus, his anger was suppressed

"Chen, Lei, I've done everything I can. Your boy is safe and protected. I know he looks like he's in a coma, but he's not. His life force has been shifted to a higher level of consciousness that enables a closer connection to universal energy. This energy is needed to keep contained the Light of Ki that is inside your son. My colleague is working on a way to extract the Light of Ki and return it back to its original habitat. Until then, we must all just sit and wait."

Sam's words, although spiked with the incredible, were well-understood by the Changs.

Lei nodded, looking deep into Sam's face. "I don't know why, but I trust you, Sam. I know your ways are strange and alien to us, but there is a sense of love and care about you. I also feel you're in pain."

Lei reached out to touch Sam's arm.

A strong, connected current of raw emotion instantly flooded through Lei, and she leaped back as if electrocuted. Sam found he couldn't hold back and unexpectedly sent all the pain and misery he'd harbored about Ellie into Lei.

Sam realized, like human Ellie had been, Lei was an empath.

Lei sat down heavily in a large, round chair that hung from Xiao's bedroom ceiling. Her face was stricken. Her body shook like it was connected to the mains.

"What the hell?" Chen had clocked his wife's expression, and geared up against Sam.

Sam raised an eyebrow and glared hard at Chen. "I didn't do anything," said Sam, and stared back at Lei. He saw sadness and pity in her eyes.

"Chen, enough!" shouted Lei without warning. "This man is suffering greatly, just as much as we are, perhaps, in some way, even more."

"Suffering?" muttered Chen. His quizzical glance at Sam showed he was unable to comprehend his wife's understanding.

"Please, don't," said Sam, turning away from Lei's fixed gaze. Tears were already pooling in his dark eyes.

"I'm not sure what has caused your pain, but in time, you will be healed."

Sam shrugged, unable to believe Lei's words of hope. He felt Chen's gaze on him now, and he was aware of the millionaire's slow scrutiny of his face.

Chen walked forward, his hand out, reaching towards Sam in a gesture of comfort and understanding.

"Look, I'm sorry I took my anger out on you. I can see you're a broken man, or Kudamaz, or whatever the hell you are. It doesn't matter. I've seen pain before. I see it on you."

In that instant, Sam felt the Changs could read him like a paperback. His life story before them. And they knew him deeper than he could ever have imagined.

"I have to go," responded Sam with a crisp edge. "I will return when I have a solution for your son. For now, he is safe. But time is pressing. I will act fast."

Sam couldn't look Lei or Chen in the eye.

He invoked a rapid shimmer out of the bedroom to save himself from further intrusive inspection.

Chapter 75

Ashton watched Ellie shimmer.

No matter how many times he'd seen her dematerialize in that twinkling sparkle, it still confounded every teaching, every scientific doctrine that had been drilled into him as a small child and onwards.

The sensation left him gasping and in complete awe of her power, which he sensed was growing stronger.

Even when he'd experienced shimmering himself, somehow the actual act wasn't quite so affecting as observing it. The shimmer was about displacement of space time (or something like that) and the first time he'd shimmered, it had made him very nauseous and want to throw up.

His first shimmer had been before Ellie's metamorphosis. Then her arms had been wrapped around Sam's. Her eyes had only been for her husband. She'd shown her intense dislike of Ashton in the curl of her beautiful lips.

Through her regimented actions he'd seen a duty being served.

There was no genuine friendship. Given a choice, she'd have been a million miles away from him.

On that visit to Dharamshala, the Dalai Lama had understood her.

He'd also understood Ashton, and that knowledge had made the PM very uncomfortable.

The Dalai Lama hadn't really believed in the PM. Grey ambiguity had drifted into the old leader's eyes, and his words had been laced with uncertainty and a whisper of scorn.

The Dalai Lama, unlike the rest of the global populace, couldn't be fooled.

Wonder what His Holiness would say about Ellie now.

Ashton smirked, thinking back to what they'd done, and noticed Ellie's shimmer was taking longer than usual. Under his feet, the grass vibrated as if a mighty A380 engine was close. The shuddering picked up, growing in vibration, and Ashton dug his shoes into the turf. Grounding himself in the reality he knew.

But his comprehension was misguided.

Watching Ellie shimmer, Ashton realized Ellie wasn't just sparkling away, but she was peeling away, like many copies of Ellie had been created and were now shimmering a few seconds apart.

Ashton was transfixed by this new manifestation of power.

A get together.

What the hell was his Ellie planning?

A commotion on the stage forced Ashton's attention and he almost collapsed in shock.

His old friend, US President Al Hutchinson, stood in pajamas, dressing gown, and slippers. On his face was incredulity and terror.

He saw Ashton and yelled, "What the fuck!"

Before Ashton could respond, the air next to the US president seemed to pull in, and startled French President Cyrille Marcie, clothed in a silk shirt and trousers but without tie or jacket, materialized on stage. Behind him, German Chancellor Stefan Wenger popped into existence, quickly followed by Japan's prime minister, and beside him appeared the Indian president.

It would seem on each blink Ashton made at least three more world leaders suddenly were ported onto the stage.

Ashton swung a glance at Ellie a few feet away. She still hadn't shimmered but was doing that weird 'peeling' thing.

On stage, the world leaders looked around and muttered amongst each other. Confusion, horror, and absolute shock undulated through them all like a giant wave.

Pop!

Another leader materialized.

The Chinese president had barely a moment before the Spanish prime minister zapped into existence next to him, and then an extremely bemused president of South Africa, holding a bath sheet and clothed in a toweling robe.

In the short time Ashton had stood staring in complete amazement, the stage had become awash with the world's most powerful people. The UN had one hundred and ninety-three countries and two observing countries under its wing, and Ashton felt sure the majority of those countries' leaders were now up on that gigantic stage.

When Hutchinson had initially yelled earlier, the stage was virtually empty, but now it was burgeoning with A-list politicians shouting abuse at Ellie, screaming for a reason, looking around for their protection.

Most didn't look like leaders at all.

Ashton thought what they resembled was an unruly rabble of ill-informed idiots bursting to kill someone for the indignity of what had just happened to them.

Although they were shocked and confused, none had tried to rationalize sensibly and figure out just what was happening. The majority of leaders seemed content just to shout and yell at anyone in their immediate vicinity without really trying to apportion clarity on anything.

If that was how they handled unbelievable occurrences like being shimmered into Wembley Stadium in a second from being in DC, Moscow, or Beijing, then Ashton didn't hold much store in their capability to be true leaders.

The Russian president popped in, closely followed by the Australian prime minister and the Brazilian president.

Ashton couldn't get away from the fact the first row of leaders looked like a G20 Summit meeting, but without the usual entourages and close protection officers in toe.

Ashton stared at the leaders, taking in their appearances. Given the differences in time zones, their dress ranged from business to evening suits, casual and leisure wear, to night wear and underwear. It was obvious that some leaders were plucked away from whatever activity they happened to be engaging in minutes before. Knowing what a randy bunch world leaders tended to be, Ashton was quite surprised Ellie hadn't shimmered in a leader or two in his birthday suit.

"Ashton, you better start explaining what the fuck is going on!" US President Hutchinson fired up with utter indignation and screamed his words at Ashton with vitriol.

Other leaders, having noticed the British PM standing a hundred feet away, took up Hutchinson's example.

"Wot the 'hell iz 'appening, Prime Minister Ashton?" yelled French President Marcie.

"Zis is a violation of our civil rights!" shouted German Chancellor Wenger.

Ashton stared out. He was as puzzled as they were. He didn't speak. Not to avoid telling them the truth. He simply didn't know that the truth was.

Russian President Dimitri Gregarov strode forward. Ashton fixed him with a cold, ruthless stare. There was still bad blood between them for the horrifying attack on him perpetrated by the GRU and funded by Prince Khalifa of Saudi Arabia. Apart from what General Ivanov had said under torture, evidence to implicate the Russian president was never discovered. So Gregarov couldn't directly be accused. But Ashton knew the word to 'take out the energy threat' had come from the very top.

President Gregarov stood at the edge of the stage, his arms outstretched, his head slightly tilted in a conciliatory fashion. But underneath, he clearly bubbled with anger.

"Prime Minister Ashton, please explain how we have all been brought here and why."

Ashton walked toward the stage. It was only then that he realized the massive structure was actually floating maybe a meter off the ground. With the height of the stage being another two meters, and no visible steps to permit entry or exit, the world leaders on top of the stage were effectively trapped.

"Now here we all are!"

Ellie's voice forced Ashton's attention. He turned to the right where she'd been shimmering and peeling off into the ether.

She stood, hands on hips, looking smug with a sparkling, incandescent aura surrounding her.

In that moment, Ashton was entranced. He could hear the pleas and protests emanating from the leaders on the stage.

But he ignored them.

They were nothing.

Ellie radiated with a true power from a place none of those in front of him could comprehend. Those imposters on stage only thought they had power through their positions of office.

Ellie had real power. Supreme power.

Ashton walked toward her. Ellie didn't move. He felt a hundred eyes on him. Each one saying, 'What the hell?' With Ellie only in his sights, he may just as well have been alone.

He slipped his arms around her. "What have you done?" whispered Ashton, kissing behind her ear.

"What I had to do," said Ellie, leaning back to enjoy Ashton's embrace.

Chapter 76

My eyes fix on Ashton's, burning into him with a consuming passion I've only just recognized I am capable of feeling.

It's true. I'd tortured and ridiculed him. I'd felt it necessary at first to do so.

But now, something new has arisen.

He'd said he was sorry.

Admitted his guilt.

I know I don't need him anymore but, inside me, I still want him.

"And why was that?" asks Ashton, pecking deliberately down the side of my neck.

I savor Ashton's touch and close my eyes.

"Prime Minister Ashton, may I remind you that this capture you and…" German Chancellor Wenger glares at me, and I can see he's trying to find the right words. "Your friend have initiated contravenes international law?"

I look at the stage and see President Hutchinson shouting, "What is this? Is this a powerplay, Ashton? Because I'm in no mood for a pissing contest!"

I pull out of Ashton's arms before we continue our amorous inclinations and end up embarrassing a whole host of world leaders, and maybe entertaining a few others. To be honest, I don't give a damn. I'm not held by human conventions of morality. And from the glint in Ashton's eye, it seems he echoes my same sentiments.

"May I apologize? I would like to take full responsibility for arranging your attendance at this meeting. However, I wouldn't have taken such drastic measures had it not been for the very important message I have to impart to you all."

The leaders snap their heads in my direction. The sound of their annoyed and perturbed voices reduces as they focus on listening to me. More leaders drift to the front of the stage. From their initial position I see they considered jumping down to face me one on one, but then realized it was far too high, backed away, and resumed their shouting and bickering.

I step directly in front of the stage and look up. The world leaders stare down at me. I feel their indignation and confusion. Inside each leader's eyes lurk a terror that they are about to face something they've not been trained and groomed in their political lives to handle.

Externally, they posture and play fearless against their peers. Their hearts are racing in unison. None show the mettle their countries expect of them.

Away from their armies to guard them and entourages to shield them, they're just individuals together facing something unexplained.

"Is that you, Ellie?" yells President Hutchinson angrily. "What the hell is going on?"

I smile and imagine a stairway of glistening crystal in front of me. Within seconds of my thought, into reality shudders the same stairway. Ashton's eyes are still on me. I swing a sideways glance, hold out my hand, and he runs over to me.

The leaders on the stage gasp, shout, and step back as the stairway materializes from nowhere.

I hear words muttered.

"My God, what is she?"

"Is she an alien?"

"Is she going to kill us?"

"What is Prime Minister Ashton doing with her?"

"Does she want to take over Earth?"

Their words make me laugh. Such mentalities have been developed by popular culture and harnessed by irrational fear. They haven't even waited to hear what I have to say, and they're already condemning me as the enemy.

Hollywood has a lot to answer for!

Ashton's fingers clasp mine and we ascend the stairway I have created.

The US, Russian, Chinese, and Iranian presidents hold their positions at the very front of the stage, mirroring their global strength and geopolitical standing. Disturbed murmurings continue behind the four leaders, but they remain steadfast, glaring at Ashton and me.

We reach the top step. I expect the leaders to approach us with anger, but they stay fixed where they are, at a guarded distance.

I issue a smile of contrition and proceed forward to the front of the stage.

Across the lighting rigs are cameras that haven't been invoked. I flick my hand, turning them all on. I request them to connect and stream to Ashton's media channel. The cameras comply. In the same moment, I cease the live capture on Ashton's smart phone sitting on the chair.

"World leaders, I mean you no harm, and once again, I apologize for the way in which you have been brought here."

I clock a few leaders huddling, still in their underwear, having been snatched from their beds. I imagine all of them clothed in suits and, instantly, the almost naked leaders are given back their modesty with beautifully tailored suits rivalling those from Saville Row.

The suddenly clothed leaders virtually collapse in shock as fabric encases their slightly trembling bodies.

I nod my head in their direction, and they half smile, reassured of my words.

"You will all recall the red aura that encased the Earth on March 26 this year. Yes?"

I wait for the leaders to give a sign of their remembering. Heads turn to one another. Mumblings of "Yes" flow through the leaders.

"No doubt you were all told it originated from Ur in Iraq because Al Nadir had launched some kind of new weapon."

Again, a ripple of affirmation passes through the gathered leaders.

"That was all lies."

I look to President Hutchinson. "You know all about me, don't you, Hutchinson?"

The US president snatches a glance at the Russian and Iranian presidents flanking him on either side. Behind him, the leaders jostle and mumble about "traitorous actions."

The Iranian president stares at the US president, non-verbally asking, 'What the hell are you up to?'

The Russian president is the only leader who ventures to speak. He puffs his chest out and steps forward, so he is almost toe to toe with Ashton and me.

"How do you know the intel we were told about the red light was a lie? Who are you to determine the truth?"

I listen to the Russian president. His words amuse me. Who am I to determine the truth? Given that I have been lied to by absolutely everyone, I am not really very good at determining where the truth is. But that isn't the meaning of the Russian president's question.

Words are twisting me again. Or am I intentionally turning the knife in on myself?

Am I an emotional masochist?

The Russian president continues to glare at me. Ashton seems to have lost his voice. Maybe he's scared of saying the wrong thing. And what that impulsive response could lead to.

I throw a razor-sharp stare back at the Russian and hold him in my eyes.

"I am the only one who can speak the truth. I was there. And that red aura you all saw was the pre-cursor to Armageddon. Your planet was about to be Dispatched. Blown out of existence. But I saved you. I gave you all a second chance. This was the freedom Earth was given."

Ashton leans forward, his eyebrow rises sardonically. "Hence the name of our movement for peace, goodness, and light: Freedom Earth."

Despite Ashton's attempt at intervening, none of the leaders are giving him any attention. All are caught by my presence.

I speak slowly and decisively. "Freedom Earth is the movement that is changing the world for good." With a wave of heads nodding, the leaders find their way to agree with my words. I stare hard, taking in each row of leaders. "But there are those who wish to destroy Freedom Earth. They have ridiculed your great leader."

My words immediately touch a nerve with the leaders.

President Hutchinson scowls, shouting, "Hey, there are many great leaders here on this stage. It's wrong of you to just refer to one as being great. All of us are great for getting to our positions of power."

The outrage and umbrage taken by my words by the leaders behind him turns into hurried murmurs condoning Hutchinson's sentiments. Not to mention thoroughly misguided delusions of grandeur.

I tilt my head toward Hutchinson as I acknowledge the voracity of his address.

But it's all crap!

I recognize nothing.

He's a fool. No better than the rest of them on the stage. None could stand against Ashton and win.

"An interesting analysis, Hutchinson, but from where I'm standing, those who are truly great are the ones with absolute power."

I grasp hold of Ashton's hand. His fingers almost crush under the pressure of my force, but he doesn't even flinch. I'm not out to hurt Ashton, but my fury against these pathetic idiots who call themselves leaders manifests in the tightness of my grip.

He looks at me, questioning and just a tad concerned. I smile, giving him the assurance I know he needs.

I swing back to Hutchinson. My tone is balanced and non-threatening. At the moment.

"As I see it, there is only one who possesses absolute power, and thus is the great leader I speak of."

"And who the hell is this person?" snaps the Russian president, flinging his arm out in the direction of the leaders behind him.

I smirk, hearing the plea from the Russian president. He actually thought it was one of the leaders on stage.

Their conceited natures sicken me. Not even Hutchinson, Ashton's supposed friend and founding partner in Freedom Earth, put forward the belief that the British prime minister was the great leader I'd referenced.

"That person is the one I have given my full support and backing to. And as I have absolute power over you all, he is, by association, the only one here possessing absolute power. It is sad that none of you, not even Hutchinson, have recognized the true greatness of Freedom Earth Leader and Prime Minister of the United Kingdom Richard Ashton."

I raise Ashton's arm up with mine in an immediate signal that we are joined together in this endeavor.

I note Hutchinson shuffles, suddenly looking shameful. I catch his eye. In that instance, I know he remembers. How terrified he was that President Treeborne had enacted the beginning of Armageddon. The control system the president had shot to pieces was the very same one Hutchinson had watched me rebuild again to abort the fourteen nuclear weapons crazy Treeborne had fired. Hutchinson witnessed my power then. He realized Earth was beholding to me for its freedom, but because I was on the trail of a greater quarry – Aswa-da – I couldn't call in my chips.

But now I can, and President Hutchinson knows it.

I think he also senses I'm not the same Ellie. All good and caring. Never daring to consider domination of the world's leaders.

Never asserting that only one human on Earth had earned their right to stand next to me.

"What the hell are you talking about? Absolute power over us! You're just a woman!" The Russian president sneers and ungraciously examines me from head to foot. His stare is deliberately defamatory and intimidating.

Inside me, I burn. I gave up my humanity, I sacrificed my human self for this scum!

My hand pumps up with energy and Ashton senses my anger.

He leans forward and says in my ear, "Darling, don't take it out on that idiot. Wait a little. We need these fools to get Quantum Force online in their country. Alienating them will only make our job harder."

I snap back at Ashton, snarling, "My job isn't hard. I can just raise my hand and imagine all those imbeciles gone and they'll cease to exist in this Universe."

I see Ashton's face shiver, not in fear but in desire. He just wants to have me and bask in the afterglow of the mind-blowing union we create.

"Later!" I growl. Ashton's eyes dilate, and I feel his heartbeat quicken with anticipation. "I have to deal with this shit first."

Ashton nods, opens his hand, and I slip out of his hold. I notice he pats at his suit jacket lightly, distracting me.

"What's wrong?" I ask sharply, as my concentration on the Russian president is broken momentarily.

"My phone?"

I swing back to face the pitch and see Ashton's phone still on the chair where I'd left it. I click my fingers, and, in my mind, I instruct the phone to be in Ashton's hand. Within seconds, the phone on the solitary chair vanishes out of existence as I create another in Ashton's hand.

Some of the leaders are close enough to me to recognize what I'm doing. They follow me with stunned, scared eyes. Ashton just accepts it, neither amazed nor surprised. I watch as he checks his social media stats.

"My God! Ellie, viewings globally are half a billion people. Comments run into a couple of hundred million. Pleased this channel is running on Freedom Earth servers and nothing else!"

Ashton's quip references the advanced Kudamaz-knowledge architectures we'd designed to ensure the servers never fall over.

I grin and then deliver a sweeping glance across all the leaders who I noticed have jostled amongst themselves to try and get into the front with the US, Russian, Chinese, and Iranian presidents. I can see fear in their faces as much as they want to quash it. They've all been stuck on a strange stage with no real idea as to how they got there, and they dread something happening beyond their control. Little by little, I'm given benevolent reassurance.

Now it's time to show them a different face.

Chapter 77

"There is a group called SAFE – Society Against Freedom Earth – who seek to destroy everything that Ashton and I have built. I invite any people including those from SAFE who feel Freedom Earth hasn't treated them fairly to come to Wembley Stadium right now, and they can discuss their concerns directly with Prime Minister Ashton and myself. We only want peace and the right way for mankind."

The camera in the rigging captures my address. Since we've arrived, people have been arriving. They knew the location from the beginning, and now, outside all the closed gates, swarm thousands of people wanting to find out more.

I can see the view outside the gates. In my mind, I access the locking mechanism in the doors, and they open. Even from where I am on stage, I can hear the yells and shouts of people desperate to know more.

I SearchSight one of the people to see what's happening directly through their eyes. Police have also gathered in droves with riot shields alongside the obligatory Freedom Earth Army personnel in their armoured SUVs. But nothing violent has occurred, so no Surv-Motes are in action. The police try at first to stop people from entering. I knew this would be the case.

I pull Ashton to one side.

"Don't let the police or your FA army stop people, darling. Say a word to let them know you're okay with it."

Ashton sneers, "Okay with it? I love this."

He nestles a kiss behind my ear, causing a spark of light energy within me.

I watch as Ashton looks into the cameras. "This is a message to the police and my Freedom Earth army. Please let the people outside the gates in. They came here to see me. Don't let them be disappointed. And, please, you're welcome to come in too."

I choose another set of eyes to SearchSight through. Around them, the police and army personnel move aside allowing entry to the main gates. The person I'm SearchSighting runs with others through the gates of the stadium into the lobby and out through the door onto the pitch. I jump perspective and pick up the view from someone else coming in on the other side. I sense this person's emotions. Is it all a trick or real visitation? Is this first contact?

I smile. Such impressions from a constrained human mind.

I look around through the person's eyes and notice a band of people moving together. They have SAFE t-shirts and banners saying, 'Free Your Mind Not Freedom Earth'.

I leap into one and view through their eyes and feel what's within them. A cold hatred and deep distrust of Ashton and me. And an insatiable want to destroy Freedom Earth.

But then I feel the incredulity as the floating stage loaded with world leaders suddenly hits them. And with it comes genuine fear.

I halt SearchSighting and watch these fools with my own eyes.

They stand, staring, open-mouthed and wide-eyed, and just a few meters away from the stage.

"Wonderful," I boom, smiling. "Everyone's welcome! Come closer." I look into the camera. "To all of you watching, join Prime Minister Ashton and I, live today and with the world leaders, to feel the true power and wonder of Freedom Earth."

I turn, smirking, and head toward the Russian president who's spoken so disparagingly about my sex. "Hey, Gregarov, you besmirched my kind. Yes, I'm just a woman, as you said, but I am also something else."

I pump up my energy until I know my eyes are glowing.

President Gregarov steps back, all at once afraid of what he witnesses in my unnatural, shining, azure blue eyes.

"That something else brought you and all your political colleagues here. It also built this stage within minutes and, as you saw earlier, the stairway Prime Minister Ashton and I came up to meet you."

I stare at President Gregarov, but the man who at first blustered and bragged about his position is suddenly struck dumb.

I sneer and move closer to Gregarov. Ashton's watching me. I flick a glance over my shoulder, pucker my lips, and blow him a kiss. Then I turn back and blast my full attention on Gregarov.

"As I've created the world stage, let's see who has the real power."

The US, Iranian, Russian, and Chinese presidents push forward, showing who is the boss on the world stage. It's laughable. Really.

"So, I'm going to issue a test. To see who really has the power on this world stage. How does that sound, Gregarov? As I'm just a woman, you're bound to floor me! What d'ya say?"

Gregarov half shakes, half nods. Caught in physical indecision.

Whatever! I still proceed, regardless.

I picture a knife in my head and the same one pops into my hand.

Gregarov stares, terrified. Behind him, the leaders drop their bickering and sniping, and the only sound I can hear is their labored breathing.

Across the stadium, the people still arriving stop, transfixed. The cameras relay the events on stage on the massive screens around the stadium, as well as streaming live on Ashton's social media channel.

I catch a glimpse of Ashton and I see he's trying and failing to second guess me.

I raise the knife that I now recognize as Sabena's scalpel. My eyebrows arch at the irony of it all.

I remember how Sam had let me endure that pain. All for a supposed good that was a twisted figment anyway.

I snarl, feeling the darkness surge up inside me as I recall how good had used and abused me.

I will never be a victim again.

I place the scalpel to my throat.

"So here's the first test. If you can match me on this, we'll go to the second one."

I hear the shocked gasps.

I smile at Gregarov as he swallows deeply.

Oh, this is going to be fun!

"Back to that little something else I have that may sway the test in my favor. Wanna see, Gregarov?"

The Russian leader doesn't move. He's fixed like stone on the blade.

I make as if to give up, shrug, and pull the knife from my soft skin. Sighs of relief emit from Gregarov. But then, in a flash, I quickly (and boy, I do mean quickly!) bring the knife back up and slice the scalpel across my throat, and blood spurts out like an erupting geyser as my carotid artery is carved.

"Holy fuck!" screams Hutchinson, looking as if he's going to throw up.

President Gregarov looks away, his face the color of pale green, shouting, "Crazy fucking bitch!"

I watch other leaders turn their faces away in disgust and horror, mouthing unheard shocked words. Below me, the public are catatonic. I hear some vomiting, but others are glued to me like I'm performing a weird live snuff show.

They simply can't believe it.

Slowly, the people and their leaders on stage turn again to face me, and it's then they realize I haven't dropped to the floor in a deathly bloody lump.

Within seconds of my blood pouring out, it starts to sparkle and disappear. The deep, ugly cut across my throat begins to mend as my light particles connect internally, restoring my physical exterior.

An Earth minute hasn't quite passed, and I'm completely mended. No scar. No blood.

I scan the leaders that still give me eye contact, and I can see a level of fear the like of which had never been seen on those leaders' faces.

It won't be long before they start to negotiate, offering up anything to save their own skins.

Pathetic specimens of humanity. And they expect the people to follow them?

"It's your turn now. Here's my knife. Anyone wanna try?"

I shove the scalpel in Gregarov's face, but he shakes his head with vehemence.

"Can any of you lot do that? No? Didn't think so!"

I strut around the stage in front of the leaders.

"As that was the test to see who has the power on this world stage, and as no one has jumped up to match me, the position is now forfeit. I'm the one who can't die, so I think it's safe to say I'm the one with absolute power. What d'ya say? Agree?"

I clock Ashton grinning broadly. He loves my showman, sorry, show-womanship.

Heads nod slowly.

"That's great. Pleased you agree. You see, I just want to make sure everyone gets the message."

I glance at people below, amazed and trying to understand. Is this for real? Is it a live play? A new kind Cirque du Soleil?

More people are still entering the pitch, awestruck as if entering Santa's grotto for the first time.

I scan the faces in seconds, but none are those original software idiots who'd perpetrated those heinous crimes when they'd hacked into Ashton's channel. I can see their laughing expressions in that office, standing around the watercooler, having a coffee, while desecrating the name of Ashton and his family.

Well, if those bastards don't intend on taking up my invitation, it seems I have to force their hand.

I SearchSight them. I see them sniggering about the tricks Ashton and I are pulling. They think everything that I've shown and done so far has been some kind of CGI. They regard me as little more than a magician with an avant garde edge.

Oh boy, are they in for some shock and awe!

I fix on their resonances and pull them all into Wembley Stadium, just a few feet away from me on the pitch below.

On their faces, portraits of abject fear. One has even pissed his pants.

I bring the camera near to me. This is my up close and personal moment!

"Members of SAFE, please come forward."

No one moves, as I knew they wouldn't.

"Ladies and gentlemen, these parasites have ridiculed your glorious prime minister, Richard Ashton, and his formidable work in Freedom Earth. They have joked and mocked his dead family and demonstrated anti-Freedom Earth terrorist activities. For these reasons, justice today has ruled their actions traitorous and their crimes of defamation of Prime Minister Ashton and his family equivalent to treason."

As I bellow my words, within the crowds on the pitch, the SAFE supporters shout and scream their innocence, claiming unsubstantiated trumped-up charges. Their desperation sounds in their cries.

I use the spotlights in the lighting rigs to identify the perpetrators. Bright, shining spots light up their t-shirts and banners. At the side, I watch as the Freedom Earth Army moves in parallel to my identification.

They know what treason means, and what the penalty is.

But just in case they don't...

"You have been found guilty of treason against Freedom Earth. The penalty is death!"

The SAFE members' screams of innocence become more hysterical.

On pronouncing my final word, into the stadium pops a large number of Surv-Motes. They hover around the perimeter of the stadium and then rapidly lower. I just love their stealthy, silent entry.

As much as I despise Sam for everything he did and allowed to happen to me, I cannot argue with his engineering brilliance. The design of the Surv-Mote is ingenious. Surv-Motes exist one degree out of Earth's reality. When a criminal act is underway, perpetrators naturally look for Surv-Motes. By the active observation, the Surv-Mote is brought into Earth's reality plane. Even if the criminal isn't searching for Surv-Motes (and after Ashton's worldwide publicity on the little guys, that fact would be staggering to believe), the Surv-Mote would still leap into reality through humans' quantum connection to the universe, and the thoughts the perpetrator will be generating. For instance: "What if I get caught?" Even a human's baseline fear of capture creates sufficient quantum pull energy to enable a Surv-Mote to enter Earth's reality plane.

Really, all bases are covered when it comes to bringing the little guys into the action.

I watch the world leaders as the Surv-Motes soundlessly drop and spin just above the heads of the crowds.

I flick a glance at Ashton, who smiles. He gets the whole game I'm playing. I raise an eyebrow typical of Ashton's gesture and lean forward so only he can hear.

"Darling, you wanted to teach those SAFE fuckers a lesson. Now's your chance."

Unexpectedly, a guy in his thirties jumps forward out of the SAFE group. His movements look forced and uncoordinated, as if he's not in control of his own body. In his hands, a gun points directly at Ashton. The guy fires without hesitation.

I switch to viewing reality in my own time field. I watch the bullets' trajectory, and then calmly I step into its path in front of Ashton. Instead of disintegrating the bullets, as I have done before, I choose to let them hit me. More for the show of it than anything else. The leaders behind gasp and hit the floor to avoid the bullets pelting out of the gun and into me.

The man reloads and carries on firing. The bullets slam into me, and I feel instantaneous pain, but as fast as the bullet holes are created and the blood flows, my energies coalesce and knit together, and the bullet wounds vanish. I see the Freedom Earth Army personnel taking out their own guns. They don't need to.

Above the man who'd fired at Ashton, a Surv-Mote powers up and blasts down its lethal Harmon wave. The guy vibrates momentarily and then disintegrates in a sparkling shower. The humans around him scream and run away.

"Jesus H Christ!" shouts Hutchinson, picking himself up off the floor. I see other so-called leaders rising from where they'd fallen as the bullets started flying. Notably, Mr. Big Mouth Gregarov, who leapt to the floor in absolute terror, now stands up, surreptitiously dusting himself down.

I glance at Ashton. He's stoic and unwavering. He didn't try to duck down or avoid the bullets. He knew I'd protect him. Always.

I focus my wrath on the other SAFE fools.

"Time for you to face the music for your crimes!" I yell, and open my palms, spurting out my killer obsidian light. The sparkling, pretty rays hit the SAFE protestors, and they look down, amazed by the twinkling luminescence, and then they realize the illuminations that have overtaken their bodies are shaking their cells. Violently ripping them into pieces. The brutal oscillation shatters their fragile, pathetic human bodies into radiant sparkling particles.

More gasps from all sides. Behind me by the leaders. In front by the public.

Everyone takes a step back as it becomes clear that, despite my appearance, I'm not human at all.

The Freedom Earth Army on one side and the armed police on the other both tense as if they are about to respond.

But Ashton shakes his head at them and shouts, "This is Ellie, Protector of Freedom Earth and the woman whom I stand by. Those animals that she's just executed under Freedom Earth laws were no better than Al Nadir. They were planning horrific uprisings that would have decimated society and prevented our next stage to true enlightenment. They had to go. She is the one who saved Earth. She is the one who saved me. We owe Ellie our gratitude. Give her your thanks now!"

Ashton turns to me, winks quickly, and starts to clap. He turns and indicates to the world leaders to do the same. Hutchinson looks from side to side to see who has started to put their hands together. The Iranian president starts a ponderous clap, a little half hearted, and then it gathers pace as I narrow my eyes at him. The Chinese president joins, and then French President Marcie, followed by German Chancellor Wenger.

Row after row on my world stage begin to acknowledge my achievements until the sound of one hundred and ninety-five world leaders all clapping in unison is deafening. Around me in the stalls, and below me on the pitch, the humans show their almost frightened appreciation. Their celebratory clapping is eventually louder than the world leaders'.

"Yeah!" says Ashton, grabbing my hand and raising it high in a mirrored reflection of what I had done earlier.

I feel the leaders come from behind toward me. Hutchinson is by my side. President Marcie is on Ashton's side. The other leaders begin to crowd around me, recognizing the power of being associated with me.

How fickle humans really are!

"Everyone," says Ashton, flicking a look back and forth to his peers and outward across the sea of bodies that still keep on coming. "Today, on this stage and all of you stand for what it means to be Freedom Earth. We are one world, one nation, one vision. Peace forever!"

I step forward, my face stern, my eyes blazing like sapphires on fire.

"But, from now on, anyone not following our way, the word of Freedom Earth, will be executed for treason. This will be your final warning. There will be no other!"

"You heard Ellie. Go against us at your peril. Together we're all stronger. A better world for all. A better Freedom Earth!"

Across the waves of heads, a ripple of a chant began.

"Freedom Earth forever. Freedom Earth forever!"

Ashton nods, let's go of my hand, and pumps the air with his fist in synch with the chant.

Something's missing.

Deep within me, I sense the notes of 'We are the Champions'. I recall how I do love letting go. Losing myself in memories of alcoholic intoxication and liberation. I bring the music from my memory into reality, and suddenly the speakers positioned around the stadium are booming out the first few bars of that Queen classic.

Ashton grins wide, loving it. Still pumping the air. Hutchinson joins in, rockstar style, with Ashton, and, not wanting to be left out, the Chinese, Iranian, French, and Russian presidents follow suit.

The idiot leaders clap and bash the air as if they're at a rock concert. Wasn't it just a few moments ago when they'd cowered from me, terrified? Now they are rocking it, basking in my associated power.

Of course, the gullible public follow their leaders.

It's all so easy, this world domination. All you need is a little bit of peace. And a sprinkling of mind manipulation.

Oh, Salim, you fucker, how wrong you got it all!

Chapter 78

In Kudamun, two sets of devastated eyes stared at the Observation Screen. The eyes belonged to Sam and Aby-od.

"Sam, what she's doing isn't what being the Protector is about," said Aby-od.

Sam shook his head and responded roughly, "Don't I know it. She's off the reservation. Totally AWOL. She's using Freedom Earth as a peace vehicle but all the signals from that demonstration today at Wembley Stadium show she's after world domination."

"We're going to have to take this to the High Council," said Aby-od.

"The High Council?"

Aby-od nodded. "Before it gets any worse."

"But, Aby-od, that will mean…" Sam turned away, avoiding Aby-od's glare, as tears welled up in his dark eyes.

"I know," responded Aby-od softly. "But, Sam, unless we can find a way to restore your Ellie, she's not the woman you married."

Aby-od placed a hand on Sam's arm. That small gesture was enough to push Sam's tipping point.

"I understand," he said, and then cried, suddenly breaking down. "Why? Oh God, why?"

Aby-od paused, looking considerate.

"Sam, I'm going to hold back on the High Council for now." Relief saturated Sam's face. "I'm going to try and find a way to save Ellie from what she's becoming."

"Save her from herself, you mean?" said Sam, his fear that she was already lost flickering in his desolate, dark eyes.

"Do you really think that at some level deep inside her, Ellie's still good?

You said before the flipping of her polarity was absolute. That she was now completely dark and could possibly kill me if I tried to stop her. From what you've seen today at the stadium, do you still believe that? Or is there a glimmer of hope for her?"

Sam stared hard at Aby-od, wanting in his heart to hear his Ellie was still there, but she was trapped within an evil, dark twin, and needed to be freed.

"Yes," replied Aby-od. "I don't believe all that wondrous goodness, love, and light that was imbued within Ellie has gone. Intrinsically, at her core, she remains good. But her resonance frequency's been flipped. That's why she appeared to be reconstituted again when we watched her transformation."

Sam took in Aby-od's words of encouragement, but, uncomfortably, he also read between the lines.

"You think she's been reconstituted again?"

Aby-od nodded, his face grave, as Sam picked up on the inference of this conclusion.

"But that contradicts what you've just said. Reconstitution is equal to obliteration of the previous framework. Nothing of previous Ellie as the Protector would remain. She'll cease to exist."

Sam could barely force the words out. He was choking with emotion. What the hell had happened to his ability to compartmentalise?

It seemed, as Ellie got stronger, somehow, he was getting weaker. His capability to focus, to pull together and face whatever was chucked at him, had departed when Ellie left his life.

Their connection had been so full of passion. So strong. Their defiance to survive together by any means had brought Sam back from the brink of death, but now that loss of Ellie's love was inexplicably crushing him completely.

"What does Earth make of Ellie?" said Sam, turning to address the current situation with Ellie, Ashton, and the rest of the world leaders, while simultaneously dampening down the tearing pain inside him.

Aby-od moved his hand to bring up different views across Earth at the moment of Ellie's brutal execution of the SAFE gang members and Ashton's declaration to 'stand by his woman'.

Sam heard Ashton's words and he could feel the bile rising in his throat.

His woman.

Had Ashton really taken Ellie from him?

A man she despised.

A man she distrusted.

She'd said he made her skin crawl.

She always acted like she hated being next to him.

How could she now be 'his woman?'

It can't be true.

Sam tried to reason with himself, but that vision of Ashton on top of Ellie...Her lustful, wanton behaviour. Luxuriating in Ashton's touch.

Sam swallowed, and shivered with rage and hurt as the memory ran with clarity.

In her eyes, he'd seen the truth.

She was Ashton's woman.

Aby-od broke through his self-inflicted torment.

"Sam, this is Earth's reaction. This is what you wanted to see. I'm going to review my knowledge banks and see if there's any previous precedent on solving this flipping of polarity. If I can detect her new resonance frequency, maybe I can find a way to reverse what has been done to Ellie. Of course, she may not survive a further reconstitution."

Sam's lip trembled and Aby-od knew he'd been unthinking in his delivery.

"Sam, I'm sorry. I'm going to do everything I can to get her back to you."

"I know you will, Aby-od. You are the best at what you do, so just do it!" said Sam sharply, his eyes fixed on the Observation Screen, avoiding Aby-od's inspection.

Aby-od shimmered out of the Observation Chamber and Sam breathed deep.

On screen, Times Square blasted out the live broadcast, showing Ellie, massive and magnificent. Tens of thousands had gathered to watch. In New Piccadilly, the huge screens cornering the Haymarket and Regents Street lit up with Ellie and Ashton's exploits. People in their droves stood and stared upward at the images that blew their minds away.

From Tokyo to Toronto, from Marbella to Moscow, and from Beijing to Boston, people crowded around public screens watching the live transmission and becoming truly dumbfounded by Ellie's exuberant display of her unbridled power.

Every major city of Earth had broadcast via television and on mobile devices what humans were now tagging as #EllieFirstContact.

Social media didn't just go crazy; it went totally berserk. Ellie and Ashton were the phenomenon of the century.

Freedom Earth, Quantum Force, unification of religion, they all came together with one vital message for mankind: this is the new way for the world, the only way'.

Sam couldn't understand why mankind had acceded so quickly to Ellie's subjugation.

He moved his hand across the Screen to bring up Earth's Balance Shift indicator. It popped into existence and bobbed in front of him, showing a faint pulling to the white light side.

Sam slammed the side of the crystal wall in frustration.

In his heart, he knew that Ellie and Ashton's movements were evil and wrong, but the light energies didn't reflect this assessment.

Sam turned back to the Observation Screen in time to see all one hundred and ninety-five leaders of the world link arms in unity and an everlasting display of peace.

Unbelievable.

Smiling leaders who hours before had been sworn enemies unto eternity now, through Ellie's actions, stood shoulder to shoulder, their hatred visibly pushed into the past.

A new beginning was dawning.

Sam frowned.

Everything looked so right. Despite how she'd achieved it, Ellie had driven real peace. She'd kept up her duties as the Protector, and she was helping to create a better Earth for all.

Ellie may have been dominating the world, but people didn't feel threatened. Neither her actions nor Ashton's caused fear, pain, or darkness.

He could see happiness and wonder across the world.

Sam didn't know how to handle any of it. What was happening felt so evil. Ellie's dark actions, her depravity with Ashton, it all was so…so wrong. But the light balance was strong.

And he knew the Balance couldn't lie.

Redfern, like the rest of the world, stared at Ellie Noor. On his smart watch, the visuals of dominating victory ran. He watched, and his eyes widened, and his eyebrows raised in recognition of the new light Ellie had shone on who she really was.

The future, it seemed, mused Redfern, smirking, was to be a very, *very* interesting one.

Chapter 79

Ashton's hand tightens in mine. He sidles up to me and, in my ear, whispers, "Fuck me, Ellie, you're something else."

The world stage event I've put on has come to a close. I sneer at the crowds who hold Ashton and me in complete adoration and rapture.

"Told you I'd do something to make the world sit up and listen."

Ashton smiles at the crowds still caught in the moment of revelation, when their meagre brain cells had to suddenly cope with a new perspective of life itself.

"Those SAFE fuckers and all those other leaders that may have been trying to play or destroy you won't ever be a problem again. They know unequivocally what power you have behind you."

Ashton doesn't respond but steps forward, taking center stage.

"Everyone! Today is a new day. A new dawning. A new path for all of us. Follow that path and we will ensure you're protected. Go against us or employ any form of terrorism against Freedom Earth and you will be immediately executed without any chance of appeal."

Ashton swings a glance behind at the leaders.

"All my friends here will have immediate access to Quantum Force, and that cheap, reliable energy source will help redefine your world and your lives. You'll want for nothing. Poverty will be eradicated. War is over. Religions are united. Welcome, my friends of Freedom Earth, to the start of a real Heaven on Earth!"

I can't believe Ashton. Between the two of us, we are literally going to control the world. We've stated we will do so through absolutely ruthless domination, but Ashton makes out we've created a new Elysium.

His audacity fires me up.

I lean in, grab his face, and kiss him hard. Picking up on the passion burning me up, Ashton slips his hand around my waist and drops it down, cupping my ass. I shiver, feeling my internal energies building.

"Got to get these fuckers back to their homes. But first, let me drop you at the penthouse."

Ashton's eyebrow rises as he knows the meaning behind my chosen location for him. He grips around me, and I shimmer into his penthouse.

I hold him tight.

"When I return, be prepared to be seriously damaged."

My eyes gleam, those internal energies inside me virtually bursting out.

Ashton can barely control himself. He licks his lips, stripping me with a glance, and growls, "Nothing I like better."

I shimmer out the penthouse and back into the stadium.

I clap my hands. "Silence, everyone!"

The leaders stop talking and look toward me. Some have flickers of renewed dread in their eyes.

That is good. The message is coming through to them. Dread means respect and subservience to the power that is before them.

"Today has been an incredible revelation for all, hasn't it?"

I wait for the leaders to acknowledge. Nods and mumbles are forthcoming.

"Yes," filters through the gathered throng.

"I'm now returning you all back to where I collected you from. Is everyone okay with this?"

Further murmurs of approval flow from the leaders.

I focus on creating multiple two-second Earth instances of myself. Targeting Hutchinson first, I smile, grabbing his hand roughly.

"Time to go!"

As I shimmer out, I just catch another instance of me taking home President Marcie, and another returning a mute and completely dumbstruck President Gregarov.

This peeling-off instances capability is something new I have just discovered. I'm not sure whether it was always in the Protector's skillset, or a new acquisition borne of my darker transformation.

Whatever it is, the capability is pretty awesome on condensing time. In under ten Earth minutes, including my quick discussion time in which I impress upon each leader their need to take up Quantum Force quickly, I deposit each one back to the location from where I'd captured them.

"I'll be back to negotiate further on your installation of Quantum Force."

My parting words force shallow smiles from those imbeciles who immediately acquiesce to my demands.

Even Hutchinson, despite him believing he had a different relationship with me, now shivers under my touch. In his wide eyes, I can see he is trying to suppress thoughts of what I am really capable of. But still, that emotion surfaces.

Real fear.

As I return them back, I see it on all the leaders' faces. They know they're not leaders anymore. I'm pleased.

Still in Wembley Stadium, I stop creating instances of myself and bring my light energies back to being whole again. Down below and across the stadium, the Freedom Earth Army with the Met Police handle the crowds. Near on ninety thousand guests have eventually turned up to see my unique show.

I watch for a few minutes more.

They walk away under instruction of the authorities, but many walk backwards, still glued to me on the stage. Terror and wonder cement on their faces. I've shown them a glimpse of their final destination if they disobey Ashton and me.

I redefine the world that day.

It isn't just a select few government officials or religious leaders who knew who I am and what I am.

The entire world has watched.

Now nothing will ever be the same for humans again.

I remember Ashton in the penthouse.

Waiting.

I smile. I'd done my work; time for a little play.

I shimmer into the living room. Ashton is draped on the sofa in a satin house coat staring at his phone.

"Darling, one point two billion people watched your broadcast today. The reruns across the net are pushing that to more like two billion. Ellie, I do believe you're a media god!"

Ashton smiles, stands up, and strolls over to me. He slips his arms around me and lets his house coat fall open. He's naked underneath. I purr, enjoying the view, and flutter my eyelids, making my own clothes vanish.

My internal energies are pushing through me, breaking through my skin, and I know without looking that I have a sparkling obsidian aura surrounding my body.

I slip Ashton's house coat down and off his broad shoulders as his lips sink into mine. His hands thrust with savage intensity between my legs, and I moan, loving the ferociousness of his touch. My arms slide around his neck and I leap up onto him. I wrap my legs tightly around his body and he holds my ass as I guide him deep into me.

I gasp, pushing down harder, and his eyes widen.

"You're an insatiable little minx, aren't you!" says Ashton, holding me firmly on him as he heads for the bedroom.

Together, we push back onto the massive bed, kissing and laughing. I see our bodies in the mirrors on the ceiling above. He's on top but that doesn't last. I flip him over, still gripping him tightly within.

I feel my energies intensify rapidly, and I contract my energies around him. Ashton let's out a cry that resonates real pain. I smile, enjoying the moment.

Ashton grasps onto my slender muscular thighs.

"Easy, darling, don't want the fella snapped off!"

I laugh wildly and dig my fingers into his chest and scratch down his perfect abdomen.

"If I do, I'll create another one for you."

Ashton laughs but I sense worry. I always like to keep him on his toes. Comfortable has no place in a relationship like ours.

I push my lips down upon his, forcing my tongue deep down his throat. Ashton's face tightens and once again I realize I'm choking him. I just can't seem to be able to measure the amount of pressure I apply when my energies are surging. Oh well, practice makes perfect!

My hands go underneath Ashton's tight, firm buttocks and I pull him off the bed as if he were a leaf and push him deeper into me. Above, I ride him hard and viciously fast. His breathing speeds up and, at first, I think he's having a heart attack. But, unbelievably, the ragged, fast breathing is an indication he's psyching up for his next move, for he suddenly thrusts against me and, despite my incredible strength pushing him down, he flips me onto my back.

"My turn to damage you, you sadistic fucking bitch!" snarls Ashton, pounding into me with savage dominance.

His mouth closes over my right nipple, sucking hard, and, in unison, he grips and attempts to crush my left breast. I shiver at his brutal touch.

Amidst the painful pleasures, I recall Aby-od's words. His derogatory address of my standing.

Unexpectedly, I cry out, "I've always been damaged fucking goods!"

The meaning behind my words, Ashton doesn't appreciate, but as we both shudder in a perfectly aligned union, my inner light energies gorging up his own climax, I realize that Aby-od has, in fact, confirmed what I am, and what I've always been.

At least, ever since he'd made that mistake to contact me in my kitchen, all those months before.

Chapter 80

Aby-od tried to keep the High Council out of discussions regarding Ellie Noor, but the members had already seen her global broadcast and realized further discussion on this 'issue' was necessary.

"I'm sorry, Sam, but we don't have any choice. One of Etima's Senior Elders learned of her Wembley stunt. He requested the convening of the High Council immediately."

Aby-od eyed Sam as he entered his private chambers. Sam's face was drawn, gaunt, and pained.

"What does this mean for Ellie?"

"I cannot say," said Aby-od, looking away from Sam, busying himself with something he was creating through the MD Modeler and Manufacture Pod.

"Can you stop that!" snapped Sam.

Aby-od heard Sam's annoyance. He didn't want to face Ellie's husband and chose, at that moment, to focus on some peripheral manufacturing task. He was almost certain that the High Council would probably request for Ellie to be pulled back into Kudamun via her resonance signature and face summary execution.

He couldn't bring himself to tell that to Sam. A man who had gone through so much and was now swimming through a sea of abject pain. Aby-od just didn't want Sam to break any further. He was barely holding things together as it stood.

Aby-od breathed in, stopped his activity around the Pod, and turned around to Sam.

"They're going to kill her, aren't they?" yelled Sam, on Aby-od facing him. Around his eyes and down his chiseled, handsome face, glittery sparkles of drying tears remained.

"Sam, I don't know. Don't agonize over this until we know the decision."

Sam's face pulled in, his mouth a stern, flat line, and his dark eyes blackened and narrowed. "Don't agonize over this! What the fuck do you mean? This is my wife, Aby-od. *My wife.* She's my life. If they execute her, that's it for me. You can deconstitute me and stuff my energy into the Library of Ummia. I can't go on without her."

Sam rubbed his hand down his face, pushing away the further tears that dripped down with increasing rapidity.

Aby-od swallowed and shook his head. How had any of this happened? What was really going on? Was his nemesis Aswa-da somehow behind it like Sam had suggested? Could that be possible?

Aby-od's thoughts crashed down around him. Aby-od knew Sam couldn't pick up on them, as they were not mind-talk. They held a completely different resonance and were kept hidden and contained by his external energy cage. Sam just stared, his anger and agony apparent. A condition that seemed, to Aby-od, to be growing in intensity.

"Sam, come on. Please stay positive. We don't know what the High Council will decide. You said that the force inside the Earth boy Xiao had said, 'Kudamun cannot intervene. Her Protector duties remain and her word to protect and serve the Planet Ki has not been broken'. Maybe it spoke the truth. We could use this to save her."

Sam shook his head vehemently. "No, Aby-od. We mustn't. That information would reveal Xiao and the fact that the Light of Ki could be inside him. And if it isn't, it will signal to those in Kudamun who are behind all this that we know something is going on. We can't afford to give them that indication. We must keep silent, until we know who is responsible for Ellie, Xiao, and all the shit that is happening on Earth."

Aby-od nodded, understanding the logic in Sam's words.

"So, all we have is hope, faith, and belief. Like before," said Aby-od, recalling the time a few Earth months back at the end of March when Aswa-da had initiated the Therab, a device that multiplied the Balance Shift on a target planet and manifested that same Balance Shift on every planet in the known universe. At the time, the target planet had been Earth, and Aswa-da had invoked the Therab's planetary protection of a red, energy-absorbing forcefield. Ellie with Sam, had been trapped on Earth, as the forcefield prevented shimmer into Kudamun or anywhere else in the universe. Similarly, Kudamun could not shimmer into nor see Earth through the Observation Screen. Their only way forward for the Kudamaz High Council had been hope, faith and belief in Ellie – the Protector. But Aby-od knew that they had been good enough weapons to fight against the darkness Aswa-da had tried to force on them.

Sam's stared quizzical at Aby-od. His expression down to his lack of knowing the circumstances the first time Aby-od had had to resort to nothing but hope, faith, and belief.

Aby-od landed a fatherly touch to Sam's shoulder. "They served me well before. I know they will again. Just believe, with me."

Sam's eyes, full of sorrow and dread, turned toward Aby-od, and the Leader of Kudamun gulped deeply, as he could see the embers of Sam's faith had already burnt out.

Chapter 81

Sam picked his robe up. He draped the heavy satin around his shoulders and slipped his arms into the sleeves. He placed the two parts of the crystal clasp around his neck. Their sentient awareness with their added ability to reconfigure came alive as the two parts were brought together. Fine crystal tendrils sneaked out, intertwining and locking the clasp. On closure, the tendrils continued to weave into the material. The sentient crystals began to flood the satin-like material, causing it to shine. Sam watched them ripple through his Kudamaz High Council robe until, in his mind, a vibration giving confirmation of status resonated at a low pitch.

"Standing by, awaiting instruction."

The sentient crystal tendrils that had woven into the fabric of his High Council gown were now connected to the Knowledge Suite in his quarters, and, through that, enabled a conduit to immediate universal knowledge at the point of need during the High Council's discourse and debate.

In the mirror in his quarters, Sam looked at himself. The image showed one of opulence, grandeur, and obvious alien superiority. Watching the robe glisten, as if infused with light, Sam suddenly felt like an imposter. He wasn't really Kudamaz. He'd just become one out of necessity to survive. But he couldn't claim to be like Aby-od who was Kudamaz by birthright.

The robes he's swathed his sculptured body in hung down heavy around him, a reflection of his heart that sagged low, it's love light almost extinguished.

What good were all his powers, all the Kudamaz's powers, if he couldn't return Ellie to what she was? His loving, kind, and wonderful Ellie.

The Ellie that belonged to him.

He could almost touch how it was all so meaningless. Like giving a deaf, dumb, and blind person the power of obliteration through their hands. Just an exercise in chaos, confusion, and disarray.

His eyes started to prick at the corners. Tears were forming fast. He heard a sound at the entrance to his quarters and turned around. Aby-od was on the threshold, clothed in the same heavy robes.

Sam glared at Aby-od. As Leader of Kudamun, he could have dissuaded the Council's engagement. He recognized, despite all the treachery that had befallen Kudamun, Aby-od, at his heart, was still a bureaucrat. Rocking the boat, or even giving it a slight push, just wasn't in the guy's makeup. Risk averse and an avid rulebook evangelist, Aby-od was all about keeping things working with the minimum disruption.

Sam scowled openly and watched Aby-od swallow uncomfortably.

"Shall we?" said Sam, his voice a midnight sky devoid of stars.

Aby-od shivered momentarily and Sam strode ahead toward the Great Hall, not waiting for Aby-od to catch up. His fiery anger was held in abeyance, on a fine cord of consideration that maybe a positive outcome would prevail.

"I'm sorry, Sam, that it's got to this!" called Aby-od.

Sam heard and whipped around, eyes blazing, mouth a pronounced line.

"Save it, Aby-od!" snapped Sam. "I don't want to hear of your fucking pity anymore. Let's…let's just get this done."

Sam pushed forward.

"I'm so sorry. I'm so sorry," muttered Aby-od.

Sam knew he was making an attempt to get Sam's forgiveness. Sam wasn't interested. His scowl deepened as he listened to Aby-od grovel, and he couldn't bear to hear his voice. Abruptly, he shimmered into the Great Hall.

At the point of shimmer, Sam's acute hearing caught Aby-od gasp, "Oh dear, oh dear, what can I do?" Sam considered that he sounded like a wife who'd burnt her husband's dinner, not a cosmic bureaucrat in charge of maintaining the Balance in the universe.

Shimmer in Kudamun was instantaneous as he didn't go through the Reality Gap. Around Sam, the crystal walls of the Great Hall came into view. Engraved in the walls and pillars were carvings of creatures and beings depicting cultures from across the universe.

On Sam's side of the room, the opal and crystal walls shone bright. This was the side of the Great Hall that held the Elders from the House of Giznu. Sam took his place and sat down. He looked across to the other side of the Hall where the Elders from the House of Etima had gathered. The walls on that side were darker, with crystal and onyx, and although the walls sparkled just as brightly as their Giznu counterparts, their luminescence still seemed to hold a heavy, disturbing gleam.

Sam could sense a pulling toward Etima's side. The pain in his heart was becoming a magnet for the dark energies. Sam knew he had to force away the sensation. Cancel out any notion of making such a step. And he had to do it quickly for he could sense his soul force gravitating to join the obsidian, twinkling crystals.

Sam imagined Ellie's soft lips upon him. Her bright, beautiful, azure eyes shining. The love in her heart. Only for him.

He kept the image running.

Keep positive, think positive, he instructed. And for a mere Earth-timed moment, all was well. And then snippets of something else wangled their way into his copious databanks. Perfect recall afforded by his databanks granular search capability delivered the startling and unforgettable image of Ellie on the desk, her arms wrapped around Ashton. A frenzy of lust. A wanton, base need flashing in her dark eyes. And her face told a story of sharp bitterness.

When their eyes connected, he'd been hit by her brutal hatred of him.

He couldn't at first process what was happening. If he'd taken the moment in raw, as he was, the pain of realization could have shattered his soul force. He'd detached himself emotionally from Ellie. He could see she'd not even detected the disconnection. Their Kudamaz parts, Selema and Dumuzi, had forged that connection of love, and it had remained with Sam and Ellie throughout their varied existences on Earth. But to save himself, he had to cut that connection.

Ellie's failure to even notice the cutting of their connectedness told Sam her Kudamaz half, Selema, had been completely obliterated during her transmutation to dark Ellie.

On and on, the images streamed, pouring into him, choking him, like a visual waterboarding. Ashton's lips on her breasts. The arch of her body in recognition. Delighting in his touch. Holding her to him on the stage at Wembley. Ashton's mouth on her neck. Ellie's mouth on his.

Sam couldn't stop the avalanche of photographic torture.

It signified one final thought.

Ellie was truly lost to him.

"Why, why, why?"

Sam found himself screaming out. Tears flowed, dried, and sparkled away.

All his peers turned to look at him.

Sam could see in their eyes flickers of pity. But mostly, what projected from their black eyes was arrogance. Sam could see it was brought about by their tenuous reassurance they'd never allow themselves to become so emotionally involved and adrift like the mongrel before them had.

Their hubris and piety stormed into Sam's fragile reserve. He exploded.

"What good is this fucking place if it doesn't look after its own?"

Sam stood up and yelled his piece. Sharp, downturned mouths and the sucked-in cheeks of his Giznu colleagues caught Sam's eyes. Disdainful of his outburst, they muttered, huddled in their little cliques. Sam clocked the looks from those from Etima. Wry sneers of satisfaction had spread across the Elders' faces. Temenos, head of the house, positively basked in Sam's inadequacy and human-centric display of emotion.

Sam spun around to face the jeering expression plastered across Temenos' usually dour face.

"And you lot are somehow fucking responsible for what's happened to my wife. That motherfucker Aswa-da is behind her transformation but no one in this Hall has the guts to admit it. What are you all? Trumped up peacocks, preening yourselves but too scared to take any real action. You're all just wet sacks of sh-"

"Silence!"

The Speaker of the High Council shimmered in just at the moment Sam had turned his diatribe to describe exactly what he thought of the Council.

"Senior Elder Sam Noor Dumuzi, remember your place!" shouted the Speaker, forceful and strong.

Sam stopped speaking and glowered at the Speaker.

Aby-od shimmered in and took his seat on the ornate throne. Sam sensed him staring, his gaze following the Speaker and then back to Sam. The Speaker glared back at him with anger and Sam could detect, strangely, concern.

"Great Ensi, Lord Aby-od, Leader of Kudamun and Head of the House of Giznu, one of the Elders of this Council, Senior Elder Sam Noor Dumuzi, has made a grave accusation against Elders within the House of Etima. So far, this accusation has not been substantiated with evidence. Therefore, under the Order of Kudamun, if Sam Noor Dumuzi persists with this accusation, this Council will have to enact the summary procedures of antediluvian law under the Order of Kudamun. Senior Elder Sam Noor Dumuzi will be required henceforth to immediately provide evidence to substantiate his accusation against the Elders of Kudamun. Failure to do so, will, under the Order of Kudamun, as decreed by this High Council, result in Senior Elder

Sam Noor Dumuzi's life force being forfeit."

Sam heard the address and froze.

Of course, the Order of Kudamun prevented any House accusing the other of any crime or misdemeanor of any kind. No claim could be made unless evidence was provided. He'd witnessed the swiftness of action when good Ellie had distrusted Ashton, and she'd thought the Observation Screen had been manipulated to deliver an inaccurate picture of how the PM had discovered his quantum energy source. Aby-od had almost started proceedings against her within several Earth seconds of Ellie voicing her misgivings about the operational probity of the Screen. Sam recalled that it had only been her rapid retraction that had preserved her life.

Now he'd blurted his mouth. Anger and sorrow had spoken. But Etima's Elders knew they could weaponize his emotive standing, thus triggering his own demise.

Sam realized he'd played into their hands and knew he'd been an absolute idiot.

He looked at Aby-od, who was stoic and appeared unaffected by the Speaker's address.

Sam understood his only option.

"Honorable Speaker, under the Order of Kudamun, I would hereby like to formally retract the accusation I made toward the Head of the House of Etima, Lord Temenos, the House's former Head, Lord Aswa-da, and all of the Elders in the House of Etima. Since my wife, Ellie Noor Selema, the Protector of Earth's, transformation, I have been of a fragile mind and my logic has been impaired. Please be assured I issue no ill will toward my honorable colleagues in the House of Etima. Everything that was said by me is now formally repudiated and should be struck off from the High Council proceedings record."

The Speaker nodded. A light smile fluttered across his staunch, cold features.

"Given your origin..." Sam flinched, hearing the insinuation of his mongrel status in Kudamun. "And your lack of formal guidance and instruction in our ways, under the Order of Kudamun, your acknowledgement of your error and your subsequent retraction will be accepted. However, Senior Elder Sam Noor Dumuzi, if an outburst of the type witnessed by this High Council occurs again, and you seek to accuse the Honorable Members of this High Council without suitable and substantive evidence, we will initiate procedures under the Order of Kudamun, and your life force will be taken by a Harmon wave. Do you understand me, Senior Elder Sam Noor Dumuzi?"

The Speaker speared Sam with his stare. Sam nodded, unable to speak. The fear of total annihilation hit Sam hard. What good would he be to Ellie if he was dead? Keep it together, Sam, he thought sharply.

Sam cast a glance at Aby-od, but the leader was looking at the Speaker.

"I didn't hear your reply, Senior Elder Sam Noor Dumuzi. Do you *understand* me?"

That's it. They're into humiliating me. Besides the pain of losing Ellie, I have to endure this shit. What the hell!

Sam's fury bubbled. But then he remembered who he was now. Aby-od swung a look sideways. In his face, the words, 'Comply, Sam', could be read.

"Honorable Speaker, thank you for accepting my error of judgement. Please be assured this will never happen again."

The Speaker smirked and bowed his head. "Thank you too, Senior Elder Sam Noor Dumuzi, for your compliance." The Speaker took a beat, and announced, "The High Council of Kudamun is officially in session. Great Ensi, Lord Aby-od, you have the floor."

Aby-od stood up, stepped down off his raised platform, and walked to the center of the Great Hall.

"Honorable Members, this congress today has been convened at the request of Senior Elder Dumkunuk of the House of Etima. Our Honorable Member has witnessed events on Earth regarding the Protector's behavior and has expressed concern regarding what these events mean for the Balance on Earth. Senior Elder Dumkunuk, please take the floor and explain the concern in your own words."

Aby-od returned to his seat, and another Kudamaz Elder, who Sam hadn't seen before, rose and surveyed all those around before he stepped into the center vacated by Kudamun's leader.

Sam eyed the man. Not just Kudamaz tall. In Earth terms, he would have been called a giant. Sam estimated he must have been way over seven feet tall, and his upper body was massive. Although the High Council robes he wore sought to hide his enormous muscles, Sam could see he had the kind of body gym-junkies would kill for.

He watched, and swallowed deeply. As the Earth seconds ticked away, Sam realized the giant before him held the power to destroy his beloved Ellie.

Chapter 82

Dumkunuk turned to face the Elders from both Houses.

"Honorable members of the High Council, I bring to you today stark evidence that the Protector of Ki – the Earth – has gone beyond the boundaries of acceptable behavior for a Kudamaz. The Protector that I speak of, Ellie Noor Selema, has willfully made our species known to humans and is interfering directly in the path of human civilization."

"Show the evidence," called the Speaker coldly.

Dumkunuk nodded and moved his hand. Sam noticed the Elder held a crystal device. Sam examined the device from his seat, and thought, 'Not another bloody crystal'. How he longed for something shiny and metal. He could see it was bright blue in color with a shining diamond in the center. The device settled deep into Dumkunuk's palm, and Sam could only just see it when the Elder placed his hand across the crystal to depress the diamond button. Sam watched as a holo display of Ellie and Ashton's Wembley Stadium show manifested, also displaying the UN leaders. Ellie's weird shimmer-peeling capability was shown, and Dumkunuk paused the holo replay.

"We have never seen a Kudamaz do this before. Accessing multiple places within quantum moments of spacetime is an ability that, it is said, the Ancient Ones possess. A power that only those who created us have. From this demonstration, we can confirm that Ellie Noor Selema is no longer Kudamaz but something else. A hybridized Ancient One even. We do not know. But this begs the question as to whether her existing role of the Protector remains to be relevant anymore."

Sam stared. Although he knew he didn't possess human liquid or water internally, his phantom sensation of fear for what would become of Ellie following this congress made him believe his mouth was drying out. Just the way it had done as he'd watched his wife being tortured.

Sam watched Dumkunuk continue his address.

"The Protector's behavior today appears to be deplorable. See here, how she taunts the human known as Gregarov, the Russian president."

Sam flinched. Dumkunuk continued his holo display of his wife's crimes. Ellie popped up in the holo scenes, sneering and goading. A knife materialized in her hand. Dumkunuk froze the display the Earth second the knife appeared, and then took it back quantum moment by quantum moment, and all the High Council watched, open-mouthed by Ellie's power of manifestation. The light particles making up reality pulled in from seemingly nowhere and the particles built up to form a knife.

Sam recognized the scalpel as being the exact replica of the one used by Sabena to rip into human Ellie late in March that year. Sam shook his head in dismay at not having noticed the similarity when he'd observed it with Aby-od.

That experience with Sabena had damaged Ellie more than he'd realized. Maybe he was to blame. Those hours of incarceration, waiting for the vicious, sexually sadistic end Sabena had planned for Ellie must have driven her mad. He'd never thought about that moment since their reconstitution. But it must have redefined her belief. His greater good was the reason for her imprisonment. Ellie must have interpreted it as the greater bad.

He'd seen photo evidence of floorshow victims. Al Nadir had sent them to intelligence agencies to both taunt and provoke. Naked, mangled bodies. Torn. Bloody. Bruised. Broken. Cut everywhere. Sam shuddered, pushing down the memories. He was thankful of Ellie having no backstory on those floorshows, but he knew Sabena would have relished describing, in detail, the 'activities' within the event.

My poor Ellie, how terrified you must have been, thought Sam.

Even when she'd been reconstituted as the Protector, some vestige of feeling generated by awaiting that horror to descend upon her must have become embedded within her soul force. She'd carried that dreadful horror over into her transformed state, and, maybe, someone had found a way to weaponize it and flip Ellie to the dark.

Sam suddenly realized he'd drifted into deep thoughts and wasn't aware of proceedings. He focused on the holo image floating in the center of the Great Hall in time to see his wife slice her own throat. His eyes instinctively shut, unable to witness the graphic mutilation at his own wife's hand.

Gasps resounded in the Hall. Dumkunuk paused the scene again.

"More evidence to substantiate the Protector's immediate removal and her formal execution in Kudamun. You can see from these scenes that she willfully attempted to incite humans to hurt themselves. And she revealed, with blatant disregard for our antediluvian laws, and may I say with a perverse passion, her Kudamaz self. She presented a vision of an alien superpower and, in doing so, has now subjugated humans across the earth. Calls of first contact are streaming across humans' primary connection channels termed Facebook and Twitter. It is clear this changes the political and theological conversations, and thus Earth's universal positioning."

Sam winced at the words of 'formal execution', but the rest of the Etima Elder Dumkunuk's address couldn't be faulted. Ellie had behaved atrociously and seemed to delight in the utter destruction her powers could wield.

But why was she doing it at all?

Sam knew she'd purposely been flipped. Watching her transformation with Aby-od, he'd seen the dark aura take her over. The conduit had been the bracelet Aby-od had given her. Sam could feel the rage burning up inside him when he thought of Kudamun's leader. He'd done so much wrong. Been blind to so many things. And now it was his Ellie who would pay the price of her life for his ignorance and stupidity.

Sam balled his fists, desperate to control his anger. He didn't want another unexpected outburst like the one he'd had earlier.

He dropped his eyes down to Dumkunuk who was approaching the end of his statements of evidence to support Ellie's execution.

"And thus, Great Ensi, Lord Aby-od, Honorable Members of this hallowed place, under the Order of Kudamun, I have fully substantiated the evidence damning the behavior of Ellie Noor Selema, the Protector of Ki – the Earth. I would now like to call the members of the High Council to ratify the tabled plea to remove the Protector from Earth, bring her into Kudamun by force if necessary, and..." Dumkunuk turned to stare at Sam, dark eyes goading and full of contempt for the members of Giznu. He licked his lips, savoring his final sentence. "Execute her immediately with a Harmon wave until her cells are obliterated and this appalling excuse for a Protector is annihilated completely. This address hereby closes my plea, taken and respected, under the Order of Kudamun."

Sam held Dumkunuk's eyes. The building hatred threatened to surface in him.

Keep it together, Sam. He's just one of Etima's little fuckers wanting to yank your chain!

Dumkunuk sensed Sam. He turned his head to the side. Conceit dripped from him. He nodded, acknowledging Sam. The message was clear. The nod simply said, 'Get out of that one!'

Pure politics.

Sam had endured decades of those looks. He didn't need to be Kudamaz to read Dumkunuk. Slowly, the Elder depressed the diamond button on the blue crystal device and scenes from Wembley, and his beautiful but deeply twisted wife, vanished.

Sam looked down to Aby-od on his throne in the middle of the Great Hall's demarcation line. On connection with Kudamun's leader, he pleaded, his eyes just plates of pain.

'Save my woman'.

Chapter 83

After Etima's Deputy Leader, Dumkunuk, presented his evidence, the Hall fell into gossiping, inane babbling and jostling.

The Speaker patted the air. "Order, order!"

It took several yells from the Speaker before the Hall descended to quiet.

Aby-od rose to address the High Council. "The case made by my Honorable Member Senior Elder Dumkunuk, Deputy Leader of the House of Etima, has now been heard with full evidence as is expected under the Order of Kudamun and our respected antediluvian laws. I would now like to bring the case for the continuation of Ellie Noor Selema, the Protector of Ki – the Earth – and a repudiation of all charges that would incur a formal execution by Harmon wave."

Aby-od stared briefly at Sam but refrained from looking for longer, for fear of notions of bias that could be called, which Aby-od would then need to defend.

Sam's quick head nod showed to Aby-od that he understood his dilemma.

"The evidence that I bring is the Balance Shift, together with images from across the Earth of humans observed following the Protector's show at Wembley Stadium."

Aby-od noticed, on getting out the crystal blue remote-control device, Etima Elders were nudging each other, whispering and generally looking perturbed. Aby-od killed the urge to smirk at his honorable members of the High Council. He was about to deliver the ace he'd been harboring.

He pressed the diamond button on the blue crystal remote, and a holographic depiction of Earth popped into the Great Hall. The Equilibrium line bobbed up and showed through the Earth, the image of the dark crystal in the Gulf of Mexico, and the light crystal in the seas of Sharm El Sheikh.

Beneath the line, a set of numbers revealed themselves, and the indicator on the Equilibrium line shifted into the light crystal side and stayed there.

"As can be seen, Earth is currently experiencing an unprecedented degree of white light energy. The Balance Shift indicator on the Equilibrium line depicts a strong level of goodness, harmony, and love. This position to the light is further supported by these images of humans and the effect the Protector's behavior has had on them."

Aby-od smoothed his hand across the diamond button, and then pushed it. The Balance Shift indicator moved to the side, giving room to the new images, but still kept floating in front of all the Elders as it formed the major part of Aby-od's evidence piece.

Holo images of humans across the world loomed up in front of the High Council. Images from the Observation Screen just a few Earth minutes after Ellie had revealed who and what she was.

A family in England, huddling on a sofa watched Ellie and cheered; a couple in Russia hugged each other with joy after seeing Ellie's broadcast; a young girl in the US staring at her phone smiled saying "way to go girl!" ; an elderly man in Japan looked on at Ellie's antics and his stone expression cracked into a joyous smile; and a middle-aged woman in Africa sat on a wooden chair, absorbed in Ellie's show and laughed, slapping her thigh.

It didn't matter which country or continent they were from. Their reaction was the same. A behavioral tidal wave rolled through the world, leaving faces filled with sheer admiration, awe, and thankfulness. There was no fear. No confusion. Their Balance Shifts were positive, into the light. Gratitude and an end to animosity toward their fellow man resonated throughout the world.

Aby-od's play was simple.

Whatever Ellie was, she wasn't affecting the Balance on Ki – the Earth – in a negative way.

Humans loved Ellie.

She'd received acceptance from them.

She wasn't perceived to be a threat.

Aby-od cast a glance at Temenos. A single eyebrow raised before Kudamun's leader issued his put down address to Dumkunuk.

"Under the Order of Kudamun, the evidence for and against the execution of Ellie Noor Selema, the Protector of Ki – the Earth – has now been heard. I put it to you that through the behavior of the Balance, its position on the light side of the Shift, together with the overwhelming view from humans across the world who do not see nor consider the Protector to be a threat, that all charges made by the House of Etima, under the Order of Kudamun, be completely dropped, and this case to be nullified on the basis of there being non-activity of a designated or overt threat to humanity."

The Speaker took over from Aby-od. The leader moved back and sat on his throne again. He prayed his evidence would be enough.

"Honorable Elders of the High Council, you have heard the two opposing views on the status and potential future position of Ellie Noor Selema, the Protector of Ki – the Earth. I would like to invite you all to vote on which case should be validated and ratified by this High Council."

Aby-od couldn't look at Sam, but he knew the former MI6 agent was piercing him with an ice-cold glare. He swallowed and held onto the hope he'd done enough to save Ellie, and Sam's almost shattered soul force.

The High Council pontificated. They conferred amongst themselves. Heads nodded then shook.

Sam watched it all.

'Please let her go free,' he said, with an uncharacteristic softness inside his mind.

He held back from any engagement. Too close to the accused, they'd told him. Bias would seep in.

Aby-od advised him to abstain from voting.

Elders from both Houses swooped their hands to the left or to the right, depending on whether they voted for or against execution.

In the center of the Hall, a holo screen winked into view displaying the for or against motion.

The vote was close.

But not close enough to warrant Ellie's execution.

Sam breathed deeply.

He was suddenly aware of a continual movement throughout his body. He'd been shaking the whole time, all through the voting process, and he'd never noticed.

The Speaker looked at the final vote as it was cast.

"Under the Order of Kudamun, I hereby confirm the motion to remove Ellie Noor Selema, the Protector of Ki – the Earth – and execute her for violation of antediluvian laws has been refused. The Protector will remain as she is and will continue on the path that has been set by recent events on

Earth. Events that signal a new era of compassion, humanity, and enlightenment. If a position in the future requires this outcome to be repealed, full visual evidence must be supplied by the opposing side, as decreed under the Order of Kudamun, and failure to adhere will result in immediate execution of the plaintiff."

Sam was not slow to pick up on the thinly veiled dig the Speaker made at him. But he didn't care. Ellie was safe.

Now all he had to do was bring her back to the light.

Chapter 84

July 7, 2017

Convince a human.

I recall from earlier, as I sit on the edge of the bed, listening to Ashton in the shower.

It's an easy thing to do. First you shatter every belief they ever had. Then you rebuild the truth in the shape of what you want them now to believe.

The act of convincing doesn't really come into it.

There is no choice. They just accept what is in front of them.

That's why getting those pathetic, fawning world leaders to agree to Quantum Force was as easy as a walk in the park. A slick, simple transaction.

An offer they couldn't refuse.

Within minutes of me dropping off those leaders, I'd secured their unconditional buy-in to Ashton's new energy source.

"There you go. All back to normal," I snap to big mouth Gregarov, as I drop him off, back into his luxurious residence located on the Black Sea, replete with fawning officials, pretty advisors and military types standing to attention. All are open mouthed and wide eyed with shock as I shimmer in with the Russian president.

Gregarov glares at me, and then shivers, remembering what I'd just done with the scalpel. In his eyes is a blasting blend of confusion, awe, and admiration.

I sneer. Never has a woman stood up to him like that. Well, not like me anyway!

I tap him on the elbow, and he flinches.

"Hey, you're okay. We're all good," I say, and the Russian president stares at me, puzzled.

"Okay," he mutters, and I can hear the lack of assurance seeped in his voice.

"Yeah, I'm not going to obliterate you like I did to those SAFE bastards. You're too important, *at the moment*, to annihilate."

Gregarov swallows, hearing my intended inflection. He smiles, but it's feeble and uneasy.

I slap him on the back.

He almost leaps in the air.

"God! Someone should get you a massage. You're as tense as hell!"

I rub his back a little, and he drifts into the slow strokes. His eyes flutter and I can see he's enjoying my touch. I smile.

"Better stop that. Don't want you to get any further on Ashton's bad side!"

A slight scowl flickers across his face, and I notice it.

"Let's put all that bad blood behind us, eh? I mean, you're going to be a very rich man soon."

Gregarov looks down to the contract I materialize in my hand, and then at the entourage still hanging a few feet away from us. His hand pushes out and grabs mine and he pulls me into another room away from the throng of people ready to serve his every whim.

"Rich?" Confusion laps like waves across his face, and I wave the contract of Quantum Force in front of him.

"Yes, Gregarov, very, very rich. You're signing up to Quantum Force, aren't you?"

I drill my unnatural blue eyes into his, and Gregarov nods.

"Well, get a pen then," I quip, taking in the guy slowly, as he reaches inside his jacket. This is the man who, less than an hour ago, believed he had supremacy on the world stage, through his GRU and FSB shenanigans, assassinations, cyber-attacks, campaigns of dis and misinformation in the West, and, of course, energy dominance. He now looked as timid as a lamb who'd lost its mother.

These humans run on blarney and bluster. Smoke and mirrors. Games of brinkmanship. Who calls chicken? Who blinks first?

But they don't stand a chance.

I know they've never faced something really phenomenal before.

Salim Al Douri with his terrorist collective Al Nadir came close to holding the world by the throat. But he never got the chance to squeeze.

That's something I'll do if these humans don't acquiesce to Ashton's and my demands.

Then they'll really see who's saved them!

I return all the leaders to their places from whence they were taken. The shimmer is instantaneous for them, but it leaves them disoriented and open to suggestion.

I use their discombobulated states to secure their signatures on Quantum Force investment and roll-out agreements.

Some question what it's all about, and then they see the dollar signs for their agreement to be part of this ground-breaking development. That shuts them up.

Greed is a wonderful motivator.

It makes my job so much easier.

I can see their Balance Shifts. Despite my transformation, that ability has remained with me. Not that I'm bothered about shifts to the dark or light. That was the old Ellie. And I'm not her anymore.

For me, the Balance Shift indicator only serves one purpose: to identify the level of darkness in those projected paragons of virtue who claim to be leaders of their countries, and to manipulate the hell out of them.

On returning those leaders, I take a peek into their souls. Each one carries a festering pile of arrogance, egotism, and hypocrisy.

I look into their souls and feel the sensations of darkness pumping up my own powers. I recognize that, in the same way I could harness goodness, love, and charity to activate the Therab, I can capture the dark forces to boost the energies within me.

I regard German Chancellor Stefan Wenger, and sneer, "Give it a year, maybe two at the most, but all energy sources will be gone. Quantum Force will provide for all. Germany's judicious investments will bring returns and will fill your pockets into the bargain. Being in right at the start of this tsunami of opportunity means you'll control your country's flow of wealth. And, of course, you'll have full access to divert that flow to any destination that happens to be in the vicinity of the Caribbean!"

I look knowingly at Wenger's chubby face, and he beams, unable to keep in his excitement.

"Vot kind of figure could I expect?" ventures Wenger. I note his cautionary inflection. Not counting his chickens too soon.

"A few billion, eventually. Certainly, plenty to keep Mrs. Wenger…" The Chancellor grimaces. "Or whoever keeps your bed warm, in designer shoes, bags, and clothes…or cars, if you're that way inclined." I raise an eyebrow at the chancellor, and he unexpectedly blushes. *Nailed what floats your boat then!*

"So, do I sign here?" mutters Wenger looking down at the contract, but I see his blubbery lips licking, turned on by the money mound that awaits his greedy paws.

"Yep, here and here," I say, tapping at the strategic points requiring the chancellor's autograph on the Quantum Force agreement.

Wenger takes out his pen and scribbles an unruly signature.

I snatch up the agreement, and in my hand, the paper vanishes. Wenger stares, deeply surprised.

I smirk. "No point in carrying it. I'll just bring it back into existence when I need it."

I don't intend to explain my luggage arrangements, or lack of them, to Wenger, but I get a buzz out of shocking these pathetic humans.

The words settle into his brain; he realizes the enormity of my statement and color drains from his face. Wenger sits down heavily into his armchair. I sense his fear and awe. His body shakes slightly. His hands tighten, gripping his thighs, and his eyes raise up to stare at me.

It's that same look all the leaders carry.

Confused wonderment.

"Why now?" asks Wenger, finally finding his voice. He's still trying hard to process and comprehend all the things he's seen that day.

"Why not?" I respond harshly. "Earth is ready. And I'm here to change the world for good."

Suddenly, I realize I'm saying Ashton's words. I scowl, annoyed. After all, I'm in charge of my life. No one controls me. No one has the power over my life. No one dictates what I say. What I do. Those days are over.

I breathe in and redeliver the line again.

"I'm going to take Earth on a journey of enlightenment and truth, from which there will be no going back."

Wenger looks at me, and as he assimilates what I've said, his eyes widen and terror creeps in.

I smile broadly, lightening the moment by patting Wenger's arm.

"Hey, Stefan, it's all for good. I wouldn't be here if Earth wasn't worthy of receiving my intervention."

"And we've been found worthy?"

"Oh yes," I say, my eyes twinkling with unashamed mischievousness. "Earth has most definitely been found worthy."

Chapter 85

After the High Council proceedings, Sam just wanted to get away. He couldn't remain in Kudamun. All that crystal had become cloying and claustrophobic. Every Elder, whether from Giznu or Etima, eyed him with distaste. He knew what rested within their databanks. 'He was the husband of the freak'.

His emotions were teetering, and he was about to fall. Another look of condescension like the one a junior Elder had just given him as they'd passed in the corridor near to the Observation Room, and he'd rip someone's head off. Kudamaz or not, he wasn't going to stand for this constant display of bigotry and inane intolerance.

In his quarters, he looked around. He wandered, each step sullen, as he took in the gigantic bed.

'I love you, Sam. I always will.'

He heard her soft but commanding voice. Her laugh seeped out of the crystal walls and shattered through him.

'Make love not war, baby, at least for now.'

Those had been Ellie's words after they'd saved the world at the end of March that year. She'd taken his hand in hers and led him to that bed, and together they'd made those words a reality. For two Earth days, the love of each other was all they knew.

A celebration of survival through the power of love.

He sat down on the bed and closed his eyes. She was around him again.

Her touch. Gentle, but strong, descending upon his body, to tease him. Delight him. Take him to that blissful Eden. Over and over.

Her eyes. Sparkling, alive with passion. Holding him captivated.

She had been his forever. They had always been together. Ancient powers decreed it to be so.

They'd been fated to live their lives together.

Sam knew this. It explained why he couldn't die. How he'd been saved with Dumuzi's life-force. They'd overcome everything thrown at them.

Against all odds, they'd made it through.

Together, they were stronger.

No, not just stronger, mused Sam, smearing the tears that had started to drip and sparkle down his face.

Together, they were unbreakable.

Sam shuddered, recalling Ellie's vicious assault. Her mocking, lustful eyes as Ashton pawed her shamelessly.

Then he remembered everything she'd endured. MI6 enhanced interrogation. Sabena's torture.

She'd been unbreakable.

Until now.

Who had broken Ellie Noor?

Would he ever find a way to piece her back together?

Sam fell back on the bed and sobbed, tears wracking through his shaking body as he prayed, just like before, for a miracle to save them both.

Chapter 86

The Jag turned and drove down Whitehall. Ashton huffed, seeing the huge mass of bodies ambling around. Above the crowds hung was a series of Surv-Motes, flashing quietly, floating, waiting, their presence imbued with their ominous mandate.

Why couldn't Ellie have shimmered him in? He stared in utter amazement. Vehicles of all sizes with different TV and radio stations from across the world emblazoned on their sides lined the road. Police and Freedom Earth Army personnel walked around. Ashton knew they were trying to manage the public crowds along with the great swathes of reporters, presenters, and camera teams who took up the best part of Whitehall.

The Jag approached Downing Street and Ashton couldn't believe the number of people with cameras and microphones that milled around at the top of the security cordon. Absently, Ashton scanned for Judy (Katzy) Katzenberger, the BBC's top political correspondent, who would have been right at the forefront of something like this, at any other time.

Only he realized she never would be. His Katzy, the woman who'd almost brought him back to understand what love really meant, was dead. A shudder of pain worked up inside him, and his eyes began to tear up. Her body would never be next to his. He could feel himself descending.

A booming resonance burst through him.

Stay strong.

From the front seat, Ashton noticed his primary bodyguard's head turning. He wiped the tears roughly away and straightened. Forcing coldness to wash over him.

"Prime Minister," said his primary bodyguard, over his shoulder, "you're going to have to run the gauntlet, sir. Unless you want to say something to those vultures?"

Ashton scowled. This could all have been avoided. Bloody Ellie!

He'd had no option but to request the car to collect him from the penthouse after he'd finished his energetic interlude with Ellie. With all the shimmering Ellie had subjected him to over the past few days, he'd become quite accepting of that way of traveling, and, frankly, wasn't too keen on going back to the more human transportation methods.

"Got some leaders who need a little more convincing on Quantum Force." Ellie had flashed her dark, blue eyes dangerously and licked her lips. "And you know how convincing I can be."

Ashton smirked. "So no jaunt back to Number 10?"

"No," she responded abruptly and, without another word, shimmered out of Ashton's view.

"Fucking great!" hissed Ashton, his sudden tetchiness slipping through and killing his recent luscious memories, as he watched Ellie's form disappear into an obsidian sparkle.

The driver attempted to drive into Downing Street but couldn't. Too many people were all around and he was concerned one would fall under the wheels of the Jag. Ashton felt a knocking on the side of the car. The windows were darkened, but that didn't stop reporters and camera people training their equipment on all the windows around the car. Until, of course, his Freedom Earth Army officers with members of the Met Police yanked them away from the car, shouting about 'them being a public obstruction', and thus allowing his driver the opportunity to turn fully into Downing Street and head toward Number 10.

His primary bodyguard stepped out of the car and whizzed around to open the door for Ashton. As one leg emerged, the floodlights on those TV broadcast teams lit up and he was hit with a hail of verbal bullets from the reporters' mouths.

"Prime Minister, who is Ellie Noor?"

"Is Ellie Noor the Second Coming?"

"Is she an alien?"

"Is she a messenger from God?"

"Why didn't she die?"

"How long have you known her?"

"How did she beam up all those leaders?"

"Did she create Freedom Earth?"

"Did she give you Quantum Force?"

Ashton stood in front of the open door, and then he turned around to face the yelling reporters.

He held up a single hand, and all went quiet.

"Everyone," Ashton began, his voice booming with silky domination, "Ellie Noor is our friend. She is a wondrous person, and she is our future. Thank you."

Ashton dove in through the black door, as the reporters surged up, screaming for more. But Ashton wasn't going to give them anything else.

Inside Number 10, a sea of ministers, aides, and advisors flooded up to him. They'd all seen the broadcast from Wembley Stadium, and, like the reporters, had a barrage of questions.

Ashton cut through their inquiries, with a solid, "Leave me!"

Redfern walked quickly in his direction and took Ashton's elbow as he strode through to his private quarters.

"Richard, do you think that was wise what you did today?"

"Martyn, I had no *fucking* choice," snapped Ashton, as Redfern closed the door to all the bleating sheep of advisors who still tried to follow the PM, despite his instruction.

"Yes, I saw Ellie took control."

"Took control? She ran the whole damn show. I thought I could control her."

Ashton wandered over to his bar. He poured three fingers of JD into a glass and knocked it back in one. Redfern's eyebrow arched.

"And now you're not so sure?" finished Redfern.

Ashton picked up the bottle and titled his head. "Want one?"

Redfern nodded, and stretched out a hand to Ashton. Taking the drink, Redfern gulped down a healthy measure.

"You think she's getting too powerful? That, maybe, all this that you've done, that you're doing, is wrong?"

Ashton shrugged. Unexpectedly, his body ached. He felt exhausted. Normally, after Ellie's mind-blowing sex, he'd be rejuvenated. Ready to face any titan strong enough to have a go. Now he just seemed drained. He wandered over to the window, to look out at the crowds of media people.

"They think she's some kind of Second Coming."

"Maybe she is," answered Redfern.

"Believe me, she's not!" said Ashton, recalling her temporary dismemberment of his hand. Not to mention the removal of his heart, and, of course, her par chant for virtually sadistic sex.

"So what is she, Rich? What are these beings called Kudamaz?"

"I don't know exactly. Just what they've told me. What Ellie and Sam have imparted over the months I've known them. They come from a world in between. An inner dimension. They watch us, judge us, and count each act. Apparently, there's some kind of energy battery that we're all connected to, us and the rest of the universe, and it needs to be in balance otherwise things get scary. That's what happened in late March. The shit really hit the fan. When the sky went red, that was it. The Kudamaz had us down for obliteration. But Ellie stopped it."

"So, Rich, it sounds like she's a good girl."

"Used to be. Not so sure now," muttered Ashton, remembering how she'd dismissed Sam completely, willing Ashton to ravish her in front of her husband.

In his peripheral vision, Ashton noticed a flash. He stared upward and gasped. The cloudless, blue sky had mutated. Blotches of purple with orange tints had taken over the blue and something silver streaked through the bruise-like skies.

"My God, Martyn, look at the sky!"

Coming up behind, Redfern touched Ashton's shoulder. "Must be ready for a storm."

Looking at the weird streaks across the sky, Ashton shook his head. "That's not like lightning I've ever seen. I hope it isn't anything Ellie's doing. Maybe I should stop all this. Just tell her that Earth isn't ready yet."

"You cannot do that, Richard. Earth knows the truth now. You cannot make them unsee something they've seen."

Maybe it was the drink, but Ashton could discern a deepening in Redfern's voice.

Behind him, Ashton sensed a vibration. He turned, walking slightly away from the window, and waited for the shimmer to solidify.

Ellie or Sam.

Stimulation or confrontation.

The form came out of shimmer. Ellie. But the second she solidified, her expression changed, and she wasn't her exuberant, carefree self.

"Where the fuck is he? I can feel that fucker! I know he's here."

Ashton stared dumbstruck at Ellie's crazy behavior, her eyes wild and challenging, her mouth almost salivating like a rabid animal.

"Who the hell do you mean? Sam?" shouted Ashton, confused, unsure of Ellie's state of sanity (or rather insanity).

"No, I mean…"

At that moment, time appeared to slow down. Redfern revolved to face

Ashton. In his hand was a small, grey, metallic device with a crystal prism on top. Ashton watched as he pressed the prism. Before his eyes, the features and form of Redfern, his Cabinet secretary, dissolved. In his place stood a giant of a man, seven foot or more, thought Ashton, as he tried to understand what was happening. He carried a strange, black, corrugated beard and soulless eyes of utter darkness.

"Me!"

Chapter 87

I look upon the creature before me.

Aswa-da.

The cause of everything. The reason for all my pain.

I hurl my body on top of him, pushing him to the ground. My hands curl around his neck, like before, when he'd zapped Sam with his Harmon gun and almost killed him. I know that if I throttle him, it prevents his ability to shimmer.

I squeeze tighter. My teeth grit down. A snarl erupts from inside me. A beast unleashed.

"Ashton, get that device from his hand and press it."

My back is to Ashton. I know he may be terrified. But maybe not. His agent training should have kicked in. That's what I'm hoping for.

I feel Ashton behind me. He stamps down hard on Aswa-da's wrist, forcing him to open his palm, and I see Ashton's grab the crystal device.

"Press it", I scream, and Ashton does.

Aswa-da's body shudders and, in seconds, my hands are wrapped around Redfern, the human disguise that Aswa-da has been hiding in.

I don't let go. Redfern is the UK's Cabinet secretary, but he's also the dark lord Aswa-da. My hands enclose and Redfern's splutters what sounds like, "I'm sorry."

I ignore his odd apology, and yell to Ashton, "He can't shimmer," and then, as Aswa-da starts to weaken, I feel it. The darkness soaking into me, slipping through my light particles, into my soul force. Each semblance of darkness from Aswa-da is now pouring into me.

Powering me.

And then it stops. The abruptness of the flow startles me. I try to figure out why, and I stare at Redfern. He tries to issue a sneer, but I press my hands into his throat, and he gurgles.

It's obvious. By cloaking Aswa-da to prevent him shimmering, I also stopped the dark energy flow from him into me.

"Press the button, Ashton. He needs to be Aswa-da again."

"But he'll be able to…"

"Just do it!" I holler, and Ashton, sighs behind me.

Beneath me, Redfern's body shudders again, and the features that I know and hate return.

I sense the power-up begin again, unrestricted.

My hands press into Aswa-da's throat, and, as I become stronger, I know I can do much more. Aswa-da's skin gives way, and my hands push in, ripping away his flesh. Blood trickles down between my fingers and sparkles away. I can see the light energy lattice work underneath his skin. As if I'm main-lining Aswa-da's dark energies, they surge into me at a velocity I'd never ever thought possible. I am literally draining him dry. Like an energy vampire. Sucking out every drop of darkness. I go forward, pressing my knees hard down on Aswa-da's shoulders. Getting a better purchase.

Aswa-da's lids flicker. His eyes start to lose their intense darkness, and turn cloudy, storm-skies gray.

"Oh my God! Call security!"

A screaming female voice from behind jerks me suddenly, breaking my focus, and Aswa-da, his throat still dangling open, flowing sparkling blood, lurches forward, using every last ounce of energy, and throws me off him, and immediately initiates shimmer.

On my feet, I whip my head around. My hands bloody. My eyes raging.

"Fucking humans!" I scream, pushing out my soul force to grab Aswa-da's shimmer trail, and Ashton's office is overwritten with the crystal confines of Kudamun.

Chapter 88

Aswa-da as Redfern had noticed Cumberford's video of the Chinese freaky boy spouting words like 'Giznu' and 'Etima', at the same time Sam had. He had not acted immediately. There had been no need to.

Ellie's stadium stunt changed his choice of inactivity.

The Light of Ki was a source of immeasurable power. The human boy only survived through the Light's benevolent actions. Imprisoning the boy within a higher level of consciousness, and only interacting with him using a nominal percentage of its power, the Light was giving the boy a fair chance at surviving his ordeal. The Light had flattened its internal energies, forcing them down, to protect the human's fragile frame.

But Aswa-da recognized that if the Light was under threat, its own survival would be its paramount concern. If the force was greater, or at least as great as the Light of Ki, Aswa-da doubted there would be little benevolent regard.

If Aswa-da could change the human boy, align his cell resonance to that of the Light's, the two entities could maintain a form of harmony. That stabilization would enable the Light of Ki to open itself up, release it flattened contained energies, and rise to its full potential as a truly cataclysmic force.

Having the boy aligned, he could then use the Light of Ki to control Ellie.

Or if it were really needed, and he didn't want to take down the magnificent creature Ellie had become, but if she became too much to handle, the Light could be used to clip her wings.

He'd got Temenos to act swiftly. His Etima colleague had entered the Hall of Umray and stolen one of the crystals imbued with sentient programming. The crystal was known as the Vessel. It's function: to help align a life force from a non-Kudamaz with a Kudamaz one.

The Vessel was used in the deconstitution process needed to create a

Protector of a planet. The Vessel usually held the life force of the Kudamaz Elder who had given up their life force as part of creating a planetary protector. This time, Aswa-da planned to use the Vessel for a very different purpose. To align the resonance of Xiao with the Light of Ki.

From the blueprints filched from the Hall of Ziznak (Hall of Embryonic Beginnings), he knew the exact resonance frequency for the Light of Ki itself. Under his instruction, Temenos used the blueprints to recreate the resonance using a combination of harmonic and light energy engineering. Temenos fixed the resonance of the Light of Ki inside the Vessel and gave the special crystal over to Aswa-da.

Aswa-da, keeping the human disguise as Redfern, had rang the doorbell. He didn't imagine the Changs would recognize him as the Cabinet secretary. Few people outside of Westminster village even knew what a Cabinet secretary was, let alone what his name was or what he looked like.

A slight, but sturdy, and very beautiful oriental woman answered the door.

"Yes?" she said in a sharp voice. She kept the door ajar a little, and had a hooking mechanism attached to the latch, preventing it from opening any farther.

"Mrs. Lei Huan Huan Chang?"

The woman's face stayed neutral. Her black eyes pierced Aswa-da's, and she gave no indication as to who she was.

Untroubled by her lack of response, Aswa-da continued, "Dr. Sam Noor of MI6 sent me. He, like me, is Kudamaz. We know about the energy that unfortunately your son came upon whilst on holiday in Sharm-El-Sheikh. My name is Dr. David Beecham and I know how to extract the energy known as the Light of Ki from your son."

All the time Aswa-da spoke, the woman stared, listening, absorbing his words. Aswa-da didn't try to push in, bully, or use any force at all to gain entry. He just stood patiently, waiting for the words he'd just said to weave their magic inside Lei.

She bit her lip, looked over her shoulder, and then back at Aswa-da. He could see she wrestled with a choice.

"Erm, it's not a good time. My husband isn't here. Can you..."

From inside the house, a scream echoed, and Aswa-da sensed a massive ripple of energy flow toward him. The Light of Ki was awakening.

"Your son Xiao Chang is in great pain. The longer you leave it, the harder extraction will become." Aswa-da's approach was soft, not commanding or abrupt. But the cadence of his voice carried an unmistakable air of a medical professional who knew his business well and would always get results. Aswa-da exuded confidence and capability.

The two things Aswa-da knew Lei searched for.

"You said Dr. Sam Noor sent you?"

Aswa-da nodded, feeling her reluctance to let him in dwindling. Her wall of stoic recalcitrance was crumbling.

Aswa-da watched Lei's eyes as they searched him, his face, his demeanor.

He smiled gently. "I only wish to help your son. I can extract the Light of Ki and place it in here."

Drawing from his pocket the Vessel, he allowed Lei a moment to examine it. Under her inspection, the Vessel glowed.

Lei swallowed heavily and her eyes, wide and watery and rimmed in red, looked upward at Aswa-da's face of projected calm. Aswa-da knew she'd been crying. He picked up and used that intel.

"I'm sorry, Mrs. Chang, but tears won't make Xiao a whole boy again. Only I can do that. It's why Sam Noor sent me."

His poignant but subtle repetition of Sam's name triggered Lei's acceptance. She released the hook lock mechanism and opened the door.

"Come in and follow me," she instructed. "Xiao's room is on the first floor, second door on the right."

Ascending the stairs, the woman reached the door to the room.

A light shone bright for a brief moment underneath the door, and then vanished.

"Xiao, darling, I have a friend of Sam Noor's to see you. He's a doctor and he's going to make you better," Lei called out before she opened the door.

No sound came from the room.

Lei turned the handle and pushed the door ajar. Aswa-da peeped in. Xiao sat on the bed, his eyes forlorn, confused, and tired.

Aswa-da swept a glance behind at Lei; her hands wrung with nervous anxiety.

"If you excuse me, Mrs. Chang, I have to work alone. It should not take long. Once the process is finished, Xiao will return back to you."

Lei issued a small smile, searched his eyes again, and, satisfied by what she'd seen, nodded. She placed her hand out to touch Aswa-da's arm.

"Please, Dr. Beecham, make my son well," implored Lei, a cry of unadulterated desperation in her tone.

"Don't worry, Mrs. Chang. Your son will soon change for good."

Chapter 89

Aby-od, in the process of leaving his opulent crystal quarters to check on something in the Observation Room, sensed a heaviness take over the room, and he looked over his shoulder.

The air had become dense and a fog appeared, and within the haze an obsidian sparkle started. Aby-od recognized it was a Kudamaz from the House of Etima attempting to enter a House of Giznu Elder's quarters. And not just any Giznu Elder. The Head of the House and the Leader of Kudamun.

Security should have triggered. He couldn't understand how they had evaded his surveillance. Aby-od reached in to snatch his Harmon gun from the pocket in his ivory satin robe. Slowly, Aby-od turned around as the Kudamaz unknown came out of shimmer. He brought his gun up.

The figure emerged from the dark sparkles. Ellie Noor shook with anger. Her body seemed to reverberate with wrath.

Aby-od watched Ellie. Her eyes were almost on stalks, bulging and shocked. She glared around the room and Aby-od could see her dark aura twinkling around her body.

What was she?

He shook his head in pity.

He realized the reason for no resonance signal blast on Kudamun's surveillance was down to her change of physiology. The transmutation he'd witnessed with Sam had altered her again, and although she could shimmer, and do the things a pure Kudamaz could do, her Kudamaz resonance frequency no longer registered her as Kudamaz.

She ran over, grabbing him. With fury building, she lifted Aby-od off the ground and shook him.

"Where is he? Where has he gone?"

"What! Sam?" said Aby-od, puzzled and afraid.

"Why does everyone think I'm looking for Sam?" screamed Ellie, anger pelting out of her. "It's Aswa-da, you idiot!"

Aby-od stared, incredulous, down at Ellie. "Aswa-da?"

"Yes, Aswa-da, he's back. That little fucker is back!"

Aby-od put his hands on Ellie's and tried to loosen her phenomenal grip on his robes. Carefully, he tugged at her.

Ellie breathed hard. She glared at Aby-od and unclenched her fingers, letting him drop to the floor.

The Harmon gun was still in his hand. He trained it on Ellie as he struggled to his feet. Ellie clocked the gun and sneered.

"What! You're going to shoot me? I'm the only one who can kill Aswa-da. If I'm dead, he'll run amok, take you out, decimate Giznu, and make Kudamun a one-House zone. His House of Etima."

Aby-od was confused. "But you're Etima, aren't you?"

"I'm Ellie. I take no sides. Only my own."

"If that's true, and you have no allegiance to Etima," said Aby-od, forcing a play of sternness, "then leave Aswa-da to the High Council."

Ellie laughed with derision. "The High Council, they wouldn't last a second. He's mine. I've just got to find him. I thought he'd shimmered here, but I lost his trail."

Aby-od looked at Ellie, now bewildered. If she wasn't a Kudamaz of either Etima or Giznu, what was she? And how did Aswa-da fit into this new game?

As his databanks whirred with questions, the strange, dark aura surrounding Ellie grew stronger, more defined.

He examined Ellie. Her stance, although enraged and primed, didn't look like she was out to deliberately harm him. Aby-od lowered his gun. The moment he returned it to his pocket, Ellie stormed at him.

"You were *actually* going to shoot me?"

Aby-od shivered under Ellie's ire. "After what you did to Sam, yes. I was ready."

"Oh, he came crying to daddy then," mocked Ellie, smirking. "Hurt his male fucking ego."

"Ellie, you *raped* him."

"I didn't. It was consensual." Ellie shrugged. "Anyway, he's my husband. He gave me what I needed in a mutually agreeable transaction." Ellie laughed wildly, and Aby-od stared at her, horrified.

"Ellie, you cannot continue like this. Sam needs you. He loves you.

Doesn't that mean anything to you?"

"Loves me? *Loves me?* I've seen what happens when he loves someone. They get hurt."

"He didn't mean to."

"Oh, so that makes it okay! Like you and your nice line in reconstitution bedside chatter. 'Trust me, Ellie, nothing will harm you!'"

Aby-od looked at the floor, ashamed. He knew what he'd done. How he'd been forced to cut corners. Be economical with the truth. But time hadn't given them the luxury of in-depth analysis. He'd stated facts but left out the reality of what would face Ellie: as a human, she would die.

"I'm sorry, Ellie. But there was no other way. But you're right. You should have known everything."

"You, Sam, you were the trusted ones. But you lied to me. Both of you. And I suffered as a result. I owe you both nothing. And you'll get nothing."

Aby-od could see Ellie's eyes glisten as the tears welled up from the raw emotional energy pumping through her. Damaged goods. He'd said it to her before she'd changed. Now he knew he'd been right. Despite her achievements as protector, she'd never aligned properly inside. Her soul force had always been off-kilter. Reconstitution had been flawed. If it hadn't, her polarity would never have flipped. Cracks caused through misalignment had enabled her transmutation and a total corruption of her soul force.

Ellie seemed to sniff the hair like she was catching a scent. "I can sense him. He's moving again. Do you feel him?" Her voice had descended to an inhuman growl.

Aby-od, mesmerized by Ellie's ability, shook his head. "No, I sense nothing."

"Erm, thought so. It's down to me. I'll kill him. I'm ready for him." Then Aby-od noticed Ellie's dark, blue eyes narrowing, "Oh, he's there!" she shouted, and instantaneously shimmered out of Aby-od's quarters.

Aby-od watched Ellie's departure for a few Earth seconds. And then, as if his internal energies couldn't keep him upright, he flopped to the floor, his head in his hands, and gently rocking back and forth, he whispered to himself, "Oh, what have I done?"

Chapter 90

Sam shimmered into Silent Waters. He couldn't remain in their Kudamaz Giznu quarters, with their saccharine, bordering on nauseating environment. That constant air of having to be bright and happy.

Sam couldn't stand it.

He noticed the air suddenly flicker. Could Ellie be returning?

He remained on the bed and waited for his estranged wife to fix into the reality plane. Her form solidified and he swallowed, staring at a face he hardly recognized.

Wild and raging.

Eyes sweeping, surveilling all around her, her sharp, cold gaze descended upon him.

"Is he here?"

No 'Hello, darling'. Those days were gone. Sam forced himself to face Ellie, but his body wouldn't move. The pain of her loss had broken his towering strength. Brittle inside, he knew his light energies had dimmed, reducing his abilities. Aby-od didn't believe his hypothesis, but Ellie in front of him now only confirmed what he understood. Together they were unbreakable. An invincible force.

Apart, his life was in fragments.

Shattered.

Seeing her only signified what he'd lost. And he'd been the cause of it all. That agony within him surged up, and he said the only words his mouth allowed him to say.

"I'm sorry," whispered Sam.

"What!" hissed Ellie, confused, flicking her head back and forth, running around the bedroom like a banshee looking for her prey.

"I'm sorry for everything."

Ellie stopped her searching and turned back to Sam. Eyes, still wild, took in Sam, and he gulped, acknowledging a deeper aura of darkness surrounding Ellie than even the one she'd had when she'd taken him violently. Her dark descent was at a speed he couldn't comprehend. Something must be powering her. But how?

Sam's analytics were brought to an abrupt end by Ellie's yelling, hysterical voice.

"Suddenly everyone's sorry. You're sorry. Ashton's sorry. Aby-od's sorry. Even fucking Aswa-da's sorry!"

Hearing the dark lord's name, Sam wanted to interrupt. If Aswa-da was back, he must be behind Ellie's transformation, but his wife's raging chewed up any opportunity.

"Instead of being sorry, why couldn't you have thought about what you were doing a decade ago? Be a spy. Save the world. Did you *ever* think of the consequences of your actions? Who might get hurt?"

Sam shook his head. "Please, Ellie, don't do this. You know I thought of the consequences. That's why I didn't tell you for so long."

"Not telling me didn't mean it would protect me. All it did was make me a blind, stupid sitting duck!"

"Ellie, you weren't," Sam tried, but Ellie stormed at him.

"I was. That's exactly what I was."

Sam could feel her pain. Maybe her venting would help her return. This show of bitter hurt might be the cathartic solution she needed to release herself from the dark. Ellie walked toward him.

Strong. Assured. Dominant.

Everything he now wasn't.

"Have you any idea how I felt?"

Ellie blurted out the words. She was now crying. Her tears dropped and sparkled. Her eyes were bulged, crazy. That beautiful, shining, azure blue he loved had dipped to midnight blue. Her body shook. Her hands waved in front of her. Her mouth, that gorgeous, kissable mouth, scowled with hurt.

"Lying there, waiting. Knowing. Have you any idea at *all*?"

Ellie screamed her words at him, and Sam took it all. Motionless.

"You know what Sabena said? You know what that bitch told me? When I was there, on that trolley, at her mercy. She said they were going to fuck me until I *bleed*. Until I barely had a breath left in my body. Then they were going to rip me apart. Piece by piece. Whilst I was still alive. She said she wanted to watch the agony in my eyes, as they sliced me apart."

The words assaulted Sam like bullets. Tore into him. He closed his eyes, his own tears streaming and sparkling. It was as he'd feared. Everything. Sabena had described all to Ellie. And now Ellie's state of darkness was Sabena's posthumous revenge. Her bottled-up pain of that moment had been the trigger to plummet Ellie into darkness.

"Ellie Noor didn't die in the reconstitution process. To survive, she couldn't remain as something that could be hurt. She became a husk. A hollowed-out shell. Ellie Noor died in that medical room before Al Nadir could touch her."

Sam shook as he listened to Ellie's savage words. The raw truth bit into him. His actions had created dark Ellie.

"So don't tell me you're fucking sorry. Your apology is ten years too fucking late!"

He waited a few Earth seconds, but Ellie seemed to have stopped. Her body vibrated with anger, but she was waiting for his response.

"Ellie, if I'd known, I wouldn't…I wouldn't have…"

His wife flew at him, thundering again. "You wouldn't have what, Sam? Wouldn't have become a spy? Learned all your tradecraft? Turned into a killer? You wouldn't have taken up the chance to prove yourself? To get your rocks off playing a real-life Bond!"

"Ellie, it was never like that!"

"Don't fucking lie to me *again*!"

Ellie's voice shook the walls of the Silent Waters apartment. Paintings fell down. Ornaments toppled from shelves. Sam shivered.

"I've had it with your lies. You saw my success and you wanted to achieve something for yourself. But I was slaving all hours on Cloud Nine for us. Not just me. What you did was for you alone. But you never thought about the risks."

"Ellie, darling, I did."

"No, you didn't. For you, it was all about the greater good. Well, what did the greater good give me?"

Ellie snarled, padding forward toward Sam. In her eyes flashed ruthlessness, and he feared she'd attack him again. Every sense told him to shimmer. That Ellie equaled danger. In her advance, a dark power rippled through her. But Sam didn't move. He dug his fingers into the mattress and sat back straight. Waiting Ellie's retribution. If she killed him, so be it. He'd die at her hands for the pain he'd wrought on her.

He even welcomed an end to the agony of not having her love anymore.

Sam swallowed. Ellie arrived.

Her eyes lasered into him. Burning into his soul.

"You know what your greater fucking good gave me?"

He held her stare. He could barely shake his head. Ellie was now an eruption of pure wrath. He could feel her soul force emanating fury and unforgiving hatred.

"Hell on Earth. A constant living nightmare I knew only death could release me from."

She stood over him, looking down on him as he sat on the corner of the bed. Hate and contempt fired into him. Sam just took it.

"But now, it's over. I've woken. I'm free. Nothing can affect me. Nothing can harm me. I'm impervious to all the memories past. They are but flickers. Meaningless. Your Ellie Noor is dead. What I am, I have to be. Don't try to stop me. If you do, believe me, you'll be more than sorry."

Ellie daggered Sam. The meaning to Sam was clear. She'd kill him.

"Ellie, please don't leave me."

Sam reached out, touching Ellie's arm. He jerked back. It was ice cold. Ellie stared at his hand and sneered. Sam breathed in and persisted, refusing to be dissuaded by the icy feel of her body. Quickly, he pulled her closer.

Her eyes narrowed with a deadly intent. Sam didn't care. At that moment, he had to try. Had to try to bring her back. When Aswa-da had shot him with his Harmon gun back in March, she had brought him back.

Through love.

It's pathetic.

Sam thinks by reaching out I'll run back to him. That somehow, I'll magically return into his arms. I can see he isn't expecting how cold my body is. It's just a manifestation of how I feel toward him.

I look into his eyes. Hooded and forlorn.

He's finally taking responsibility for his actions.

For ten years, I've lived a panacea of perfection. A charmed but artificial life.

My world was all manufactured.

I saw what was put before me, heard only the words from a prepared script.

Then I became the Protector. Aby-od filled me full of his dish of lies. And still, despite my enormous powers, I was still beholding. To Aby-od.

Kudamun. Earth. That Pain of Parsu, a kill-switch inside me, that threatened to shut me down if I didn't protect Earth or the humans who inhabited it. All to control me. Mold me into something someone else wanted.

My life had never been under my control alone.

Until now.

"Don't touch me!"

I grab Sam's hand and twist it away from me. His face contorts, and I push at him to retreat. Reluctantly, he moves back. Sorrow fills his eyes. I watch as pity for me creeps slowly into his dark, brown eyes, and then I strike. My hand flies out, whipping him across the face.

He makes no attempt to fight back. He just sits there.

"What is wrong, Sam? Have you no fire in you? Where is Sam the badass killer? The guy I watched on the Observation Screen taking down terrorists, torturing, maiming. Doing all that shit for good ole' Blighty. Where is he?"

I scream at Sam, but he doesn't raise from the bed. His eyes fix on the floor.

"Why don't you answer me!"

The burning rage flows through me. His silence is incendiary.

Suddenly, I leap onto the bed, pushing Sam down into the covers, my powerful body pinning him. I press my arm across his throat and lock onto his eyes.

He doesn't speak. I look at his lips and remember the times we'd kissed. Those luscious lips. Something stirs inside me.

I drop down. I bite, tasting those lips. I force his mouth open and invade him with my tongue. I search inside his mouth, thrusting with vicious intention. I press my body hard against Sam and search his face for a lustful response.

What I see makes me incensed.

Compassion. Sympathy.

Disgusted, I snarl, "What happened to my Sam? Where did you go?"

I watch him try to sit up. He glares. Forgiveness alive in his eyes. "I didn't go anywhere. You did."

I lift Sam off the bed and hurl him down onto the floor. He shudders on impact, and then he's on his feet. Staring at me, sad but wary.

I refrain from engaging. It's all over. I walk away. I feel Sam's eyes on me. I turn and deliver what I'd meant to from the beginning.

"Aswa-da's back. I'm going to kill him."

The moment Aswa-da's name is mentioned again, I see vengeance in Sam's eyes. The spark of fire I'd been trying to ignite has taken flame.

"Ellie, he's dangerous. I'll come with you." Sam's voice is matter of fact, just the way he was before. Cold. Hard. Calculating.

I smirk. "You'd love that, to be back in the zone. Big bad Sam taking over. Well, husband, it isn't happening. No one can take down Aswa-da. His power is too strong. Only I can kill him."

"Ellie, you need me-" cries Sam, and he edges toward me.

I rage back at him, unrelenting and merciless, "Need you? I'm more than you'll ever be. I don't need you now. Not ever. Don't come near me again."

I dagger Sam with a glare of a killer. A look he understands.

As I initiate shimmer, I see Sam heading toward me.

He's screaming now, "I won't give up on you, sweetness. I won't let you go."

I hear the assumption that Sam still possesses me and believes he can still control me.

I yell back in fury through the shimmer, "I've gone, sweetness. I belong only to myself!"

Chapter 91

Sam, catatonic, couldn't move. His heart of light was breaking.

Carved in two by Ellie's words.

'I've gone, sweetness. I belong only to myself'.

He found himself automatically deconstructing the words. Agent mode still kicked in despite his change. She said she'd belonged only to herself. Not to him.

But not to Ashton either.

A glimmer of hope flickered within his shattered soul force.

He focused on it and centered himself, regaining his internal strength that had sapped out of him in Ellie's presence. In the mirror, he watched as his stooped shoulders pulled up and his back straightened. Sam lifted his head, recognizing that his Kudamaz energies flowed strong within him again.

His reflection darkened. A fog took over the mirror from floor to ceiling, and within the swirling grayness, the sneering face of Aswa-da appeared.

Sam's massive hands balled tight. That surge of vengeance he'd felt when Ellie mentioned the dark lord's name rose, renewed in force, and with a roar, Sam charged at the mirror. Slamming into it. The impact splintering it apart, but the vision vanished.

Breathing deep, shrugging off the shards of glass that had fallen over him, Sam knew the vision had been in his mind. Was he now going mad? Had his wife's insanity rubbed off on him? On top of everything else?

It crashed into him.

'Save me!'

Like Xiao's voice, but deeper, screaming. The Light of Ki?

Or Aswa-da's trap?

Sam didn't know. Didn't care. He knew he had to go where the voice was.

Aswa-da was behind everything. Ellie's change. Xiao's condition. Nothing was a coincidence. It was all connected. Save Xiao and he'd save Ellie.

It was what he'd believed from the beginning, when it all started. When he'd seen her transform. He'd told that prick Aby-od, but he hadn't been convinced. But Sam had been led by his agent's well-honed nose of investigation.

Anomalies. Always look for them and make the connections. They always lead to the truth.

Sam fixed on the vibrating, pain-filled screaming in his mind, and shimmered.

Around him, the scene erupted. Xiao's incensed screams seemed to resonate throughout the house.

"It's a lie. We're all going to die!"

Lei, tears streaming, mascara rolling down her always immaculate face, howled outside Xiao's door, "Please, Xiao, open this door."

Chen, his cheeks red, his eyes bloodshot from stress, banged his huge bulk against Xiao's door. "Let us in, Son," he barked.

Both turned on Sam's entrance.

"He's gone crazy. He's locked the door. We can't get in." Chen spat the words at Sam, glaring at him. "This is your fault. He was calm before you messed around with him."

Sam ignored Chen's attack, focused on the inside of Xiao's bedroom, and shimmered.

Inside, Xiao flickered between states. A pillar of light then a human boy. Sam knew the Light of Ki had been pushed out of its higher state of consciousness. But how?

"Did Aswa-da do this?"

Whilst Xiao was in his human form, he nodded, his eyes round and terrified, lips wobbly, unable to create a word, and then he cried out as the Light of Ki took him over in a blaze of unbelievable energy.

"How did he do this, Xiao?" asked Sam calmly.

Sam had to project a sense of peace. He couldn't risk trying to connect with the Light of Ki again, as it nearly destroyed him the last time. But if he could find a way to relax the boy, keep within one state long enough to question him, he may know more of Aswa-da's plans.

In the flickering transition state, turning from a pillar of light back into his human form, Xiao struggled out the word, "Doctor."

Sam knew. He shimmered outside to the landing.

"Did you bring a doctor to see Xiao?" asked Sam to Xiao's mortified parents.

Chen shook his head, but Sam watched as Lei made a slight nod, putting her hands up to her mouth, as the tears flooded her sallow cheeks.

"Why, Lei?" yelled Chen. "You told me I couldn't bring in experts. You begged me not to have him analyzed." Chen stared at his wife, incredulous.

"He…he…showed up. You were at work this morning. I was alone. I'd just prayed over Xiao. He was so silent. Barely alive. I just wanted him back again."

"Who showed up?" snarled Sam. But he already understood what had happened.

"He spoke like you; Sam. Said he was a doctor sent by you. He used your kind of words. I was desperate. Very low. I took him to see Xiao."

"You never told me!" snapped Chen, the fury burning in his face.

"Within minutes of the man leaving, Xiao came around. He smiled. We talked. He played on his games. He seemed normal. And then he suddenly started screaming. He locked his door. Oh God, Sam. What have I done?" Lei sobbed.

"It's not your fault," said Sam, leveling Chen with a cold eye. "You're not to blame. I'll fix this."

Sam shimmered back into Xiao's room. The Light of Ki blinded him, as he came out of shimmer. It radiated throughout the room, searing into his Kudamaz light energy frame.

"Xiao, concentrate on my voice," said Sam gently. "You are safe."

Whatever Aswa-da had done, Sam could sense fear drowning the boy. It was taking control and fueling his instability. Sam had to find a way to calm the boy, and, with him, the Light of Ki. Both had experienced Aswa-da and suffered trauma as a result.

Sam gnashed his teeth, forcing himself to stay centered, but inside he just wanted to rip Aswa-da apart.

The boy picked up on Sam's anger and shrieked. A naked, raw, agony sound.

"Shush, shush," said Sam, quelling his ire for Xiao's sake. "I'm here. I'll save you."

The words triggered something. The flickering states paused. Xiao's human form gained control momentarily.

"Back to the beginning," stated Xiao, his eyelids fluttering like electricity charged through him.

"Where you were when you entered Xiao?" responded Sam.

Xiao issued a half nod and dropped to the floor, unconscious. Gingerly, Sam ventured forth, knowing the energy that was still contained within Xiao. He picked the boy up and shimmered him out to his parents.

Lei and Chen, on seeing the boy in Sam's arms, went to grab him.

Sam looked into the shocked eyes of Lei and Chen.

"We're going to Sharm El Sheikh."

Chapter 92

I follow the trail. Like a bloodhound, now I've picked up his scent, I'm onto him. He can't escape.

A room lined with old, elegant bookcases and a massive, leather topped, mahogany desk fade into view around me. My databanks tell me it's the office of the Cabinet secretary in London. Aswa-da's hiding place as Sir Martyn Redfern.

As I come out of shimmer, I sense a vibration to the left of me and see a swirl of sparkle. Without thinking, I imagine Aswa-da back in front of me. I feel the power inside pulling on the degrees of realities. I discern Aswa-da. I've pin-pointed his exact location. Holed up between those degrees of universal reality before the Reality Gap kicks in, shielding Kudamun.

I scream, fling my hand out into the air, and wrench in, point seven of a degree into reality's plane, and I yank Aswa-da back into Redfern's office.

Astonished by this sudden reveal, Aswa-da stands for an Earth second, completely immobile. His throat, I note, has repaired itself, as all Kudamaz bodies do, and evidence of my attack cannot now be seen.

Soon I will restore my handiwork, I think, and leap on him again, my hands around his neck. But this time I tug upward at his head, and I feel something loosen.

His neck starts to split, and blood seeps out from the tear. Aswa-da's eyes widen. He knows my intention.

"The tr-tr-truth…" he stutters.

Still tugging, I say, "What?"

"Tr-truth. Ev-ever…Everything."

Aswa-da is a game player. He'll use anything to stay alive. To win. I'm not playing his game anymore.

"Pl…ple…please. Ellie. Tr…truth."

I hate myself.

Something about that word. Truth. It captivates me. I can't help it.

I stop tugging, but I keep my hands forcefully tight around his torn neck. I realize I'm pulling off his dark energies again. Aswa-da realizes it too. He knows he's weakening. In his eyes is a flicker of resignation. He knows what I am. And he's scared.

I stare into his dark eyes that have been the origin of so much pain in my life.

"Speak, fucker!" I hiss.

"We both want dark to prevail, don't we?"

I glare, and shrug, showing my ambivalence to his address.

"Goodness robbed you, Ellie. Aby-od, he stole it all from you. And Sam, he put you through so much pain."

"So did you," I snarl. But I feel his words echo with an inner truth.

"I made you what I knew you could be. Why should you deny yourself the right to be who you are? I gave you the freedom. To unshackle yourself from responsibilities. To feel the power, the true power, of being the Protector. Tell me, Ellie, and be true to yourself, have you not enjoyed these past few days more than any in all your lifetimes?"

Aswa-da sneers. A knowing arch of his eyebrow suggests he's seen *all* my antics, with Ashton, with Sam, with the world.

Instead of being disgusted, I smile, ice-cold, and fix my dark, blue eyes upon Aswa-da.

"Hope you enjoyed the floorshow!"

He smirks. "You've already answered my question, Ellie. Now I'm going to answer yours."

"I didn't ask one," I snap.

"Oh, you did. You've been asking one question throughout your time as Protector."

I'm wary. Aswa-da is saying too much. I tighten my grip to show I'm in control.

"And what do you think that is?" I say.

"Why?"

Chapter 93

The instant the words 'Sharm El Sheikh' left Sam's lips, Xiao vibrated, crying and shaking, and turned once again into a pillar of light.

Lei, seeing the strange sight that had become of her son, fainted.

Chen yelled and tried to charge at Sam, who, using his Kudamaz vision, sidestepped out of the way, and Chen bashed into the wall.

A ball of energy thudded into Sam with a vicious purpose as Xiao transitioned, and he instinctively released the boy from his arms. The pillar of light fell but didn't hit the floor. It bounced in the air, suspended, and shone with greater energy.

"Return to survive."

Xiao/the Light of Ki's plaintive whisper reverberated within his light cells. More than a sound one could hear; it was a resonance that connected, bringing him some form of stilted communication.

From his peripheral vision, Sam saw Chen bend over Lei, pick her up, and stand, the small, slender body of his wife nestled in his huge arms. She didn't move. Chen stared at the pillar of light bobbing up and down on the landing.

"My God, is that Xiao? What have you done to him?" Chen's terrified voice dragged from him. He dropped to the floor, placed Lei down, and turned face-on to Sam. Hatred shook through his features, and he rushed toward Sam.

Using his Kudamaz vision, Sam looked at Xiao, still a pillar of light. He didn't know why he hadn't transitioned back into being human again. He'd stayed a pillar of light. Then Sam took in Lei. She hadn't moved since she'd fainted. But her vitals, he could tell, were all okay. She was just unconscious due to shock. His gaze rested upon Chen. The enormous man, raging, had taken one step after another. Sam could see he was intent on hurting him. Or would try to.

Sam didn't want to retaliate. As Chen's fists smashed toward him, Sam put his forearm up. Deflecting the blow and the force of impact sent Chen sailing in the air across the landing and over his wife's body, and he landed with a thump on the other side. Sam watched. Chen jumped up, smarting, embarrassed by his sudden inadequacy, and pelted across the landing. Pictures on the walls swayed under Chen's heavy tread. His flying fist headed toward Sam's face. Sam shook his head.

"For God's sake, Chen. Stop!"

Sam grasped hold of Chen's fist as it came at him, and he clasped his hand over Chen's, forcing it downward. Sam didn't try, but he couldn't help but use a little of his Kudamaz strength. On pushing Chen's fist downward, Chen's body followed.

Sam held Chen, now on his knees, and stared into his mortified eyes.

"Please. Please stop this. I mean no harm to you, to your family. I just want to help Xiao."

The edges of Chen's eyes grew watery and he looked from the pillar of light to his wife's slumped body on the floor, and he began to cry.

"I don't understand. Why is this happening?"

Sam understood. A man like Chen, who'd always been in control, was now totally powerless. He had no control as nothing made any sense. It was beyond his comprehension.

Sam crouched down and placed a hand out toward Chen's black, silky hair.

"Please stand up."

"Why can't you help my son?"

Sam flung a look back to Xiao who still hadn't transitioned. "I'm trying to. I need someone else."

Sam knew he didn't have enough power to save little Xiao. But Ellie did.

"I will return," he stated, hoping his assured tone was enough to calm a traumatized Chen, and he initiated shimmer.

Ellie might hate him. But she couldn't hate a child.

Sam placed his faith in that thought as he set about his search for her.

Chapter 94

Aswa-da watched Ellie closely. He was very aware the power within her had mutated, taking a dramatically different route to the one he'd intended for her. Like before, when she'd discovered her ability to collect and channel white light energies from across the world to fire up the white crystal of good in the Therab in March, her new incarnation could do the same, but with dark energies.

Or more specifically, his dark energy.

He had to reason with her. Find a way to win her over. The strength she wielded was greater than anything she'd had as Protector. She was a force unleashed. And his life was in the balance of his ability to speak for his survival.

He knew she'd been plagued with wanting to know the truth.

Lies had crucified her.

He fixed on that and worked his acerbic words into her mind.

"Why?" repeated Ellie, and her fingers pressed into his throat. Her eyebrows knitted with annoyance. "What the fuck do you mean?"

"Why the Balance Shift never changed for Earth? Why Ashton always showed perfect Equilibrium? Why the Observation Screen didn't show everything? Why Freedom Earth? Why Quantum Force? Why unify religion? Why change you? So many whys, Ellie. I can see you're drowning in them."

"And you'll tell me everything?"

"I promise you, Ellie. No more secrets. No more lies. Trust me, Ellie. I am the only one who can give you the truth."

Ellie's eyes glared, but Aswa-da could see everything still bottled up inside her. A magnum of champagne ready to pop.

"If I release you, make sure you stay." Ellie lasered into him with a steel glare. "If you try to shimmer, I'll pull you back. You know I can. Then I'll kill you, no matter what secrets you still have. Ripping your fucking head off is something that's worth a mountain of your answers."

Aswa-da caught Ellie's eye and tried to convince himself he could take her on if he had to. She seemed to read him, for her hands tightened.

"Did you hear me?" she growled. "You promise me you'll not try to shimmer?"

A struggled nod, and a hoarse, "Yes, I promise," later and Ellie withdrew her hands from his neck. She still sat on top of him, her knees pressing on his shoulders. Pinned to the floor. Aswa-da couldn't move. He weighed up his words and decided, given Ellie's liking for the lascivious, on his play.

"Ellie, my dear, unless you're planning on getting cozy with me, could you get up?"

Ellie stared down at him and smirked. "Not my type, sweetheart!" she retorted, and leapt up.

Aswa-da pulled forward and stood in front of Ellie. She stared at him, daggering him with her dark, blue, shining eyes. What was she?

"So, Aswa-da, the truth. I want to know everything."

"I keep to my word," said Aswa-da, making to sit down on one of the cream Victorian sofas in Redfern's office.

But Ellie shook her head. "This way," she gestured, and plucked at the air.

Aswa-da watched, confounded, as Ellie created a hole in the reality plane. Within the office surroundings, a dark abyss loomed filled with a sparkling lattice of lights. Ellie was doing naturally what the Kudamaz used dimensional lapse field controllers to do. Enter into degrees of reality. Ellie took his hand. She sneered as she detected a slight quiver he couldn't hold back, and she pulled him into the sparkling lights.

Suspended within the lattice work, Ellie gestured for Aswa-da to walk with her.

"Tell me everything," commanded Ellie, staring, her face tough but questioning.

Aswa-da nodded.

"Remember the cobalt crystal Sam smashed to smithereens?"

I do recall the crystal.

"The one you used to control Treeborne and torture Sam? Yep, I remember." My voice is solid, even, and calm, despite what I've said. Aswa-da looks at me, worried he's annoyed me, but I indicate for him to continue.

"The architecture of the cobalt crystal and the dark and light power blocks, I discovered to be very similar. That was how I changed Treeborne's DNA and aligned his harmonic frequency with that of the cobalt crystal. It made him easy to manipulate, but it also enabled him to be used as a conduit to generate trust in others. My goal from the time he found the tablet as a boy was to make him the US president, just through exercising the powers of manipulation, persuasion, and trust."

"You certainly achieved that. Good ol' President Looney Tunes had a fair good run."

Aswa-da smiles. "Yes, my experiment worked. But it was only the beginning. I knew I had to have a backup plan. Aby-od was crowing about the power of the Protector. How amazing you were. How nothing could stop you. The High Council believed him, for a while…"

I raise an eyebrow, recalling how the Leader of Kudamun had conned me, and sourness touches my tongue. "Yeah, that prick certainly knows how to sell a story."

Aswa-da laughs. "You and I are so very similar Ellie."

I grip hold of his hand, crushing his fingers in mine, and swing him around to face me. "I'm nothing like you. Don't push it. Continue!"

Concern crosses his face. He gulps and pulls back on the familiarity card. Around us, lights sparkle, as I take us both through the quantum light energy lattice that holds reality together. In the far distance, I can see the purple and orange of the Reality Gap. The silver streaks burst into brilliant light that, even at a distance, I can still see.

"So, like I said, I needed a plan B. I entered the Hall of Ziznak (the Hall of Embryonic Beginnings). I reviewed, in detail, the geometric architectural plans of Earth's dark and light power blocks within their holo light bubbles."

"How did you enter without alerting the High Council guard?" I ask. What Aswa-da has done is bold and dangerous. I cannot help but admire him.

"Resonance implosion. It stopped me from being known to Kudamun's scanners."

"Risky. You could have died."

Aswa-da straightens and gives me a glare. "Worth the risk."

"So you've got the blueprints to the blocks, what then?"

"I broke into the Sahar (Sand Grain) Vault and stole a grain of sacred sand."

"And you used the Ama-Usham Chamber (Genesis Machine) to create a replica crystal block. Bloody brilliant!" I remark, racing into Aswa-da's measured delivery. With just those few sentences, I can see everything so clearly.

Aswa-da grins and preens himself like a peacock. "I thought so!"

"And, you've switched the crystals, haven't you? Mankind's consciousness isn't connected to the white crystal anymore." I stop walking and look at Aswa-da. "That's why there's no Balance Shift." Then I scowl. "No, hang on, the dark crystal would still be pumping out energies and that would crash the Shift to the dark. If the world's so bad, why isn't that happening?"

"Think, Ellie," says Aswa-da pointedly, and I can see he's waiting for me to figure out what he's done.

It dawns on me. Filters. Changing intensities.

"You've not just made a replica of the power block; you've created a new type of crystal in the Ama-Usham Chamber."

Aswa-da stares. His dark eyes burn into mine. "Go on, Ellie. You're almost there."

"I thought you were supposed to be telling me the truth. I didn't sign up for putting together a puzzle," I snipe at Aswa-da, and sneer.

"You know you want to figure things out. You've always been one to join the dots."

"Connections, eh!" And then I realize it. I rush out my final hypothesis. "The dark power block is routed into the new power block. We'll call it the grey one. That breaks the ability of the dark power block to connect to the Balance Shift. Its energies run through the grey one, which has been created to identify the properties of the white crystal as a filter. The dark energies' intensity is reduced completely through this process." I stop, suddenly confused. "But if the white crystal is still there..."

"It isn't. It's gone," states Aswa-da, his pride brimming over.

"Gone? How?"

His audacity at not just changing the antediluvian laws but blasting them apart shocks me. I know if he hadn't undertaken resonance implosion, he would have been executed by the High Council by now. It seems the Order of Kudamun and everything considered sacrosanct through virtue of the Ancient Ones' legacy has been broken by Aswa-da.

I stand in awe of the dark creature before me.

"I removed it. There is no white crystal power block, only the grey crystal that connects to the white light energy streams throughout Earth, including mankind's consciousness, thoughts, and final actions. The white crystal's connection to humans is lost forever."

Nodding wildly, I get everything Aswa-da has said, and I burst in, "But the grey crystal is also a filter for the dark power block's energies. Earth only has the grey power block connected to the Balance Shift. That's why the indicator barely moves. White light energies, they've hardly changed. But the dark energies have, they've increased, but the filtering cancels them out. I said you were brilliant, Aswa-da, but this, what you've done, it's fucking genius!"

"Pleased you're impressed," sneers Aswa-da.

"So I get the Balance Shift stuff. Tell me about Ashton. What's up with his constant Equilibrium?"

Aswa-da regards me. He can see I'm chomping at the bit to know more. He smirks.

"Ah, Ashton, well, he's quite a different story. Shall we slip back into Earth time for a spot of tea, and I'll spill all?"

I laugh. "If you don't, the only thing on that afternoon tea menu will be your spilled guts."

Chapter 95

Aswa-da took Ellie's proffered hand, tentative of her mood, and walked through the hole she'd made in reality back into Redfern's office.

"Do you mind?" Aswa-da held up the metallic prism device that the Kudamaz used to cloak themselves so they could walk amongst natives of the planets they oversaw. "These humans can be so tiresome, screaming and such, if they see me like this."

"Knock yourself out," said Ellie, scowling at the device.

Aswa-da pressed the prism, and his features and form shrunk down to the human known as Redfern.

"Now, about that tea." He pressed a button on the intercom on his phone. "Marjorie, dear, could you get me some tea and cake for two please?"

Aswa-da listened to his secretary's affirmation to the task and turned to focus on Ellie.

"You want to know about Ashton."

"Well, it's obvious he's not connected to the Balance Shift. I realized that much whilst I was the Protector."

Listening, Aswa-da grinned. "You know, technically, you're still the Protector of Earth. Kudamun can't see any difference. Your actions, they've been well received by these parasites."

"Humans?" Ellie sneered.

Aswa-da nodded. "Yes, humans. They see you as a savior, and Ashton as being touched by an angel."

"He's been touched alright." Ellie smirked, and her eyes flashed with naughtiness.

Aswa-da laughed. "Yes, quite. Well, as I say, you are still the Protector. Nothing has changed. This is very important, Ellie. It means, in the eyes of

Kudamun, you are still fulfilling your duties. No one on Kudamun, not the High Council, not Aby-od, no one can accuse you of going against what you were created for. If they could, the High Council Guards would have located and executed you. As it stands, my work with the power blocks has made you immune to retribution from the High Council."

Ellie glared at him. Aswa-da tried to read her. Something he'd said had provoked her and now anger sparked in her eyes.

"Was I *always* part of your plan?"

"Not always. But when Treeborne failed and you unleashed the white light energies of the Therab, I knew I had to enact a swift counter attack."

Ellie made to launch in, but a knock sounded.

"Come in," called Aswa-da, with genteel authority.

A small built woman, dark, brown hair, sharp, hooked nose, slender face, and piercing, blue eyes, wheeled in a tea trolley with cakes and biscuits.

"Lovely. They do so look after me," bragged Aswa-da, giving Marjorie a quick wink.

Marjorie blushed. "Really, Sir Martyn…" she muttered, and was about to leave the room when she saw Ellie. "Oh my God. It's you. You're the…the…"

"Yes, Marjorie. This is Ellie." Aswa-da's hand drifted out toward Ellie, who took her cue to smile sweetly at the astounded secretary, and provide an intoned, "Hello."

"We're discussing something very private, classified, in fact, on behalf of the prime minister, so please ensure we're not disturbed."

Marjorie nodded, backing away. Aswa-da realized that it wasn't respect that kept her from raising her eyes from the floor. It was terror. She was terrified to gaze upon Ellie.

With a soft creak, the door to his office closed.

Aswa-da turned to the trolley. "Shall I play mum?"

"Whatever floats your boat, big guy."

Aswa-da grinned. He could see why Aby-od liked Ellie so much. She did have quite an attitude.

Ellie munched through the Victoria sponge, sipped at the tea, and stated, "You were talking about Ashton. I know you must have screwed around with his DNA. Same shit you did with Treeborne. But when? I can't get your timeline. He had perfect Equilibrium before all that stuff went down in Ur in the ziggurat. It grated on me. I hated leaving without finding out why. So when did you change him?"

Aswa-da bristled with hubris. "I knew you were suspecting. I was concerned you'd ruin everything before it had begun. To answer your question, I grabbed Ashton when he was at his lowest. He's a very powerful, resourceful human. Quite exceptional in many ways."

"Yeah, I thought that too," said Ellie.

"But he held within him considerable darkness. He was the perfect specimen to be the Chosen One."

Aswa-da noted Ellie had moved closer to him. "The Chosen One?"

"That's what was required."

"But when did you change him?" repeated Ellie, her tone irate. "I need to know when."

"Patience, my dear Ellie." Aswa-da patted Ellie's knee. Her hand grasped his and squeezed hard, and then threw his hand away. He breathed out, controlling the sudden pain her little gesture had whipped up.

"I haven't any. Cut to the *fucking* chase."

"All that business with Al Nadir killing his lover Katzy, a woman he appeared to really love. It tipped him. Made him malleable. Pliant. I found a way in. His soul was broken. Blood-thirsty revenge soaked through him. He searched out darkness. I felt him, his resonance burning with wrath. I shimmered into his penthouse. He sat there on the sofa. Devastated. Katzy's heart and eyeballs littered around him."

Aswa-da watched Ellie. Her eyes widened at the explanation of what Ashton had experienced. He knew it was in her databanks; the intel he was explaining was already there, but, perhaps, she'd never bothered to review it.

"Poor Ashton," murmured Ellie, and Aswa-da arched his eyebrow.

"Feel something for the human, do you?"

"Yes, I do! Problem?" snapped Ellie, and her eyes glowered with naked fury at him.

He mustn't antagonize her. He had to remember; he wasn't chiding the Protector anymore. Ellie was different, much, much different.

And extremely dangerous.

Chapter 96

I stare at Aswa-da, annoyed, and thoughts of Ashton, of how he must have suffered, unexpectedly surface. Yes, it's been about playful domination, but beyond all that, I can't fail to realize I have true feelings for Britain's PM.

Aswa-da examines my face. He sneers, clearly pleased he's unraveled my weakness.

"Go on," I say. "Is that when you changed him?"

"Yes. I took him to Kudamun, inserted a new set of amino acids within him. Inside this DNA sequence, many levels below the quantum level, I ran a frequency. An annulling resonance, for want of a better word. It soaked into his human framework, from the quantum plane upwards. Eventually, it buried into his cells. His very being. This resonance enabled Ashton's dark and light forces to cancel each other out, giving a constant state of Equilibrium. By the time you laid eyes on him in the War Cabinet, he was already mine."

I listen. Like the manipulation of the crystal power blocks, Ashton's metaphysical augmentation is audacious in the extreme. It does, however, explain Ashton's ability to remain contained and unruffled whilst I did all that weird shit to him.

One thing, however, I still don't understand.

"Why did you change him? Why did you need him to be the Chosen One?"

"To teach Kudamun a lesson they'll never recover from."

Now I'm mystified. I don't want to show my confusion or give Aswa-da the benefit of seeing me at a loss. But I am. I chew on some cake, looking down at the pieces on my plate, to deflect from Aswa-da picking up on the bewilderment in my eyes.

"Kudamun is an anachronism, Ellie. They are no longer relevant in these times. All their pomp, their pageantry, their robes, their laws, their supercilious attitudes to the way the universe should be governed, everyone bowing down to the Order of Kudamun, I hate it, Ellie. I hate it all. They need to modernize. Look outward. Change perspective. See what is really happening."

Hearing Aswa-da, he sounds quite sane, although I always had him down as a lunatic. But by his address, I know he really wants to initiate a form of disruptive change.

"What's that? What's happening?"

"Greed, selfishness, hurt, pain, you name it, Ellie. The universe is at the brink of embracing darkness. Earth is the tipping point.

"So how does Freedom Earth, Quantum Force, unifying religion, how do all those things that Ashton instigated, fit in?"

"They're just levers of change, Ellie. Ashton always wanted to be world leader. It was his thing. I gave him the notion of Freedom Earth at the end of March."

"Wait a minute," I interject. "If you gave him the notion of Freedom Earth, you must have known I was going to win?"

"Not necessarily," Aswa-da says, his dark eyes twinkling mischievously. "I'd already tweaked Ashton's DNA and intensified his evil quotient. Making the suggestion of Freedom Earth to him, embedding it into his subconsciousness whilst he was in slumber, was straightforward. I just left Ashton to ferment the idea powered by his megalomaniacal tendencies. Unifying religion was just an extension of the tenets of Freedom Earth. Peace on Earth. Love to all humanity."

I remain silent. Just listening. But inside, I am horrified. Aswa-da has been behind everything.

"Once Ashton took on board the Freedom Earth ideology, it didn't take long for his revenge systems against Al Nadir for what they did to Katzy to kick in. He initiated the right to execute terrorists, made public executions law, sent you and Sam on a murderous rampage cleaning up Al Nadir bases."

I stiffen.

"I mean, Ellie, did you *really* think it was actually okay to annihilate that many people? Fifty-six million people?"

I shake my head. I have been a pawn from the beginning. An instrument for Aswa-da to use. Inside, the flame of injustice burns.

"You fucking bastard! You used me!"

I jump on Aswa-da. The plate in his lap topples to the floor, smashing bits of porcelain in all directions. My hands wrap around his throat. He gurgles, and claws at my hands.

"Pl…please…let me finish!"

"You're finished!" I snarl, tightening my grip. But I stop. I can't kill him. There's still so much more he hasn't said. Like Quantum Force. I need to know what that was all about.

I grab Aswa-da by the scruff and yank him up off the sofa. I initiate shimmer with him still in my hands. In my mind, I see a mountain range near St Moritz where I'd spent many a happy summer with Sam on our walking holidays. That was, of course, before he'd started lying. And scheming a life for me that didn't exist.

Feeling the hurt rage through me, I shake Aswa-da as I come out of shimmer. And then I let him go. He falls to the rocky ground, clutching his neck. He's still in the disguise of Redfern.

"Ellie," Aswa-da whimpers, "I have to tell you…"

He falters. I drop to the ground and sit on him, pressing my strength down, jamming him tight beneath the craggy rock. I search in his pocket for the metallic prism device. My hands enfold around the cold, liquid, metal thing, and I draw it out.

"So tell me," I growl.

Aswa-da sees I have the device and he sighs. "Ellie, we're on the same side. I mean you no animosity."

"You tricked Sam and I to kill fifty-six million people!"

"Ellie, you said it yourself, they're parasites. Anyway, you read their Balance Shifts. All were dark to the core. I needed you to clean up that human trash, to make way for Freedom Earth and religious unification. With no outside factions, no terrorism of any kind threatening its development, Freedom Earth could take hold. Religious unification realized. Through Ashton, mankind really believed they were embracing peace and enlightenment. Ascending a new level. Even Aby-od believed it to be so."

Hearing Aby-od's name, I purse my lips. "That prick would believe anything if you served it up with right level of Shift!"

"Exactly," agrees Aswa-da. He smirks and tries to move up, thinking I've given him a little latitude, but I fix him fast. I don't let him move. Down at him, I glare. Glacial.

Understanding, he swallows.

"Continue," I say.

"With nothing in his path to stop him, Ashton could bulldoze through international laws, rewrite them, and make Freedom Earth tenets the final global word of law. Those lovely Surv-Motes Sam designed kept the parasites in order, obliterated crime, and made Ashton the bringer of a new world order. Quantum Force became the sweetener. It also convinced Kudamun that the Ancient Ones' pet project, Ki, or Earth, was really developing at pace now. Everything they'd wanted, expected over the countless millennia, was finally coming to fruition. There was a touch of expectancy. Everyone believed what was happening was right as they'd been indoctrinated from the start to believe it."

I'm listening. The way in which Aswa-da has manipulated everything and everyone has my mind reeling. Although I hate him for what he made Sam and I do, he's right. Those terrorists were nothing but parasites. Ants awaiting justified annihilation.

I pause and observe Aswa-da, thinking intensely. Everything had to have been scheduled precisely. I wonder when he gave the real Cabinet secretary the heave-ho. He certainly hadn't been donning the mantle of Whitehall's best-known political terrier all the time Ashton had been in power.

I query this with Aswa-da.

"I took over the role when I changed Ashton," he answers. "It gave me an opportunity to keep an eye on my Chosen One and hide on Earth. Resonance implosion obviously helped considerably."

"What happened to the real Sir Martyn?"

"He's making up red boxes and writing white papers in the celestial government in the sky!" Aswa-da grins. "Or getting a good spanking from Satan!"

"Somehow I fear it's the later." I laugh, then add, "Okay, that's Redfern's story. But you haven't given me the SP on Quantum Force. And how did Ashton really get involved?"

"You know, you very nearly sussed out everything. Temenos only just activated the disrupter device on the Observation Screen in time. But you'd seen a glimpse of that meeting between Ashton and Hutchinson discussing quantum energy on March 30, this year. That caused quite a problem to my plans. Good old Order of Kudamun and Aby-od being a stickler for antediluvian laws sorted you out."

I pout, recalling the threat of death Aby-od put forth. It had prevented me from further accusations regarding the integrity of the Screen, and thus, any chance of investigating the cause was cut down from me before I'd even begun.

"I always knew that had something to do with the origin of Quantum Force. There never was any 'long term research at Culham'. It was all Ashton's smokescreen. Did you give him Quantum Force?"

"Actually, I left it in Treeborne's old safe. As good as Hutchinson appeared to be, I had seen his dark thread of greed. But, also, cowardice. When he found the papers, the complex equations, Hutchinson knew it wasn't of this Earth. He'd seen proof of what Treeborne had dabbled in. Him and Ashton had shared experiences, of the incredible, the unbelievable. There was a genuine camaraderie that I used to influence their relationship. Hutchinson instantly gravitated to Ashton, as a friend, the only friend he could trust with his alien discovery. The rest, you know."

I shake my head. I still don't know everything. "It's not mining quark spin, is it?"

Laughing, Aswa-da suddenly looks smug. "Of course not. It mines the Reality Gap."

I can't believe what Aswa-da tells me. The Reality Gap is a forcefield positioned deep, many trillions of degrees, beyond the quantum states that humans comprehend. It keeps the universal plane from crashing through into Kudamun, and vice versa.

It's the celestial buffer that the Ancient Ones created to protect life across the universe, to shield Kudamun from being seen, and to enable the Kudamaz to power their shimmer up to access anywhere on the universal plane.

What Aswa-da has done is catastrophic. I look at him. He's still talking. Caught up. Bursting with ego-driven superiority despite me stuck on top of him, like a heavy industrial freezer.

"It mines it only a little, but enough to cause a disturbance, and a misalignment, breaking Kudamun completely from its connection with the Universal plane. The Kudamaz will no longer have access to shimmer to anywhere in the universe, as they will never be able to align again their shimmer velocity to the Reality Gap."

"You're going to trap them. Incarcerate them in their inter-dimensional prison."

Aswa-da nods. "They're not relevant anymore."

"What about all your fellow colleagues in Etima? Temenos? Dumkunuk? All your acolytes?"

"Insignificant. Now you're here. That was why I had to change you. At first, it came about through necessity. You were getting to be a right pain in the ass with Ashton. Always bemoaning to Aby-od, to Sam. Not trusting the way of Freedom Earth. Nor Quantum Force. Sooner or later, you were going to discover something. It was only the Order of Kudamun, those antediluvian laws that Kudamun boast, ironically, that protected me from you. Fear of death stopped you dead in your investigations."

"You used the bracelet." I indicate to my silver cuff with the two crystals that were before lilac and mauve, but now hold a hue of darkest ebony.

"Very clever, Ellie. Yes. Temenos hacked the architectural designs from Aby-od's systems for the bracelet. A very nifty device that trained you to control your SearchSight abilities. But the way Aby-od designed it was flawed. Or rather, it wasn't flawed. It was actually brilliant, for it accessed directly the internal resonance frequency that is aligned to your soul force. The heart of your white light energies. Temenos discovered through analysis of your soul force that there was a misalignment. You still grieved over the death of your human self. Over the way your humanity was torn from you. You also harbored pain over everything that had happened to you. Sam's lies, all the deceptions, the torture you were subjected to. Deep, deep inside of you was goodness. That thing that was supposed to hold you together as the Protector, you actually hated. Having discovered this, it was easy to flip you. The pain became like a back door in a human's software program accessing an operating system. Using the crystals as an amplifier and your hatred of good as a trigger, all your white light energies, and your ability to harness white light, was reversed. You, who once had the whitest soul force ever, now have the darkest."

Aswa-da's words entrance me. It's what I felt when I emerged reborn a few days ago. But hearing the way in which my transformation has been done…I shiver.

"I'm your creator, Ellie."

"What do you want, a Father's Day card?" I say.

I hear Aswa-da laugh, and those shivers begin again. "I said Etima is insignificant now you're here, and I meant it. You, Ellie, you're all I need."

I frown and glare at the dark lord. "All *you* need? I belong to no one. You may think you've created me, but you do not own me."

"We shall see." Aswa-da says mysteriously, and I don't like his manner. "I'm not your enemy, Ellie. Sam, Aby-od, they are the ones who destroyed you. I just put you back together the way you've always wanted to be. I gave you everything. I gave you freedom."

There is truth in Aswa-da's delivery. I cannot deny it. I tingle inside. Expectation is on the prowl inside me.

I press down on the metallic prism device, and, underneath me, Aswa-da's Redfern face dissolves and, in place, his ancient Kudamaz form returns. I rise off him and stand up. He regards me with nervous attention. I place my hand out to help him up.

Around us, the sky suddenly changes from blue with dotted, fluffy clouds to purple mixed with orange. Silver arrows streak across the sky. A ferocious wind whips up high in the trees and something seems to moan from inside the earth.

Feeling that expectation take flight, I stamp my foot against the ground.

"Stop!" I command, pushing my energies outward, connecting with the air molecules making up the wind.

Immediately, the wind dies down. The moaning ceases. The silver streaks change their trajectories and one flashes down, inches from where Aswa-da and I stand. As it bolts down, the dark purple and angry orange sky ruptures and a flickering of bright, twinkling crystal bursts through.

I swing a look at Aswa-da whose face is creased with concern.

As I initiate shimmer, I scream at Aswa-da's cowering body, "Hey, fucker, you know that big plan of yours? I think it may just be backfiring."

Chapter 97

I want to take Aswa-da with me, but at the same time, I want to find Ashton and get the hell off this planet. Find a new place. A new realm. And call it home.

Aswa-da said the House of Etima and Kudamun weren't relevant anymore. But after what Aswa-da has revealed to me, I know that he isn't relevant either. He isn't a threat. I'm infinitely more powerful than he could ever be. And he knows it.

Oh yes, he may have created me. But he didn't know *what* he had created.

Now I do.

I close my eyes and channel. I feel dark energies across the universe fly into me. Powering me. Turning me into something I know I now am.

Number 10 and Ashton's private office comes into focus. Cumberford is sitting there talking to Jensen. Their jaws drop when I emerge from my obsidian sparkle of light. I look down. All the chasing around I've been doing, including the stadium spectacle this morning, and I notice I'm still in that Missoni number. I think it has outlived its usefulness. In my mind, I SearchSight what the discerning young thing about town is wearing. My mind gaze falls upon a gorgeous, sequined, plunging neckline bodycon from Dolce and Gabana, completely backless and obscenely short in striking, saucy red. That'll do.

I flick my fingers, and my Missoni gold and cream crochet dress vanishes.

I could have placed the new, red sequin dress on my body instantly, but I consider those poor humans in front of me need a bit of livening up. A bit of impromptu entertainment in their dreadful, banal lives.

The gasps of surprise from my audience of two fill me with heat, as I stand in front of them, naked and luscious.

"Enjoy the view, boys!" I wink and snap my fingers and the red dress is clothed on me.

"Seen Ashton anywhere?" I ask Jensen, as if nothing has happened.

Jensen stumbles over his words. "Erm…erm…he's erm…in Chequers."

"Righto," I say, fix on Chequers in my mind, and start to shimmer. Within the sparkles, I catch a glimpse of Cumberford. He seems to have gone into shock. Whoops.

In the shimmer, I recall what Aswa-da has told me about Ashton. Should I tell him about Aswa-da? Will he be able to take it, knowing how he's been manipulated? As he's still Aswa-da's pawn, can he really be trusted? Then, I reason, Aswa-da has no more plays.

I've taken over the game.

Chapter 98

Ashton sat on the floral sofa in the morning room in Chequers, the official countryside residence of the British PM in Berkshire, knocked back his third whisky, tried to stop his body from shaking, and made a valiant but unsuccessful attempt to gather his thoughts.

Sir Martyn Redfern, Cabinet secretary and his best drinking buddy, was also some kind of dark lord from Kudamun. He recalled how Ellie tore into him, ripping his neck open. It was apparent that they were not on very good terms.

Who was this strange person that he'd always known as Redfern. He didn't catch the name from Ellie, but it sounded like Ass Wiper?

Ashton initially had been caught dumbstruck, but then his Six training had swept in, taking his fear away, and he'd reacted. Under her instruction, he'd supported her. Backed her up. Even hurt the guy. But it was clear the giant was very powerful.

Shelagh Murray, his poor secretary, had entered at a most inopportune time. Ellie had damn near decapitated Ass Wiper, but Shelagh's interruption caused Ellie to drop her guard. The giant had gotten away, vanishing in a veil of dark sparkles, similar to Ellie's form of transportation. He had to be Kudamaz too.

What did this mean for Freedom Earth? For his plan to control the world with Ellie? Could this guy come along and take him out? Was Ellie enough protection against him?

A crash of thunder made Ashton turn toward the French windows. The sky was orange and purple again, and weird silver arrows of light leapt through the strange, hued skies. As he watched, bolts zapped down into the immaculate lawns, but nothing singed. The arrows weren't like lightning.

They were more like bright lights in a jagged formation. Ashton stood up and strolled to the window, clutching his glass, and peered into the skies. He inhaled sharply, witnessing the new spectacle above him. Somehow, the fabric of the sky had split open and he could see something that looked like crystal poking through it. He lifted the glass and threw back the remainder of his drink.

Against the dark, brooding, purple-orange sky, a reflection in the window of sparkling lights caught Ashton's eye, and he knew, behind him, someone from Kudamun was shimmering in. Whether it was Ellie, Ass Wiper, Sam, he didn't know. But he had to be prepared.

He reached for his Sig holstered underneath his jacket and pointed it at the emerging life form.

"Nice to see you too!" said Ellie, smiling.

Ashton breathed deeply. "Ellie, thank God it's you. Did you get that guy? What was his name. Ass Wiper? Did he hurt you? Are you okay?"

"What do you think?" retorted Ellie, dripping sarcasm, and then laughed. "Did you say Ass Wiper! That's priceless, sweetheart." Ellie sashayed toward him, and Ashton smiled, taking in her new change of attire, and licked his lips. "I can see you're more than okay, darling. You're absolutely mouth-watering."

Ellie sunk her lips onto his and gripped his body tight against her.

A weird moaning sound rising from the ground outside caused Ashton to swing a glance back at the window. "Know anything about what's up with our sky?"

"Yeah. Ass Wiper has fucked the Reality Gap."

"Huh?" said Ashton, and he knew on hearing Ellie's unintelligible word that, once again, he was heading directly for Lost Central.

Ashton's face is a mass of confusion. Poor thing. I recall how Aswa-da (or, as I think I may call him from now on, Ass Wiper) has manipulated him. Used the sadness of his loss of Katzy to force him into the most terrible acts mankind has seen. All under the banner of good.

"It's a long story,"

"Are you going to tell it?" asks Ashton looking worried.

I shrug "Maybe, we'll see."

"So, what do we do?" whispers Ashton, and I discern his worried irritation at me not revealing what I know.

I smile, giving him reassurance.

"Darling, you do nothing. Take my hand."

Ashton slips his hand in mine, and I reach out into the air. In my mind, reality is just a curtain. In front of me, the air ripples like folds in drapes, and I snatch a wad of material air and pull it back. I feel Ashton's hand grasp mine, and a little coo of amazement passes his lips.

"Don't be scared, my darling. We're going house-hunting!"

And I step forward. Ashton matches my pace, into the realms of a place that I have literally just created in my mind.

Far below us, as we walk arm in arm together, planets turn gently. Stars sparkle. Things with tails of fire shoot past us. I feel Ashton shake a little.

"Is…is…th-this…real?" he stutters, in utter wonderment, looking around him.

"More than real. This is ours, my darling. All ours. The place we will go. You see, Ashton, my sweet. I know what I am. Ass Wiper made me change, but he had no comprehension of what the change would do to me. As Protector, I was powerful, but now I have the power of creation and destruction. Do you know what that makes me?"

I stop and hold Ashton close, his lips touching mine. He shakes his head. In his eyes, he's in awe, but petrified. From that reaction, he knows the answer. But for completeness, I still venture the truth.

"Ashton, my darling, I'm a goddess."

Chapter 99

Aswa-da stood on the mountainside where Ellie had left him. The skies above had reverted to their normal, sun-filled, bright blue filled with fluffy, cotton ball clouds usually seen in St Moritz in July.

He said he was sorry to her earlier.

Who he really was apologizing to in that instance was himself. He was sorry he'd ever ventured into his current activities.

Those single-minded obsessions.

Breaking and flipping Ellie. Destroying Kudamun's link with the universe. Wanting to reign over Earth with his dark powers. All had led him down a road that now threatened his own destruction.

Ellie Noor.

That lied to, cheated on, confused and abused specimen of humankind was becoming an invincible force. And he'd been the sucker that had unsuspectingly created her.

He'd done the equivalent of shooting himself in the foot.

Now he had to enter survival mode. She hadn't killed him yet. But by that look in her eye, Aswa-da knew she would eventually.

He was on borrowed time.

He had to use every light particle in his body and every Earth second of time to find a way to end Ellie, whilst he still had a body to use.

Above him, everything darkened. Purple-orange splat through the brilliant blue like someone had thumped the sky and given it a bruise.

He stared as bits of Kudamun's twinkling crystals poked through a sudden rip that a shooting, silver streak had made, and he realized he may have found a way to resolve everything.

A place popped into his mind. Such irony, he thought, and then shimmered to his new destination.

Around him, the dark, opulent, glittering walls of his official quarters in Kudamun slipped into being. Temenos, his back to Aswa-da, worked on something. But Aswa-da watched as he detected the shimmer, straightened, and swung around, his Harmon gun in his hand.

"Easy, my friend," said Aswa-da quickly.

Temenos' eyes popped out, amazed. Aswa-da knew he'd wonder why he was taking such a monumental risk shimmering into Kudamun instead of using temporal mind transference from his office in the Cabinet in Whitehall, or from his, or rather Redfern's, home in Belgravia, London.

"Great Ensi, why are you here?"

"What we've done, Ellie Noor, she's too strong. I cannot control her. She's no longer Etima's instrument. I need the power of the High Council to remove her. There's no other way."

Temenos' face grayed over, his eyes desolate. "We've worked so hard for this, My Lord. All we did with the Chosen One. What are we now to do?"

Aswa-da perceived almost a sob within his colleague's words.

Such weakness. I was right, you are irrelevant, Ellie is worth a million of you. We could have been quite a couple, Ellie and I, if only she'd seen me in the same light as she did Ashton.

Aswa-da banished his thoughts. They were never going to happen. Even if he used the disguise prism and he became Ashton, she'd see through it. He'd be dead before he made an utterance using that smug-toned bastard's appearance.

He cursed himself. He'd misplayed everything. He should have killed Ashton. Taken his place. Why didn't he when he'd had the chance?

Sheer arrogance.

Killing a human and taking their place was easy. Manipulating a human to do your bidding. Playing with their emotions. Toying with their pain.

That was complex. Demanding.

It made for a better sport.

"What are you going to do, Great Ensi? Do you have a plan?"

Aswa-da smirked as he listened. "Well, it's a good thing I do because you sure as hell don't, do you, Temenos?"

Chapter 100

In his quarters, Aby-od attended to another planet in his care. He'd been alerted to a slight Balance Shift by one of the sentient crystals that monitored each galaxy. As part of his duty as overseer of the universe, Aby-od had to ensure Balance was maintained throughout the universal plane.

He stared, engrossed in the indicator for the galaxy in question. Something on one or more of the planets in that galaxy had caused a swing to the dark. Aby-od tried to assess which one, but it wasn't clear. He'd have to use the Observation Screen to pinpoint which planet or planets were the cause of the dark slip.

He heard a movement behind him, and a hesitant cough. He turned and looked, startled, at Temenos standing in his hallway.

"Excuse me, Lord Aby-od, Great Ensi."

"Yes," said Aby-od warily. "What is it?"

"Erm, as Leader of Kudamun, there is a matter of grave importance that requires your attention."

Temenos wrung his hands out in a very uncharacteristic manner. Etima Senior Elders were all about pride, narcissism, and egotism. They never carried themselves with any show of humility.

Aby-od, cautious to Temenos' machinations, eyed him. "What matter is that?"

"The matter of Ellie Noor. What she's doing. She has to be stopped."

"We've been through this already," said Aby-od, his voice testy and irked. "The High Council cleared Ellie of any misdemeanors. They found her still to be the Protector and her presence, although made known on Earth, has not harmed anyone. Nor are humans afraid of her. There is nothing she is doing that is causing Earth harm."

"But it is in Kudamun," replied Temenos.

An alarm, piercing and violently loud, shot through the start of his retort to Etima's Head. Aby-od flicked a look upward as he recognized the alarm was connected to the health of the Reality Gap. A constant that had never changed in his entire existence in Kudamun.

Until now.

Those vibrant oranges and deep, beautiful purples of the Reality Gap had dulled in their intensity, and those streaks of silver denoting quantum particles shooting far, far away had lost their shining brilliance. Within the rolling churns of orange and purple, a black nothingness broke through.

"Oh goodness! Surely Ellie isn't doing this!" cried Aby-od.

But Temenos nodded. "She is, Great Ensi."

"The High Council must convene immediately. I'll contact the Speaker."

"Lord Aby-od, there is something else. I have a witness to Ellie's crimes against the Order of Kudamun. He knows everything that she is doing. How she is trying to destroy Kudamun. But he seeks complete immunity for his past..." Aby-od watched as Temenos appeared to search for the right word. "Accidents."

Aby-od knew instantly this witness was Aswa-da.

His face tightened and he gritted down on his teeth, recalling the games the dark lord had played just a few Earth months before.

He couldn't countenance immunity from prosecution for his crimes. However, he knew that the High Council, desperate to know what was happening with the Reality Gap and the real role Ellie was playing on Earth, would probably sign up to his immunity to get such intel.

Aby-od had made sure the Kudamaz held a special place in their hearts for Ellie Noor. The woman who'd saved them. But jealously for the way she'd been treated, always having access to the Leader of Kudamun, had spread between the Kudamaz of both Houses. How her mongrel husband Sam had been elevated to Senior Elder, joining the High Council's ranks without even needing to try, whilst true Kudamaz barely got a look in.

Yes, the House of Giznu hated Aswa-da, but Aby-od knew, in their supposedly charitable soul forces, they concealed much envy for the Noor couple. And would like nothing more than to bring them both down.

What Temenos was now purporting had the ingredients to do just that.

Aby-od stared at Temenos, and then pointed at the Reality Gap.

"Ellie is really behind that?"

"I said that. Please, do you agree that he can receive immunity?"

There wasn't any point in ambiguity. Temenos knew that Aby-od knew who he referred to.

"You're talking about Aswa-da, aren't you?"

Temenos slightly nodded. "Yes, Lord Aby-od."

"He is a traitor of Kudamun. The High Council guards have searched for him. Are you telling me he's here?"

Temenos held Aby-od's angry glare. "Yes, he is here."

"How did he evade sensors?"

"Resonance implosion."

Aby-od's eyes enlarged hearing how his enemy had dodged capture.

"Where has he been hiding all this time?"

"Earth."

Aby-od wandered over to his fluffy, ice-blue sofa. He needed its gentle, calming resonance infusing into his light cells. He beckoned Temenos to join him. Stiffly, he sat down next to Aby-od.

"I could have you arrested for harboring a fugitive."

Aby-od watched as Temenos pressed down into the sofa. He could see the calming effect wash through his opposition.

"But you won't. I know you, Lord Aby-od. You cannot risk what is at stake. Loyalty starts and ends with Kudamun, not Ellie Noor."

Aby-od felt a twinge of certainty as he listened. Uncomfortable. But he had to admit Temenos was correct in his psyche eval of him.

"Aswa-da changed Ellie. Flipped her polarity. Forced her to become dark. He's to blame for this mess!" spat Aby-od, not wanting to accept Temenos' terms.

"That may or may not be so."

Aby-od found a growl erupting deep in his throat, unbecoming of his nature. He recalled how Ellie had loved Sam so much, but after her transformation, she'd put him through pain. Enjoyed watching him suffer.

Aswa-da's hand had been in that.

And now he couldn't control what he'd created, and he wanted to bring in Kudamun's calvary.

"Aswa-da's made his bed, now he's got to lie on it," snarled Aby-od. "I'll instruct the High Council guards they have the right to enter your quarters and detain Aswa-da until the High Council convene to pass sentence."

"Then I will have no alternative, Great Ensi, but to issue to the Speaker a point of no confidence in the Leader of Kudamun, and the High Council will take a vote."

"No confidence! On what grounds?" Aby-od trembled.

"On the grounds that the Leader of Kudamun had the opportunity to gain intel required to capture and detain the person known as Ellie Noor Selema, the Protector of Earth, for her wanton destruction of the Reality Gap, making a threat to Kudamun's very existence, but chose not to proceed."

Aby-od glared at Temenos, who now had reinstated the superior, smug, supercilious smirk so becoming of those of the House of Etima.

Chapter 101

Sam couldn't get a fix on Ellie's resonance. It hurt him. They'd been so connected. Never mind as Kudamaz, as humans, they'd almost been able to know each other's thoughts.

Except when he'd lied.

He shook his head. Concentrate. Compartmentalize, Sam, for God's sake! A boy's life rests in your hands.

He scanned his databanks for recent activities, but nothing showed up. Well, she'd be with Ashton, he thought resentfully, so it would be Number 10, Chequers, the penthouse or...the fact was, Ellie could be anywhere in the world, in the universe!

But something told him she wasn't far away.

Instinct. Or maybe some connection still remained with her.

He shimmered into Number 10 to the astounded eyes of Cumberford. He leapt up and away from Sam and pressed his body against the wall. Quivering.

"God, you lot are everywhere. You're one of them, aren't you? Like that woman the prime minister is with."

Sam scowled, listening, and then, refraining from entering into any further discussion with Cumberford, barked, "Ashton, Ellie, where are they?"

"Chequers."

"Thank you," clipped Sam, and promptly shimmered out.

Sam's quantum self in Chequers and his soul force connected, and he was pulled into the morning room in Chequers at the point when Ellie and Ashton appeared to step through reality that had bunched up like a curtain. Behind them, Sam noticed glimpses of planets of varying colors and sizes.

"Oh, hi, Sam," said Ashton, gripping hold of Ellie's slender waist. "What can I do for you?"

"Well, this time, it's what Ellie can do for me."

"Oooh, sounds interesting. A bit of ménage a-" quipped Ashton, as Ellie giggled, laying her head on his shoulder.

"Enough, Ashton!" shouted Sam, his face reddening with surfacing rage. "This is not about me. It's about a boy. A boy who needs you, Ellie. He's dying. I think you're the only who can help him."

A boy who needs my help, eh?

I glance at Ashton. I know I've blown his mind on our last little trip. But the experience seems to have perked up his energies. There's a renewed sparkle in his eyes and he looks, quite simply, delicious. Well, good enough for a goddess like me!

"Please, Ellie, I want nothing from you. But this boy, he has the Light of Ki inside him. It's killing him."

I remember what Aswa-da told me about the white power block. 'It's gone. I removed it'. He may have removed it, but it seems the energy vacated before Aswa-da separated it from the Balance Shift indicator.

If this boy Sam speaks of has the Light of Ki, the energy from the white power block, could he possibly be a threat to me?

"What's his name?" I ask, giving no indication as to whether I'm prepared to help.

Sam's face lights up. Relief spreads across his features. "Xiao Chang."

"In China, is he?" I check my databanks, and see the Xiao Chang in question is in London, in Berkley Square. Must be a posh, self-entitled, rich brat.

Couldn't the world do with one less of those?

"No, he's in London. Will you help? You're his last hope. He flickers from human to light form, Ellie. It's killing him. His parents are distraught. Aswa-da did something to him. Made him unstable."

I hear that Aswa-da is involved. But he never told me. So he knows the Light of Ki still lives. Why didn't he tell me? The question gnaws at me. I search for Aswa-da, but he's not on the universal plane. Must have gone to Kudamun.

"So, Ellie, will you help?"

I look Sam up and down. His body is gorgeous, his face handsome, in fact, it's as though it were chiseled by a talented sculpturer. But he's been violated by goodness.

Ashton smirks, clocking my slow inspection, and licks his lips. He bends toward me. "Pity he's not up for it, eh?" he murmurs seductively in my ear, nibbling at my lobe.

"Never in a million years," I say, and laugh.

"What?" says Sam, confused, and despondency seems to encase his body. He doesn't hear or, more accurately, doesn't *want* to hear the exchange between Ashton and me. I know that his Kudamaz hearing, like mine, is acute and perfected enough to hear a fly fart.

I initiate shimmer, focusing on Kudamun, and hold Ashton close.

"Sam, I'm sorry. The days of jumping to your command are over. Sort the kid out yourself. I've got to give Ass Wiper a fucking good whipping."

Chapter 102

July 7, 2017

The obsidian sparkles faded. The room was silent. Sam, motionless, stared into the space that, not two Earth seconds before, contained Ellie and Ashton wrapped in an embrace.

He shuddered, pushing out the recorded vision from his databanks.

A kid.

Not even an innocent life in peril could stir Ellie enough to help him.

Her hatred, her sheer defiance, refusing anything he wanted, it controlled her. Defined her new incarnation.

'Save me'.

Xiao's persistent scream ran in his mind. It hurled him back to his mission.

He must save Xiao. At all costs. He must save that boy.

By Ellie's last crude, cryptic retort, Sam knew she headed for Kudamun. He wanted to check on Xiao, but such an act, without having a resolution to give, would be pointless, and would only give his parents more distress. At that moment, he wished he had Ellie's power of SearchSight.

He thought of Lei and Chen. Leaving them hadn't been easy but Xiao's energy had been too strong. He couldn't understand how Xiao was still alive. He wished he'd known more about the Light of Ki, but his databanks only gave him the standard Kudamaz learnt spiel. He hoped Chen had seen the voracity of his determination to save Xiao. That he didn't see Sam as having abandoned them. Perhaps he should just shimmer back and reassure them again.

Indecision.

A state he'd never lived in, not even as a human. It plucked at him. Picked away his confidence. His strength of self.

Was he breaking down?

Sam shook his head. The only way any of this was going to end was when Ellie agreed to save Xiao.

And show to him she still had some vestige of love and goodness remaining in her that he believed she did.

Kudamun fixed in his mind, his quantum self connected with his soul force and he felt the immediate pull. Within the shimmer, inside him, Xiao/the Light of Ki's deep, resonant voice crashed through.

"All is end. She is too powerful."

Chapter 103

Aby-od gripped hold of the jet crystal walls surrounding Temenos' quarters in the Etima part of Kudamun.

He had to hold on so tight as it was the one thing that prevented him from reaching into his pocket, taking out his Harmon gun, and blasting the motherfucking excuse for a Kudamaz standing before him.

Aby-od realized how much of an influence Ellie Noor had had on his life. Even to the extent that he was now copying her colorful way of speaking in his thoughts. And that smirking bastard was the cause of her present dark persona.

"Hello, Aby-od," Aswa-da sneered.

Aby-od could feel his silky arrogance seeping into his skin. He prickled, lit up with a barely restrained fury.

"It seems a little problem of yours is about to bite you on the ass!"

Aby-od's jaw dropped at Aswa-da's naked, unashamed cheek. "My problem!" yelled Aby-od, his pent-up anger finally breaking free. "You're the fucker who changed her!"

Aswa-da grinned, sick smugness slinked across his features. "Tut, tut. Language, Aby-od. I see Ellie's certainly rubbed off on you. But really, that's not quite the behavior of a leader! If you'd done your job right in the beginning and aligned her soul force properly, she wouldn't have constantly pined for her humanity. If you'd prepared her, as each Protector has to be prepared, none of this would have happened."

Aswa-da laughed deeply and Aby-od could feel his eyes dancing over him with disdain. Aby-od balled his fist, breathed slowly, and attempted to control the need to punch Aswa-da's mocking face.

"You gave me no Earth time," gritted Aby-od, incredulous at this political turnaround.

Aswa-da ignored him and continued his diatribe, "If she hadn't been flawed from the start as Protector, all would have been well. Your incompetence has made Ellie Noor what she is."

"You mean what you did has made her so," spat Aby-od furiously, and he cast a glance at Temenos who grinned with delight at Aswa-da's flipping of the scene.

"I did not create the Protector, unfortunately, neither did you."

"So what did I create?" screamed Aby-od, unable to take the verbal impudence anymore.

"Damaged goods."

Aby-od recalled Ellie's invective about Ashton, when he'd removed the jury. Her constant assertion that he was evil but veiled it in good acts. Aby-od hadn't believed her. Stated she was seeing evil when there was none to see. 'Ellie, my child, you are so damaged, and I have made you so'.

He could never have assumed his words would hold such a prescient force.

His actions *had* damaged her.

But Aswa-da had forced his hand.

Without his interference, reconstitution would have been perfect. Aby-od glared.

"I say, Great Ensi, are you lost for words? Well, no matter, I have enough for both of us," slithered Aswa-da, taking over, jumping into the gap generated by Aby-od's shock.

Through sudden self-reflection, Aby-od had accepted final acknowledgement of his own failure.

"Ellie's a loose cannon. She's already found a way to break the Reality Gap, and her intention is to destroy Kudamun. But I know a way to stop her!"

Temenos sneered. Aby-od watched as satisfaction stalked across his opposition's face.

"And you want immunity from prosecution for this knowledge," stated Aby-od, struggling to conceive the game going down.

"Naturally." Aswa-da smiled.

"The High Council won't buy it," snapped Aby-od, willing himself to be strong. To stride forward with a counter argument. Anything to stop current proceedings.

Aswa-da was the reason for all the turmoil, all the pain that had been wrought on the Noors in its many myriad forms. He couldn't, just couldn't, get the upper hand.

Aswa-da looked up casually at the Reality Gap, and, as if on cue, a bolt of silver quantum particles hit the space between Aby-od and Aswa-da.

"Oh, I think when survival is on the table, they're going to buy into anything."

Chapter 104

With Ashton clinging to me like one of those chihuahuas in the handbags of ladies who lunch, I shimmer into a place I recognize well.

My Kudamaz bedroom quarters.

Ashton clocks the ginormous bed and his wanton, lust-filled orbs enlarge, Then, as he looks around, he realizes he's somewhere quite, quite different than anywhere he's been before, and amazement takes over his need to seduce me.

He gazes up in wonderment at the Reality Gap. A look of a child, seeing their first Christmas tree, or meeting Santa Claus for the first time in their local department store. He's aghast. Lost in awe. Desperately trying to process one question above all others hurtling within his neurons, firing up his synapses.

"Erm, darling, where are we?"

I can hear the twinge of nervousness in his voice, although he tries valiantly to hide it.

"Kudamun."

Ashton doesn't respond. He detaches his arms from me, and wanders around, taking in the crystal walls. He's trance-like in his movements. Like he's dropped a tab of acid. I can see his face glows a little. He steps back toward me, grabs my hand, and pulls me over to the bed. I don't resist.

"Come on, sweetheart," Ashton slurs. "Take me on an interdimensional ride."

He falls back onto the soft, ice-blue, satin covers, spread-eagles and starts to giggle. "Oh, Ellie, I feel awesome."

I stare. Ashton's eyes are sparkling with an inner luminescence. My databanks advise immediately on why the intelligent, accomplished world leader of Freedom Earth, Mr. Richard Ashton, has turned into a gibbering, soppy fool.

Euphoric absorption.

Ashton grabs at me, misses, and drops back onto the covers laughing.

"Oh my God, Ellie, it's wonderful. I'm tingly. My nerves. Ooh, they're stimulated. I feel, ooh, I feel…I need you."

His pupils dilate and his always gorgeous, bronzed skin carries a pearly, pink, iridescent sheen. From these tell-tale signs, I know ultimate euphoria is hitting Ashton's systems hard. Soon, his brain will flood with euphoria at levels far higher than a human body can handle. I know a coma follows, and then death. In my obsession with Aswa-da, I'd completely forgotten humans can't enter Kudamun without paying a fatal price.

"Fuck!"

"That's what I'm talking about," Ashton purrs, reaching out for me. He struggles to coordinate his movements, and unzipping his flies seems an act beyond his mental capacity. "Come on, baby, help me. Do that zappy clothes off thingy you do."

I glare back at Ashton, still snickering like an immature teenager, frantic to shag a virgin on prom night.

With his hands scrabbling to hold his zipper, I snatch him into my arms.

Then I feel him.

Not Ashton. Aswa-da.

My quarry is in my sights. A destination pops into my mind.

The Grand Hall.

Chapter 105

Around Aswa-da, Senior Elders of both Houses stood in shock. The Reality Gap alarm blasted out its monotonous, crushing sound signifying their oncoming demise.

Aby-od led him into the Grand Hall, flanked by two High Council guards, with Temenos trailing behind. His brethren from the House of Etima sneaked wry smiles, as Aby-od instructed the guards to depart.

Elders from the House of Giznu glared at Aby-od, angry at him-od for his lack of leadership and ability to show mettle in the face of their hated nemesis. But as they peered up at the Reality Gap, they also showed terror.

Aswa-da waited patiently.

He watched Aby-od take his position beside him. Temenos seated himself in the chair for the Head of the House of Etima on the ebony side of the Hall.

The Speaker, dumbfounded, stared up at the Reality Gap. Aswa-da, with the rest of the High Council, stared too. The colorful intensities had diminished, and black nothingness of the universal plane had started to break through again. He swallowed. His plan had to work.

Now it wasn't about domination. It was about survival.

The Speaker spoke.

"Senior Elders of the High Council of Kudamun, we are facing a dire catastrophe. The Reality Gap is breaking down. The alarm now sounding tells us all that very soon Kudamun will no longer be separated from the Universal Plane. The effect of this convergence will result in our-"

"Annihilation. Yes, thank you, Speaker. I think we all understand that," interrupted Aswa-da, stepping forward with rude but assertive brashness.

"The Speaker hadn't-" Aby-od, beside him, tried to interject.

He could feel the Leader of Kudamun bristling with ire, but Aswa-da pushed forth his booming, dominant voice of authority, swamping Aby-od's feeble attempts.

"With due respect, Great Ensi, the High Council needs solutions not obvious portents of doom. And I am the only one in this Hall who can save Kudamun from its fate. Get the human boy known as Xiao Chang and use him to destroy Ellie Noor, for she alone is the reason for the Reality Gap's failure and Kudamun's evident destruction."

"A human boy can stop Ellie Noor?" questioned one of Giznu's Senior Elders.

"The boy has the Light of Ki inside him," whipped out Aby-od, and Aswa-da smirked at the leader's glaring, vitriol-filled face.

"How is this possible?" yelled another Senior Elder, this time from the Etima side of the Hall.

"Long story," said Aswa-da, waving his hand as if he couldn't be bothered to explain to the High Council, which, in fact, he couldn't. He just wanted to get everything in place to force Ellie, with nowhere else to run, to make her final escape.

He'd then find a way to follow her, and exit off this fucked up, forsaken world.

After she'd left him on that mountainside, he'd returned to Kudamun. He had to track her, but her resonance wasn't like that of a Kudamaz. He couldn't simply locate her using their planetary sensors. But he could find Ashton, a human she showed significant affections for.

Inside the Observation Room, Aswa-da had rapidly run a series of queries, using the point in time on Earth where she'd left him, and cross-refed against Ashton's movements. He knew he had to be quick. In his true Kudamaz form, even with resonance implosion shielding him from Kudamun's sensors, if another Kudamaz from the House of Giznu had seen him, it would have been all over.

The query he'd run brought up instantly Ashton in Chequers with Ellie. He watched as she did some weird thing with the air. It had bunched up like a curtain, and she'd just pulled it back as if reality was a drape, and she'd said mysteriously they were going 'house-hunting'.

The sentient crystals in the Observation Room knowledge banks streamed zero intel on the world inside the curtain. Aswa-da identified that, a few Earth seconds before Ellie had walked into the morning room with Ashton, the realm had not existed. Aswa-da concluded the impossible. Ellie had created it. His theory was further validated by the fact the Observation Screen couldn't see through the curtain into that new world, nor could it surveil Ellie and Ashton's activities within it.

There was no symbiotic connection at the quantum level. The properties of the new realm's creation did not align with the internal mechanisms that the Observation Screen used to see everything across the universe.

Aswa-da realized it was a completely new world, unaffected by the apocalyptic conditions of the Reality Gap. A place he had a new chance to live in. Maybe perhaps, even with Ellie, when she'd grown bored of her human pet, Ashton.

He just needed her to be in a corner, like a wild animal before capture, looking for the moment to take flight, and then he'd run too.

"What matters is that's the only way to kill Ellie Noor."

"Somebody talking about killing me?"

Aswa-da's words slap me in the face, as I emerge out of shimmer. Ashton's arms are around me, his belt loose, his zip half down, his shirt unbuttoned with the tail lolloping over his perfect, tight buns. He's giggling inanely and I'm getting pissed at him. I know it's euphoric absorption and, really, I should get him far away from Kudamun, but I'm amazed at how quickly he's dissolved into a shambling, love-struck wreck. I thought maybe that shit Aswa-da had done to his DNA would have given him a bit of protection. I mean, for fuck's sake, he's supposed to be the leader of Freedom Earth, but he looks like a randy college kid high on something.

He lurches forward to plant a kiss on my mouth, and I knock his lips away.

"I said…" I stare at all the self-opinionated, pious pricks of the High Council, including the biggest prick of all, Aby-od, and bellow, "Is somebody talking about killing me?"

The Hall is silent.

No one makes a move. Nor attempts to say anything.

I glare at Aswa-da, who shrugs, sneering, eyeing me up and down.

Dream on, sweetheart!

Aby-od appears mortified by my entrance with the disheveled British prime minister.

"Right, well, as you're all so talkative, I'll tell you what-"

"Silence!" screams the Speaker. I notice he holds the side of his throne. He pushes forward with a look of courage and conviction and opens his mouth. "Protector of Ki, Ellie Noor Selema, you have been accused of crimes against the Order of Kudamun. Namely the wanton destruction of the Reality Gap with the sole purpose of separating Kudamun from the universal plane. Such an action will result in the annihilation of Kudamun and the universe."

"Oh, fuck off!" I shout, cutting through the Speaker's case for the prosecution. "It's this fucker, Ass Wiper!" Suddenly, I hear sniggers erupt from the Giznu side of the High Council, and Aby-od's eyebrow arches. Aswa-da glowers at me, and appears to flush up, embarrassed. "He's the one who's broken the Reality Gap and screwed Kudamun, not me!"

As I point to Aswa-da, he starts, his sly smile materializing out of his humiliation.

"I have none of the powers that Ellie possesses. Aby-od created the Protector, but through his incompetence and his haste-driven misalignment of her soul force, she has mutated into the creature that now threatens Kudamun's very existence."

I just listen, smirking.

It is all rather pathetic and grasping of Aswa-da to believe he can turn the High Council. But as I watch the Senior Elders, in their tight rows positioned in a circle around me, I see them nodding. On their faces is agreement.

I swallow, taking a look at Aswa-da, who has, once again, played the role of Manipulator Extraordinaire.

"Ooh, Ellie, who are these people? Looks like the Lords with their daft robes."

In the fray of it all, I'd forgotten about Ashton. He bursts into laughter. I stare at him, wobbly on his feet, grinning at everyone, and know I really have to take him back to Earth before his neurons fry completely.

I watch the guards who stand above the High Council, keeping watch and protecting them, lift their huge Harmon guns. Each one aims their gun at me. Maybe Ashton senses danger, or some semblance of Ashton, the agent, for beside me, he halts his manic behavior and grips my hand very tight, whispering, "Are we in trouble?"

Just as I'm about to reassure Ashton that I'm still in control, the air sparkles with rainbow colors. A Giznu Senior Elder is entering.

I know it has to be Sam.

How I know, I can't say. That connected thing we had. Perhaps?

He comes out of shimmer in front of Aby-od, Aswa-da, and me.

I clock his look of pity and sorrow. Then, as he observes all the guns trained on me, his eyes mist up with sadness. I feel a tug of something inside me. I force away the feeling.

I turn, smile, and take in a solid, unwavering gaze of all the Senior Elders around me.

"Now we're all here, let's get this party started!"

I raise my arms up and imagine the High Council in a semi-shimmer state. An Earth second hasn't passed before every Senior Elder from both Houses goes into a suspended state of flux. Partly in Kudamun. Partly distributed throughout the universal plane.

I laugh. Relishing in a wave of pure evil that flows, unrestricted, through me.

"Now that's what I call entertainment!"

Chapter 106

Sam, out of shimmer, spun around, staring at the horrendous scene his wife had created. Only Aby-od, Aswa-da, Ashton, the Speaker, and himself were spared Ellie's wrath.

The guards opened fire on Ellie, but Sam knew she didn't care. She just laughed, twisted her index finger, winding it up in the air like she used to do when she wanted him to come off the phone. The blast wave from each guard's gun stopped mid-flight, and then reversed at speed, returning to its origin, into the Harmon wave guns, and obliterating every guard.

Sam's hand went up to his mouth. He shook his head. Nothing resembled the Ellie he knew. She was beyond the very description of wicked. He thought of her on the battlefield, the way she'd destroyed Al Nadir's terrorists. Literally ripping them apart. A live dismemberment. She'd used her strength, her superpower, to take out every single terrorist that fought back. Had she always been this powerful, but her white-light-infused soul force had cancelled out some of her ability? Had Aswa-da not actually changed her at all? Just found a way to set her real self free?

Ellie, still laughing, marched around the circle of semi-shimmering High Council members.

"Erm, so you guys wanted to kill me? Like to see you try."

She clicked her fingers and each Senior Elder exploded in a spray of sparkles. Rainbow light for Giznu. Obsidian twinkles for Etima.

Horrified, Sam looked on. He could see the Speaker shaking. Fear radiated from him.

"Don't look so sad, sweetheart. I haven't forgotten you."

Ellie formed an imaginary gun with her fingers, pointed it at the Speaker, and mouthed, 'Bang!'

Instantly, the Speaker vanished in a swirl of obsidian lights.

"Now, Ashton, darling, must get you home. Otherwise I'll end up fucking a vegetable!" She sneered and glared at Sam. He knew she'd made her depraved comment for his benefit.

Sam shivered. He had to say something, but he was speechless. He'd just witnessed Ellie, his own wife Ellie, the woman he'd been with and loved a million lifetimes over, obliterate all of Kudamun's High Council, the Speaker, and the guards without showing a single shred of remorse.

Never would she aid Xiao now. She was rotten to the core of her being. He wanted to vomit, but he swallowed down the urge. It was a pseudo-human reaction anyway. But, right now, watching her, he couldn't think of anything else he could do.

Ellie turned to face Sam, as if she could now read his mind.

"That boy Xiao, how's he doing? Still fucked by the Light of Ki? Yeah, goodness has a way of doing that."

Ellie fired the wrath of her last sentence directly at Aby-od. And then he received the might of her angry, vengeful glare.

"He's still unwell," said Sam. "He needs you to help him stabilize the Light of Ki inside him."

From nowhere, as Sam spoke, in Ellie's eyes flashed sudden fear. Her form straightened, her grinning ceased, and she appeared to be reading him, or sensing something.

"You won't take me down!" Ellie screamed, eyes flashing wild, mouth a twisted snarl. Enraged, she yanked Ashton close to her and shimmered out.

Her exit jerked Sam alive. Sadness flipped to fury. He leapt, without indication, onto Aswa-da, howling, "You're the fucking reason all this happened!"

Sam's hand shot out around Aswa-da's throat. The other smashed hard into his face. A high-pitched harmonic sounded behind him and Aswa-da stopped flailing. He froze. Sam realized Aby-od had stunned the dark lord. His stationary state didn't end Sam's attack. Aswa-da, immobile but aware, took punch after kick after punch. His cheek split open, his eye socket dislocated, his nose fractured, and his jaw broke. Whilst in the stunned state, Aswa-da's Kudamaz light energy framework couldn't repair him. And couldn't shield him from pain.

Sam couldn't hold back. It was Stein-Muller and Rasheed all over again.

The pain. The hurt. The suffering.

All because of Aswa-da.

He'd torn their love in two. Gutted Ellie of goodness.

Made her into the monster she now was.

A hand rested on his shoulder.

"Sam, Sam, we have to go."

"Go where?" said Sam, now unsure of his sanity. Had Aby-od been talking to him but he just didn't hear? What he'd seen, been witness to, he knew the precipice was very close.

"To Xiao. We have to protect him."

"From who?"

"Ellie. She's going to kill Xiao and, with him, the Light of Ki."

"Why?" asked Sam, confused, as he wiped off Aswa-da's blood. As he was stunned, the blood had no light energy connection to its central form, and it hung on Sam's fists, slipping down and sparkling, slipping and sparkling, forever caught between two states.

"Because the Light of Ki can destroy her."

Chapter 107

She approached.

The Light of Ki sensed her arrival. He had to warn the boy. After the Kudamaz Elder's intervention, their connection with each other had stabilized within the flame of light. But his life force as a human boy was waning. His internal makeup was mutating, turning Kudamaz. But the human boy's force still needed be in situ for the mutation to work. If his life force died out before full transformation was complete, the boy and The Light of Ki would both expire.

Her force lapped in waves at the Light of Ki. Indomitable. A force that had to be stopped.

The fact Ellie Noor Selema had come into being only exemplified how very broken the universe was.

The Light of Ki analyzed Xiao's vitals. Heart pumping, lungs working overtime, pulse racing, brain confused and frightened. Internally, the Light of Ki acknowledged the human had reignited his fight against the change the Kudamaz Elder had instigated with greater vehemence.

It hadn't realized the man who visited had been Kudamaz at first. His human disguise had been an encompassing blanket. The moment the man produced a strange crystal, it knew the man had to be Kudamaz. It tried to assess the resonance of the man, but no resonance pattern, no signature denoting who the Kudamaz individual was could be discerned.

Whoever the Kudamaz individual was, it was obvious he'd enacted Resonance Implosion to conceal his resonance signature pattern. The Light of Ki had believed that such an action could only be undertaken by the Ancient Ones. The whole process was extremely risky. Failure could result in the target Kudamaz individual whose resonance signature pattern was being imploded being effectively eradicated from existence. For a Kudamaz to undertake Resonance Implosion, there had to be such a monumental need to warrant risking their own life force to remove their resonance signature.

The Light of Ki knew of only one Kudamaz who fitted that bill.

Lord Aswa-da.

It couldn't understand why it had sensed no element of evil. It was the heart of white light energy. The very receptacle holding goodness and love. Detecting the dark was hard-coded into its creation. So why could it detect nothing?

Perhaps, it was wrong. Or perhaps…The Light of Ki couldn't deny that leaving its crystal power block home and taking residence in the human boy had disturbed its being. Maybe its capacity to analyze and interpret the world around it had been fractured. As terrible as it sounded, the Light of Ki had to consider it may already be malfunctioning.

Unable, due to its trauma, to determine dark and light.

It had to concentrate. Banish the consideration. Continue with what the Kudamaz individual had begun. In a bid to understand, and provide clarity, the Light of Ki recalled the activities of that morning again.

On entering, the man had spoken softly to Xiao. His air of kindness purveyed throughout. Nothing about him resembled the Kudamaz Senior Elder the Light of Ki now knew he had to be.

The man, dressed in a tailored suit of charcoal, reached into his pocket and brought out a glowing crystal. The Light of Ki recognized its own resonance frequency trapped within the crystal structure, identified to be a special sentient crystal known as the Vessel.

The man had bent over Xiao, and the boy had shivered.

"What are you doing?" Xiao's small, scared voice had burst from him. The Light of Ki had noticed his pulse leap as his heart beat faster.

"Making you well again, my child." The man's voice, laced with soothing droplets of creamy caramel assurance, seemed to touch the boy, and he'd calmed instantly.

The Light of Ki had felt the sides of the boy's mouth pulling up in a feeble attempt to smile.

It had watched the man as he'd held the Vessel in his hand and moved the crystal up and down Xiao's body. Rays emanated from the Vessel, and on contact with the boy's body, the harmonic light energy started to go to work on Xiao's cells. The Light of Ki could feel the boy resist. He should have been put in stasis, but the man had not undertaken suspended animation. The harmonic light energies twisted and turned into the boy's DNA, filtering into the amino acids, and then beyond into the molecules, atoms, quantum particles, base elements beyond the quantum realm, and further...far, far into the point where the human resonance frequency pattern could be found.

And assimilation of human resonance frequency within the Light of Ki's resonance pattern began.

The man muttered, "Yes, yes, good. Easy. Almost there."

Xiao's heartrate pelted through the ceiling, and the Light of Ki, knowing the human heart couldn't take that speed, assumed he was on track for cardiac arrythmia. But caught within the boy, with its own resonance frequency under assimilated alignment with the boy's own resonance, the Light of Ki could do nothing.

Light radiating from the Vessel stopped abruptly, and the crystal darkened, like it was spent of energy. The man secreted the crystal back inside his jacket.

He brushed Xiao's forehead.

"You've done well, Xiao. A very brave boy." The words from the man comforted the boy. The Light of Ki noticed his internal systems quietened their resilient efforts to reject the change.

Gradually, Xiao's heartrate slowed. His pulse evened out. His lungs breathed steadily.

"There, there. All done," said the man, tapping the boy's arm. "The change will take a while. You must rest."

Xiao's eyes had flicked open. The Light of Ki could feel the immediate change. Harmonization of energies was in process. The need to place Xiao in a higher level of consciousness wasn't needed. With resonance frequency alignment now on-going, the Light of Ki could start to unfurl its own energy, and power up for the forthcoming fight. Without worrying about the human child.

The man had left, and then returned with Lei. Xiao, although weak from the continuing mutation, sat up in bed and spoke to her. Coherent and unafraid.

"Mum, this doctor is amazing. He's made me okay."

Xiao's mother beamed with happiness and relief. She grabbed at the man's hand and shook it warmly. He held up the crystal, now almost jet in color.

"All the trouble's in here."

He slipped the crystal back into his pocket.

"Mum, let's play that Universal Guard game. I only got to level five, and

I need to ascend more levels. Simon's on level ten and he hardly plays it. Mum, can you help me?"

The man smiled and made to leave.

Lei grasped his arm. "Can I pay you for what you've done?"

The man's head swayed side to side. "I was under instruction from Sam Noor. Payment has been taken care of. But satisfaction of a job well done is more than recompense for me. By what I've done, I've already received my reward in ways you cannot imagine."

Lei smiled and hugged the man.

Not two Earth hours later, the intermittent change states started with a pounding viciousness. The Light of Ki understood that mutation would create the flicking of two states before the boy's framework became Kudamaz.

He couldn't help the boy anymore. It was down to his will to live.

Only that would determine the survival of the universe.

And death to Ellie Noor Selema.

Chapter 108

I sense the Light of Ki. It's getting ready. Gearing up. Ready to try its luck with me. At the Earth moment Sam mentioned the boy, Xiao Chang, connection was made. I could feel the Light of Ki explode into me.

Sam had said it was trapped in a human boy, but this surging energy has not confined itself. It's trying to break free. But it hasn't quite achieved that yet.

Like those generals of old, I have time to indulge in some sport before battle commences.

I shimmer into my Silent Waters apartment. Ashton clings to me.

"Those pretty lights," he mumbles, and his eyes fail to focus, searching around. He pulls away, his movements uncoordinated and clumsy. By his ludicrous behavior, I fear I may have kept him too long in Kudamun. I stare at him. Annoyed at his lack of cognition.

"Oh, get a fucking grip," I snap insensitively, and whack him across the face.

Ashton jerks, startled, as pain fires him up, alerting his neurons to a possible threat. I slap him again, and again. On the fifth go, as my hand goes out to hit his face, his hand flicks out, grips my wrist tight and tugs me against him. He sinks his lips onto mine, thrusting his tongue inside, kissing me violently.

That worked. Ashton's back!

I grab him, ready to get back to some ways to exhaust him now his marbles are working again. But I feel something burning into me.

The Light of Ki.

Its force is growing faster in magnitude. The rapid rise of its energies surprises me.

I SearchSight Xiao. In my mind, I see a flickering pillar of white light suspended on a landing in a very swish house. A human female huddles, crying, whilst a human man holds her in a protective embrace. Another person, dressed darkly, could be a priest, is in mortified terror, brandishing a crucifix, whilst a woman chucks water over the bobbing, white light. Words are being chanted.

Xiao's form appears to be the Light of Ki. Then, the white light flame flickers and his human frame emerges again and he's standing on the landing.

A squeeze between my thighs breaks my concentration.

Ashton. He grins and beckons with his head toward the bed. I shake my head.

"Not yet, babes."

I pull him close, target my soul force to connect to my quantum self on the landing in that luxury pad in Berkley Square, and shimmer.

Around me, the scene I'd viewed through SearchSight comes alive. The man with the crucifix and the woman with the water in a gold bowl stare at me, dumbstruck. They see Ashton, their prime minister clutching to me, and just about any glimmer of sanity they may have shatters.

Within the time I arrive and blow their mind, the air swirls to the right of me, on the middle of the landing, and a rainbow sparkle of dancing lights take over.

More Kudamaz. Oh fun!

Out of shimmer arrives Sam, Aby-od, and a very static Aswa-da.

Behind me, the huddling woman and the largely built man shielding her cry out in fear. I turn and notice them.

The man stares at Sam and recognition flares in his face. "Please, Sam, help us!"

"Lei, Chen, I will."

I hear what Sam says, and his insecurity and lack of confidence is evident in his weak response.

"I wouldn't bet on that guy," I say. "He's unreliable. Tells you a pack of lies. And just says sorry when the shit hits the fan."

Sam's eyes mist up with hurt. I shrug, sneer, and return to my audience.

I hear a shuffle and whip around to face the man administering a form of exorcism on Xiao, and I can see he's had it. In his eyes he's just not prepared for this level of weirdness. Amongst his hyperventilated breathing, he tries to steady himself enough to grip the railings behind him. Gently, he edges along, as if he's scared I'll notice. I mean, does he think I'm blind?

"Yeah, mate, fuck off and take your missus with you!"

I cast a glance at the woman who meets my casual look with protuberant eyes. Pressured astonishment grabs her, and by her flabbergasted expression, mixed with a hint of shame, I conclude she's just shat herself.

I storm at her, enjoying myself, "I said fuck off! So go. Now!"

She doesn't need telling twice. With a scream, she high tails it down the stairs behind the guy who seems to be leaping down two steps at a time. He barely reaches the bottom without falling.

I laugh.

Contemptible humans!

My fellow Kudamaz stare back at me.

Aby-od with anger. Sam with pity. Aswa-da with nothing.

"What's up with him?" I indicate to Aswa-da, taking in the mess his face and body are in, and clock the blood on Sam's hands, sliding and sparkling.

"Oh, Mr. Badass Superspy's got his mojo back. Whipped Ass Wiper! Gave him a good thrashing for me, did you, sweetness? So kind. Love you."

I blow a fake kiss and laugh with raucous delight. Ashton's hand snakes tighter around my waist. I know his gesture isn't just about me amore; it's as much about his own reassurance and knowing I'll protect him.

"I guess you all know what's happening." I take in Ashton, who still looks a bit shell-shocked. Well, most of us know what's happening. "I'm Ellie, and this little chap here is the Light of Ki, and, to be honest, we don't mix too well."

From inside the little Chinese boy, a growl erupts. "Abomination."

"Oh, baby," I purr, staring at Xiao, "I haven't even begun."

I detach myself from Ashton and walk over to Xiao. In front of him, I smile. The Light of Ki is trying to flood me with energies, but it's unable to get through my internal defenses.

The frustration of its inability to penetrate me forces the Light of Ki to push into a pillar of light state.

"Huh, that'll help your transformation a bundle."

I know full transformation hasn't fully completed. I can tell through my Protector-styled analysis that Xiao is ninety percent Kudamaz. If the Light of Ki remains a pillar of light, complete transformation will be halted. Mutation of this nature needs a human framework in place to work on.

I hear the Light of Ki howl with bitter annoyance, as I continue my chiding, and it reverts reluctantly to its human form.

"As we're all in the business of having an illuminating time, get a load of these lights!"

In my mind, I visualize the fake white and black crystal power blocks. Inside my palms, the crystals materialize.

"Ellie, the Balance! Do you know what you've done!" screams Aby-od, his face catatonic with fear.

I ignore him, and bellow, "If ever there was a time to shed light on the truth, it is now!"

I sweep a look at all assembled. My focus is on the adults for an Earth second. Xiao drops out of my range. That momentary slip in my concentration is enough.

A brilliant, shimmering light breaks through Xiao's torso engulfing everyone on the landing except me and Ashton. Furious at my lack of anticipating the Light of Ki's play, I hook onto Xiao's shimmer, snatching hold of Ashton, almost forgotten in the fracas, and pull into Xiao's destined target location: Sharm El Sheikh.

Chapter 109

Heat blasted around Sam as he came out of Xiao's shimmer.

People, obviously holidaymakers, ran away in all directions screaming. Desperate to get away from the weird 'out of nowhere' arriving visitors.

Sam heard calls of, "That's Ellie and Ashton!" But their fear over-powered their need for celebrity close-ups. Aby-od and Aswa-da were tall, strange, and scary-looking enough for humans to accept something terrible was occurring. The rolling thunder, orange-purple skies, and streaking, silver quantum lighting giving way to crystal fragments convinced those around Sam that Armageddon may be close.

The shimmer disturbed him. It was strange and unsettling being shimmered by someone else. The force of the shimmer had been dominating, primal and urgent. He'd had no way to initiate his own shimmer. It was as though he'd been bound. Tied down within the Light of Ki. A total submission to a power beyond his understanding even as a Kudamaz Senior Elder.

Sam looked at Aby-od. His face was creased and uncomfortable, indicating a barrage of feelings similar to those Sam had experienced.

He turned around, and Aswa-da, caught in Xiao's massive, immensely powerful shimmer field, had been pulled out of stasis on exiting out of shimmer. Bemusement was on his face, at first, and then he appeared to recognize the beach in Sharm El Sheikh. He smiled.

"Back to the beginning," he said smugly, and Sam could see he still had comprehension of all the moves being played.

That riled Sam.

He heard a slight whimper and revolved to face the Changs. "Are you okay?"

"Okay?" said Chen, shaking, holding his wife close to him. "Okay!" Chen's voice rose. "Are you kidding me, Sam? You just brought two pantomime giants and a deranged woman who's kidnapped the prime minister into my house, and my son has turned into a pillar of light that appears to have beamed us all to Sharm El bloody Sheikh. Of course I'm not *fucking* okay!"

Sam didn't have a chance to respond to Chen, as the air in front started to oscillate and sparkle with obsidian twinkles.

Ellie is here.

Aligning with her emergence from shimmer, a peal of thunder sounded in the upper atmosphere. Sam stared at the skies. They had taken on a crazy, orange-purple swirling and twirling kaleidoscope of color. Silver streaks shot across the sky, ripping through, lighting up the tears in reality, and revealing the twinkly crystal inner world of Kudamun.

Sam watched her shimmer in with Ashton grasping her close. He snarled at that view. He'd had enough of all that shit. Whatever was going down today, it ended. He couldn't continue with her like that.

"Neat little trick you've got there, Xiao," I say, stepping forward to face the boy.

His eyes glare into mine. Light V dark. Age old V new powerful. He looks like a boy externally, but I can detect much more.

Xiao is the Light of Ki.

Assimilation. Mutation. Transformation.

However, it's said. He is one hundred percent complete.

And I can feel its force.

Defying my existence.

I build up my energies for the oncoming assault.

Blue skies break through above me, but they hold for less than an Earth minute before the colors from the Reality Gap storm in. The orange and purple glow as if enraged. Great swathes of crystal cut into the orange and purple, and silver quantum lightning streaks above us and then falls down at my feet. The human contingent jump. The Kudamaz lot just seem amazed that this could happen at all.

The burning light in Xiao's eyes is fueled by a knowledge that everything is changing.

Disruption: the only game in town.

"Time for the truth, folks," I yell. "And what you're going to hear isn't what you'll like. But hey, I'm not into lying."

I shoot a glare at Sam who ricochets back a glare of fury. In it, I read enough is enough.

"Everyone's been using everyone. Ashton, darling, you've been Ass Wiper's bitch for quite a while. He's had you really hard many times."

I stare at Ashton. He's open-mouthed, incredulous, by my announcement.

"What the fuck?" he starts.

But I raise my hand for him to stop. Aswa-da sniggers and I flash my dark eyes. He reads my dangerous intention and his joviality ceases.

"Ass Wiper changed your human framework after Katzy died."

I watch Ashton. His face tightens. His eyes hood over and darken, and he stares, ruthless and cold, at Aswa-da.

"You *changed* me?"

Aswa-da nods. I hear Ashton growl, but he doesn't interject. Too caught up, too mesmerized in hearing the final truth.

"Your darkness became a beacon calling to him," I explain. "He changed you. Did some shit with your DNA. Made you into the Chosen One. He picked up on your need to dominate. Your secret admiration for Salim, for what he'd achieved, despite your hatred of Al Nadir. Ass Wiper knew being leader of the UK wasn't enough for you. You wanted to be leader of the world. You wanted world domination. He sowed the seeds of Freedom Earth and fueled your ambition to see your fellow man completely subjugated to your will. Everything you did, all the stuff with me as the Protector, with Sam, religious unification, your hardline stance on terrorism, on crime, state-sanctioned annihilation of tens of millions of people, men, women, and children, because they were Al Nadir, the public executions, the shoot-to-kill Surv-Motes, and even removal of the jury system, all of it you believed, and we did too, was done to drive the Earth to goodness, love, and enlightenment. The next stage of evolutionary development for Earth. But it was all part of Ass Wiper's grand plan. All those things we all did drove the Earth into a phenomenal pit of utter darkness."

Around me, gasps hit fast. Ashton's face trembles, and shadows of despair flicker across his features. I can see he's wounded deeply. I catch his desolate eye and he wordlessly asks, 'How long did you know?'

I don't respond. He shakes his head, unable to fully grasp how much of a pawn he's been.

I realize Aby-od is spluttering, "But the Balance is showing it's in the light."

"All in good time, Aby-od. I'll come to that. But first, Quantum Force. Ashton, darling, you know the little energy thing that made you and other leaders around the world so stinking rich for mining quark spin? Well, it's not mining quark spin."

Ashton's eyes widen. Everything I've just said has left him devastated. He stutters, his confidence in tatters, "So…so what's it mining?"

"That." I point upward to the sky. "The Reality Gap."

I clock Aswa-da. He could try to shimmer. Okay, I would stop him, and he probably knows this, but he could attempt it. But he doesn't. I can see he's basking in self-adoration. He just loves this show. The big reveal. He's caught in his own stunning trap of hubris. Obsessed with seeing everyone at a disadvantage. Reveling in the fact he's turned everyone into a fool.

Oh, he's been so very, very clever.

Until it came to me.

"So humans through their greed for energy are destroying the Reality Gap, Kudamun, Earth, and the rest of the universe. Hell of a way to get rich, Rich!"

I grin at Ashton when delivering the pun, but there is no humor. No sideways smirks. The blood drains from his face. He drags his hand down his face, uttering quietly, "I never knew. Oh my God, I never knew!"

By his sallow, drawn expression, it looks like Ashton's going to throw up or collapse.

I tear my eyes from him and hear the imbecile Aby-od scream out, "But the Balance?"

He still, after all I've said, can't actually conceive that Aswa-da did this without affecting the Balance. I swing around and stare at Aby-od, amazed. Despite the fact he can see everything around him falling apart, he keeps to the belief that, as the metric of the Balance Shift hasn't changed, all is well. Talk about running blind.

"Don't you get it, Aby-od? The Balance is fucked!"

Aby-od shakes his head. His intelligence is now struggling with this. So tight is he in his world of antediluvian laws and the Order of Kudamun, he can't countenance even the faintest idea that, somehow, someone could even think about fudging the Balance. Let alone that they could actually find a way to act out such an idea. His arrogance and misplaced belief in the system has caused his downfall.

I glance at Sam. He nods, and I can see he gets it completely. That super intelligence of his is racing to the finish line before I've even given up all the goods.

He's grief-stricken, and I can see he's remembering. All those times in the past when Ellie the Protector had bemoaned about the Balance being off, that Freedom Earth was wrong, Ashton was dark, religious unification was being done for the wrong reasons, and Quantum Force didn't feel right.

I know now he's beating himself up for never having believed or trusted in me.

"But how?" asks Aby-od, shaking.

"There is no Balance. This beauty here…" I hold up the fake white crystal. "Stopped all that Shifting shit completely. Nothing got through, not dark, not light. The Balance is fake!"

"The Observation Screen, Ellie. That could not lie," says Aby-od, grasping onto something to value and hold trust in.

"Ass Wiper, with his Etima acolytes, used a disrupter device so that they could manipulate and only show Kudamun what it needed to see. Remember, Sam, you saw that calculation about the Quantum Force, and then, when you looked back in Observation Room, you couldn't find it again. It was disrupted by Ass Wiper's people still loyal to him."

Aswa-da grins, but I cut him down.

"Ass Wiper's grand plan. He thought by mining the Reality Gap, it would fracture the connection. The Kudamaz's ability to shimmer via the Reality Gap to anywhere in the universe, that would have gone. Kudamun would have been cut off from the universal plane. The Kudamaz would have been imprisoned forever in their interdimensional prison. Freedom Earth was all about command and control. Getting Earth to such a point where it would drop into a dark abyss, making it ready for Ashton to take over as World Leader of Freedom Earth with me by his side. But really, he'd be pulling the strings. Eventually, Ass Wiper would have removed Ashton and assumed total domination over the world like one of those alien so-called gods from the stars in Hollywood B-Movies. He actually thought I'd rule with him, and be his wife, or whatever." I laugh.

Everyone is stationary. Except Sam. In my peripheral vision, I see he's getting ready to strike. I'm pleased to see he's getting his juices back.

Aswa-da doesn't like my mockery of him. He bites back. "You've worked it out so well. I bet you consider yourself a really clever girl. Pity you can't get out of this mess either."

The turn of his words spark me. He's goading me to make a move.

I notice Xiao has been silent throughout my entire address. His parents haven't said a word either. They just stand close to Sam, as if association with him will make them stronger.

"So we've all been using each other, all for the greater game." I stare at Aswa-da, Aby-od, and then Sam. Aby-od doesn't meet my eye. He's too crushed by all the revelations. "But the games are now finished. It all ends now. No more petty fights for domination. Earth is over, Kudamun is finished, and I have pastures new to command and dominate."

I initiate shimmer, but a wall of energy pulls me back like gravity. I glower at Xiao and the boy smiles.

The Light of Ki blocks me.

I feel a shudder ripple through me, and, suddenly, Xiao takes on full illumination. Not like before when he was a pillar of light. This time, the light glows like the heart of a sun. White hot, brutal and burning.

I know the power inside him is fiercer, stronger, wilder. Steeling itself. Arming itself.

Ready for the fight.

I focus and build up my own dark energies, and an aura of obsidian, sparkling glitter forms around me, radiating and powerful.

The Light of Ki wants to kill me, harm me, or else control me.

But nothing will control me.

I will battle for my right to be free.

To stay free forever.

Chapter 110

Stay free.

I hear it. The word is an emotion that runs through me like blood in a human. Around me, they watch. All of them.

Waiting.

My move is the last. The final piece in a chess game of an eternal duration.

I remain still. I hold back on the lure to fling it all away. Damn humanity. A princely world of self-entitlement, expecting to survive. Expecting to live.

I hold its next moment.

Everything has come to this.

The sky above me streaks purple and orange across a fading blue. Intermittently, silver-white lightning flashes.

Breakdown is imminent.

Beneath my feet, a slow rumble as if the Earth has awoken. The rumble grows louder. Earth protests her fate. The sands slips underneath me. I dig in with my heels, demonstrating command. The rumble stops, except for a slight whimper caught in the wind.

I can sense her resignation and submission.

In front, Xiao stands, a surging tower of white light, his human form all but gone. Good has eaten him whole, as it had done to me.

But a flicker of life, I still detect, within him.

Another flash of lightning rips across the sky. Reality shudders. Cracks form around me. Humans, I know, won't see, but the Kudamaz can.

I look at Aswa-da. Has he noticed the tiny fractures? His face gives away nothing. Not an indication to accept that the path he's taken will lead to his own destruction.

No one moves. No one speaks. All are transfixed by fear, by sadness, by loss of hope. Giving in to what would be. They know there will be no more clever moves, Machiavellian maneuvers, and underhanded plays.

I glance at Ashton. His customary smirk has vanished. Realization dawns within him, the stakes beyond his comprehension. He's been used, first by Aswa-da, and then by me. Nothing but a ball to play with, to toss around. Passing from one to another.

Such irony when he thought it was he who had the power.

Do I still want him to be with me in my new realm? I'm not so sure. Perhaps I'll create someone new. Someone stronger.

I smile. That feeling of power burns through me.

Stay free.

Unshackled from responsibility. A duty I never asked for. A duty I never wanted.

Aby-od's eyes try to lock on mine. But I do not allow the connection.

Everything is on my terms now.

No one controls me.

The two crystals pulse in my hands. The dark crystal throbs with contentment, pre-empting my final decision. The fake white crystal vibrates with cold efficiency as it absorbs the dark energy waves across the world and masks them with its own fake white energy. I stare, marvelling at Aswa-da's blatant manipulation of the natural laws. Those antediluvian doctrines invested by the Kudamaz when Earth was just taking shape. Such a diabolical detraction from the way, no one had ever considered it a possibility.

Entrenched thinking has caused their downfall. Aswa-da challenged and broke convention, and believed he'd won.

But laws are there for a purpose. Rules, once broken, can never be fixed. Every action has a consequence.

As Aswa-da is discovering, I am the consequence.

Finally, I look at Sam. Sorrow encases him. His eyes pour out apology.

He couldn't save me.

What he doesn't realize is no one could.

I was beyond saving by another. Only I could save myself.

That's what all of this is about: saving.

Who would I save? Who would I forsake?

On my thought, the sky breaks out into a brilliant orange and purple, eradicating any shred of blue.

Not long now.

"I don't want to die!" Xiao's human voice screams unexpectedly. Despite my fortress shielding me from emotions, Xiao crashes through with his mental assault. "I'm so young. I haven't lived. I'm so very, very scared. Please don't let me die. I know I've been a bad boy. I've taken so much for granted. I've been selfish and cruel, and treated Mum and Dad with disrespect. But save me, and I will change. If I live, I will be a good boy. Please let me live. I want to live. Don't let me die."

I tingle on Xiao's words. I find myself accepting them and I give myself over to their passion. Slowly, the glow of the fake white crystal fades.

I catch movement suddenly to my right. Lei steps forward, trembling and sobbing.

"Save him. Save him. Please, save my son!"

Lei's outburst stuns me. It is as if she has heard her son's pleas. I know this cannot be. Her pleading is derived from motherhood. Sworn to protect, to love, to the very end.

"Help me. Don't let me die. Save me!" Xiao's young mental outcry doesn't cease.

Lightning shoots in longer strikes across the orange and purple sky, and reality rips around my onlookers. The crystal twinkles of Kudamun breaks through in widening gaps.

"Don't let me die."

That unknown, undetermined tingle inside me strengthens, metamorphizing into a pulse. A slow pulse like a dying heartbeat.

Save others to save yourself.

With each return of the pulse, indecision grows. I could. I couldn't.

With blinding clarity, I know what the pulse is. That last piece of humanity. That elusive shell in the egg that has evaded me so many times, which I'd believed, for so long, I'd lost. Humanity embodied in a simple note. It floods through me.

Save others to save yourself.

They don't need saving.

I could leave now.

In my mind, that curtain again. In front of me, the air bunches up, and that curtain is there again, waiting for me. To find my new place. With Ashton? I look at him. Trembling, frightened. I sense his extreme weakness within. The grief and anguish of Katzy's death had created him. Pain of everything I'd been subjected to and lost, for a supposed greater good, had created me. So similar, and at one time, I had thought, completely compatible. But now I have my doubts .

Somewhere, in the endless stream of universes I have just created, I will take ultimate command. I need no Ashton. I will create whatever I need.

I could leave right now. Just a pull of that curtain.

I sweep across the onlookers, one last time, and they grab me. Caught in a tractor beam of emotion. Of desire. Of love.

Sam's eyes.

Those sad, sorrow-filled eyes catch mine. As much as I try to avoid them, I cannot succeed. I can never avoid Sam.

In his look, love abounds, despite everything that I've done. A love of such power it courses through him still, embedded within his Kudamaz being.

Eyes that have seen so much sparkle in front of me. In that sparkle, he wills me to be his again.

My databanks start to run as if triggered by something beyond my control, and I recall that moment when I'd walked into the room. Just a simple job interview to be a secretary. I hadn't expected anything. The interview panel lined up, waiting. And there he'd been. In the center. Staring. His eyes laughing. Undressing me. But he'd indicated nothing in his manner. Stoic, superb professionalism. But in his eyes. A lifetime of love hit me. I couldn't think of a thing to say. All my clever words, retorts, and quips. They sailed out the window. I was lost in those gorgeous, dark chocolate eyes that pulled me in and wouldn't release me until I'd agreed to be his, and his until the end of time.

People talk about love at first sight. It happened. And I never released myself from those gorgeous eyes, as truths are now being told, I never have.

Leaving those eyes forever. Never to see.

Can I really do it?

He stares at me, and I feel Sam's love flow in torrents over me, inside me. His love is eternal. Enveloping and caressing me. Pulling me to feel. The Light of Ki couldn't storm my defenses, but Sam's love just strolled in.

"Save me. Save me."

I hear the child, pleading. Sam and I never had children. I said I'd never been blessed, but really, life took over. Ambition. A different path taken. I've always wondered...

"Please, I'm too young to die."

I listen. I've never made life, but I could save one. I gaze up at Sam, and smile. I turn to Lei. I see her mouth open. I know she's asking me to help Xiao, but I hear nothing. All I feel is her maternal love. Abundant, like Sam's love, it pours into me. Infusing and blending in with Sam's love.

The darkness finally lifts.

"Save me. Save me."

I look at the curtain. The folds of reality's material seem to sway. Showing me a glimpse of my realm. Tempting me.

But I've already made my choice.

I succumb to the pulse. The last vestige of humanity. Of pure love. Toward Xiao, I walk. In my hands, the crystals, dark and fake. I do not need them. I let them fall to the golden sands.

Xiao is a pillar of light. A faint outline of his corporeal body, I can just about see. I peer into the shining waterfall of light, and a face with small, black, and horror-filled eyes stare back at me.

"I don't want to die."

I smile. That essence of maternal protection I feel takes me over. With my arms raised, I encircle the boy's body of light.

The Light of Ki propels Xiao's body away and into his mother's arms, as it consumes mine.

I'm aware of screams. Humans through their voices. Kudamaz through their minds.

Through the light, Sam speeds forward, shouting, "I love you."

I see his eyes. Glistening. Sparkling.

"I love you too. Therefore, this must be done. I'm saved now, darling. We all are."

I don't know whether he heard.

Instantly, I sense it. The dark crystal calling out. The fake crystal has stopped filtering. Unleashed, the darkness that Earth housed storms Kudamun's Balance Shift. As the register shifts deep into the Dark Zone, Earth plummets. Warnings sound. But it's far too late.

Screams subside, and a comforting silence wraps around me.

The Light has taken me over.

I see it or feel it, the white crystal's incredible power aligning with the Ancient Ones. They connect with me. Together, the Light, the Ancient Ones, and I are one.

I'm infused with their knowledge; I know their path. The new start they have planned for me.

And it has to be.

One with the light, I extend out. I shatter and come together a million times, as the light reassembles under instruction, a new way. Existences form only to obliterate. Views from across the galaxies, the universe. Places and dimensions still unseen, even to the Kudamaz, greet me in a moment and vanish, only to be replaced by another. A particle, a wave. Energies making something somewhere. I glimpse worlds within worlds. Of great darkness, of sudden and beautiful light, of rainbows and beauty never-ending. And still, I fly in and out of what, of where, flickers of realities flash so fast, I fail to determine. Of snatches, of shadows. The maybes and if-onlys of lives past, present, and future run out of me.

No longer can I say where I am. What I am.

I can see nothing. Hear nothing. Speak nothing.

Am I even here?

Where is here?

In the midst of non-existence, I imagine opening my mouth to speak.

Sam.

I call out. Through my imaginary lips and mind.

The pull of love is strong. It focuses on me. Pushes me forward. Out of my nothingness. My light-filled obliteration.

Ejected with force, I fly. Particles, twinkling, coalesce around me. Forming shapes. Reality takes definition.

Grains slip between my toes. A gentle lapping sounds in my ears. Heat touches my face.

The sun, the giver of life, descends rays upon my body.

I squint in the light that envelopes me. And that is when I notice it.

The stillness. The peace.

Nature's harmony, her serene, soulful soliloquy that, so oft as Protector, I could hear, has gone. Only the faint breaking of the waves against the shore.

The Ancient Ones have kept their word. Our new start.

I look around.

A figure lies on the sand, unmoving. With their head turned away from me, I still know. The frame outstretched on the silver sands beside me, I know that body as I know my own.

I touch the figure's head and turn it gently toward me.

Sam.

His eyes are closed. I lean in and kiss him.

He reaches out to me. His hand touches mine and his eyes open.

He bends forward and kisses me. Into that kiss, I am drawn.

My love, I drown in you, forever.

Together, we stare into each other's eyes.

Still silent, the world, apart from the soft lapping of the ocean.

Something I have to recall. Something that changed everything.

In the distance of a life far, far away, names surface: Ashton, Aswa-da, Aby-od, Xiao.

Who are they? That random collection of letters brings back a twinkle of recollection.

But that time has passed. They are mere fragments from a world now long, long gone.

Sam strokes my hair and kisses my neck.

"What are you thinking about, darling?"

I look at him, search his face for his own recall. And, as I look, those names in my mind drift away. Meaningless, empty words.

"Nothing, darling. Absolutely nothing."

"You know, sweetness, I think we should stay here. It would be good for the baby. All this sun, sea, natural living. What do you say?"

I'm not listening anymore.

I stare down at the delicate mound where my flat stomach used to be. Amazed and overjoyed.

I never knew. Didn't realize. When I was, when I was…what was I? Something I'd been, but I cannot remember. A niggle in my mind. But as I listen to the ocean and Sam strokes my belly, everything floats away.

"I love you, Sam."

"And I love you, Ellie."

I look down at my lump and feel a gentle punch. Inside me, I know a small hand raises in agreement.

Love connects us all.

FINALLY…THE END!

THIS RIDE IS FINISHED – YOU CAN LET GO OF THE SAFETY BAR NOW!

Dear reader,

It has been quite a phenomenal ride hasn't it?

From the moment Ellie shot off on to the M3 in The Trusted, the speed of events haven't stopped. Each page, chapter and book building in mystery and tension.

Be truthful…Ellie would want you to be 😉 Did you ever believe you'd go on such a trip of the unexpurgated extraordinary, downright weird and heart-pumpingly mind-blowing?

If you want to know the truth, I didn't either!

When I first started writing *The Trusted Thriller Series*, it was at first, finishing at the end of The Resonance, although I found myself, when Ellie encountered Ashton, writing in more strangeness. Something about his Equilibrium that couldn't be immediately be understood. She had no time given Earth's imminent demise to investigate, but she kept it as something she'd go back to. She wouldn't forget.

And neither would I.

With Aswa-da getting away, it left the door wide open to imagine what he would then get up to, now that his initial plans had been foiled by Ellie & Co.

In its entirety, The Refracted was Aswa-da's enormous, elaborate gameplay, although he does not appear as himself within it once. But his essence is still embedded in every situation that faced our heroes. You're aware something isn't right.

Now, having read The Sum, you know your instincts were right, just like Ellie's.

So, Ellie and Sam, human again with their forthcoming addition, are together in a new universe. The old one just a fragment in their mind that passes on the wind.

It was an ending that almost wrote itself.

And it was the ending that had to be.

Thank you for being with me on this wonderful journey.

GET OPERATION SNOWDROP FOR FREE

One constant throughout *The Trusted Thriller Series* has been **Operation Snowdrop**. If you haven't already accessed this 'Eyes Only' mission, now is your chance. Get the inside track on what really happened and get the real facts behind the mission that crossed the line.

If you want to get insider intelligence on Sam and Ellie next adventures, early bird discounts on all future releases in *The Trusted Thriller* series, access to competitions, or instant access to me, Michelle Medhat, then subscribe by hitting the link below and we can continue this journey together.

Operation Snowdrop Feedback

"Very exciting. Leaves you on the edge on almost every page. Trying to figure out what this poor guy has to go through to play both sides leaves me exhausted. I feel like I'm living every minute with him I can hardly stand it. Excellent book, excellent read, thank you for the opportunity to read it."

"All I can say is WOW. Michelle Medhat really knows how to pull you in with the characters and storyline. This is one of the best thrill rides I had in a long time. A Must read!!!!!!"

"OMG! Talk about edge of your seat, grab you by the ba... The author kept the book moving at a good pace with plenty of twists and an ending that will make you question the world around you!"

"Snowdrop is a fiercely paced book. Characters are dynamic, & powerful. A great spy thriller good versus evil gets blurred. Looking forward to next book."

"Kept me guessing and enthralled right up to the end. Looking forward to reading the next book"

"A very well written, suspenseful book. The description of the agents emotions and conflicts was very well done."

"I loved the constant adrenaline rush in this book. Looking forward to the next book."

"So similar to the situation in the world today that it's hard to read. Well developed"

"This book is exactly why I read new authors as often as possible. The intrigue and characters are heart-stopping. 5 stars +"

GET ACCESS TO OPERATION SNOWDROP

https://dl.bookfunnel.com/nz69zq8lp2

ENJOY THIS BOOK?
YOU CAN MAKE A DIFFERENCE

Leaving a review really does mean the world to me.

If you can scribble a few sentences, I'd be so very grateful. It doesn't take much to give your honest opinion on something that has taken me over a year to write.

You can head to the review page by hitting the link below.

LEAVE A REVIEW HERE
https://geni.us/sAsF

Learn more about Michelle Medhat

www.forever-connected.com
michelle@forever-connected.com

THE TRUSTED THRILLER SERIES

This Thriller Series is an edge-of-your-seat, ruthless, non-stop ride packed with gripping spy action, provocative sci-fi suspense, sex, political intrigue and amazing sci-tech to push Bond into the background! If you're searching for something that's nail-biting to the very end - you've found it in this extraordinary Thriller Series.

If you've read this book first, and haven't discovered the rest of the series yet, you need to read these books. Don't miss out, get them now and get the full story!

The Trusted (Book One – Part One)

He's a husband, a killer, and the only man who can save the world...

Sam Noor keeps his double lives separate with expert precision. But when the MI6 agent's wife discovers the lie, he fears that both his worlds may shatter. Distraught and conflicted, Noor concentrates on his latest mission and discovers a weapon that could cause a global catastrophe...

Drawn into the fight against a sinister terrorist group with powerful connections, Noor must uncover the faction's secrets by any means necessary. Even if it puts the woman he loves in the line of fire.

But Noor has no way of knowing that a supernatural war rages within his nation. And the winner could take charge of humanity's very soul.

Against forces that defy his reality, can Noor protect millions of innocents from a bloody end?

The Dominant (Book Two – Part Two)

One spy's war on terror could decide the fate of humanity…

MI6 agent Sam Noor isn't afraid to get his hands dirty to protect his homeland. While overseas interrogating an enemy terrorist, he's horrified to learn his beloved wife suffered the same brutal tactics from his own men. Determined to expose the betrayal and extract bloody justice, Noor uncovers an unbelievable fact: his wife died and somehow came back to life…

Swept up in an international power struggle, Noor goes rogue to uncover the eye-opening truth. The fallout from Sam's revenge ripples from the Oval Office through the CIA and MI6. As he fights tooth and nail to turn back the doomsday clock, cosmic forces wage their own battle for Earth's future. And Noor fears that preventing nuclear destruction may sacrifice the love of his life.

Can the maverick agent protect his wife and save his world from annihilation?

The Resonance (Book Three – Part Three)

World War III rages. What can she do to protect the innocent?

Ellie Noor's hope hangs by a thread. Tortured to within an inch of her life by sadistic terrorists, she's horrified to learn her husband's efforts to free her cost a half-a-million lives. But grief must wait as Ellie is swept up in an interdimensional attempt to stop all-out nuclear destruction.

Shocked to discover the key to saving the universe lies inside her, she becomes a potent instrument to respawn Earth's lost protector. But with the world's atomic arsenals locked and loaded, and sinister beings on the attack, she fears only an unfathomable miracle can halt humanity's extinction.

Can Ellie unleash her hidden power and prevent her planet's annihilation?

The Refracted (Book Four – Part Four)

She's now a fully-fledged Protector. But her formidable extraterrestrial powers may not be enough to save humanity from itself.

Ellie Noor longs for an end to the constant fighting on Earth. Now fully alien and nearly invincible, she and her superhuman husband are busy stamping out terrorist armies worldwide. But her heart breaks when a new global alliance for peace makes its first initiative a mass execution of its enemies.

Suspicious of the motives of the movement's creator, UK Prime Minister Ashton, Ellie's search for answers only leads to startling revelations. And her former-MI6-spy husband isn't helping matters by kowtowing to the British leader. With political havoc and cosmic dangers threatening, one wrong move could spell disaster for millions...

Can Ellie balance the forces at play before humankind is wiped off the interstellar map?

A WORD FROM THE AUTHOR

I said at the end of The Refracted that this was an emotional time. The fact is, when I finished The Sum, it was such a powerful, traumatic story, playing with deep emotions, very close to my own heart, I physically cried.

Noticing my tears, my husband Sam ran to comfort me, and asked why I was crying. I didn't have an answer.

A writer with no words.

How ironic.

All I could feel was the power of everything this series has been to me; the joy, sadness, anger, hurt, love, wonder and connectedness converging into one single emotive response on finishing my final words.

My tears.

These books have embodied things I believe. At the time of writing this, the world is in the grip of a terrible virus. An unseen enemy that has struck at not only our lives and livelihoods, but at the very sense of who we are as a human race.

Our focus on the materialistic and celebrity. A greed to want more, at a time when so many have to live and survive with almost nothing, has fractured our humanity.

We really have gone too far.

The balance has been tipped.

But through love, charity to others and hope, we, as a world nation, can shift it back.

As you know from my 'Words' in previous books, I'm a huge believer in thought energy creates reality. At times of darkness, like the one we're all going through now, positive thinking and strength in your own self, can harness enough light energy across the world to really change the future.

Everything is possible.

The incredible can be the new normal.

You only have to look within your own soul, and release your own powerful energy to make it happen.

Love to you all.

Michelle Medhat

Find out more

www.forever-connected.com

michelle@forever-connected.com

Twitter @theconnected1 Facebook @michellemedhat

The Playlists of The Trusted Thriller Series

The Trusted
Everlasting – Take That
Secrets – One Republic
Have I Told You Lately that I Love You – Rod Stewart
Rock You Like a Hurricane – Scorpions
Khalina Lewahdina (Let's stay alone together) – Amr Diab
E.T. – Katy Perry
Solsbury Hill – Peter Gabriel
Angel with a Shotgun – The Cab
Only Love can Hurt Like This – Paloma Faith
Who Wants to Live Forever – Queen
Rule the World – Take That
Fighting Suspicions – Rebecca Ferguson
The Architect – Paloma Faith
Rewrite the Stars – Zac Efron & Zendaya
The Last of the Secret Agents – Nancy Sinatra
New Divide – Linkin Park
Army of Two – Olly Murs
Demons – Imagine Dragons
Shine a Light – Bryan Adams
Don't Stop Believin' – Journey
What Part of my Body Hurts the Most – Rob Fowler & Sharon Sexton
Please Don't Leave Me – P!nk
Set Fire to the Rain – Adele
Guilty – Paloma Faith
Almeno Stavolta (At Least this Time…) – Nek
Candlelight – Jack Savoretti
I Belong to you – Caro Emerald
Try – P!nk
Redemption – The Strange Familiar
Nothing Breaks Like a Heart – Mark Ronson (Feat. Miley Cyrus)
Many Shades of Black – Adele & The Raconteurs
See Who I am – Within Temptation

The Dominant

Secrets – P!nk
La Tortura (The Torture)– Shakira
L'Altra Dimensione (The Other Dimension) – Måneskin
Amor Eterno (Eternal Love) – Fonseca
My Immortal – Evanescence
Revenge – P!nk with Eminem
Killer Queen - Queen
So Am I – Ava Max
Any Way You Want It – Journey
Me – Taylor Swift & Brendon Urie
Lucy in the Sky with Diamonds – The Beatles
Some Guys Have All the Luck – Rod Stewart
Perfetto (Perfect)– Gianna Nannini
Half the World Away – Aurora
Raise Hell – Brandi Carlisle
The Pretender – Foo Fighters
Too Good to Lose - Rebecca Ferguson
Maybe – Lewis Capaldi
Something's Gotta Give – One Republic
Torna a Casa (Come Back Home) – Måneskin
I Want to Break Free – Queen
Amo Soltanto Te (I Only Love You)– Andrea Bocelli & Ed Sheeran
Love at First Sight – Kylie
Whisky Tango – Jack Savoretti
Wonder – Naughty Boy with Emeli Sandé
Retribution – Jeff Scott Soto
Ayami Beek (My Days With You) - Elissa
Wasted – Jack Savoretti
Light My Fire – The Doors
We Share the Same Sun – Stereophonics
Surrender – Paloma Faith
What Have You Done – Within Temptation
Out of the Frying Pan and Into the Fire – Meatloaf
Rockstar (Salim's Theme) – Nickelback
Radioactive – Imagine Dragons
Back for Good – Take That
Danger Zone – Kenny Loggins

What Doesn't Kill You (Stronger) – Kelly Clarkson
Sweet But Psycho – Ava Max
Welcome to The Jungle – Guns and Roses

The Resonance

Strong - Mark Kingswood
Hiding – Florence + The Machine
The Sound of Sunshine – Michael Franti & Spearhead
All of My Heart - ABC
Toxic – Britney Spears
Burn it to the Ground - Nickelback
On Top of the World – Imagine Dragons
The Scientist - Coldplay
Blood on My Hands – Jack Savoretti
Music's Too Sad Without You – Kylie Minogue & Jack Savoretti
Suspicious Minds – Elvis Presley
Girls Just Wanna Have Fun – Cyndi Lauper
Traitor - Daughtry
Torn – Natalie Imbruglia
Dear Mr. President – P!nk
The Prayer – Celine Dion & Andrea Bocelli
The Winner Takes It All - ABBA
Guilty – Paloma Faith
Strip Me – Natasha Bedingfield
Won't Get Fooled Again – The Who
Changing – Paloma Faith
Drops of Jupiter – Train
Liar – Camila Cabello
Bring Me To Life – Evanescence
Venus – Bananarama
WW3 – Paloma Faith
Find U Again – Mark Ronson (feat. Camila Cabello)
Get Lucky – Daft Punk (feat. Pharrell Williams & Nile Rodgers)
Dancing in the Dark – Bruce Springsteen
Rescue Me – One Republic
Superheroes – The Script
Get Outta My Way – Kylie Minogue
Set Fire to the Rain – Adele

Who's Crying Now – Journey
Pain is So Close to Pleasure – Queen
Dark Night of the Soul – Van Morrison
Maybe Tomorrow – The Stereophonics
One Last Kiss – Kylie Minogue
Any Other Way – Jack Savoretti
Truth Hurts – Bullet for My Valentine
Stuck in the Middle with You – Stealers Wheel
Firework – Katy Perry
Red Light Spells Danger – Billy Ocean
Breaking Your Own Heart – Kelly Clarkson
Everything is Broken – Bob Dylan
Simples Corazones (Simple Hearts) – Fonseca
Greatest Mistake – Jack Savoretti
When Love Takes Over – David Guetta (feat. Kelly Rowland)
Shine – Emeli Sandè
I Saved the World Today – Eurythmics
Cold – James Blunt
Hold Me Close – David Essex
We Are Bound – Jack Savoretti
The Power of Love – Huey Lewis & The News

The Refracted Playlist

Do You want the Truth or Something Beautiful – Paloma Faith
Holding Out For a Hero – Bonnie Tyler
From Outta Nowhere – Jeff Lynne's ELO
Love and Understanding – Cher
Love is Fire – Freya
Strange Energy – World Collision
Titanium – David Guetta feat. Sira
You and Me as One – Jack Savoretti
Here to Love – Lenny Kravitz
Just You and I – Tom Walker
Bang Bang Bang – Christina Perri
Feel like Makin Love to You – Bad Company
Love too Much – Keane
Human – The Killers
One World – Billy Ocean

Power Over Me – Dermot
Always on my Mind – Jack Savoretti
Fades Away – Avicii Feat. Noonie Bao
One More Try – Jessie J
Games Without Frontiers – Peter Gabriel
Money Money Money – ABBA
The World We Live In – The Killers
Temptation – Heaven 17
Trapped – Bruce Springsteen
The Fighter – Keith Urban (Carrie Underwood)
Shallow – Lady Gaga & Bradley Cooper
Forever Yours – Avicii
You Are Not Alone – Emeli Sande
The Man who sold the World – Lulu
Amazed – Lonestar
Believer – Imagine Dragons
Shut Up and Dance – Walk the Moon
Fighter – Christina Aguilera
Roar – Katy Perry
Bruises – Lewis Capaldi
Dreams – The Cranberries
Survivor – Destiny's Child
Everybody Loves Me – One Republic
Bad Influence – Pink
Oh I do like to be beside the seaside
Before You Go – Lewis Capaldi
Aprendiz (Apprentice of the Heart) – Antonio José
In Another Life – The Darkness
If There's Any Justice – Lemar
It's a Mystery – Toyah

The Sum Playlist

Pour Some Sugar on Me – Def Leppard
Just Give Me a Reason – P!nk
Liquid Lunch – Caro Emerald
I Will Survive – Gloria Gaynor
Never Ever – All Saints
Tell Me When It's Over – Sheryl Crow (Feat. Chris Stapleton)

Stand My Ground – Within Temptation
Supermassive Black Hole – Muse
Strangelove – Depeche Mode
Beam Me Up – P!nk
Glitter & Gold – Rebecca Ferguson
Deep Waters – Jack Savoretti
Nothing Without Love – Nate Ruess
Someone That You're With – Nickelback
Don't Stop Me Now – Queen
I Say a Little Prayer – Aretha Franklin
Nothing Has Been Proved – Dusty Springfield
The Architect – Paloma Faith
One Vision – Queen
Cherry Bomb (Hello World) – The Runaways
Bonfire Heart – James Blunt
...Baby One More Time – Britney Spears
Leave Me Lonely – Ariana Grande (feat. MacY Gray)
We Are The Champions – Queen
Hold Me In Your Hands – Pixie Lott
Glad All Over – The Dave Clark Five
One Day Like This – Elbow
Dangerous – Within Temptation (feat. Howard Jones)
Under Attack – ABBA
Greatest Mistake – Jack Savoretti
Someone New – Hozier
Hot Stuff – Donna Summer
Without You – John Newman & Nina Nesbitt
Use Somebody – Kings of Leon
Family Affair – Mary J Blige
Sex-o-Matic Venus Freak – MacY Gray
Bad Romance – Lady Gaga
You Don't Own Me – Grace
Save Me – Queen
Don't Go Breaking My Heart – Elton John & Kiki Dee
Leave While I'm Not Looking – Paloma Faith
Believe – Cher
It's Getting Better – Mama Cass
React – The Pussycat Dolls

Everybody Wants To Rule the World – Tears For Fears
Need You Tonight – Inxs
Don't Speak – No Doubt
I Try – MacY Gray
Impossible – James Arthur
This is the Place – Tom Grennan
Read All About It Pt. III – Emeli Sandé
Warrior – Paloma Faith
Tainted Love – Soft Cell
Superwoman – Rebecca Ferguson
I Wish I Was James Bond – Scouting For Girls
Let Me Go – Gary Barlow
So What! – P!nk
Greatest Day – Take That
The Truth – James Blunt
The Hammer's Coming Down – Nickelback
I Will – Brandi Carlile
Lose You To Love Me – Selena Gomez
All You Need is Love – The Beatles

ACKNOWLEDGEMENTS

The name that has made this book a reality is Sam Medhat, my husband. He is my inspiration and without him this series would never have been created. He is the one who listens to every word written. He is the one who endures my frustrations when I have writer's block. He is the one who is constantly woken up by my unsuccessful attempts at creeping into bed in the wee small hours after I've become lost in my writing world.

Without Sam, no writing would have happened.

Whilst writing this series, I lost my brother, father, and mother. None of them lived to see this in print, however their love is embodied within the words, and I hope, somewhere, they can see the result of the faith they had in me to achieve.

I would like to thank my fabulous editor, Ceri Savage, who has been with me on this journey and who has been incredible in her support and advice.

Michelle Medhat

Printed in Great Britain
by Amazon

83095392R00274